BAD MOVIES

PETER JOSEPH SWANSON

Stonegarden.net Publishing
http://www.stonegarden.net

Reading from a different angle.
California, USA

ISBN: 1-60076-078-3

StoneGarden.net Publishing
3851 Cottonwood Dr.
Danville, CA 94506

First StoneGarden.net Publishing paperback printing:
October 2008

Visit StoneGarden.net Publishing on the web at
http://www.stonegarden.net.

Cover art and design by Peter Joseph Swanson

More from Peter Joseph Swanson!

Hollywood Sinners

The Joan Crawford Murders

Prologue

I was packed into the most expensive beaded gown that I'd ever been packed into. With my knees bound together, I hop-skipped up the wide steps to the vast glossy stage. I was accepting my 1976 Celluloid Intelligentsia award for best supporting actress in a comedy. The comedian host made a face at me like it was too amazing an upset to be true. I was now the world's biggest sex change star. I wanted to bolt the other way. I wanted to run to the bathroom. I kept saying to myself, "I *really am* worthy," though I didn't quite believe it.

Smiling graciously, I seized my award. It was far heavier than I'd expected. I felt the big block of metal slip through my greasy fingers. It caught against a press-on nail, which for a sickening moment I feared might pop off and fly across the stage. I turned to the crowd that was so big I couldn't see anybody. In my distinctive voice that could be a bit like a frog, I went into a gushing litany of heartfelt thank-yous to those craftsmen who'd made me clever, beautiful, and almost always in focus.

The instant I was backstage, an incredibly beautiful young woman with the most ludicrous cotton candy hair skedaddled up to me. She grabbed my award and said, "We need this back. It's not your real award."

I questioned her. "What?"

"You have to return this. It's just a prop. We'll send you your permanent one. Let go! See? We'll get you one with your name stuck right *there!*"

"Huh?" I didn't hear her. I was so out of it. I was high on myself. I thought she was trying to steal it. Of course I held on for dear life. My nails popped all over the backstage floor as we both jerked this way and that with it. Then a heavy cinderblock fell from high above and struck the beautiful woman on the head.

I'd been a fool to think she'd been brainless.

Lights started falling onto the floor with explosions of glass. Sparks showered down, igniting the dust on a curtain. A man in a tux ran by. He was screaming and holding his bloody forehead. If he were a big movie star, I couldn't tell. One end of a long metal catwalk dropped down and swung out and hit the backside of the set. It ripped a swath out of it. As it swung back in, the comedian host of the show was stuck to it. He dragged across the backstage floor. There was blithe applause from out front. The comedian host pulled himself off the catwalk and scrambled to get back on stage, but the fire curtain that sealed the stage away from the audience dropped like a guillotine. He was knocked on his belly. The audience screamed in alarm. All was dark backstage until rows of ceiling work lights finally clicked on. I looked up and spotted a man in a yellow leisure suit in the ropes. He was dropping, slowing his descent by keeping himself tangled in them. When his feet finally touched the stage floor, I saw that he was very ugly.

He pulled out a pistol and shot at a charging security officer, stopping him dead in his tracks, if not killing him. Then the ugly man quickly turned and looked straight at me. His eyes were cold. I was mortified. I watched his finger squeeze as he fired his gun deliberately at me. The bullet was stopped by the award that I wouldn't let go of. He aimed and fired again. I was hit in the shoulder but didn't feel it yet. I just stood like a dummy. I must have been hoping someone would yell, "*Cut!*" They didn't. He aimed again—he fired again. I dropped the award. I gasped in indescribable pain as the award crashed down on my pedicure. When I looked at the gleaming block of metal on the floor, I could see two bullet dents in it. The man aimed at me again and all I saw were his tiny mean eyes.

Then, like one of those science fiction movies that have a budget, several men stormed in and shot the ugly man with strange long guns that set off electrical bolts. The man convulsed and fell. As people still ran around screaming, more curtain dust flashed briefly into flames. The men in black grabbed the electrocuted man and dragged him away, while the colorful "Singing While You're Swinging" backdrop fell over all of us like a long parachute. I somehow just stood there under the crinkled blue sky.

When I woke up, I was being wheeled through a white tiled hospital shower room. I was still dripping with water as I was being shoved off to somewhere else in a wheelchair. A grinning doctor stepped up to me and handed me a glass of champagne.

"Congratulations," he said.

"Bless you," I said, grabbing the glass. Then I grabbed the bottle. The bullet was dug out of my shoulder on local anesthesia. I was awake so the cops could ask me impossible questions. I meant to ask, "How did I get shot?" But it came out, "How did I get the award?" A frowning lady cop shook her head like I wasn't anybody, and hadn't deserved either.

*****

The next morning, I felt so sick that even the gravity was horrible. As I sprawled on my best friend's couch, toes and shoulder bandaged, I moaned, "I've been shot, I got the award," over and over. I wasn't sure which was more significant. The champagne headache didn't help.

Andernach looked down at me and finally said, "Soon you'll be getting residuals enough to pay for your own apartment. *Love it!*"

I nodded to agree. I said, "Now the studio jerks won't be able to come up with reasons why my run-away hit isn't making any real moolah." I randomly flipped off the room with my middle finger as if the studio heads were all there. The phone rang. Andernach did a lame two-footed pirouette and then plopped the phone on my lap.

It was Mom. She said, "Hey stinker. Why did everything go to hell just after you were on? How do you do that?"

"I dunno."

"And why do you think you were the only one in that film to even get a nomination?"

I thought fast. "Um, because while I was on the set, I think I was the only one to pass up the maryjane. So, I was the only one who wasn't assuming that things were funny."

"You were a hoot," Mom agreed. "You looked genuinely bewildered. You looked downright constipated. I couldn't stop laughing at the look on your face."

"Thanks, Mom. I think. I thought I was pretty."

"You are, when you aren't looking so lost. And, you were just as lost on the award show last night. It was as if *you* were the one who made all hell break loose."

I couldn't tell her I *had* made all hell break loose. It *was* me that was the target of that man's gun, though I wasn't sure about the details. I wasn't a sleuth.

Mom said, "You must be terrified. That gunman may be after all you show biz women. I'm glad my TV's black and white. They say your dress was an awful shade of tan that made you very rude. They said that if it wasn't for the sequins you would have looked like you weren't wearing anything at all."

I said, "It was expensive. So it was OK." My stomach flipped, recollecting all the other mysterious murders around me in the past year. I wondered what their pattern might be. It was certain now that I was the psycho killer's next target. And his final target. I looked over to see that the apartment door was chained.

Mom continued, "Back when I saw your movie, everybody laughed at your name when it finally came up in the opening credits. They just couldn't believe *you* were in such a real movie. Not after all that incompetent trash you've been in. God you've made some bad movies. So when your name came up on the screen, everybody laughed. Except me of course. I saw your name up there and I just was so proud of my little… my little… girl. But then the movie started. Then you really stole the show. You just looked so turned-around… just ready to bump into things."

"*Mo-om*!" I lost patience. I was now a star. I was somebody who'd been so grandly awarded the top prize and then shot. So I finally felt like I had some sort of power. So I forced the chat short with, "Bye, time for my bullet hole to be looked at again."

Andernach and I did indeed look at my bullet hole again, since a real bullet hole looks so much more horrible than a movie bullet hole.

"*Eeew!*"

"Gross!"

'I'm gonna throw up!"

"I'm going to die!" Then I re-read the *Movieland Nova* and *Slanderbox*. They were the big competing trashy tabloids. They told me all about what I'd just attended. I was so happy that my snapshots were larger than anybody else's. That was probably because I was the underdog sex change star that had been shot. Also, my mascara was dripping. I looked like I just fell out of a big plane crash in a very hot jungle. "What's more important," I asked Andernach. "Getting this award or getting shot?"

"Both," he answered without a second thought. "*Love it!*"

I double-checked again to make sure the front door was chained against the psycho killer. I made sure my very sharp fondue fork was still at my side to protect me lest he push his way in. It was. So I closed my eyes. I tried to remember how I got to this place of such big celebrity and mortal danger.

Part One
Movieland or Bust

Chapter One

"I'm *soooo* nervous!" I said to the stranger sitting next to me on the bus. "I've never been out of Plaksville much. Not on my own. Not like this." Though he never encouraged me, I couldn't stop talking. I finished a small bag of *Corny Peso* corn chips as I continued, "Things come to *us*. The carnival comes to the parking lot every summer just after school lets out. I *loved* the woman who only has a head, because she was in a car crash. And she was decapitated! But she's somehow still alive!"

"What?" *That* finally jarred the man out of what he was probably really thinking about. He looked at me.

"It's true. I saw it! You look through a little window and you can see her head sitting right there on a shower-mat up on this table thing. She lips right back to the teenage boys who ask her dumb stuff. Like how she can poop. It's great!"

The man nodded again, seeming irritated, but I just couldn't shut up. I felt so odd riding in such a cold bus being taken so far away. I said, "Once I won a pageant as Miss Milk. It was at the Town and Country. It was a promotion for the dairy there. *Delly Dairy*. And they said I was the prettiest Miss Milk they've ever had. So, heck! Why not try my luck in Tinseltown! No?" I pulled at my brown hair, wishing it was thicker and longer. All the while, I looked again to make sure my purse was still between my feet, that it hadn't slid away on a hill or had somehow been cleverly stolen. The strap was tightly wound around both ankles. So it was silly of me to worry so much about it. I worried.

"I don't believe a person only wins something once in life. I'll win again. Has anybody ever gotten hypothermia from an air conditioner?" I hugged myself. I glanced out the window at the endless tan desert. This new frontier seemed so primordial and savage compared to the lush cornfields of home. I began to question whether I'd like it much out West. My brave enthusiasm was starting to fade. My jaw tightened. There was only one thing to do about that.

Talk. "Jill Marohn, that's my name. You'll see it in lights! By '75, I'll be all over the papers." I noticed a tiny town ahead. "Is that it?" I asked anyway to be dumb. Out the window I saw a couple of Indian women selling blankets and jewelry. "Injuns," I whispered in awe. These people were the closest anybody could ever come to Creation. At least that was according to the Indian Creation documentary I'd once seen on a TV after-school special. So I told the man sitting next to me all about it. I concluded, "And then the Indian boy jumped off the mountaintop, but he didn't die. He turned into an eagle."

At the other side of the tiny town, where the desert picked up again, the bus squeaked to a stop. Indian women were peddling. It dawned on me that they looked nothing like movie Indians. They were not Irish stagehands slapped in braided crepe wigs and stiff fringe pajamas. I bravely stepped out into the furnace heat to shop. "How much is that turquoise-like ring?" I asked, pointing to a modest stone.

"For you, dear, two dollars."

Smiling in relief, I unwound my purse strap from my wrist and bought the ring without noticeable commercial or racial incident. When I put the thing on, I felt inaugurated into this brave new world. Who'd heard of turquoise in Plaksville? I smiled as warmly as possible and thanked her, for the first time really looking into her face. Her eyes somehow seemed as incinerating as bonfires. "You have a bit of the two spirit shaman in you," she remarked. "What's your favorite color?"

"Peach," I smiled. "It's so *now*. So soft. So nail polish and lipstick."

"No. It's *purple*. The color of twilight. The color of the crossing of the heavily guarded abyss between the sexes, making the transformation of the *Nadle*."

That utterly puzzled me. "What's that?" I asked, trying to look deep in her eyes again. I could see the entire desert reflected in them. She just watched me, cryptically. It wasn't a rude look, like an *I-should-know-it-and-feel-dumb* kind of a thing, like Mom would do. No. It was a look that suggested that I'd learn it, somehow, from the inside out. Or at least that I shouldn't act like such a bimbo when I shop. Shivering in the blasting heat, I took one last look at Creation. I finally noticed that many of the cacti had bright red flowers. There was an odd dry sweetness in the breeze. Exhilarated and very frightened, I hurried back into the icy bus.

The Indian woman's voice came back at me. It needled my memory of something. I couldn't tell if I was remembering a past event or an old bad dream. I was in Mexico with Mom and I had a weird deformed badly circumcised penis. The damn thing blew up like a red water balloon when I tried to pee. It even caused endless kidney infections. Of course I decided I was remembering a really *really* bad dream, and as soon as I decided to forget it, I forgot it. I was looking at my fingernails and thinking about how pretty they were.

*****

I must have approached the big city from a bad angle. The buildings were just massive and bland. I'd been hoping that such a place as Tinseltown would have looked more like a sparkling futuristic movie miniature city, one of those places that shone like a rich person's Christmas tree. But I was now seeing too much dust, white concrete and sun bleached stucco. The glare hurt my eyes. I walked into the large ugly bus station. Agents were not lying in wait for me. They were not crawling all over themselves to meet me like I knew wouldn't really happen, of course. I'm not retarded. But I did have the small hope that they'd save us both time and make things mutually convenient. I *was* the fresh face. It *was* people like me who were the logs that fueled this town's brilliant fires.

"Would you like to buy a flower?" a brown-skinned man asked me. He boldly held out a paper flower for me to take. "It's only a quarter." I ran away to a cab, feeling lost, with "victim" surely flashing over my head for all the conmen and rapists to see.

My motel was in a cage of very tall palm trees. With my room key in a death grip, I went in circles, passing the same ice machine and the same view of the pool a few times over. I was all turned around. That was probably because I was trying not to ogle the parade of tanned bodies more than I was reading room numbers. After feeling like I'd just flunked both math and a beauty pageant, I found my door. It was on the back of the building. The palm trees there were brown and dying. They faced an ugly parking lot that faced another ugly parking lot.

My room's cinderblock walls were painted in a glossy bright lemon color. But they weren't cheery. I yanked the curtains shut to run around naked in a wild frenzy. I was just trying to break in the room—and city. I thought if I broke it in well enough, then it would be a little bit in my control.

After collapsing on the cold stiff bed cover, an incredible monster of loneliness crept into me and overwhelmed me. I couldn't believe how insignificant I felt. Outside my door, I heard people laughing as they passed by. I felt jealous of them. I imagined them already having great jobs and spouses. As I listened to the traffic honks and sirens, I felt jealous of all the people out there in cars who were going someplace. A sign on the TV warned me that if I moved it, an alarm would go off. So being extra careful that I wouldn't fall into it and knock it off its simulated-wood metal stand, I turned it on. I let its electric colors and noise fill me with some bland semblance of proper universality and comfort. The denture commercial was the same as at home.

All night long, plaintive sirens wailed like sad ghosts in the distant hills. They pressed closer and closer, louder and louder. The suspense became unbearable. I shivered. Maybe my door would smash open and the violent army men from my hospital dreams would come back for me. I had been in the hospital more than once. I was brought back to life a few times after they'd removed things. And then a hypnotist told me to forget everything. So I have no idea what I'm talking about, except it had something to do with something in Mexico with Mom, and it was all very illegal.

Chapter Two

Morning was silent in a creepy way. After checking my door key a few times to make sure it really did work in the big silver doorknob, I bravely walked away and went to a cramped dim corner drugstore. I found a couple of cool postcards of that scary gothic silent movie actress with the impossible name, Dunkel Morgendammerung. She was that exotic star who had also been the mother of those far scarier mass murderers, the Twins Of Evil. I wanted to buy the cards, liking the look of her, but then I decided mass murder might not be a good first message home. "I'll be a star, tomorrow," I scrawled across the back of a happier beach card. I wrote with a groovy pen that constantly changed its ink color.

I picked up a newspaper and spotted an add for *Derriere Modeling*. I decided to go there, thinking aloud, "Oooh… so la French!"

In the door, I said, "Hi, my name is…"

"Take a number. Park it there," a receptionist ordered me.

I did and felt shamed. I sat unmoving in the narrow room on a metal bench for a few horrible hours with a bunch of other nervous, but haughty girls. I looked at the rows and rows of hundreds of black and white photos of smiling models all over the walls. They all looked so much alike that it was unnerving. In fact, my mind was so stimulated with anxiety, I finally had a profound realization. "Wow. We really are all the same species."

"Are you on drugs?" the doll-like girl next to me finally asked.

"Nope," I assured her, closing my mouth. "Just thinking." Suddenly the room began to vibrate, roar and shake. I wondered if I was feeling the first warm-up of some horrible earthquake. Then I noticed it was just a big garbage truck driving by the front window, rattling it. "I thought that was an earthquake!" I said nervously to her, and then laughed.

"When one of those hits," she said, "you'll know."

"How?"

She smiled tightly. "The stunt people come out and run around."

When my time came to talk to a representative, the sullen woman didn't seem impressed that I'd heard of them through the paper I'd paid good money for. She was an uppity blasé snot about everything else. I left feeling humiliated. The same went with all the other agencies the paper took me to. "Where have you modeled before and who was the designer? Italian or French?"

"I was Miss Milk. They thought I was very dairy-like. I wore my Mom's sweater. She knitted it with red, white and blue knitting needles."

"Please sit down over there. No, farther down. Yes. Way down there."

This went on a few times over and, "Yes," they said I was perfectly pretty. "Yes," they liked my perfect measurements. "Yes," they approved of my perfectly petite nose that bobbed just a bit, but not too much. They even wanted to praise a plastic surgeon who didn't exist. They were charmed at my perfectly wholesome smile that was not stained by coffee vices. My imperfect voice that "sounds like you have a cold" got mixed reviews. My hair was too fine and thin and blah. "Get a hairpiece." After a few days of this, I started to feel unreal. They were going to change that somehow with expensive classes. Yeah right. I left. I wept. I felt sick. I just couldn't push back the self-doubts anymore.

I looked in the mirror. I yelled at it. "You ugly cow! You need more than lipstick! You need to have never been born!"

Horrible days later I was at a donut shop, reading useless actor help-wanted ads.

Wanted, experienced only. New York soaps or Broadway roles will do.

Then an older man wearing a green polyester golf shirt and holding a big fat cigar in his hand approached me. "Anybody sitting here?"

"Nope." Since the cigar wasn't lit, I was thankful. I smiled big.

"Do you have a job?" he asked. "Right now?"

"You an agent?" I asked, feeling like that girl from *Fade Away* who was discovered while provocatively sipping a lemonade fizz. Then she went on to become such a brief but bright star, they called her *The Shooting Star*. So on her thirtieth birthday she set herself on fire, then jumped off the roof of her tall hotel. Thinking of all that blazing glory, I tried to sip my iced water from my little Styrofoam cup in a way that would bring out my cheekbones. *"Hmm?"*

He said, "No. I'm not an agent."

"Oh." I was sad.

He was looking mostly at the two sunflowers on my t-shirt. "I own a business selling aluminum siding for houses. We're at the trade show at Palm Spree and I need a pretty girl to attract attention. You sure are pretty, in that epic movie sort of way. It's a shame you weren't around when they made movies with chariots. You a lesbian?"

"No. But thank you for the compliment… about being pretty. Of course I'm not a lesbian. Can't you tell by my nail polish? It's the most darling shade of peach. Don't you think?" I felt cheered since agents all own houses and have to buy siding. Now agents would be coming to me. "When can I start?"

"Today," he said. "The show started yesterday and I thought I could've done it myself. But damn. I forgot that standing so much is hell." He showed me his ankles. His fat purple varicose veins seemed a bit like an interstate road map.

*****

I found the Palm Spree shopping mall and quickly realized the show wasn't exactly a *show* in the way that I'm accustomed to thinking of the word show. No costumes or wigs—no special makeup—no stage floor—no music, glitter, disco or spotlight. It was just a tiny booth like at the Quonset building at the county fair. All I had to do was stand at the display and ask shoppers if they'd like to sign up to win a free siding job for their inadequate houses. I soon realized that flirting got me the most numbers. "Can I have your phone number?" I asked wholesome looking dads, holding out my forms just below my knockers. I got them—hook, smile and sinker. Then, a homely sort of woman with red hair and freckles actually walked up to *me* without my having to cast a line. "Hello," I smiled in a nice girl-to-girl way. "Would you like to win free siding for your lovely home?"

"Have you worked here long?" she asked, her eyes narrowing in girl-to-girl distress. "I hope you're not expecting to get paid for this. I used to work for the old rip-off, myself. You probably won't even see a check to bounce. All he cares about is those cards people fill out. Then he calls them up on the phone and spins his phony web. He never gives anything away, of course. There's no drawing. He don't give anything away, not even a wage. He just wants everyone's phone number, everyone with a house. Period."

"Oh!" I said. "What do I do? I worked so hard for these cards!"

Her eyes narrowed. "How many phone numbers you got?"

I started pulling the cards out of the box. "I think about… um… lots… so far."

The woman held out her hand. "Just give them all to me and I'll throw them away for you. Just take this as a learning experience. Don't trust anybody around here. *Anybody*!"

I gave her all my cards that had been filled out. "Thank you!"

She added, "Live and learn." She gave me a sympathetic smile, girl-to-girl, like when the apple pie has burned. "Now get the hell out of here, honey, and find a real job."

I left the mall. Once outside I jolted. I realized I'd left my purse behind in the cabinet of the booth. I quickly went back in to fetch it. With its strap tight around my wrist, I then decided to go further into the mall to get a pop and bag of corn chips. I was hoping they had my favorite brand *Corny Peso.* A few booths past the hot tubs, to my complete alarm, I saw that the honest-looking red-haired woman who'd taken all my cards was sitting at *her own* aluminum siding booth. She couldn't help but notice my abject horror. She said, "I told you not to trust anybody." She smiled and then casually flipped me off, giving me the middle finger. "Thanks for all the free leads. How are you going to explain this to the old man? It'll break his poor old heart. And he has a very weak heart."

I couldn't help but feel as if a brick had just hit me. I ran, but not so fast as to draw the attention of the police, and once outside in the relentlessly cheery sun, I collapsed on a concrete bench. After numbly watching gorgeous, tanned shirtless boys on skateboards going around on sidewalks, I pulled out a compact. I began to rejuvenate my eye shadow. "I will not *look* like a loser, at least!" I said to myself, trying to muster up some pride. "You're not the first girl who's been bit by a bitch." I wished Mom were here. She'd fix everything. After I added a lot more color to my eyes, even penciling baby blue underneath, I felt better about myself.

"Hello, hi! My name is Andernach," I heard a guy say and I could just tell it was directed at me. My heart skipped. I wondered if I'd have to fight, flee or be flighty. I looked up and saw a young man in trendy feathered hair, cool shirt, an even tan, and nice white teeth. He'd have looked trustworthy if I weren't having such a sour day.

"I don't trust anybody so don't talk to me," I said, trying to sound like I had authority. But my voice already had a low enough register so I may have overdone it.

My bluntness made him step back. He finally busted out in a bright festive laugh. "Good for you! I don't trust anybody either, especially those who call themselves friends. For some reason, their jive is the worst."

"Are you a spy from the aluminum siding people? Just don't ask me for anything."

"I was going to," Andernach admitted, smiling nervously.

I quickly fingered on some more cherry lip gloss. I wanted to dazzle him in the sun.

Then he did a corny two-footed pirouette and asked, "Have you ever modeled before?"

"I was just modeling aluminum siding."

"I'm a nobody photographer and I want to do some outta-sight nude layouts to get into the girly magazines. Nudes are a good way to get started in photography, you know. Jump in."

"Hah! I'm lady-like," I protested, "I don't do that sort of thing." I stiffened my posture.

Andernach said, "I didn't mean to accuse you of being a jive turkey, or anything. You seemed cool enough. That's why I thought you might make a good model for this sort of thing. You've got eyes that could tear holes in a poster."

I quickly looked away. "You're full of bull."

"What I mean," he started to talk faster, his shoulders hardening, "is that nude layouts are… are usually not supposed to look too, you know, *witchy*—for most magazines, if you know what I mean. It's supposed to… you know… not be nice but look nice. You know, man. *Love it!*"

"No, I don't know. No thanks," I said, starting to get up. "I'm going to be a film actress, not some sprawled-out slop. Not some grinning hooker."

"Here." He pulled a scrap of paper from his pocket and put his name on it. It looked like a grocery store receipt. "My name's Andernach. Remember that name. I'll be a famous photographer, someday, and you have to start with nudes. If you ever change your mind, ring me up."

"How do I know you're not just trying to get me in the sack?"

He looked at me oddly before he blinked a few times in astonishment. Then he blushed. "Oh. Oh, I'm gay as red shoes, can't you tell? *Love it!* Don't you know a gay guy when you see one?"

This was the first time I'd met anyone who admitted to such a thing, so I stammered like a dork, "H-h-how d-do you know you're really… that?"

He blinked a few more times, this time demurely. He slowly smiled, crookedly. "When I look through the men's section of the catalogue… at the underwear… I just *know*. I look real hard. I look at that underwear for a real long time. You get my drift?" He laughed then quickly got serious again. "I just want some artsy-fartsy nude layouts, without showing your box, of course. Call me if you change your mind. That's unless you're not hip to your body, or something. Are you from the Midwest?"

"I'm not shy." I took the number from him. "I'm not some Midwestern prude! I'll call you if I decide it's the smart thing to do. And by the way, how much would I get paid? What about the *money!*"

"I can't give you anything right off," he admitted, suddenly not able to look at me. He looked plaintively at the half naked boys on skateboards. I was turned off. He looked at his feet and continued, "I'd have to wait and share what I get if I sell. If you don't trust me, you can write the goddam contract, yourself."

I wondered how a person would go about writing a contract. "Residuals?"

Andernach nodded. "Crumbs probably. The money thing all depends. Who knows? This town is so goddam all-or-nothing fickle. There's no middle, here. Either veal or doggy-nips."

"You're not too good at making wild promises," I accused him, darkening my dark voice.

He shrugged flippantly. "It just gets you into trouble. It's easier to work with strangers. In the long run, if you're just up front about what's expected, and cool, then there's no train crash at the end of the line. Friends are the ones who have the power to give you grief. They expect twice the favors in return. Friends act like you owe them till the day they die."

I wondered if he was he trying to warn me that he was a jerk. I stood. "I'll let you know if I decide this is what I want to do."

Andernach said to me, while watching the skateboarding boys, "It takes only a few weeks in this town before you realize you're pumping winter."

"Sure, whatever." I wondered what he could have meant by that expression in this glaring concrete desert. I looked up at the sky and crinkled all my makeup.

*****

I found a furnished efficiency apartment (nothing like the spacious apartments in sit-coms). The pad didn't even provide bad art, but if I leaned far enough out the window to look up the street, I could see two palm trees. To me, that was exotic. The instant my phone got connected, I made a call. "Andernach?" I asked into the receiver, nervously, picking at my dark orange nail polish. "It's Jill. Remember me?"

"No, sweets. Who's Jill?"

"The chick you met outside of the mall. You liked men's underwear."

"Who? Underwear? Whose? What party was this? If you're trying to bust me for those French doors at Biff's party, forget it. Just because I was found sleeping underneath them doesn't mean I was the one who went flying through them. I could sue! I didn't smoke a thing and the vibrator needed new batteries anyway!"

"*What?* No, not that. No, no. How can you forget me?" I asked. "Oh, I guess I never told you my name. Well, you gave me your card, sort of, scribbled on a scrap of paper, a receipt—you spent sixty-eight cents on groceries—rice and beans and petroleum jelly."

"Oh!" Andernach laughed, sounding relieved. "*That!* The mall! Outside Palm Spree! I remember now. You were that model… jilted! I remember you!"

"Jill. You've got the right me. I was wondering if you were still interested in shooting my charlies."

"Your *what?*"

"My knockers," I clarified. "My assets."

Andernach asked, "Oh. Why do you call them charlies?"

I explained, "There was a perfume commercial. Long story. It's just something I made up for myself."

"Oh sure," he said. "Like how I call my belly button my knitting machine. But anyway, the shoot. Um, sure, I gotta think fast now. How about tomorrow? I'm too hung over today to run all over and I need a day to shop for a new light bulb."

"Tomorrow is soon enough. Is there anything I can do, besides losing weight?"

Andernach asked, "How much do you weigh?"

"None of your friggin' business!"

"Sorry!" he said. "I'm sure you'll be fine… but say… how about if you bop down to the drug store and pick up some bleach for your hair to num-num it up a bit. We're just mad about blondes around here… you know what I mean?"

I'd always harbored a lurid desire to bleach my hair. So this seemed to me the magic key to tell me that this man was right for me and my career. "Bleach? Isn't that a bit cliché?"

"Sure, welcome to town. Anyway, it'll soften your face."

I loved him for that, but warned, "I'll go bald!"

"It's fine. We'll just fluff it around and it'll look like you have as much as you want."

I loved him all the more. On the way to the shoot, I made the mistake of thinking I could do a little last-minute eyebrow plucking on a bus with jerky brakes. As I walked up to Andernach's building, all I could think of was shoving the top half of my face in ice. Up four flights of crumbling stairs, Andernach greeted me at his door. I asked, "Why is this place so smashed up? Was there an earthquake?"

"Yeah. Once. Isn't it lovely? I'm just so glad there's a dent in mopboard. It gives the place some personality. Come in. Watch the last step. I tried to fix it with some school glue. It was all I had. It didn't hold one day."

"Oh my. What a booby trap." I took a bit of a leap and entered his one-room studio with a tub sink and hotplate in the corner.

Andernach sized me up. "You're kinda tall for a girl."

"I hear that tall women make great models. The fabric just falls for miles. I guess I shouldn't bring up fabric now." I admitted, "I'm a wee bit flustered."

Andernach said, "Oh, there's nothing to be nervous about. It's easy being naked once you get naked. Don't be a fuddy-duddy. Just don't start streaking, either. There's so many naked people running around outside, just for the fad, it isn't even cool anymore."

I said, "I didn't see any streakers." I found a mirror on the wall that was at crotch level. I crouched down and started to fluff my hair. "Why are there drops of school glue on your mirror?"

Andernach pulled me away and pulled up on my hair with his fingers. "Your hair's turned out great."

He twirled again in excitement… or nervousness. Then he started hanging clear plastic sheets around for a backdrop. "You really sucked out that pigment."

"Pigment?"

Andernach said, "The pigment in your hair. You've really lightened it a lot from what it was before."

"Oh. Sure. Say." I asked him, "What's a two-spirited shaman?"

He stopped what he was doing. "Why?"

"An Indian woman called me a two-spirited shaman."

"When? Where? Is she right outside?"

"No," I clarified, "on my bus ride here. We stopped and I bought a ring from her."

Andernach rubbed his chin. "Could she have been trying to call you *cheap?*"

"I don't think so."

"Neither do I. *Hmmm.* She could have been serious. It can only be one thing. You've been called a *dyke*, I think."

"Ha! *Me?* I can't be one of those. I don't have any scars, not on my face. I don't drive a truck. When I see a pretty woman, I only think one thing. I just think… *I'm glad I'm thinner than you…* or I think… *you goddam thin bitch!* And so you know what that makes me… a true blue woman." I flipped my hair in a girly way. I looked at my pretty nail polish for comfort. Then I kicked out of my clothes. I did it quickly, so I wouldn't think about how dumb it felt. Then I powdered a few moles and small body scars with my compact. "You better shoot me through a thick filter."

"I wish I could afford a pretty filter. They have filters that make stars and fog and all sorts of things. They have filters that make everything look gold. I'd be Midas then. I'd make everything gold! Get it?"

"Get it."

Andernach added, "I just wouldn't be able to cash it in."

"Get it." Looking down at myself, I decided, "A pop bottle will do. I've just got a few nicks here and there. I'm clumsy."

"We won't see those beauty marks." Then he looked at me oddly. "I'm an expert on boy butts. Girl, you have a boy butt."

I glared at him. "Is that good or bad?"

He shrugged. "It's just the way you are."

"Then please call it a *tiny* butt, if you will. My butt is mine and I already told you I'm not a lesbian!" I fluffed my hair and then showed him my pretty nail color.

"Sure. Toga up in that long piece of plastic," Andernach directed. "Peek a boob. Now, look over here so the light hurts your eyes."

I looked right at the light until it hurt. I didn't really mind the pain of the glare. So I knew right then and there I had what it took to be a star. "All I see is spots."

He squinted behind the camera. "Something's wrong now. It's not foxy."

I'd already re-fluffed my hair, and my makeup certainly hadn't slid places yet. Maybe blood was shooting out of my eyebrows. "How is something wrong? Aren't my lips shiny enough? Hand me my purse, I brought my cherry lip gloss. I could gloss them again. Hand me a spatula."

"No, no. The shine of your lips could light all of Tinseltown's tinsel."

"You sure?"

"You got so much lip gloss on you smell like a giant punch bowl. No. It's your eyes!" Andernach said. "Something's not jiving. I got it! Your pupils! They've shrunk down to pinholes! You've been looking at the lights too much!"

Now feeling utterly blind, I offered, "I'll close my eyes for a few minutes then. When you're ready, I'll open them and you can snap before they shrink again."

"That should work... *love it.* You're a natural... just granola!"

I waited an eternity for him to give his cue. Then I opened my eyes wide and foxy. It hurt, but I refused to squint.

"*Great!* You look cranky! It's great! *Love it!*"

After a while, Andernach said he was bored with the set-up. He left the room to try and borrow Christmas lights from some neighbor in the building he was on borrowing terms with. He came back carefully untangling a string. "We'll wrap you in these. That'll be so *bad!*"

As I was wound, I cried, "Hey guy! I'm going to electrocute!"

"Now, now, don't punk out on me, not yet. Five more snaps and the roll of film is spent."

I posed my best, counting the camera clicks, so if he'd lied, he was out of luck. After four, I got up. "Hand me the camera," I ordered, "The last one's of you."

"Great idea! Just wait a moment." He ran behind a table. He took off all his clothes and quickly fashioned himself a totally see-through loincloth with a strip of clear plastic. "When I'm famous, this shot will be so scandalous!" He held out his hands to embrace the world as I carefully composed the shot. I didn't want to whack off his head at the top, or what I could see through his plastic wrap at the bottom. He asked, "Do I look hot? Don't I have a great basket?"

"Like that, it looks like something in the meat department at the grocery store. All we need is a Styrofoam tray under it all."

"How modern."

I snapped. We dressed.

On the way out, Andernach declared, "Look to the stars and connect the dots."

"Gotcha." I had no idea what he was talking about.

*****

Two weeks later I was sobbing into the phone. "Mom, I'm coming home to ya!"

I hung up and began to pack my bags. Then the phone rang. Andernach was on the other end with a voice that was too excited to listen to. "Slow down!" I scolded him. "Please lower your voice to a human frequency. Talk like a person. Now what are you talking about?"

"We're invited to a party and…"

I interrupted him. "Now pretend you're a Butch Thornton-like and talk to me like a calm cowboy."

Talking more akin to a strangled songbird, Andernach took an impatient breath and started over.

"We-are-invited-to-a-*party!* Snako, the owner of *Spy Your Skin* magazine has invited us *both* to his next pool party. He *loooooves* the pics! Well, a few of them. He thinks he has a new star in his… er… *on* his hands!"

"Sure he does," I said without care, not believing that for a movieland minute.

"It's a get-to-know-everybody party. There'll be all kinds of industry people there. You know, producers and cool stuff!"

"*Oooh?"* I got excited. "I'll bring my best bathing suit."

"No," Andernach said, "I want to wrap you up in clear plastic. I think that would draw the best attention to you. It's the new hip image I created for you."

I didn't care. "As long as we all become famous and make more mad money than we know what to do with." After I hung up, I stripped off my yellow T-shirt and looked at myself long and hard in the mirror. I turned this way. I turned that way. I remembered how I used to be embarrassed of my breasts and I'd slouch. Mom said the lurid items were there to stay. She said that girls have to get used to them. "From straw to gold," I said to myself. I ran my palms across them and smiled. "Boys are so dumb."

Chapter Three

The pool party was cheap. The only nod to fantasy was sun-faded molded-plastic Chinese lanterns. I felt letdown. I cried inside. I said, "This is *so* cheap."

Andernach assured me, "You look great. Like art. Creative. That's big these days."

"Art?'

"People need art to distract them from their own crap in life, at least for a little while."

I tried not to consider that my clear plastic toga wrap might also look cheap. I pulled on it where it was sticking to me from where I was sweating. I looked around with a big celebrity smile. Andernach kicked off his blue jeans and arrogantly swished around in such a sheer little red bikini that it left no doubt that he'd been circumcised.

"Do you have a problem with exhibitionism?" I asked him. Most the other men on the small patio wore baggy shorts with cartoon tree palms on them.

"Love it!" He looked down at his bumpy crotch and then grinned at me like a proud loon.

I smiled as if all were perfect in the world even though the concrete beneath my feet was burning them to hell. That made it easy to bop to the music coming from the 8-track stereo inside.

Andernach said, "God girl, I could swear you really do have a boy butt."

"Shove it."

I was offered treats. "What's that?" I asked. "A baby's first poop?"

"Guacamole."

"What's that?"

"Stuff."

Andernach walked over to Snako, the deeply tanned owner of *Spy Your Skin.* I was amazed how Andernach's butt crack had sucked up the fabric of his swimsuit. He looked so naughty both coming and going. Andernach said to Snako, "She's a natural in front of the camera. She can be your next big super-skin star. She treats the lens like raw sex. And baby kittens. And homemade macaroni and cheese. All at the same time. *Love it!"*

"Oh really?" Snako muttered, gazing at me like I was racetrack horseflesh. I got the willies. Snako added, "I'm also going to take over operations at my brother's movie studio, Flicker Farm. And he don't know it yet!" He laughed cruelly. "I'll need some new stars to rub it in his face even more."

Andernach said, "She'll be a great star for Flicker Farm. She'll polish all the apples in town. A real doll! She's not a damn snot. She's not like the other dolls we've tried to put on a poster."

I carefully mounted a clear blow-up sofa in the water. I didn't want to think about Flicker Farm. It was the cheapest studio in town, with Dixie Dawn Don as their number one star, and she looked like dried up trash.

"What do *you* know?" Snako asked, looking at Andernach's swimsuit. "You're just a fudge-packer, right?"

Andernach paused a moment to pose. "So? So, I'm as queer as red shoes. But I still know what assets look like. Look at her! *Love it!"*

I was now demurely poised in the middle of the pool on the float. As they looked over to me, I slowly took a sip of my warm beer from my flimsy plastic cup. I tried to sip in a way that would bring out my cheekbones. The beer went down the wrong pipe. I convulsed so that half of it splashed out of my cup and went over my wrist. But I still waved and somehow said, "Hi, fellahs!"

"We're not so different," Andernach continued saying to Snako. "We know what to look for in a doll. Look at her! Look at her legs! Long as a pony! Any boy, girl or *it* could figure that out. *Look!"*

I smiled back at them. It was amazing to see people look at me like that. I rested my head on the blow up pillow and let the coastal sun evenly flood my fair face. Then I noticed there was somebody else I hadn't spotted before. He was taking photos. He was a sort of nice looking man in cute gray briefs. They were not as naughty as Andernach's, but not as shapeless as the baggy shorts. "Nobody pee in the pool!" he hollered.

I smiled. I'd already committed *that* great crime. I could smell chlorine in the water enough to kill scabies—let alone skin, nails and hair. So a little pee was but a small revenge. Besides, there was no way I was going to attempt to unwind and then rewind my wet plastic wrap just to visit the porcelain.

"Hey, sweets," the man called out to me. "Arch your back! Show us your hooters!"

Confused, I wondered if Andernach would call a duel. So I glanced his way. Andernach seemed pleased. He winked at me—I winked at him—though I didn't know why. When my divan floated to the edge of the pool, I grabbed the blue tile edge. The man in grey briefs swaggered up to me. Since I saw him approaching, I took it upon myself to say *hi* first. He stood at the very edge of the pool. His toes were hanging over. From my angle up between his legs, I had a rather formidable view. I was flustered and looked anywhere else. *Pig-like*, I concluded.

"*Eh*. My name's Bod," he said as he squatted low, knees too wide apart, holding out his hand. "I'm a small time, but *not* forgettable, movie producer."

"How nice." I wondered why his side-burns looked like pubic hair.

"Ever heard of *Babe My Way?*"

"No."

"Heard of *Crap Land?* That's my classic! It stars Dixie Dawn Don. *Eh!*"

I smiled, annoyed. I totally *hated* Dixie Dawn Don. I hated her entire lowbrow white-trash drive-in career. "Was the movie about crap?"

"Gambling."

"But Dixie Dawn Don was in it so I'd first think of crap."

"You don't like her?" he asked in a manner that suggested he didn't understand why everybody wouldn't always hate her guts.

"I hope the drive-in she plays at also has a carwash. So people have something to do."

Bod looked stupid. "You don't like her?"

I said, "And if I ever cross her path, *ever,* I'll tell her so!"

"Where you from?" Bod asked.

"Plaksville."

"Where's that?"

I pointed east. "That way. Across the desert."

"Ha, you're a poet." Bod smiled.

"Everything's across the desert," I reminded him. "Are you big?" I asked, accidentally directing it directly up at his swimsuit.

"I'd be a really big producer, now, if *Twins Of Evil* had gone through."

"Oh! I heard of them." I splashed water over myself. "They were the kids of that scary silent movie star, Dunkel Morgendammerung. *Ooooh!* She was the most glamorous movie goddess, ever. At least of the silent days."

Bod nodded sadly. "As soon as my script was done and the deal announced, I got lawsuits. They were all from that old hag, Dunkel fuck. She was afraid of more bad press, as if I could do anything more damaging than her own kids' book. I could've won the stupid lawsuits but I couldn't afford a lawyer. Not after all I'd spent getting the production started. I already had a script I wrote myself and it took me a long time. I had no money. That old bag owns several oil wells. I couldn't fight that kind of power."

"Is that why there haven't been any movies made about the Twins Of Evil?"

Bod said, "Oh there's been a few. But they changed them to avoid litigation. So now you wouldn't recognize them. Remember *Satan Sisters in Blood?"*

I nodded. "I think so. I think that was the one that came to the drive-in as a double feature. It was with *My Mother's Blood of Evil.*" I never saw it.

Bod nodded. "Both those flicks were based on the story of the Twins Of Evil. But they changed them so much they even cast the killers as women in one of them. They turned the other one into a western."

"That's very strange."

"Well, I'm not drunk enough yet to get stuck in past failures," Bod said, rubbing his palms together. "What do you say we make some plans to get rich?" His eyes twinkled. They seemed like vibrant windows to a greedy cash-register mind.

"Me?" I splashed water on myself again. I was thrilled, but knew it couldn't be so easy.

Bod asked, "Can I tie a deal with you? Would you like to be the star of my latest flick?"

In spite of my excitement, I had to look at him as if he wasn't even capable of tying shoes. "Right." I grumbled in disdain.

"You a lesbian or something?" he asked. "*Eh*."

"Nope," I snapped back. "Why?" I flashed my sparkly fingertips at him. "What lesbian would have this kind of glamour?"

"The sun's going down soon," he smiled and rubbed his thumb across the front of his suit. "I've always wanted to do it in the pool after dark."

"What?"

He looked shameless.

"*What?*"

"I want to boff you right here."

I pushed away from him. I hadn't considered that a pool could turn into a cold wet casting couch. I went to the ladder and heaved myself up out of the pool. My plastic toga wrap held so much water that I gushed all the way to the house. I didn't care. It was all so stupid. I changed back into my two-piece, bell-bottom blue denim pants suit with bright sunflower patches on the knees, and my sunflower hat. Stepping back outside on the pool patio, looking for more snacks, I thought I looked hip.

"Why are you dressed?" Andernach asked. "The sun hasn't gone away yet. You haven't even been out long enough to get a good tan."

"I just didn't want to get chlorine shot up my pooky." I gave Bod a dirty look. "I hear it's bad for you. How chemical."

"What're you talking about?" Andernach asked.

I complained, "This man wanted to ball me right there in the pool in front of everybody. Ick!" Andernach shot Bod an over-acted incredulous glare.

"Um," Bod mumbled. I saw the light in his eyes go out.

I loudly added, "They should have set some rat poison out, before we came."

Andernach said to me, "You're too smart for this town."

Bod stood up and tried to act nice. "I didn't mean to freak anybody out. I just love to ball chicks, you know how it is for a guy." Then he gave Andernach a dirty look, peering down at his little red bikini in utter disgust. "And I'm not a weird rump ranger either," he added, "I'm normal. What normal guy doesn't like to cozy up to some nice wet mink?"

Wet mink? I tried to think of something clever to say again about rat poison. I drew a blank. The question didn't deserve a response, anyway. I walked toward the house.

"You're overdressed for a pool party," Andernach said.

"Did I say I would stay?"

"You're not famous enough for haughty exits. Sit, pose, and be nice."

Not wanting to be Midwesternish, I went back in and changed yet again. I stripped a bed and made myself a colorful G rated toga. It made everyone laugh when I did my fashion show; the cartoon footballs on the sheets helped to make it all the more silly.

When the sun went down, most of the people left. Just Bod, Andernach, Snako and I sat inside. A Country Western 8-track tape played so loud, we all had to yell at each other. We started to play cards. Somebody in a *Mano Mano Monster* rubber mask and powder blue leisure suit came to the front door. I could see it clearly from where I was sitting. Snako laughed at the rubber mask and went outside to talk with him. A short while later the lights flickered. We thought nothing of it as I went on losing pitifully at the game. The men kept insisting I was going to pay with my doing a minute of hula-hula dancing for every one of my losses. Yeah right. Then the lights browned out and stayed that way for about five seconds.

"It's the energy crisis," Bod declared. "We're running out of it."

Andernach said, "Downtown smells like something you could put in a gas tank. Maybe they should start using that."

I asked, "Do I hear splashing?"

"No," Bod yelled back. "The 8-track is a little warbled here where the machine once ate it."

"Oh!" I said, "And I thought I heard somebody yell."

"No! That's the song! Dummy! Don't you know this song?"

Andernach tried to do a pirouette. He was too drunk. He fell to his knees then crawled out the back door to the patio to refill the beer pitcher from the keg. Over the blare of a song, we heard him scream like a ninny. "Was that a scream?" I yelled.

Bod agreed. "Yes!"

We ran out to find Snako dead in the pool, floating on his back, still jerking grotesquely with electrocution. The molded plastic Chinese lanterns were flashing and melting. Their cord was wrapped tightly around his neck. "A *murder!*" I gasped.

"Who could have done this?" Andernach cried, pulling the plug out from the side of the house. The rest of the lights came back up to full.

I blurted, "It was the man in the rubber mask! A monster mask! He did it—he had to!"

Bod asked, "What monster mask?"

I asked, "Didn't you see it? Remember somebody came to the door and Snako went out to talk to him? He was wearing a rubber monster mask and the ugliest leisure suit! I could see it from where I was sitting. Couldn't you?"

Bod rubbed his lips. "Oh that's right." He puked a lot of beer in my direction. "No. I don't remember."

Leaving the body in the water, we called the police and waited for the inevitable interrogations.

*****

The next day, Bod called. "*Eh.* Remember me?"

I said, "Even retarded people have memories."

"What's that supposed to mean?"

"I just said it."

Bod asked again, "What's it supposed to mean?"

"Nothing," I grumbled. "I'm just tired from being in a police station all night talking about murder and stuff. I feel like I dreamt it all. Did I? I have odd dreams all the time. Sometimes I dream a green space baby is in a hospital. It's stalking me. And my body parts are being ripped out of me. And I'm brought back to life like a movie monster. But this was real. Right?"

"You toke a lot? *Eh.*"

"Toke?" I asked.

"Smoke pot."

"No! *Peeee-ew!*"

Bod said, "The murder was freaky."

"Freaky?" I asked. "That's all you can say? Didn't it give you nightmares?"

"The guy wasn't nice," Bod said. "People like that can have things like that happen to them. You know? And I didn't see anything until we found him in the water, so… so that's what happens. Sometimes."

"Are you next?" I asked. It was rude but he was far removed by a phone line. I didn't fear him. I should have been terrified since I hadn't been able to get him out of my head since the party, which made me seriously question my sanity. "Now why are you calling me?"

Bod boasted, "I got on the horn and drummed up a film for you."

"Yeah right," I said, wondering if it was on his pukey bed with a ten-dollar, made-in-Japan, super-8 movie camera. "And I'm the star?"

"Well, I didn't mean it was the starring part. In fact it's a bit part, really. That doesn't mean it's nothing. It's a pretty splashy part, really. Only if you're up to some good sport and want to have some fun. And make a few bucks."

"Oh? Bucks? You mean *make real money for once?* Tell me what's involved. How much do I make, and believe me it better be at least a month's rent. They better have snacks all over the set, like corn chips. I love corn chips. And what is it that I do? Believe me, it better not be getting balled by you in a pool! Wet mink, my ass!"

"No, no, no, no!" Bod assured me, but still sounding too nervous. Red flags went up. "First, can you tap dance? Can you hoof?"

"Of course, where do you think I came from? Clodhopper city?"

"I don't know? I just thought I'd ask. Some people can't, you know."

"Well, I can dance like anything," I lied, not caring. I figured real dancing had little to do with these parts.

"Great. I guess that makes me your agent, now."

"Oh," I said after some deliberation. "I guess it does. I wonder if I'm lucky."

"Have you been to the beach, yet?"

"Oh!" I said. "I can finally wear my real bathing suit. I was just wondering when I'd ever see the beach. I always knew there was one out here somewhere."

"It's a nude beach."

"Oh." I was silent for a spell, not knowing if that meant something culturally really good or really bad, or just really dumb.

He asked, "So, *eh*, you wanna go? Eh?"

I became resolute, if not angry. "I'm not doing it in the ocean with you. You can plug up a navy seal butt for all I care, goddam you, but I'm a real lady, especially about that kind of thing!"

"I won't touch you. What are you? A friggin' prude?"

"What do you mean?" I asked.

"I don't know," he said. "What do you all do in the Midwest? Wear sweaters in the bathtub?"

Another spell of confused thinking passed before I finally conceded to his gig. "Okey-doke."

*****

"Will be star soon!" I scrawled on the back of a postcard to mom. "But first, my dues. Am going beachy today to take in some local culture. I bet there aren't any cornfields there. Ha Ha Ha. And don't worry, I'm taking my vitamins like a good girl so I stay pretty."

They really weren't vitamins. They were hormone pills. They helped replace what all my surgery had chopped away. Or maybe it was a botched abortion. Was it cancer? I was only eight or nine years old at the time so female trouble was unlikely. But I couldn't remember any of it anyway because a hypnotist told me to forget. But it's hard to forget how hot it gets in Mexico. "You *bad little boy!*" I yelled out into the room for no good reason. Then my rage passed. I forgot about it. I cupped my perfect breasts. "You good little girl. Mommy likes you better this way. You make such a pretty girl." I touched-up my nail polish and waited.

Bod finally drove up.

"You're late. I hate you."

"Here's your money."

"I love you!" I took my movie money and hid it in a plastic bag in the toilet tank like I saw in the TV movie, *Spotchers*. If the place burned down while I was gone, the money should be spared. We got into his noisy little white bug of a car. It was peppered with enough rust spots to give it the impression of an animal skin. The way he shoved around traffic amazed me. He should have caused collisions in his wake. I ended up putting my hand over my eyes, pretending it was to shield them from the sun, even when it wasn't in front of us. I asked, "Do you think somebody who knew Snako killed him?"

"Why?" Bod asked.

"If he was a relative then he'd inherit something, right? Like his magazine?"

"I don't know."

"People always kill other people over the last will and testament. It's always in the movies, anyway. It makes the best plot. Because everybody is family. And nobody can razz you better than your own family. Even a small dumb comment can ruin your life if it comes from your mother. *You* can call me an old fat ugly cow and I'll just think you're a rude jerk, and I'll forget all about it after I've forgotten all about you. But on the other hand, my *Mom* can ask me when was the last time I washed my hair, and wait until we're at the shopping center to do it, and I'll be completely devastated for the rest of my life."

"*Eh*. Family can be mean."

I nodded to agree. "Even mean enough to murder."

Bod said, "Snako's brother owns a movie studio. His name is Os, but he's not mean. He's bananas."

"Oh? Which studio?" I perked up.

"Flicker Farm."

"Oh, *that!*" I moaned. "*That* trashy studio. Oh! I remember now. I remember Snako saying he was going to take it over from his brother! His brother did it! Os did it! Os is the murderer. I just know it!"

Bod shook his head. "Flicker Farm is a great studio. I made a few movies there since the big studios wouldn't give me the time of day. And those two brothers have fought too much for actual real murder. Those two gangsters would never kill each other."

"Fighting stops murder?" I asked, puzzled.

Bod nodded. "Eee-*yep*. You'd have to know them. *Eh.*"

We rode a while longer in silence, until I finally admitted, "I don't know if I'll even get a good night's sleep again. I've never seen a real murder before. That was so gross the way Snako was getting shocked and he was jerking around like that in the water and blowing bubbles all like that. So gross!"

"Yeah," Bod agreed. "That was pretty freaky, huh. I wish I could remember it. I was pretty hammered."

"You were drinking your beer way too fast. Your puke was still cold and carbonated."

"How would you know?"

"I have very sensitive feet."

On a gravel road, we slowed down and wound around some tall sand dunes. "This is it?" I asked. My heart sank. I wondered when movieland would start looking like the movies.

"Almost," he said.

We topped a hill. All at once, with a loud gasp, I saw the ocean before me. It was in its blue glorious infinity. It was as if I'd come to the edge of the known cosmos. Sure, I'd seen the ocean all the time on TV, but this was so much wider. "*Omigod*!" I gasped. "Look at it!" When I finally stepped out of the car, I'm sure I looked just like a gaping idiot. "Look at that! Look! Just look at it!"

Nothing could have prepared me for the sight of the real thing. The wind blowing from it had a scent that I couldn't describe. It was sort of like stale salty corn chips and dirty motor oil and rotten seafood. The sand was littered with many dead fish and lobsters and crabs and pop-cans and their pull-tabs. "Oh my god! A syringe. A junkie was here!"

"Or a nurse."

"Why are all these dead things here?" I asked, pointing to a big snail shell.

Bod shrugged. "They get old and die, I guess."

"So we're, *aaah,* walking through a giant seafood graveyard?"

He gave me a "smarty pants" look, kicked off all his clothes and walked on. Nice! I thought, taking inventory of his body as if I hadn't just seen him in a swimsuit, save his pubes, meat and potatoes. They were now all in shocking detail.

He noticed me figuratively putting my eyeballs back in. I blinked. I smiled. I said, "Oh. You have a dick."

He said, *"Eh."*

I looked around at the landscape. I noticed most of the other nudes were not in the magazine shape Bod and I were in. My ego liked that. I tossed my own clothes into the back seat and skipped up to him. He coolly looked me over as if seeing me for the first time, and his face showed approval. "*Eh.* Foxy," he murmured. I'd have punched his lights out if he'd thought anything else. I followed him, careful not to step on dead fish, glass, pop can tabs, or needles. I loved the way the warm sand yielded sensuously under my bare feet. I forgot everything when a frothy wave finally washed over my feet. "Shit! It's *cold! Ahhhhh!"*

"Of course. What did you expect? Bath water?"

"I don't know." The more the waves washed over my feet, then legs; I began to feel I was undergoing some sort of Tinseltown baptism. I held my arms up and yelled, "I've reached the end of the world! Here be dragons!"

"*Here* be a dragon," Bod tried to brag, wiggling it at me. I only thought of a limp rag.

When I got too cold we got out. We walked the sand dune trails. "Did you remember to bring any snacks?"

Bod shook his head like he knew he was in trouble for it. After stepping on enough thistles and pop can pull-tabs, we returned to the car to drive home. I realized, first, that sand was well wedged under my seven remaining press-on nails. They'd all have to go. Also, my skin was on fire. "I have a burn!"

Bod said, "You're not used to the desert sun, yet."

"Screw you!" I replied. "Don't laugh. I'm in pain."

"Sorry."

"How can I do the scene with blisters all over myself." I moaned. "Oh no. I'm ruined."

"It'll be fine," he assured me. "The color will help you photograph."

"I'm glad pain doesn't photograph." Then I noticed my hair felt thick and stiff. "What was in that water?"

"The oils are good for your hair. Consider it a free condition."

"Oils?" I asked, "Like jojoba and sunflower?"

"It's an ocean, stupid. Motor oil!"

I frowned. "Gross." At home, I had to wash it several times with dishwashing detergent before it felt like hair again. Then it smelled like lemon.

*****

Bod dropped me off at the set. It was just a rec room in another cheap nondescript pressboard ranch house. The room had oddly chewed-up lime green shag carpet. I found out I'd somehow committed myself to topless tap-dancing. I would tap up on a pool table. It was a bachelor party scene. I hadn't read anything about the film in the trade papers. The topless part was easy; I had what was needed in doubles. For modesty, I was to wear two big yellow "smiley face" stickers over my nipples. I'd never done tap before and no one had thought to hire a choreographer. I figured it didn't matter, really. When "Action!" was screamed at me, I just tapped like in those giddy 30's musicals. I pounded the darn pool table as if it were a drum. Men with open shirts and gold chain necklaces stood around the table and screamed their praises. I didn't care. They were down there and I was up there and I had the center stage. "Cut!"

"Like it?" I asked, pushing against both smiley stickers. They felt like they wanted to pop off.

"You don't tap dance, do you," the cameraman said.

"Why?"

He grimaced. "Because you're about to put a hole through both the goddam ceiling and the table."

"So?" I shrugged him off and rubbed the top of my sore head. The ceiling was surprisingly hard. "If they want a professional-like dancer," I added, "they'll have to pay union scale for one."

He wagged his finger at me. "Don't bring up the union here. Who do you think you are? Some kind of star?"

I said, "I'm the kind of person, like, the union was designed to protect! And who are you?"

That was my end in pictures, I assumed. But the very next day, while getting high on a big bowl of delicious fake banana flavored sugar cereal, I received a call from Bod. "*Eh?*"

"Oh. You."

"Great knockers!"

"What?" I asked. "What about my lead feet?"

"No one was looking at your feet."

"You mean no one could see my feet," I corrected him. "I already knew that. I had figured it out. All those guys were in the way of them. The camera didn't have an x-ray lens."

"You're pretty smart," Bod declared

"I'm pretty insulted."

Bod said, "Why would anyone look at your feet?"

"I was dancing, creep! Crap! My feet were like two bricks!"

"You weren't hired to dance! *Duh!*" Bod said. "I hired you for your looks. They bounced. I now have a great scene. Thanks. It's the best scene in the whole damn boring film. It's about some dope fiend having a tedious mid-life crisis. Who cares?"

I felt a thrill. "I'm the best part of the film?"

"Yes. Completely. Most of the film is him going to different boring places. And he talks to boring people. All the while, he refills boring vending machines. And who cares about feet. Who cares if you dance like a cow."

"I'm the best part of the film?" I was thrilled. Something was completely wrong with me that I wasn't furious.

*****

That evening, Bod came over to my apartment. In the middle of some obligatory small talk about oceans and beaches and dead fish, he seemed to become restless. "Bod? What's wrong?"

"I, *er, aaah –*"

"Bod? Your eyes don't look right."

"*Aaah.* I. *Aaah…*"

"Bod? What's wrong."

"*Eh.*" He wiped the sweat off his upper lip. He pulled on his pant leg. Then he stood up and stripped. I was very surprised with what I saw. He was so much more than before. Without thinking further, lest I spoil the *Woodie's Feathers Nature Show* mood, I quickly shed my faux patchwork caftan. But then I decided I wouldn't give away something as big and important as this, my mink, not to a mere man. So I put out my hand. "Give me your watch!"

"What?"

"You're not touching me until I have your watch for this."

Bod argued, "It's too expensive to just give away."

I stood firm. "Give it to me and I'll know you respect me."

"But I do!"

I put my hand on my hip. "If you want to get this mink wet, then you give me something real!"

His breathing became heavy. A trickle of sweat ran down his side. Then he trembled and his eyes didn't look right again, like he needed glasses. He licked his lips. He tried not to regard his rearing male member, but then he just grabbed it and moaned pathetically. His breathing became spastic. His blood vessels seemed to become more prominent under his skin. He ripped off his watch and tossed it toward me. I didn't see where it rolled.

"Hold your breath, woman!" He didn't even kiss me. At first he seemed very angry, as if I was supposed to be punished for something. Maybe it really did irk him that I made him give me his watch. But then, after a few of its minute-hand twirls, we slammed to one roaring hoedown. We got lost in our own floating, sloshing, squeezing, soaring, lifting, sweating, dipping, plunging, ultra big budget 3-D cinematic wide-screen stereophonic blue film.

Afterwards, in the bathroom, while we were mopping up each others' honey pots, we were barely able to hold back euphoric giggles. I wondered how I could not only have *allowed* all this, but definitely *wanted* it—and badly. I could smell his sweat and it stunk. But it wasn't horrible at all. I couldn't believe I wasn't gagging. I was smiling! I felt gloriously human. I felt like I'd finally figured out something, but it didn't have words. I tried. "So, the fairer sex wants it, too, I suppose, just as much as the ape-like sex. Jeez!"

"What'd you say?"

"Talking to myself."

"You said something about an ape."

"Talking to myself."

"Oh. *Eh.* You have any beer?" he asked.

"Nope."

Then his eyes zoomed in on my hip. "What's that?" Just like a lover after the rose colored glasses are ripped off, he quickly found my mortal flaw.

"Oh, it's nothing."

"What's that scar?" Bod asked, digging his finger into a small imperfection on my hip.

"How can you see such a tiny scar through all the bruises you just gave me?"

"How'd you get a scar?" Bod repeated.

"I fell off the roof of my house onto a wagon when I was a dumb kid."

"You did *what*?"

I shrugged. "You'd think I didn't value my own life. I don't know why I do some of the things I do. I guess I don't think, sometimes."

He asked, "Don't think? How could you be so retarded?"

"Sue me." I thought about how I could have died. That would have been my second out of three escapes from the Grim Reaper. The *Dim* Reaper. I was always getting away. Maybe four times in all by now. Mother told me that the first time I almost died was when the doctor dropped me on my head and that was why I was the way I was. And finally I had a space alien growth removed while I was in Mexico. But they didn't get it all out so they tried again in High School and Mom said I really was dead for a while. That's why I was a stinker. "I was a very dumb kid," I admitted. "It's a miracle I'm even alive. In fact, come to think of it, I fell off that roof two times. I also have a scar on my scalp." I showed him. "Can you see it through the lump on my head from where you tried to pound me through the headboard?"

"I did what? I did?"

"You weren't paying attention to my head."

Bod asked, "Why did you climb the roof?"

"I had to. The house had trellises." Then I had the oddest memory. I was actually trying to kill myself. As a child I was always trying to do something dumb like that. For some reason my body was in a lot of pain and it drove me mad. My mother was calling me a bad *boy*, over and over. And the nurse pulled my pants down to stitch me up, and she screamed at the hideous sight of my naked body. And then Frankenstein clomped out of the dark woods and dragged me away by my hair that was now long like a fashion doll. *That's* what the hypnotist had said. He'd called me a fashion doll. So maybe I was.

Chapter Four

That was not my first and last rendezvous with this flim-flam film man, but this was the beginning of my new life as an adult. I was finally a woman and finally away from home. I worked on teaching him to be a bit gentler like a romantic ballet, and he worked on teaching me to get real and take it like an army tank. I knew that life was far more than this itch and scratch. I badly needed to get some semblance of a career on the road. But for now, our balling took up a lot of our time. You'd have thought we were newlyweds.

"Life is great," I wrote on the back of a postcard with an unusually bold and sure handwriting. It looked like a man had written it. I ripped it up. Mom would not have liked to see me writing like a man. Not after all the work she'd done to make me such a lady. I tried to think about what that could imply, but then I forgot.

The end of the month came and Bod asked me to move in with him and be his chick.

Every fiber in my brain said, "*NO*" don't do that, but every fiber in my mink said, "*DO IT! DO IT NOW!*" The part of the brain responsible for logic must have wept bitterly as my legs flew out from under me. But it's a miracle what that groveling, low, indignant posture can do for a girl's self-esteem. And, besides, rent was due. If we were going to behave like newlyweds, we could live like it. He pays.

He said, "Now if we're going to live together then we must promise to never lie to each other. Never."

I said, "But I thought white lies keep the world going around."

He said, "No. Lies are sad. *All* lies are. Even the white ones. People are so different from each other. Especially men from women. So even when we only speak the truth, we'll still never agree on what reality is. But that's as close as we can get to it. So we can at least try not to lie. Trying is all we have."

"Oh, so you're telling me that I'll never agree with you." I got in his spotty bug of a car and he zipped me out to his "*ranch*." His *ranch*, as he called it, *ha ha ha ha HA!* It was an upscale squirrel's nest. It could've been mistaken for a trailer home except they're built better and aren't shoved over the side of a hill like you're trying to get rid of them. "You've got to be kidding."

"If I'm funny, then *eh*… laugh."

I got out and looked down. I laughed. Since he lived on the side of a tall steep hill, the back of the house was perched high on two metal stilts. "People can sell the side of a cliff as real estate?"

"It's not a cliff. It's a hill." Bod walked up beside me and took my shoulders. I wondered if it was to keep me from falling forward and dying in his backyard. He said, "Welcome to *Indian Hill.*"

I wanted to say something nice. I just couldn't. It came out, "This is a place where real estate is definitely not choice."

Bod tried to use his logic. "Then why call it something so fancy? *Indian Hill! Eh.*"

On the very top of another hill was a tall sculpture of a totem pole topped by a cigar-store Indian, looking forbiddingly toward the expensive real estate. The good land was many miles away above a distant reservoir barely visible through the hazy smog that smelled chalky in a stinky way. Below it was a row of billboards that faced some unseen highway. Behind them were ragged faded plastic flag garlands for a closed car dealership whose parking lot had cracked off and slid halfway down into the ravine. "Bod, people can't live in this!" I said worriedly, tapping very carefully on the outside of his thin wall. "It's like… *um*… a birdhouse or something."

He unlocked the front door and jerked it open. "In a few days, you'll wonder how you were ever able to live anywhere else," he assured me, squeezing my toosh. "Come look at the bitchin' balcony." First thing in the door, Bod ripped off all his clothes and told me to do the same.

"I'm not balling right now," I said.

"No, no," he explained. "This is a nudist house."

"What? Why?" I moaned, wiping sweat off my face.

"It's just more comfortable. *Eh*."

I kicked out of my clothes as he led me through the tiny house to the balcony. He didn't mind stepping outside with his ding-a-ling in full view because back there, all we faced was an ugly concrete culvert that serviced a bone-dry creek bed. Beyond that, across a vast field of colorless sand and sad yellow weeds, there was a power plant that looked like it could be the view for a futuristic movie.

"It's got a dome!" I said, pointing to it and feeling a hot dry breeze blow over me. "You've got to make a futuristic movie there, like that one, *Tresspassages*, where they had those big white plaster domes over everything and they got radiated on purpose for having their own thoughts. And then everything blew up at the end. Well, at least the toy train models were shooting lots of sparks. Did you see it?"

"Everything always blows up at the end in those types of movies, dummy. That's how you know it's going to be over soon and you can start trying to think about where you parked your car."

"Well, they won't give you permission to blow up their power plant so you'll have to come up with an original ending. Unless we make a plaster model and blow that thing up. I read an article in a movie magazine that said it looks real if you film miniature explosions and models in super slow motion. That's how they do it. The film just runs through the camera super fast. It goes through the camera a lot faster than it later goes through the projector. That's what makes it seem like it slows down."

"I know all that," Bod said, "and they don't let you film anything at all at power plants."

"Why not?"

"It's all top secret military government stuff."

"You mean power plants aren't regular business-like places?"

"No," he answered. "And I should know. There was a protest rally out there last year. Lots of dorky hippie songs were sung about atomic whales. And stuff. And then wham, *hundreds* of cops came out and beat the living tar out of everybody they could get their hands on. They carted them off in dozens of city buses that said, 'out of service' up on top. Scary. The stink of teargas blew over the whole neighborhood. The dog next door wouldn't shut up. It was just a fiasco. Then the FBI pounded my door down asking for my camera. I didn't have one, but they checked anyway."

"Scary." The house was filthy, layered with dust. Luckily, it was enough of a matchbox so it wouldn't take me long to do my cleaning thing. "Is this thing earthquake proof?" I asked.

"Sure. Everything around here has to be. It's a law."

"How can a house on stilts be earthquake proof?"

"Here, look, I'll show you," he explained. He went to the bookcase and yanked at it. "See? It's bolted right to the wall, and not just in the dry wall, but in the studs. So in an earthquake it won't tip over on your head and kill you."

"Why would I be under a bookcase in an earthquake?" I asked. "It isn't like there's any books in there. It isn't even like you read."

"I read scripts. They go in a filing cabinet, dummy. Just because it's called a bookcase, doesn't mean you actually put books in it. That's just what it's *called*."

"Whatever," I said, not interested, regarding how the tall metal filing cabinet was probably the most expensive thing in the house.

Bod looked at me funny, again. He picked me up and took me toward the bedroom. He hit my head on the doorframe. It didn't hurt; the frame was so flimsy. I let him get his devil out on me while I tried not to seem like I was looking around at his room as much as I was. When he finished up, like he wanted to pound the house off its stilts, I said, "Thank you," and then went at the place with my soap and water.

"What are you doing to my house?" Bod asked in dismay.

"Dodo… cleaning!"

"Well, be careful," he warned.

"Careful of what?" I asked as I bleached the outside of the toilet, hoping the thick stinky carroty colored stains would soften enough to remove.

"I don't know, just be careful."

"Yes, dear." I wondered if he meant that soap could accidentally dissolve the house. "Can soap dissolve glue?" I asked.

"Sure." He shrugged.

"Well, how prefab is this place?" He didn't get the joke so I just went back to scrubbing, feeling happy as sometimes menial work can put a person into a pure state of Zen. With my back turned, it didn't take Bod long to rummage through my stuff and find my pills. "Don't take those!" I warned. "Those are my special vitamins! I promised Mom I'd take one a day!"

"Special?" he smirked. "If I pop one, will I get a bigger boner? *Eh!*"

"You're already a total one," I said, then warned him again, "If you pop one of those pills, you'll grow charlies like mine, so *don't!*"

"Vitamins make you grow jugs?" Bod asked doubtfully.

I nodded. "Mom calls them vitamins, but it's girly hormones. I had some surgery. Stuff was cut out of me a couple of times in my life where I almost died. The pills make it so it doesn't matter."

Bod gasped, "You had *cancer?*"

"Don't say it like it's contagious. And maybe I did. I can't remember. It was all very traumatic. Oh… I don't remember. Look what all this cleaning has done to my nails!"

"Then maybe you're not really *you*!" Bod suggested. "Maybe you're somebody else and you forgot!"

I nodded. "Yeah! That's it! Maybe I'm a princess and belong in a real castle!"

"Eh," he vacantly replied. I expected a better resolution to our conversation, since I wanted to talk more about my being a princess in a castle, but he just grabbed a beer from the fridge and then walked away to pee off the back balcony.

The next morning, the instant Bod let me get out of bed, I lunged for the bleach and rewashed the kitchen. "I want all the bugs to know they're not welcomed!" I reached as far back behind the stove as possible. "What's all back here?"

"Oh, a stupid spice-rack fell," he answered. "Screw it. Hot sauce goes in the fridge, anyway."

"Here goes." I held my nose and gritted my teeth and poured gobs of bleach all behind the stove.

"Good *God* girl!" he exclaimed. "Watch it!"

As a pungent mudslide oozed out from under the front of the stove, dozens of stunned cockroaches zigzagged out with it. "I think I found them!" I smiled, proudly.

"Eh!" Bod went into a cockroach stomping frenzy, shaking the whole house a bit.

When he was done with that, I tanked up on instant coffee so much I felt dizzy and had to sit on the floor. I turned on the TV. There were of shots of burning fields and houses. It all looked filthy, so I went to the bathroom and picked at my face trying to find clogged pores to punish. My face was good and blood red when Bod finally tried to kick me out. "You're a manic chick!"

"No, just too much caffeine." I skipped to the balcony to do sit-ups, and then collapsed in a fraying lawn chair.

Bod stepped out, righteously announcing, "You're gonna be a star, right? So you need a name change."

"*What?*"

Bod rubbed his biceps. "As your wise agent, I say you need a name change."

"I do?"

He rubbed his chest. "*Eh!*"

"I do not. My name is Jill. Good enough," I insisted and would've soundly slapped him, but I really didn't care to get up. Getting in and out of frayed lawn chairs is so very bad for them.

"My name was once Bob," he confessed, "but I changed it to Bod. Wasn't that clever? It makes it more memorable."

"It does?"

"It draws attention to my bod, since I've got a great one. So why not press my advantage?" he continued, flexing his arm muscles and looking utterly stupid poking at his belly. "Don't you just want it?" He flexed his arm again.

"No thanks, *Bog*! I like my new girl name, *Jill*" I said. Then I was puzzled why I called my own name *new*. What had it been before, if

Jill was new? *Sammy* came to mind, but as I looked at my pretty nail polish, I couldn't imagine ever being named *Sammy*!

Bod said, "My name makes me more memorable in this shit town of everybody trying to get their loser name remembered. Remember that." He released a loud burp. "So now it's your turn. Your name sounds like some retard who falls down a hill with a pail of water. Fix it."

"With my grace and this hill," I said, peeking over the balcony, "I just might."

"Don't ever say I pushed you."

I flashed him a dirty look. "So, what's my name? Diamonds? I'm sure as hell worth it, because I'm so… fab-dazzling."

"Diamonds?" He smirked. "That's a drag queen name."

"Well then, what?"

"Something organic from your own name like mine, *Bod* from Bob," he said like it was the neatest thing.

"What? *Chill* instead of *Jill?* Please!"

He admitted, "I've been giving it some thought."

"What!" I wondered, dreading what it might be. I closed my eyes tight and in the giant black empty sound stage of my mind, I heard my mother screaming, "*Sammy!"* at me when I was too tiny to obviously remember it right. I hoped with all my might he wasn't about to say *Sammy*.

"Jilly," he declared.

After a long pause, I laughed.

"I'm serious," he said. "It's so original."

"It's too cute! I want to be something grand. Something like Dunkel Morgendammerung!" I tried to make a sophisticated pose. It was hard in a lawn chair that was ripping apart.

"Jilly," he repeated.

"What are you calling me?"

"Jilly."

I insisted, "That's not a name!"

"Of course; it's *your* name."

"No!" I persisted.

"Sweetie, get used to great stardom."

"With that sort of language? I believe not." I got up from my lawn chair, hearing a strap tear from under my leg.

"*Jilly*," he said again as if it were profound.

I thought I smelled smoke, so I leaned way over the balcony to see if I could see what the neighbors were up to. "Who's she?" I saw three people lighting up a barbecue and wished I were there.

"You."

"Have you ever thought of marriage?" I asked, not only desperate to change the subject but also wondering if any woman had ever tolerated him as long as I had. I wanted a measure of how stupid I'd been.

He scoffed. "Marriage will always be sick as long as there is such inequality among the sexes."

I was surprised at such a pat answer. "Are you sure you're not just suddenly using jargon for your own selfish good?"

"Don't feminists?"

I mulled that one over, not going to let him have the last word. "Well, then, everybody is a feminist," I snapped right back. It didn't have the ring of truth I wanted so I added, "Get your finger out of your nose."

"It itches. You're so uptight." He left the balcony, releasing another huge belch as if there were nothing at all wrong with that. I walked into the bathroom to lower the seat since I knew it had been left up. I turned off the light since he always left it on. I somehow suddenly felt like my whole life was a big wasted goof up and wondered what might have become of me if I'd gone to New York instead.

I began to weep. "I just threw my life away!"

*****

At the grocery store waiting in the long line for a free sample of a new translucent blue ketchup gel (they were putting it on quarters of cherry red hot dogs!), I heard, "It's *her*!" He pointed at me so everybody looked.

I smiled. "Hello."

Another man said, "She's in that girly magazine of that dead guy."

"In the very same pool! Gross! She was in the same water as a dead guy!"

"What a slut."

"Cool!"

At the mall, with Bod, we heard a man yell out, "It's that lady from the pool table! She jumped up and down like a crazy slut!"

Bod patted me on the toosh, for show. "You're going to get a lot more of this as you become a bigger and bigger star."

I looked through a selection of postcards. "It would be nice to see my face on one of these."

"Soon," Bod assured me.

"Can I have your autograph?" a man asked, smiling like a lech.

"Certainly." I nodded graciously, like I'd seen the Queen of England do on TV.

"You're sure nice for a porn star," he said.

"I'm not a porn star," I kindly corrected him, my face reddening. I turned to Bod and gave him a look that was darn close to screaming. "*Porn?*" I showed him my nail polish. "Isn't this nice?"

"Doesn't matter," Bod assured me. "There's studios all over that don't do family pictures. And I've been talking with Flicker Farm about you."

"Flicker Farm?" I stopped dead in my tracks. My heart sank. My bubble popped. My bottom dropped out, figuratively and almost literally. I scampered to the toilet. When I returned, the box of rocks named Bod was still nodding his head enthusiastically. It should have been a sad nod. "*Them?*" I shrieked.

"What's wrong with Flicker Farm?" Bod asked, becoming defensive. "You can't start out at the top, you know."

"Flicker Farm is the cheapest studio in town!" I complained. "The *world*! And they're not even in town! Don't they literally shoot out of an old barn? It's in the desert!"

Bod said, "What does it matter where they shoot? Many stars have started there."

"Who?" I demanded.

"Dixie Dawn Don," he said.

I slapped my hand over my mouth like I'd vomit. "*Aag!*"

"Well, *eh*, she did make us money."

"That icky *thing* can't act!" I argued. "And she's so gooey… so full of herself, she's just so *me me me,* I just want to gag! She's such a fake! So *icky*! All that *freaking hair*! It's like a lapdog curled up on her head and then got run over." Just then I spotted the wig shop, so I paused. "Wait! I can have bigger hair than her!"

Bod frowned. "What. You don't need a wig. That's for old ladies."

"They have wiglets and hairpieces here, for sure," I explained as I tugged him in. "It doesn't show up like a wig. All of my hairline is still mine. I just blend my real hair up into it and nobody knows the better."

Bod said, "I can't go in there!"

"Why not?"

"That's a wig shop. I'm a guy!"

"Don't be silly. You have to buy me a fall or I'll never become a star. Big hair is as important as big boobs!" How could he argue? We went in. The shop smelled like plastic. It took me awhile to find the right pale blonde wave-on (as they're called) for my head of straw. "Does this look natural?" I asked Bod. Of course the cross-eyed clerk said it did, but he just wanted a quick sale.

"Looks good to me," Bod answered without even looking. "Eh. Let's get out of here. This place is too poofie for me."

"Don't flatter yourself."

Bod insisted, "Hurry! Let's look at footballs. You play catch?"

"Screw you," I said. I flashed my nails in his face to remind him that they were far too fabulous to be getting smashed up catching a football. "That's a boy's game. Give me some time, here. This is important. I have to look like a star!"

"You should have come with Andernach. *Eh*! He'd love these things. You could have *both* tried them on. I'm a producer type of guy. I produce. I don't do hair and makeup. I don't do wig shops very well."

"Andernach would've been more help and more fun." I glared at Bod as if my eyes could shoot bullets. He glared back like all women are mentally ill. I glared back, anew, like all men are pigs, then turned away from him and looked at my head carefully in the mirror. I tugged at the plastic locks, pulling them carefully down around my ears.

"It looks fine," he said, "and I'm *not* just saying that to hurry you along."

"You're right," I agreed. "I look younger with big hair. Pay 'em and let's get out of here."

"Yes ma'am," Bod drawled in a tone that belied the fact that he didn't like shelling out good money for hair.

"Oh, honey," I added, "and I also need a new set of press-on nails. I just keep losing them all over the place." The way he looked at me, I knew it was not the time to be greedy. "Maybe later," I surrendered. We went and looked at footballs.

*****

The phone was ringing when we pulled up to the house; we raced for it. Bod had never heard of ladies first through a door, so while I rubbed my sore shoulder, Bod grabbed the phone and chatted for a while. When he hung up, I jumped on him with excited questions. It hadn't taken much eavesdropping to figure out that it was about me and my career. "Slow down, slow down," he said. "Let me pour us a drink, first."

"All we have is beer. Cheap."

"Put it in fancy glasses and it won't matter. It has fucking bubbles." I grabbed the two-piece, snap-together, clear plastic champagne party glasses that he'd pulled out of the neighbor's garbage after one of their barbecues.

"Who was it on the phone?" I asked. "The studio boss?"

Bod went on to explain how he arranged to get me a Flicker Farm film.

"I didn't give him a chance to say much. I jumped up and down and screamed over and over, "I got a part! I got a part!" I had decided to accept Flicker Farm on the drive back, so the timing was just perfect.

The next day I got the script. To my lack of enthusiasm, it wasn't a big part. The phony stupid bimbo, Dixie Dawn Don, had that—the *me, me, me* phony tramp who looks like she really needs a glass of water. She just had to, *of course,* hog the show. The *hog!* I was so irritated I can't even say, the evil twit!

Looking over the script (shot full of spelling errors), I noticed the film was a western. Men were mostly shooting at each other, with guns, and the ugly stupid Dixie Dawn Don was trying to make peace while the front of her shirt keeps getting wet.

"Where's my part?" I asked.

"Keep reading."

"Okay." I read. "Hey, where's my part?"

"Keep going."

"Oh, there I am, page sixty-two. Sixty-two minutes of the movie has passed and here I finally am. Most the audience has already left to get appendicitis because of having to look at Dixie Dawn Don while eating popcorn! So I play to an empty theater! I am going to become depressed!"

Bod said, "It's a great part."

"*The bimbo.* And it's spelled wrong." I went on to read about my scene when the boys hit up a saloon to get their rocks off. "Figures. But then again, nobody would want to touch that Dixie Dawn Don. She's just too icky. But still, to you guys I'm just two knockers on legs."

"Eh!"

"But I want my part to have character."

"Acting is not how you got the part," Bod explained. "Who do you think you are? So far, as of today, you're just a pretty rack." He went on to assure me that I had to give the civilians of our nation what they really wanted or face their fickle wrath.

I certainly didn't want to impose my own brick wall with a prudish opposition to partial screen nudity. I hadn't before. I had shed my Midwestern cocoon. So I decided to get enthused. I thought back to TV *Wild West Ho* episodes that had saloon dances and realized I'd have to learn to dance for real. So I started a strict stretch program. I cried in pain as I sat and yanked and yanked and yanked.

"Are you OK out there?" Bod called to the balcony. Moments later, "Do you think you'll ever stretch yourself into a state of talent?"

I yelled back, "Do you think this balcony could be tilting away from the house?"

"Why do you say that?" he asked, popping his head out the door.

"Look." I took a pencil and put it on the floor and it rolled away from me. I didn't catch it in time and so it rolled right off the balcony. It flew through the air and vanished into the scrawny yellow weeds far down the hill. "See? It just went to Hell."

"*Eh.* You're wasting good pencils and they're expensive, like everything else made with real wood these days."

I complained, "The balcony is tipping away from the house. When was this thing built?"

"I don't know. Five years ago?"

"Well, it's obviously falling apart at the seams."

Bod looked confused. Again. "Well, I'll be…"

"See?" I said, pointing to where I'd wasted a good pencil. "It didn't do that before."

"Well get off of it, dummy," he suddenly spoke with some alarm. "Just stay off the balcony before it falls and takes you with it."

"Oh, don't be jumpy. I don't think it'll come down anytime this week."

"*Eh*," he agreed.

That night, there was a wind so ferocious it rocked the entire house on its stilts. The wind howled like a tomcat fight. It was so fierce it even brought in the smell of the ocean (dead fish). I wanted to bury myself under the covers. I was surprised at how cold it could get on a windy night in a desert. "Do you think this house could be blown off its legs?" I asked shivering and feeling my hair blow. "The house seems so light."

"We're fine," he assured me, not even fully awake.

"Is there a window open?" I asked, scared of the house rolling down the hill with me in it.

"No, it's just a drafty house."

"Sure is. Glad we don't have winter, here. We'd die."

"*Eh.* The ventilation is good for us. That's why the people out here live so long."

Another chilly gust slapped the house and a framed picture of two too-cute dogs playing pool fell off the wall. "You're OK," he murmured, not realizing our life was in peril.

I asked, "Why would anyone build something so cheap on the side of such a shitty hill? I don't think we're safe. I'm getting sea sick."

Then we heard a terribly loud crash and felt the house jerk. We both jumped out of bed. "The balcony!" I pulled a pink fuzz-trimmed robe on and hurried out to the living room. When he pushed open the sliding door, a gust of wind blew grit in my eyes.

"It's gone!" he yelled.

"Close that door!" I screamed. Pages of my script and my Cindi May wig catalogue blew around the room. "Close it! *Close it, now*!" He closed it, but remained looking through the glass.

Bod sadly said, "Goddam it! It's gone!"

I spotted thin strips of wood splintered down the bottom of the hillside. "I'm sure glad I wasn't stretching my legs out just now."

"In the middle of a wind storm?" He looked at me oddly.

I shrugged. "You know how much I like to practice." I turned and began to pick up the pages of my script.

*****

In the following days, I danced my legs into near paralysis. I needed alcohol rubs and Epsom salt baths to soothe them. I was that hell-bent on being the best dancer in all of moviedom, taking my pain as proof of my worthiness to the pantheon of the stars.

"Get out of the bathroom!" Bod screamed at me through the door. "I need to shave, and I don't mean from my eyebrows to my toes like you do every morning. So it won't take me two days!"

I screamed back at him, "I'm soaking my muscles. I hurt! I've been working hard!"

"I hope you prune!"

When I finally got out, he handed me a ring. "What is this?" I asked. "Engagement?"

"Hell no," he said. "It's a mood ring. You wear it and the color of the expensive crystal tells me your mood."

"What in the hell is that?" I asked.

"I told you. It tells me your mood, in a ring."

I asked, "Why would you need to read my mood in a ring?"

"Because you're so secretive… always keeping things to yourself… like all uptight Midwestern chicks.

"What about you?" I challenged. "Where's your ring? How am I to know your mood?"

"If you want to know my mood, just look at my schwanz," was all he offered before he slammed the bathroom door behind him.

I suddenly had the oddest memory of a bright red blowfish sticking out between my legs, spouting urine and infection in painful violent fits. I was screaming. Mother was screaming. The nurse was Mexican and she was screaming in a foreign language. After more confusion than a person should have to endure, the hypnotist told me to look at my pretty fingernails. I had always wanted pretty fingernails. It was a dream come true. I was so happy. Now I knew I could live happily ever after, like a princess.

Chapter Five

When Bod finally drove me out to Flicker Farm in his spotty bug of a car, he kept giving me dirty looks. He finally said, "You stink like an old bag."

"Thanks for the pep talk." My aching legs were liberally swathed in menthol arthritis cream. "They hurt. I practiced too hard."

"What did you do?" Bod asked. "Douche?" I looked at him as if I couldn't believe boys could be so stunningly dumb. Actually, the more I looked, I believed.

When we pulled off the highway towards the "studio," Bod said, "Be grateful. You're getting what so many girls have come to Tinseltown for. So many come here and get nothing. You get a chance to be a star. You get a part in a film."

"Sure. I'm grateful. I'm no ingrate." I looked around. I could tell that Flicker Farm had once been a real working farm. We went down a long gravel driveway. First we passed a 1940s type flatbed truck with bullet holes all over it. The house had burnt down and what was left of it hadn't been carted away. The barn still stood. It was a proud monument to adaptation, though its walls were so weathered there was very little red paint left. Its roof missed a few patches of shingles and a few hay doors were gone. But this building was obviously the center of production. Lights, stands, carts, boxes, set flats and furniture lay festively higgledy-piggledy about it in clashing myriads of colors. A hay wagon, like I would've seen outside my hometown piled with hay, was piled with weather-beaten pillars.

Bod parked front and center of the barn doors. I asked, "Is Dixie Dawn Don going to be around? I think I smell her. I smell something. Oh. There's an outhouse over there. Never mind."

"Don't worry," Bod assured me. "She's not in your scenes. And if you do see her at a party or something, just keep your fat mouth shut."

"I'll run over her fat hair with a lawnmower." I walked inside two sliding wooden doors. My eyes adjusted.

Parting a plastic tarp, and stepping into the barn aisle, a man said, "Hi!" He was cute-as-buttons. He had brown-skin with pouty lips and heavy-lidded eyes sporting shiny blue eye shadow. He walked up to us.

"Poof," Bod scoffed.

He ignored Bod as if he wasn't even there. His eyeballs went obstinately the other way. "I'm Candy Cane," he introduced himself to me, "and I'm bad." I nervously held out my hand so he could see my new pink press-on nails. "I need to take your measurements for the costume," he continued.

"You sew?" I asked.

"I do everything around here. You name it, I do it. It's all very serious, man." He wrapped me tightly in his tape measure.

I asked, "You Mexican or what?"

"You ca-ca?"

"You don't sound like it," I marveled. "You don't have a funny speedy little type accent; you sound American." Then I had a flash of lucid memory. "I used to live in Mexico. Or I visited there once with Mom. It was hot and the gardens on each side of the sidewalk grew like crazy and everything smelled like flowers and I told Mom that I loved flowers, but she already knew how girly I was. And for some reason, I was wearing *a dress!*"

Candy Cane looked at me in worry and put his hand over my forehead, like I really would be all right. He said, "American is a really screwed up language. Seriously. But I manage. The other day, a car tried to run me over in the crosswalk, and I yelled at it that I was a pedophile. I thought it meant I loved to walk. Then I realized I wasn't a pedophile at all, but was a pedestrian. Who would have known they were different."

"I love corn chips. My favorite brand is *Corny Peso*. Does that make me an honorary Mexican?"

He put his hand up to check me for a fever again.

I felt stupid, so I blurted out, "I hope I'm not too fat."

The plastic tarp slapped aside, again. An older thick-necked man walked through. He'd been too busy poking at a little futuristic calculator to put his hand out for shaking. "You must be Jilly," he greeted me warmly.

"Yep I am," I said, "and you must be Oscar, the owner of this nice place." I tried not to stare at his hair, or what little there was of it. He was bald on top with wiry tufts of grey hair around his ears, and, I dared notice, some of it was coming *out* of his ears. Candy Cane looked at him like he was dirt, turned way, and left us.

"Just call him *Os*," Bod said with a cordial slap on his broad back. "Everybody does. *Eh*."

"Everybody but Bod," Os slapped Bod in return, and much *much* harder. "To him I'm *Mr.* Os!"

"Why you wearing black?" Bod asked. "Who died?" Then his face crunched up as he realized what he'd said.

Os said, "This fool always chokes on his feet. He's just bananas."

My face went grey. "Oh, that's right. Snako was your brother."

Os nodded, sadly. "Now I have nobody to fight with." He gave Bod a dirty look. "Nobody worth fighting with, that is. Nobody with a brain bigger than a lizard."

"I'm so sorry," I said. "I was there, at the pool party where it happened… in the very pool!"

Os frowned at Bod and then poked him in the chest. "So was *he*. I'd think *he* was the psycho killer if he wasn't such a klutz."

I said, "Bod has an alibi. He was with me and he was so upset. He even puked his beer on me he was so upset. Do you know anybody who walks around in rubber monster masks?"

"My son used to." Os frowned. "He was bananas. He loved to wear monster masks because he was so ugly. As a baby he fell into an iron. But he's dead. They torched him along with the elevator he was riding up in. He was messed up with the mob. They don't live long. Now it seems there are other crooks out there trying to copy him. It seems that wearing monster masks around town to scare people has become a fad. Nowadays people only like fads. Nobody wants to copy honest hardworking businessmen like me."

I said, "I hope burning elevators don't become a fad. It's bad enough to just worry about them falling."

"Cool calculator," Bod said to try and lighten things up. "*Eh!*"

"Twenty-eight dollars. An eight digit gizmo," Os said like a salesman. "Ain't she sexy. Florescent display with a floating decimal. It's the future!"

"Wow." I tried to picture a decimal floating around and why anybody would want that, but dared not ask the certainly stupid question.

Bod elbowed me in the gut and gloated. "So, I brought you the merchandise. Ain't she great? Hon, lift up your shirt and show him the goods." I froze and turned all twelve nail color shades of red.

"Leave the girl alone," Os ordered Bod. "We all know by now what her gifts look like. I saw her film. Bad film. Good film when she was in it. Bad film. But everybody went bananas when this lady came on. There's something edgy about you. I can't figure out what it is, but there's something about you that just isn't same-ole same-ole. You a lesbian?"

"No. I've always loved to wear pretty dresses. But, thank you. I think." I made sure he caught the sight of my press-ons, lest he still doubted how genuine I was.

He looked upon me benevolently and smiled. "This will be a great part for you. You put *yourself* on the map, but *The Plunder* will keep you truckin. It's a cheap piece of banana garbage for the stupid public, sure, but they just love cheap pieces of garbage. That's why movies are the way they are. You got to make them really stupid or else you'll have a lot of empty movie theaters."

I said, "The world before movies must have been totally dark ages."

Os smiled as if it were all a joke. He said, "Back when I was a kid, baby, there was a math show on the radio. You could sit there and listen to it all and actually follow it because it was radio—all in the head where your marbles are. Movies don't stretch the imagination.

Movies are all *show me*. So we don't have dry junk like math because how in the hell do you show *that*? We have gunfights. We have tits. We can only do stuff that hits a guy below the brain, usually below the belt. Any dummy can feel." Then he pulled a tiny packet of white powder from his pocket and handed it to me.

"What's this?" I asked. "Is it good for ring-around-the-collar?" I glared at Bod's collar.

Os shook his head. "Don't you know?"

"She's kind of backward," Bod said, snottily. "Plaksville."

I looked to Bod for meaning. "Huh?"

He looked at me like he was smarter than I was. "*Eh*."

"It's cocaine," Os explained to me. "You're a little fleshy, if you don't mind the expression."

"I'm a toothpick!"

"You're never skeletal enough for the camera. And everybody knows that there's nothing better for a diet than this stuff. 'Snow' they call it on the streets, but this ain't garbage from the streets. This is good old-fashioned stuff from Doc Brown. See, it's white. That means it's clean."

"What do I do with it?"

"I'll show you when we get home," Bod said as he happily rocked up and down on the balls of his feet. "*Eh!*"

"Hell if you do," Os interrupted, stepping between us and putting his arm around my shoulder.

"What?" Bod said.

Os said to Bod, "Are you bananas? You'll just snort it all for yourself, pig. I know you. This is for the little lady. She does all her snorting here at the studio, so I know whose pretty nose I'm spending my good money on."

"I can have *some*!" Bod said.

"You can snort my socks!"

I offered, "I'm sure I can find a cheaper way to diet. I was reading about carrot juice..."

"Nonsense!" Os's face flamed. "That's commie propaganda!"

"How?" I asked. "The commies want us drinking carrot juice?"

"Not that!" he said. "The commies want to control our supply and demand! They want to tear down capitalism at its very core!"

"I don't figure," I admitted, smiling, wondering how we'd slipped from the smart topic of dieting to the stupid topic of politics.

"The commies are making things illegal, just to control what's out there to buy."

"So." My mind raced to get us back on the subject, if I could just remember what it had been. "So this drug is good for dieting?"

Os said, "Nothing faster and it's all natural. That's such a trend out here, now, you know. All the actresses who are with the trends use this. Now snort!"

He handed me a straw. I snorted. Though it was through my nose, it tasted like a bear trap on my whole head. "*Ah!*"

"God bless American freedom," Os loudly proclaimed.

After the confusion of feeling like cold steel girders had been shoved completely up my nose and down my throat, with blunt icicles attacking my eyeballs from behind, I felt my mind expand to the size of a snowflake, which I know makes no sense when one is sober, but it seemed like something at the time. All the while a wild grand hysterical euphoria swelled up in me like I'd never felt before. I shook out my foot. And then circus animals went off in my brain and I couldn't shut up, but I have no idea what I said.

*****

The next evening, Os did something Bod claimed he never did. He took Bod and me out to supper at a modest but lovely little restaurant at the top of one of the canyons north of downtown.

As soon as we were seated, a wine list was handed to Bod by a waiter who wouldn't even look at him. Bod asked Os, "What the hell do I do with this?"

Os asked the waiter, "What's your cheapest white wine?"

The waiter's face fell just enough to reveal some snobbery. "We have a Chenin Blanc that is from these parts of the…"

"We'll take it," Os interrupted him. "This country can grow a goddam grape as good as any French banana!" The waiter nodded and left us.

"The cheapest wine is always the best," Os told us. "It's a trade secret. The restaurants are just trying to make a fast buck on wine. Don't ever let them get the upper hand. Don't ever let yourself get ripped off by those bugger waiters who've been drilled and drilled as to how they can rip you off." I felt ashamed, having completely bought the waiter's spiel about the French wine and hadn't even thought to think. "They say that in this town you either drink champagne or you die of thirst," Os added, "Which is true enough of the *big* studios where everyone is overpaid and heads roll like marbles. Flicker Farm has never lost any money, though, because first we have to spend something to lose something. We're happy with our humble lot in life. We don't get greedy. When you get greedy out here, like most do, you end up a headline. This is a town full of broken hearts dulled with sex, cults and drugs. I hope your work with us doesn't go to your head, Jilly. I'd hate to hear that you'd gone bananas and slashed your wrists, one day."

As he wagged his finger at me, I shook my head at him in a way to assure him I wouldn't dare. "There's no king-of-the-hill at Flicker Farm," Os continued. "Just work, work, *work!*" Then he gave an evil eye to Bod as if for him the warning was double. "People who killed themselves were expecting too much from life. You have to expect what crap you get, because everybody gets it, and nobody wants to hear you cry about it. Everybody has enough crying of their own!"

I couldn't decide if I was being given advice or was being threatened, so I smiled as if it could be either.

*****

The next day at the studio, I felt fat from having had a fancy night out. My costume was a saucy gold painted bustier trimmed with red feathers. I worried that it wouldn't fit anymore. I felt dread as I stepped over the tangles of wires, cables and extension cords that snaked across the barn floor.

I noticed a black woman sitting on a low stool; she was plugging a microphone into a socket. "Hi," I said to her. "Do I look fat?" I hadn't seen her before and wanted to be nice. And I adored her simple vibrant orange skirt and top. Her dark skin looked so dramatic against it. She nodded at me in a weary manner. "You're on the crew?" I asked. She nodded again. I asked, "What's your job?"

She looked at the microphone just before her. "Sound."

"You don't sound enthused about sound."

She shook her head. "I want to do camera."

"Well, then," I suggested, "Why don't you just ask Os to let you learn the camera. He's a very nice man and I'm sure he'd…"

"I already know the camera," she stated. "Os just says, 'no banana mama is gonna touch my honky camera.'"

"*What?*" I gasped, not able to believe Os would say something so harsh to a lady. "He said *that?*"

"Yeah, he's a freak." The black woman nodded. "Take a look at all them ofay camera boys around here that he breaks in, letting them apprentice."

"You sure?"

"Sure I'm sure. It don't take blue eyes to see things."

"But Os seemed so nice," I insisted.

"What's nice?" she smiled, painfully. She had a very grand smile. "Sure he's nice. Who ain't? So what?"

I briefly glanced around to make sure no one was near. Then I said to her in a conspirator's tone, "Why don't you try a different studio?"

At that, she let out a loud explosive laugh. "Shit girl, Os is the most liberal son of a bitch in town! He may have said, 'no touch my white camera you banana woman,' but look, he lets me do the sound. That's totally radical! This is otherwise a white boy's business, only. Even the sound."

"It is?"

She nodded. "Before I met up with ole Os, I could only get gigs at the majors as miss jungle bunny for that friggin missionary movie I refuse to mention by name. Or I could only be a thievin' junkie hooker in that friggin cop movie I also refuse to mention by name. Or I serve the crew coffee and sweep up the sets in *Rome in July*, which was an OK movie but I didn't even make the credits. I wouldn't ask much. I wouldn't expect them to keep it up long. I wouldn't even e*xpect them to use my name. Just make it big.* CLEAN UP DONE BY *NEGRISS* WITH *NAPPY HAIR!* Hell, an intelligent woman's self esteem only spreads so thin before she gets a little pissed off."

"You are truly inspirational," I said in awe.

She put her hand out for me to shake it. "I'm Molita, the entire Flicker Farm sound department."

"Oh, that's a beautiful name." I smiled as I took her hand. "I'm Jilly."

Molita explained, "My beautiful name means a way of making coffee. You can imagine how pissed I got when some bozo would say, 'Hey Coffee, bring me some molita.' Ha ha. Like I'm not even a friggin person. Have you ever contemplated savage murder?"

"Oh, that's awful! What did you do?"

Molita smiled wickedly. "Ever hear of cowboy coffee?"

I gasped. I smiled. "Spit?"

"No! You don't filter out the grounds."

"That's a good one." I chuckled. "I have to say I really like your outfit. You look so hip in it. You look so fab in that rich color. A white girl could never pull off wearing such a great shade of orange."

"Thanks." Molita smiled. "I used to have the meanest afro. It was bright red and heart-shaped. But I had to cut it for this job."

"Why?" I asked. "Os is prejudiced against afros? That ass!"

"I'm the sound department," she reminded me.

"So?"

"Headphones. Who's gonna try to fit headphones over a giant heart-shaped afro?"

"Oh!" I laughed. "Oh, of course!"

"And what do you do around here?" she asked. "I hope it ain't coffee serving or sweeping up. I'd pity you, even me."

I laughed, suddenly feeling very embarrassed. "I'm the star of the day. I'm the lead saloon girl."

Molita stopped fiddling with her mic pole and grinned. "Well, eat my pig ear, you lucky ugly little ofay girl. I'm so pleased to have met you without airs. You're not like that little pale slut. That white fart. That bitch Dixie Dawn Don, at all."

I smiled. "Oh, I'm not that special. I'm just a regular ole dumb person like anybody else. And yes. Isn't Dixie Dawn Don just a dirty whore? And stupid! And her lips look like old dried up apricots!"

"Of course you're like everybody else," Molita agreed, "but some of those drugged-up sluts up on the hill seem to forget that their crap stinks just as bad as mine. And I can tell right now that your voice isn't gonna make my ears bleed like Dixie Dawn Don. Somebody needs to dub her. She sounds like somebody wound up the chipmunk and sat on it."

"What do you think of her record?" I asked wickedly.

"I'm not into Frisbee so I'd have no use for it."

"You're groovy," I laughed as I reached out to touch her shoulder. "I just hope my singing doesn't hurt your ears. Gotta run and see if my costume still fits."

"And why wouldn't it fit?"

I confessed, "I went out with the boss for supper last night!"

Molita's eyebrow raised. "Where was I? That *cheapshit!*" She made a ferocious face. I nodded as I took a few steps backwards. She laughed, then instructed me, "First, go over your song with the piano man, as loud as you're gonna do it. I want to listen in and adjust the mic levels."

"Sure." The upright was out of tune, probably since good money wasn't going to be used to correct it. For this scene it was just perfect. As I belted out my song like a big stupid frog, Molita twisted a dial until she nodded her approval and I then skipped off to the dressing rooms. They were the old horse stalls with sheets hung up between them.

When Candy Cane came in to dress me, he was in full saloon drag, himself, looking exotically pretty. I howled. "You're going to be a showgirl with me?"

"Camp, huh?" he said, nodding and smiling. *"Si."*

"I'm not sure what that means."

"Si? It just means *si!"*

"Camp."

"Oh, it just means camp. You know. Camp. Ca-ca. *Camp* is when you find beauty out of the grotesque. And what is more grotesque and more beautiful than Mexican *moi* playing an extra. Especially in a sick film like this for no extra pay. It's all very serious, man!"

I was overwhelmed and not sure what to say. "An extra?"

He grinned big and back-kicked a heel. "You bet. Bad, man. I'm an extra!" Then he grabbed a roll of duct tape and unrolled a long piece with a loud crack. "Take it off," he said. "You're getting a corset like mine."

"Huh?"

"A duct tape corset. It hurts like hell when it comes off, but it's worth it." I slipped out of my polyester blouse that had pictures all over it of Victorian people. I sucked in my gut. He wound two strips around me; I didn't have to worry about looking fat anymore. When Candy Cane started to button up the back of my outfit, the frilly item zipped right up without resistance. "You've got gorgeous shoulders. Ca-ca! You a lesbian?"

"No. Why? Have my nails popped off?" I saw that I was still all together and sighed with relief. "But thank you… I think… but I can't breathe," I protested, growing concerned. "I'm supposed to sing."

"Opera?" he asked.

"No."

"Then don't worry about it." Candy Cane stepped back. He looked at me in admiration. "After a few layers of a little more makeup, you'll be fantabulous enough even for a Flicker Farm ingénue. Seriously!"

"What more do you think I need?" I asked, thinking I'd already done a fine job.

"Where are the deep contours of your eyelids?" he asked, "or the chisel of your cheekbones? Look at how I did it. Where is your lip line? Where are the outside corners of your pitiful eyes? Exaggerate, girl. Exaggerate! Pump it!"

"All right, all right," I conceded, for he indeed had painted his own face into an exquisitely delineated mask. After the re-do, including turning my wiglet backwards for an explosive effect, and with my teeth glossed up with petroleum jelly, we headed for the set to warm up our fishnets.

When Os saw Candy Cane saunter onto the stage taped-up, gooped-up, made-up, and dressed-up as fantabulous as the three other chorus girls, he screamed, "What's this bananas? Where does it say that a goddam jumping bean fag is in the scene?"

"Screw you, nazi ca-ca," Candy Cane exclaimed. "I'm in the scene because I'm entirely beauteous!"

"What?"

"Si, I'm seriously pretty." I held my breath in horror. The boss had just been called a name by a mere peon and I couldn't believe how scandalous it sounded to my decorous ears.

"That's just bananas! If you don't get off that stage," Os growled, "I'll..."

"I'm in the scene and you can't stop me!"

Os hollered, "You're trying to ruin my movie!"

"I'm in the scene, seriously, and you're a commie!" Candy Cane yelled. Os stormed off the set. I looked at Candy Cane in pure horror, not believing he'd just been so out of line. "Os loves me," he cooed.

Os returned with a gun. "Get off that stage or I'll blow you off."

"You're gonna shoot me dead?" Candy Cane asked, blinking his big eyelashes like he was flabbergasted. "That's *bad*. That's really serious, man!"

They stared each other down again. Os aimed the gun, but Candy Cane didn't budge a cell of his corseted body. Os stomped off again. Candy Cane looked a bit flustered, with beads of sweat above his perfectly painted lips, but he shrugged indifferently.

"Get off the stage, Candy," the cameraman moaned, "so we can just get on with it."

"Screw you, man!" Candy Cane screamed. "I'm a show girl, now, and nobody's going to take that away from me! Especially not some little nobody focus-puller like you!"

"Just let the guy be in the scene," one of the other showgirls spoke up. "I think it's funny."

"Yeah," I chimed in. "Candy deserves this. He's done so much for this studio, I'm sure. And he looks great!" The other girls joined our mutiny. The cameraman shrugged and positioned himself behind the viewfinder.

When Os returned, he was beet red. We were all deathly silent. He handed me a small bag of coke and pointed to his nose. He gave Candy Cane the finger and left again. I shared with the girls (Candy included) and snorted my own sinus-full. I reeled at the alpine avalanche that thundered my brain to pieces, before the cameraman told us we were ready.

I picked up my props, a bottle of whiskey for each hand. Then the cameraman cued the sound, "Sound." I looked up and saw a mic dangle directly over my head. Another camera operator was discreetly placed at a table, holding a smaller 16mm camera, catching extra footage.

Molita loudly yelled her order, "Sound!" Through the glare of a light in my face I could see her in the far corner hovering over a big old-fashioned '50s reel-to-reel tape machine, her eyes closed, her hands cupped over each ear of her headset.

I heard, "Camera." Then the cameraman looked at something on the side of the camera before responding to himself, "Speed." Then he said, "Action."

The piano started banging out of tune, and in our bliss and energy, we all nearly kicked the roof in, dislodging a few feathers about us, as I bellowed the song, sometimes losing control of it and yacking like a big stupid frog on coke. I did my best. I tried to project directly into Molita's mic without looking at it or the camera.

On his cue, the cowboy stuntman flew at me from across the barn on the hay claw. It was slightly raised on its pulley as he hit the middle of its swing so his boots wouldn't wipe out a few tables.

When his feet hit the stage, I saucily kicked him back away, right in the crotch. He feigned surprise (his tender parts were perfectly safe beneath a hard plastic cup). He flew back onto some conveniently waiting straw bales as I finished my ditty and we all struck our tarty poses, turning to flip up our frills. We mooned the camera. Of course, we had no panties. "Cut. Print."

Molita squinted at me and said, "You got a boy butt."

"I have a very petite heinie," I agreed. "Don't I?"

"What are you?" Molita continued. "A sex change?"

"Of course not, don't be stupid."

"Are you sure? I never get stupid, but you all always confuse me."

"I think I'd remember such a thing." I caught my breath and asked, "Are we going to do it again?"

"Just a few bits," the cameraman answered as he checked dials on the side of his camera.

"Why?" I asked. "I think we should do it all over. Another take." I noticed the 16mm camera was still rolling, shooting close-ups of some leering cowboys at the tables.

"Too expensive," he answered while he started to write in a log. "You didn't flub."

"But I sounded horrible!" I insisted. "Didn't I sound terrible?" I asked Molita.

"For an ofay girl, you can sing," Molita said, "But I'd get your throat checked for cancer. Do you smoke?"

"It was fine," the cameraman said, not looking up from his writing. "It's a take. Now let's just get a few quick extra shots that don't eat up a bunch of film."

"Who's the director?" I asked. "I want to consult with the director."

"Os is the director when he ain't busy," Molita explained. "And he ain't around right now so he must be busy."

I asked, "You mean we just filmed without a director?"

She nodded. "Yep."

"What? Can you just, like, do that?"

"Just did," the cameraman said, closing his logbook.

"Yep." Molita added, "If Os agrees with you about you not being up to snuff, then you can re-dub it. Just re-do the sound part. That's cheaper than re-shooting the whole thing. Besides, who cares. It's just a cheap honky western for the rednecks."

"Oh." I hadn't thought about the possibility of not sounding good, but still looking good, and then only redoing the sound.

"It sounded great, though," the cameraman insisted. "You're very good at spontaneity. Really. It sounded real."

I said, "Oh. Is that why I can't really remember what I just did?"

"Sure." He nodded.

Candy Cane asked, "But what if *I* want to do it again?" He was ignored.

We did a few quick close-ups of my face, me now silently lip-synching to the fresh playback tape Molita had rewound and cued to a few spots.

"That's fine," the cameraman said. "Bye."

"You sure make a choice girl," Molita added, winking to Candy Cane. Then Molita winked at me. "You too."

"Of course I'm a girl!"

Candy Cane blew her a kiss then turned to us and shooed us off towards the dressing room. "Let's go."

I said to Candy Cane, "That Molita called me a *sex change*!"

"You *are* a little *elbows out into the world*."

"I think I'd know if I was a sex change." I looked pensively at my fingernails. "So pretty."

Candy Cane snickered, "I think you'd know that, at least. You can't forget that. Snip snip. There's nothing more, serious, man, than that! Seriously!" He undid my corset.

Troubled, I asked Candy Cane, to change the subject, "Do you think Os is going to can you, now? *Aaaah!*" I roared in pain as he ripped the duct tape from around my waist.

"Hell, no. *Hold still*! We love each other. Not in *that* way, we don't go all kissy-face on each other, but you know what I mean. Os is so bad. He's always trashing the suits. That man puts the seeds back in apple pie."

"What's that mean?" I asked. "Seeds? Huh?"

"He's a little subversive, himself."

I gasped. "He's gay?"

Candy Cane loudly slapped his own ass cheek. "No! Not *there* in his pants." Candy Cane spanked himself again. "In his wallet! He's a bit of a gangster. And a free thinker at that. It's all very serious, man! Welcome to Flicker Farm!"

Chapter Six

Back at home, it was stifling hot. But I was still vibrating from all that jarring cocaine. I decided to take a long walk around the strange looking power plant domes. Amongst the loud chattering of zillions of insects that darted away to avoid getting stepped on by me, I bellowed my saloon song over and over again. I let my Jilly voice crack and wail and do its crazy thing:

"*Up to the bar, order some swill.*
Drink it up fast, go out and kill.
Come back to bed, tip me your hat.
Toss me your gold, we'll go to bat.
Guzzle your whiskey, we can be rough.
Till yer time's up, dance in the buff."

I sang it at least twenty times. After circling all the way around the radioactive domes, I was plumb tired. When I made it back through the door, Bod was sprawled out on the couch in the light of day with his privates all drenched with lotion. He scowled at me as if in disgust, and said, "Take a bath."

Though breathless, I mustered great fury towards him for being so horrible. He was playing with my most expensive hand lotion that was almost all gone. The pig! I screamed hysterically. I stormed out the back sliding door. I completely forgot the small fact that the balcony had left us.

"*Bod!*" I wailed, as I stepped out onto thin air. I plunged feet first onto the weedy slope where I continued my descent with a few sloppy somersaults, leaving the plastic part of my hair behind on a scrubby bush. I stayed on my face until Bod pulled on his swimsuit and ran out and rolled me over.

"You OK?" he asked in genuine terror.

I breathed in the dry hot dirt and gasped in great pain, "Can't move."

"You sure?" he yelled in my face then started shaking me and dragging me around. "Move! Move! Get up and walk!" Luckily, my spinal column hadn't dented, otherwise I'd have never moved ever again thanks to Bod's ignorant resuscitation technique.

"I think it's my ankles." I cringed in anguish. "I heard them snap. I think I sprained both real good. I heard them go off like two firecrackers. Oh *man*! And stop smashing me up and down. It hurts! Bod! You're going to break my neck! Stop!"

"No! Oh no! Oh god *no!*" Bod screamed, terrified, still desperately trying to shake good health back into me. "You have another scene to do in the film! We've got to get you up to the house. Ice! We've got to pack you in ice!" He dragged me all the way up the hill and into the house. He packed frozen hash brown bags around my already purple swollen ankles.

I asked, "Did you get my hair?"

He grabbed it from the table and shook it at me. "It was hanging from a goddam bush for all the neighbors to see! Do you know how much this piece of shit cost me?"

I cried, feeling nothing but acute pain. "I want to die. Please, Bod, just shoot me in the head. I can't take the pain."

"I don't know if shooting you in the head would do very much damage."

"Screw you, Bod. Just get a knife from the kitchen and cut off my ankles. I want them as far away from me as… *oooooh!*"

"Be lucky you're coked up," he said, "Or this would hurt really bad."

"It hurts! It hurts!" Then I realized that the coke probably made me so stupid that I would walk out into thin air. "I want to die, I'm so embarrassed."

"I'll call Os and have him postpone your scene. They've just started shooting and have a lot of other things they can shoot in the meantime." He was on the phone; I heard loud swearing. When he hung up, he explained. "They have to shoot it all tomorrow, because then they go out to the desert. It's all location from there."

"I want to die."

"You're in bed most of the scene anyway," he assured me. "You only jump up on your feet and hop around the room when the gunfire starts, so we can all see your hooters bounce. You can do that much!"

"No. I can't"

Bod said, "You'll have to."

"Can I just be rolled around on a tea cart?"

"Don't be stupid."

"I want to die!"

"You're not going to die. You're just going to suffer a lot."

I said, "I feel sick to my stomach. How could this have happened? My career is ruined. I am over. I might as well just kill myself. I feel so horrible!"

I didn't know what hurt more, my physical injury or feelings of doom, dread, incredulous stupidity, and self-reproach. They all hurt like hell.

*****

The next day, Bod tightly wrapped my fat red ankles in elastic bandages and threw me over his shoulder. He carried me to the bug and drove me to the barn. There, they shot some painkiller up my arm. They gave me a few snorts of coke. I had one sip of beer. I don't remember the rest. It seemed like seconds later, I woke up feeling like I was dry heaving two wiglets, my pancreas, and a few sagebrushes. "Bod! Bod! Where am I?"

"*Eh*," I heard his voice. Then with a click, the lights came on and I saw I was home in the birdhouse. And it was wobbling. I heard wind howling.

"What happened! Is it me or are we wobbling?"

Bod said, "You were great, hon. I should have been jealous, but you were great. You two caught the damn bed on fire."

"My feet are on fire. What happened?" I moaned, suddenly dreading the worst.

"Don't you remember? Damn! I'm sure Rex Manson will never forget!"

"W-what are you talking about?" I stammered, feeling fear well up in me almost as strong as the toxic hangover nausea.

"You jumped up on top of him and then did the old go-horsy-go for real. For real! You *have* to remember *that* part."

"I do?"

Bod continued, "We thought his eyes would pop right out from surprise when you climbed on. It's all on film! I think they even got his expression when his gun went off. You nearly gave that old geezer a heart attack! I think you even gave him chapped lips!"

I sat a moment in silence. My scorched crinkled brain slowly descended from the ceiling and returned to my throbbing head. "I don't even know this guy," I said. I groaned, not able to remember even meeting the star. Not even a hello. "How old is he?" I asked.

"Oh, about seventy-three or eighty."

I wanted to vomit. "Is that possible?"

"Old stars always do it to young chicks on the screen. Don't you know? It's tradition."

"I'm never leaving this house again," I said. "I can never show my face again."

"Are you that ashamed?"

"No! I'm going to die. I think my liver is moaning."

Bod offered, "I'll make you some Chinese tea and you'll be able to get your head off the pillow by tomorrow."

*****

After my poor squashed liver finally started back up again, with a few chugs and angry back-fire explosions, I crawled into the wheelchair. Flicker Farm used it for camera shots that moved. I went to the barn. I wanted to watch the work print of my infamous unconscious performance. I watched the footage unspool on a TV sized screen on a fancy thing they called a movieola, or an electric flatbed editor.

"Woooow!"

I was amazed as how together I appeared. I slurred a bit, but who's to say I wasn't playing a drunk whore. After all, I was only dancing with a bottle in each hand the scene just before. "I'm so glad there's so many shadows where they are," I told the assistant editor who was turning the knobs for me on the movieola, going forward and backward. "I'm so glad you can't tell we were really balling."

"What?" he asked, being an older gentleman and a tad hard of hearing. "Really doing *it?*"

"That's what Bod says," I said loudly. "He says I really got boned. I was too stoned on painkillers to remember. I blacked the whole thing out. I don't even remember meeting the star. I'm so creeped out about that."

"You were *not* really doing it," the assistant editor said. "How could you? Rex can't get it up, you know. It's a medical thing, I guess. He likes the ladies and all. He was a real tiger in his day. But he just can't get it up anymore. Everybody in town knows it. Poor devil."

"I wonder why Bod lied to me about that. How odd."

"It happens to a lot of guys when they get that old. My dick has turned to dust and I'm only sixty-five. Rex must be eighty by now."

"He doesn't look that old," I said, looking at the screen. "All that hair."

"It's a wig."

"Oh, of course." I marveled. "He's so active. He's been around before movies?"

"He started in the wild west shows of Colorado. He's a real cowboy. He never did hardcore rodeo, though. That's why he could still walk after thirty. Shame he has to end his career with total garbage like this. No offense, lady."

I was confused. It hurt my feelings that Bod could lie to me about something so dumb. "Then why did Bod tell me that?" I asked him. "Why would he do that?"

The man shrugged. "If you don't believe me, you can ask Molita. She was there with her mic; she knows the scene. You were so on the moon that you slobbered all over her. You kept telling her how cool you thought she was."

"I did?"

"And how you wished you could be a black girl like her."

"Why would I want to be a black girl?"

"So you could pull off wearing the color orange that she does. You were crying, bawling actually, about it. You really wanted to be able to pull off wearing bright orange!"

"Oh my gosh!" I gasped, mortified. "What did Molita do?"

"She just looked at you like you were a dope fiend."

*****

Back at home, I flipped through the pages of an outdated wig catalog as I waited for the ill-fated Bod to return. It was stifling hot outside. That helped me fume with psycho killer murderous thoughts. I wanted to put on a rubber monster mask of Franken-lady and stab him to death with a butter knife. But then, as I became absorbed with the catalogue, I became amazed that the same woman could look so different in the various wigs. I then realized that that was the secret of those character actors who play so many different people. "It's their different hair! That's all it is!"

When Bod finally returned, he was skunk drunk. He was so wobbly-legged that he smelled the room up enough to make one fear a match. "You're drunk," I said.

"I was out getting even with you," he slurred. He walked sideways into the wall and cracked his head. "*Eh*."

"What?" I asked. "What's that supposed to mean?"

"*You* boned somebody else—*I* boned somebody else!"

I was shocked. "How could you? Who?"

"Some slut in a silver miniskirt. *Aaaah,* what a dish. She was in town for a science infliction. I mean fiction. A convention. She wanted pork while she was in town, so I porked her alright. I made her whole goddam summer."

I gasped. "How could you cheat on me!?"

He shrugged like an asshole. "Have you ever heard of a get-even?"

"You hypocrite!" I gasped in alarm. "You want me to be your girlfriend and then you cheat on me?"

He said, acting all righteous, "At least a hypocrite has high standards to fail to achieve. You could never be a hypocrite; you have no standards at all to fail at! You have no *blewerf - iiiin - ack* - " he lost his balance and hit the side of his head against the wall again.

Oh, so that's his game, I thought. He was going to try and stun me with drunk logic. I was hurt but knew I couldn't show it. I had to think very fast and be very wise. "That's only fair," I agreed with a charming smile. "Fair is fair."

"Yeah. And don't you forget it. You screwed the old actor. So I screwed a little science fiction slut. I had to. To get even. Life has to be made fair!"

I sadly nodded. "Fair is fair."

"*Eh!* You know it *plister… sssssisiter!* Fair is fair. Damn right, sssssssister!" He stumbled around the room a bit more. He finally realized how bad off he was and put his hand on the wall to steady himself, missing a few times, first, and hitting his head a few more times.

Since I couldn't very well take his stupid dick back from where it had been, I decided I would just have to accept the fact and roll with the punches. "Rex called me today," I lied in my best acting, which took some effort to keep even-tempered. "He called from… some small gas station out in the middle of the desert to thank me for curing his terribly famous impotence. Wasn't that sweet of him to give me all the credit?"

I could tell Bod was confused. "What?" My invisible brick had hit him square in his soggy head.

I nodded, smugly, even though I was really a wreck. I started sweating even more than I had been before. "He said I was going to go down in his autobiography as one of the most important women he'd ever known." I lied on, "And can you imagine it's all on film? I hope your budget motel scabies was not as important to the history of movies as what I did. I'm going to a have a few pages about me in his autobiography. What press for me! He's the man who pioneered the western! It's a very big deal."

"He's full of shit. Full of shit!"

I vapidly shrugged. “I would think so, too, but his story went right along with yours. Otherwise, how would I know? I was *gone*, remember. I was completely *gone*. I don’t remember a thing. I’m just going by your word… and his.”

“You’re lying twerping *fnert*!”

“If I’m lying, then you’re lying.” I smiled.

“And you’re a tramp running around with no clothes on in front of a camera!”

“The lighting was so bad you wouldn’t have been able to tell one way or another! The lighting was so bad you could have painted me up like a zebra and nobody would have guessed.”

“*Baahlee-youwe-marf!*” He grumbled something more, then stomped away and crashed onto the bed like a jet with more turbulence than altitude. He began to snore. I started to bawl—very loud. I wondered if the cabinet in the bathroom contained a strong drain cleaner I could pour into his mouth.

I went to the couch for the night. The eerie sound of the wind kept me awake, and I could feel the whole place shake on its stilts. “Bod’s a jerk, Bod’s a jerk,” the wind might as well have been saying since it burned so bright in my mind. I tried to think of distracting thoughts to lull me to sleep. I tried to think of pretty lush wigs full of complicated curls. But I found it hard to keep from thinking of how Bod had lied to me. I wondered if he’d ever lied to me as my agent. I wondered if he’d rejected great big studio parts meant for me, or stolen my money.

“Don’t trust anyone in this town. Don’t trust anyone in this town,” kept flipping through my head again and again. I remembered the aluminum siding people at the mall. That woman had lied to me. I started feeling such unbearable shame that I thought I’d have to sit up and rip out a good scream. “Write mother in the morning, first thing. Write mother in the morning, first thing. Get new postcards. Tell her again that you’ll be a big star soon. Assure her that everything is OK. Nothing is OK. Bod is going to come out this very minute wearing a rubber monster mask. Bod is too drunk. He can’t move. Shut up, brain. Don’t worry. The sun will come out. Think of wigs.

Think of wigs. Lovely wigs. Under the bed is probably stashed a few dozen different rubber monster masks. It's Bod! Bod committed the murders! I bet he's the killer! He has to be the one! He's rude enough! He's pig enough! He's got a big fat chip on his shoulder! *Aaaah!*"

I heard something bang under the house like a shutter. The house had no shutters. Maybe the whole underside of the house was peeling away. Maybe the couch would fall through with me on it. Finally, despite the sound of the wind turning the house into one big police whistle, I dropped off to sleep.

I woke up to bright sun blasting through the dusty yellow windows. I wondered, as I looked out the back of the house at the steam pouring out of the nuclear plant, what I could've been so upset about. The late night hours, I decided, now dismissing my fears. Darkness plays tricks on the mind. It amazed me how such sinister thoughts were utterly impossible in the glaring light of day. "Honey?" I called out. "Could you please make me some coffee?"

"I'm too hung to move," he moaned back. "Make it yourself."

"A little green at the gills?"

"Eh."

"Never mind, dear." I smiled to myself, overjoyed that he was sick as a dog.

There was a soft knock on the door. I saw a woman, maybe five years younger than me, peering in through the screen. She had a headband, two cute Indian braids and fringed clothes. That suggested to me that she was one of those alternative people who didn't touch meat and sat in impossible pretzel positions for God.

"Come in," I called out. "I can't come to the door. I'm all crippled. I hurt my ankles the other day."

"Oh, OK, groovy," she answered and pulled on the door. "I'm Sue from the Nuclear Action Committee," she introduced herself, and then seemed momentarily startled by my sheer nakedness. "What happened to your boobs?"

"Oh, nothing. I just taped them up so gravity couldn't get at them. I'm feeling baggy today."

"Oh," Sue said. "Well then, why not just put on a bra?"

"My bozo in there," I gestured to the bedroom, "Won't allow clothes in the house. He's into bringing nature indoors. It's always hot enough to make sense. He hasn't ruled out cellophane tape, though. So I taped them up."

"Oh," Sue smiled. "I love nature. But, you just walk around bare all day?"

I nodded. "Sure. My mink gets to breathe a lot."

Her face took on a frightened expression. "But… but… what about the seat cushions. What about when it's *your time.*"

"You mean *of the month*?" I asked.

Sue nodded, looking gravely concerned. "Yeah."

"Oh." I shrugged. "Bozo in there is real boy-dumb. He didn't think of that. Doesn't matter, though. I'm so lucky I don't have to worry about all that any longer. No more cramps. No more bleeding with the moon. Not after they ripped half my innards out when I was in the hospital in high school." I paused, puzzled, because I'd just lied. I'd never had a period, which made no sense. So I looked adoringly upon my pretty fingernail polish. "I don't have periods and isn't this a pretty color?"

"What?" Sue asked. "You had surgery?"

"I already told you that. But you never listen or remember or care!" Then I realized I was getting weirdly hysterical about what I couldn't remember. I tried to appear normal again. "I'm OK."

Sue asked, "You had cancer?"

"*I never said I had cancer!*"

"Whatever," the hippie girl said. "Sorry. You had polio? Lead poisoning?"

"I don't want to talk about it. I'd much rather talk about a good black and white mad scientist movie than my own hospital hell. I kept dying, they told me. I don't remember. It's hard to remember being dead."

"*Ooooh*. Groovy. You went to the light?"

"Something like that. It didn't look much like Heaven, though. It was like a weird roller skating rink with lots of disco lights. I just rolled round and round until they brought me back to life. And I kept waking up. I would look at the surgeons and they would look at me as if it was rude to watch, and it was all very nervous and painful. I don't think you're supposed to actually feel all the cutting and sewing when they put you under. I think it's supposed to really put you under. "

In a low private tone Sue asked, "Was it a hatchet abortion? What was the address of that doctor? Did he have a real license to practice?"

"I don't want to think about it. Call it chainsaw surgery. I don't know why they kept chopping chunks out of me; there was a whole line of doctors waiting their turn at me. Then the whole military. Well, I was on a lot of drugs so I'm not sure. But I do know they weren't going to stop chopping until I got better, I guess. Hell, I don't know. You know doctors. But I don't want to think about that. It's a miracle I can still swallow with all they removed. I dream at night that they found a tiny werewolf or space alien hiding inside me, or something. They wanted to send all they could to the giant secret lab under the White House for testing.

Sue firmly stated, "There is no such place!"

"Oh, well anyway, I kept waking up. I kept seeing these faces in goggles and masks… and the *pain!* Oh the pain was just amazingly weird. And intense! When they cut and stitched me up they just pulled and jerked so rude like I wasn't even a person at all. But then I think they thought I was asleep so they didn't think to be careful."

"Oh *groo-oovy!* You should just thank nature and the Goddess in your heart that you're alive," Sue said, wide-eyed, now making a point of acting like a hippie again. "Do you miss your womb and things?"

"Do I miss my ovaries playing ping pong once a month? Do I miss my intestines doing macramé? Do I miss bleeding? Do I miss being paranoid? And all at the very same time every friggin month as if I'm some big fat bloated joke of nature? I don't think so. Besides, look how trim my tummy is with all that junk gone."

"You don't even have a scar. Groovy."

"I've got some of those from other things. But they did the radical H thing right through my honey pot."

Sue asked, "Can you still have a big O?"

I frowned. "I'm not sure. Sometimes when I'm having sex, I just feel like a bowling alley. My boyfriend once tried to ring my bell but he just pushed me like an elevator button and that was about it."

Sue winced. "He's not good in bed?"

"Oh, he has a rather athletic rhythm thing going on when he's balling. It's a good thing I'm not made out of tissue paper. I'd be found in three states by now. But the radical H thing toughened me up, I think. I feel tough."

Sue looked at my tummy and nodded as if I were, indeed, a woman raised from the dead, like the movie *Voodoo Blood Night. "Wooow,"* she said in a timid whisper.

"Sit here on the couch," I offered, "Just don't scratch-n-sniff it, first. Bod sat here, too. Now, what would you want with a poor naked cripple?"

Sue sat cautiously on the armrest and asked, "What happened to your legs?"

"I stepped out the back door," I said, as I rolled my eyes in mock embarrassment (to hide real embarrassment). "Say, could you make me some coffee while you're at it," I added. "I can't. My ankles."

"Sure. And the reason I'm here is to talk to you about radiation. That power plant is nuking us all. We have to work together to shut it down. The atoms are spreading out."

I nodded to agree. "I don't want atoms anywhere near me!" I glanced toward the back door. "How is it nuking us? What do you mean? I'm not an expert on those things. I wouldn't know an atom if it bit me."

Sue pushed on her headband. "That power plant uses radioactive nuclear power to turn water into steam. It's very dangerous."

"They can do that?" I imagined sequences of big bright neon orange mushroom clouds going off inside there and melting big ice cubes hanging from the ceiling—something amazing. "*Cool!*"

"It's radioactive," Sue said, unreceptive to my amazement at the nuts and bolts of science and public utilities, "and the radiation will give us all cancer."

I doubted that. "I'm not sure I understand. Doesn't radiation stop cancer? Don't they radiate you every time you go to the hospital to check for cancer things?"

"No, no, no. That's something different." She went to the back doors. "There's some kids down there at the bottom of the hill and they're pulling on the boards of a fallen balcony. Yours, I can see."

"Honey?" I called out to Bod. "Honey! There's kids out there trying to steal our balcony! Chase them away!"

"They're getting radiated!" Sue added.

Bod stumbled out of the bedroom, looking like hell. Sue was shocked at the sight of his semi-boner. She looked at her feet. When his eyes, that were also swollen, fixed on Sue, he asked, "What is this? Some kind of satanist coffee hour?"

I repeated, "Shut up and chase those kids away. They're trying to steal our balcony."

"Let them take it all," he grumbled. "Who cares?"

I shrewdly suggested, "If we can't stick it back on the house then we can sell it off as firewood. It could bring in a bit of mad money." Bod didn't hear me. He loudly dry heaved a few times right in front of us and then fell limp back into the bedroom.

I asked Sue, "Go yell at those kids, will you?"

She stood at the sliding door and shouted down to them, "You're going to get cancer!" They ran away.

"You can tell they felt guilty," I said. "Look at how they ran."

"So, are you going to help us with our campaign?" Sue asked. "You are one of the closest residents to the plant. Do you know if your neighbors are planning on blowing it up or anything… or any other sabotage? Have you been having secret meetings to do anything about it? Do they take photos? Do you have any photos? Do you know if your neighbors have photos and where do they keep them in their houses? What drawer? Do you ever hear Russian accents? Do you ever hear Russian sounding names? Do you ever see cameras? Has anybody ever stopped their car to take pictures of the plant? You must tell me!"

I gave her a dubious glare. "Do you think they'd tell me if they were going to blow up a nuclear power plant? Wouldn't they move to Austria first? Or is that Australia. Or wherever it is below the border, below the top half of the planet, or however it is. I looked at a globe before, sure, but I just get confused. There's just too much on it. Do you know how it works?"

She shrugged and looked very sweet and vapid. "I dunno."

"So what's wrong with nuclear power?" I asked. "If the government supports it, it must be safe. I haven't heard of any trouble, yet."

"*Yet!*" Sue warned, her eyes narrowing, her hands pushing against her Indian braids as if they might pop off. "Do you know what the government plans to do with the waste? Hydrogen bombs! And the Russians are always spying!"

"No! I don't believe that." I knew that you mixed hydrogen with ammonia to bleach hair, a fact as clear as the hair on my head, but I didn't want to argue with the poor girl.

"Jilly!" Bod shouted from the bedroom, "I need some scrambled eggs! *Now!*"

"He's a baby when he's hung over. Could you make some scrambled eggs for me? I mean him? He's hung so he'll probably want them real greasy."

"Sure," Sue said with some hesitation. "I'm not a very good cook, but I think I can do greasy scrambled eggs."

I agreed. "Anybody can make greasy scrambled eggs. It's the fluffy omelet as light as air that sends us straight to hell! Anyway, I don't think Bod will notice if you're a bad cook. Not this morning. I don't think he'd notice if I spit in them."

"I want some eggs!" Bod yelled again.

"Shut up and wait for them to cook!" I yelled back. "Or you'll get them raw! And pelted!"

"Fuck you!"

"Sugar is the devil," Sue warned, "Remember that. So is whole milk."

"And oatmeal is the worst," I added.

"Huh?"

"Prison food," I firmly stated. "That's worse than anything. Could you be a dear and hand me the phone? I need to call the studio."

"Do they have drugs there?" Sue asked.

"Just for dieting," I said. "And painkillers for my acting."

She handed me the phone. "Are there *drug* drugs?"

"I'm so glad you stopped by," I said, shrugging off all the nosey questions. "I don't know what I would've done without a little helper."

"Do they do drugs at the studio," Sue asked again, seeming to become a bit older than I'd first guessed, and a bit scary. Some gut feeling made me wonder if her Indian braids were real.

"I suppose, why not, it's a movie studio full of high strung artists. But don't you run down there thinking they'll get you high. I really don't know much about it and they're all so busy making art."

"Oh." Her face darkened.

After the eggs were finished and she had served them to Bod along with milk, aspirin, and an ice pack, I had toaster pancakes with three syrup packets. After she had tossed the gingham paper plates away and wiped off the top of the stove and counter tops, Sue excused herself.

"On the way out, could you please please, *pleeeeease* take my garbage with you? Thank you!"

She did and was gone, acting a little snippy and perturbed.

Chapter Seven

I dialed the studio. "Os!"

"Hi, Jilly," Os said. "How's Bod?"

I laughed. "Hung-over today. Real bad. He's like road kill on a bad day."

Os warned me, "He's a dead banana when he's impaired. Just dish him up some beef bouillon made with vodka. Have any? That'll paste him up. That's my secret."

"I'll try that," I lied, wanting him to suffer. "I'm calling you about the western. How's it going? Did you tape it together yet?"

"We don't use tape, we use glue to edit it."

"Oh yeah, I stopped by when they were cutting one of my scenes. The stuff smells real plastic like. Like model glue."

"Same idea. It actually melts the celluloid together. But anyway, yeah, we'll do an advanced screening next week sometime after the sound is mixed. Molita has added a lot of sound effects that made the picture look like a lot more than it is. Her gore effects are a hoot. She punched her fists through a few watermelons and got some great splatter sounds. I won't allow the immoral waste of food, of course, so when she was done I saw that she ate every drop."

"I can't wait to see the movie… and *hear* it!"

"It's been changed," he said. "We moved the saloon stuff to the beginning because we badly need something to start the movie. So stay clear from Dixie Dawn Don for a while. We bumped her scene till later. She's lit a little too harsh and we can't have her coming out right away and scaring everybody. You should hear how she goes bananas on you behind your back now that you're giving her such a run, and you got the film's song. We're going to play it three times, including the opening and closing credits. We don't waste anything."

"What could *that icky horrible nasty woman* possibly say about me?"

"The usual cat fight stuff. Forget it. If I got a nickel for every star fight, I'd be floating in dollar bills."

"I suppose." I frowned. I had wanted dirt on that vile woman. "Thanks for the compliment, though. And don't worry. I'd never trash any Flicker Farm star. That most precious Dixie Dawn Don can just be out on her own. She can just make herself look bad. I've never said anything to those syphilis-lips. No, not to hurt her. And isn't her face starting to look like it's made out of tree bark? What is going on with her? Is that what happens when you're such a drunk slut all the time? Is that what happens when you go down to the docks every night after the bars close to get balled by half the longshoremen?"

"That bananas Candy Cane is even great," Os continued, ignoring me. Either he knew I was a giant liar or didn't care. "I could kill him sometimes but he always keeps everything together, don't he?"

"Sure," I agreed, though I would rather he'd told me how he thought Dixie Dawn Don was yucky. I wanted to hear how she'd been over-padding her bra. I wanted to hear how her bra was so padded you could sell admission to it as a funhouse ride. "If Bod can only get me as famous like he promised. She got famous. Now it's my turn, and I'm not even icky."

"Bod's scraping by," Os warned me. "He swam with the sharks and lost a few legs."

I asked, "What's his problem?"

"He would've been a big, *big* director right now if *Twins Of Evil* had gone through. I'm sure he's griped about that project, to you, about a billion times by now."

"Yep." My eyes began to glaze over at just the thought of it. "He went on and on and on. That Dunkel Morgendammerung really has great power, doesn't she? She's the ultimate old star. And nobody has even seen her for years. I wonder if they ever will again. I wonder if she's just propped up dead somewhere."

Os said, "It really made him bitter when that project was yanked out from under him by all those criminal lawyers. A whole army of them just swooped on him. His pre-production was done, his script was done, and he was ready to shoot. What business do lawyers have in this town? They aren't artists! They just get in the way of the free market. Ship them to a rock quarry in Siberia where they might be put to some use!"

"Oh, Bod tries," I said. "Sure. If he'd made it big on that movie I probably wouldn't have even met him in the first place… and he wouldn't be working for you."

Os had to agree that Bod should be there for just *us*.

*****

The Plunder was a smash hit, or at least, *I* was, in it. Critics said I was a welcomed fresh face in this tired old desert town of tired desert westerns.

Timothy Cline wrote such, so nicely in the Movieland Nova:

"Jilly, vibrant new actress with two assets pert as personality; hope finds bigger better parts for bigger better parts soon. *The Plunder* waste of talent for all. Dawn Don looks lost so far from hot tub."

I had to giggle. I read the last part several times because the writing seemed a bit odd.

"Rex Manson appeared propped in saddle; all feared he'd fall and shatter his papier-mâché. Why storm intercut with nylon sock clothesline, never know. Phone us."

I shoved the review in Bod's face, literally, and he just said that I wasn't to let it go to my head. Too late. My head didn't swell beyond door spaces; it just filled my entire body with an energizing joy. For once I felt like my life had some hope to it.

*****

After my ankles healed, I decided I didn't get out enough. So I shopped. Even at the supermarket, one or two strangers came up and told me how wonderful they thought I was. I agreed as I dilly-dallied at the free samples. Not everybody knew who I was, of course, but savory hotplate items can stand on their own.

"Will you date me?" a pubescent boy asked. Before I could tear his heart out with a sad shake of my head, he smiled shyly and scuttled away. Sweet boy. I could have pinched his cheeks, his face not included.

On the way home, I stopped by a drugstore and saw a gorgeous postcard of Dunkel Morgendammerung. I said to a passing shopper, "She ruined my boyfriend."

The shopper gasped. "That is the great German silent screen star who raised criminals for sons! Cross yourself when you even think of her name!" He rushed away.

The photo was from the fifties. Dunkel was out of movies and doing cabaret, except for that part in *Quake* where she stands in front of the obvious miniature of the czar palace set burning down. She says what she would repeat in real life. "I will never be in pictures, again. I'm just too old for this cw*aaaap*." Though she was in her fifties, her skin looked as eerily flawless as a plastic fashion doll. In the postcard, Dunkel was slithering up against a clear glass column, pencil thin and dressed in a shimmering white beaded gown that made me prune with envy. I decided to buy the card for a change. I felt like I was growing ambushed by happy sunny beach pictures that depicted more nature than glamour.

"So *your* lawyers ripped up my little Bod," I said loudly to the card. "Ha. Ha. Ha."

At checkout, it amused me to hear from the drugstore clerk that Dunkel Morgendammerung translated into American as something like "very gloomy morning" and her real name was Hilda Norda Burger. In spite of her glamorous pose under dramatic lighting, the back of the card didn't even mention that she'd been a film star or had followed that achievement with decades of live stage. It read, "Dunkel Morgendammerung, mother of the Twins Of Evil".

"What do you know about the Twins Of Evil?" I pressed the drug store clerk.

"What do you want to know about them?" he asked. "I know everything about all the has-beens."

"They still in prison?"

"Nope, didn't you hear? About ten years ago they were murdered there. They were just too sick and twisted for even *that* perverted place. Good thing they got a chance to write that book first."

"What book?" I asked.

He looked at me like I'd been living under a rock. "It was a bestseller. Where've you been? It's classic. It says so much about life in these times. It was all about how those two monsters killed those poor stand-ins, and how their rotten mother abused them with cold coffee enemas. She tried to protect herself from evil by rubbing rare herbs all over her body. Didn't work, *heh?* Evil! Evil! Evil! They all went down the big fat toilet of evil!"

"What?" I asked doubtfully. "Why would anybody give their kids cold coffee enemas?" I was not even able to imagine how people carried out such tasks.

The clerk explained, "She claimed it cleaned out the liver. Why kids would need their squeaking pink little livers cleaned, I don't know. What did she feed them? I don't think dog food could even fuck up your liver. She was pretty loony. They say she had a goat. They say she took it to bed with her. I think it was the Devil! That's what they said… that she made love to the Devil. And she ate raw goat meat! Once she was chasing one of her goats with a fork and it escaped only to be hit by a car outside her home, and her gig was up. Everybody knew, then, how crazy she was."

"They should make a movie about it," I said, to test that soil.

He shook his head in angst, then dug into his ear for some wax as if that was what he always did when he was so upset. "Nobody will touch it with a ten foot pole; producers have tried but died in mysterious accidents. They say the whole thing is cursed."

I said, "Maybe it's just lawyers."

"Well, then, that makes it a giant honking conspiracy. Either way, a film isn't going to be made about the Twins Of Evil until their old witch mother dies. Then the curses will stop. Then the producers who try to make a film won't die in mysterious, bizarre accidents."

"Like what?" I asked.

"There was this dumb bozo named Bod who used to work for those two-bit gangsters at Flicker Farm. He was on his way to her house to have her sign some papers. On the way, on the highway, his convertible crashed under a truck trailer and he had his head sliced right off. God knows why he didn't duck. They say they never found the head. They said it just sat in the middle of the road for an hour, because the ambulance took forever to get there… you know how traffic is. But then it was gone! It was somehow snatched when everybody looked away at the same time. They say it's in Dunkel Morgendammerung's closet, now all dried up and shrunken! That's what they say! They say she has an entire shrunken head collection in her basement chapel! Hundreds of shrunken heads! Hundreds! Like a Nazi camp!"

I was confused. "Bod dead? "When did this happen?"

"Oh, years ago."

"Oh." I frowned. I realized Bod had become a Tinseltown ghost story and it wasn't even true. I walked out.

*****

When I got home, I told Bod that he had a shrunken head. He looked down at his dick and then said, "I don't understand. It looks OK to me. I think you're trying to be a bitch."

I didn't want to explain that people also thought he was dead. It was all too weird and he would just probably call me a *bitch* again. So I promptly made *Starpop* popcorn, making my house smell like the greasy movie theater lobby the label had promised. I got out the movie star postcard and a pen and told Mom that I'd wedged one knocker in the door of stardom, but the door had slammed on it.

Then I noticed for the first time that our neighbor had a dog. I'd never even heard it before, but it started barking and barking as if it was really spooked, causing a red flag to pop up somewhere in my head. But I couldn't land it. So I asked Bod, "Why is the dog barking? Maybe they're being broken into over there. Maybe there's a psycho killer loose over there with a rubber monster mask and a pickaxe. I've never heard that dog do that before."

"Oh, I'm sure it's nothing."

I insisted. "I got the creeps. With all that's going on around here, it could be a mass murder!"

Good neighbor Bod slipped on his bathing suit and then picked up a baseball bat from behind the door. He announced, "*Eh.* I'll be back. Don't worry." He flexed his arm muscle and rushed off.

I sighed and waited impatiently for his return, wondering if I should just call the police anyway. When I couldn't stand it anymore, I did. "Hello? The dog next door is barking like crazy! So something might be, you know, like something might be kinda wrong. Right? My boyfriend just went over to check it out, but it may be another mass murder-like thing or something, so could you please just, you know, just come over and please check it out, because this isn't normal."

The officer told me, in a voice of total unconcern, that they don't send squad cars out to noisy dogs when there's too much else going on. I felt so stupid.

"Fine, thank you, can I get back to you if my boyfriend has also been slashed?"

My imagination conjured up the ghosts of the Twins Of Evil in matching rubber monster masks slashing Bod to total hell so that his head rolled down the driveway as perfectly as a basketball. He came back to me in one piece. "Nothing," he said. "The owners are home and they just can't get their dumb dog to shut up. That's all."

"That's it? What took you so long?"

"I had a beer."

"Oh. And the dog just barked?"

"Eh." He nodded. "A strung-out dog. This town will get to anybody."

"Oh, could be rabies," I suggested. "Happens all the time back home. I bet Valium would help."

*****

Bod said he needed sex. While I was in the bathroom doing a special hormone douche, he was in the bedroom quickly doing himself. I walked in just to see him finish.

"You pig! That's my expensive hand lotion! And why couldn't you wait for me?"

"I'm in a hurry." He changed into jeans and a t-shirt and left the house. I was glad he was gone. I redid the dishes, since he had done them. All the while I wondered why the dog now sounded like it was crying. Did it have nasty owners? I started to feel pukey and was ready to scream and the dog was making me feel worse and worse with every passing minute. The dog got louder. Then it seemed as if the house had been bumped into by a car. It lurched forward. I threw my towel down to storm out to scream at Bod for being such a dumb driver as to bump into a house on stilts.

As I turned from the sink, another jolt caught me off guard as the house lurched again and all my dishes popped up about a foot into the air before crashing back down into the rack. Luckily they were plastic. Still, though, it was so bizarre that my heart leapt. I stumbled forward, grabbing the sink to steady myself. In the stillness that followed, it dawned on me that I had just survived my first movieland earthquake. I looked around and had to notice that nothing really that bad had happened. Everything looked just fine. It wasn't like the movies at all. I laughed.

Then, suddenly, with a loud explosive crack, the house jolted again and this time it wobbled side to side. The cabinet doors swung open. All the stuff in them rolled out at me all at once like an angry haunted house. Everything just wiggled and screeched so terribly that my feet flew right out from under me. I hit my chin on the edge of the sink. The wood around me crackled brightly, sounding as if it were all being shoved through a giant laundry wringer. I scampered towards the front door on hands and knees, not really ever able to gain footing as I was now on a rolling, waving, bucking fun-house rodeo roller coaster ride on springs. The vacuum cleaner ran over my fingers. By this point I was too hyped-up to feel a thing. I kept scrambling. The couch crawled across the floor all by itself. It blocked my way. As I jumped it, I heard glass break behind me. Curtains fell in my face so I grabbed them to wrap around myself. At the door, the curtains snagged on something. I left them behind and hobbled outside to the driveway, in the buff. How earthquake glamorous!

I turned to look towards the atomic power plant just as the sickening rocking stopped. To my utter amazement a dry geyser of dirt and sand had just finishing blowing up and out from the field, past the culvert. The dry spray was awesome. It must have been at least fifteen feet high. After it settled for a few minutes, and the sickening sound of rock crunching under my feet had completely stopped, the dog finally shut up. I slowly crept back to the front door. My heart was racing like I'd just snorted way too much cocaine and I was going to die. The air smelled like a vacuum cleaner bag had exploded, and rotten eggs.

I moaned in despair at what I saw of the inside of the house: an unholy mess unlike any mess I'd ever seen before. A wrinkled tube of toothpaste and a bottle of aspirin lay at the front door. They'd been way over in the medicine cabinet. I bent over and tugged at the curtains to unsnag them. But I found that they'd caught on nails that had almost worked their way entirely out of the wood. I hunted for my pink fuzz trimmed robe, hoping that having it wrapped around me would help make me feel safer. It did, but only a little.

Finally, I just broke into a good cry, thinking, "Leave it to jack-off to be out at a time like this." He was probably pinned under a bridge or something. Maybe he was dangling off a melting skyscraper, except in the movie that was a painting that was obviously bending in a flexible mirror, but this wasn't a movie and the mess wasn't just a painted backdrop. I kicked at some of the crap on the floor and got a bit of toothpaste on my foot. I collapsed on the couch, which now faced the opposite direction. I noticed the sliding doors were gone. The sight of the gaping hole on the back of the house made my heart feel all the more sick.

A man came to my door. "Everybody OK in there?"

I turned and wiped my eyes. "*Yah*. Who are you?"

"I'm your next door neighbor."

"Oh." I'd never seen any of my neighbors before, so I was surprised. "Are *you* OK?" I returned the concern.

"Shaken up, but we're fine."

"OK, thanks," I said and turned away from him. I hadn't finished my crying yet and wanted to get back to it as soon as possible. He went away and I thought about how the entire city must be a ruin and my neighbor and I might be the only people left alive. I supposed we'd be seeing much more of each other, then.

About a half hour later, while I was still sitting in the same spot but done crying, somebody else was at my door. "Hello?"

"Yes, I'm fine," I hollered back. "Thank you. Are *you* OK?" If he needed a bandage, who knew where I'd find it.

"Excuse me, but I'm from the Seismic Institute," the man introduced himself. "Can I ask you a few questions?"

I turned. I was amazed. A scientist? I wondered why he'd be at my house when there must be a yawning crack dividing downtown and changing east from west. Half the state could even be one big cracked-up island out in the middle of the ocean by now. That must be far more interesting. I stood and stepped over the obstacle course to the door.

"Can I ask the questions *now?*"

"Hello!" I said to the nice looking man with a big mop of black curly hair. "You don't want to come inside. It's just a freakin mess." I was surprised at the tone of stress I heard in my voice. I wished he would hug me. I decided that I wanted him to make total love to me. I wanted a man as close to me as he could get, I was so shaken. "No! Do come in! Please! Come in and make yourself at home!"

He didn't pick up my vibe. "This area has just had quite a jolt," he said. Maybe seismologists make it a rule not to go in earthquake houses, and there would be some common sense in that.

"Is the whole city just a pile of ruins?" I asked, tears pushing at my eyes again at the thought of all the dead bodies squashed under billboards and concrete. I wished he'd hug me.

"No, they didn't feel a thing," he said very calmly to assure me. "It's the absorbent quality of sand. Only *this* area was shaken. The epicenter seems to have come from right here."

"What? The earthquake came from under my house?"

"Close; it came from the field out there where the power plant is. Great place to build a power plant, huh."

I spotted a lot of people running in and out of the power plant that now had even bigger plumes of bright white steam coming out of it than usual. Big silver trucks were pulling up. I said, "I saw a big incredible geyser-like fountain of junk shooting up out there. Well, like, I caught the end of it anyway," I recalled, excited, grabbing his arm and taking him to where I could point it out. It was obvious where it had blown, since it left a mound of gunk. "It was the weirdest thing I'd ever seen in all my life!" Since I'd already grabbed his arm, I decided to hug him. He finally pulled away.

I said, "I'm not married you know, and I've had such a fright. And I feel so alone! I'm just shaking!" I tried to send telepathic messages to him that I wanted him to drop his pants.

He jotted some stuff down. "Anything else? Can you tell me what you experienced?"

"Wait a minute, do you mean it was a small quake? I couldn't even keep on my feet!"

"Small, yes, in that it was very localized. You were in a stilt house. It magnifies the effects."

"Then why do they build these horrible things?" I asked, rubbing my sore fingers. I'd forgotten that they'd been run over by the vacuum cleaner, but they didn't forget to hurt. I rubbed my sore chin, too.

He frowned. "Real estate and wise public planning never go hand in hand. Now tell me what you experienced."

I took a deep breath. This would tax my drama skills. "Well, um, I'm like washing the dishes, you know…"

He interrupted me. "Did anything funny happen with your water flow?"

I paused to think about that but then finally just sighed. "I don't think so. It's hard to tell. Our water pressure is never even. But yes, it was uneven, then. Very uneven. I even yelled once at the faucet, if you must know."

"What did it do… exactly?"

"It just exploded water at one point and scared the bejesus out of me. And then it only dribbled for awhile."

"OK," he scribbled. "Go on. Then what happened?"

"Well, first the house jerked a few times, you know, just *boom!* Everything flew up into the air really weird. It wobbled back and forth, back and forth, first scooting against one wall and then the other. It built up momentum. It was slamming back and forth harder and harder, left right, left right, until all the contents of the entire house were completely stirred around, just freaking awful, you know. I got out as fast as I could, like, like, you know, just friggin awful, you know, trying to dodge the furniture. It was all shoved from one wall to the other. Dishes were falling and then rolling back and forth. It was nothing like in a disaster movie where the set just crumbles here and there. No, this was all at the very same time and coming at me. Nothing held still. And it was happening everywhere at once! I didn't even have time to scream." I paused to take a breath. "How's that?"

He scribbled. "There was a jerk and then a wobble? How were they different?"

"Oh, I don't know," I tried to remember, more calmly this time. "It all happened so fast and it was just crazy. I do remember that there was a few jerks and my stuff in the kitchen just jumped high into the air. It went up about a foot or so. Really scary. Then I thought that was it. But then after a few seconds of calm, everything just wobbled like crazy."

"Up and down or side to side?"

"First up and down and then side to side," I answered. "Is that weird?"

"No," he said, sounding very interested as he scribbled. "That's the usual pattern. Anything unusual happen the rest of the day, before the quake?"

"Well let's just see," I mulled, looking up into the clear bright sky, thinking how ironic it was that an earthquake could happen on such a fine day. There should be lightning and clouds the color of blood.

"This place is always crazy. I found out that my neighbor has a noisy dog. He's quiet again. Is that caused by earthquakes?"

He perked up, interested. "Maybe. Tell me about it."

"Earthquakes cause noisy dogs?"

"I don't know," he said. "Just tell me about it."

"There's nothing to say other than the dog wouldn't shut up for a few hours before the quake, and I remember the sound of his barking made me feel really sick."

"You felt ill?" he asked.

I nodded. "I may still have a heart attack after all this is all over, though. Just watch me."

"We don't know, yet," he said, "But maybe earthquakes cause stomach upset, before it's even gone off. Maybe gases are pushed from the ground in greater quantities, like radon, causing symptoms in some people and animals. Maybe it's sound frequencies. We just don't know. That's why I'm asking. But some people, who are very sensitive, feel sick just before an earthquake."

"I'd have never thought feeling queasy meant something bad was about to happen. Maybe the dog and I are psychic? Well, you never know."

"No, you never know. Did you see anything else odd?"

"Have other animals acted weird in earthquakes?" I asked, curious, if not utterly fascinated, wondering what the dog knew that I didn't.

"My worse case I ever reported was a poodle who jumped off a fourth floor patio minutes before a quake that didn't do any building damage. But anyway," he asked, again, "you can't think of anything else?"

"Well, now that you mention it, I think that the sun may have reflected weird."

"What? The *sun?*"

"Why? Is that odd?" I asked. He looked at me like it was. "Well, it was like it had changed directions or something. The sun can't do that, can it, it hits the planet all at the same time, right?"

"What do you mean?" he asked with great interest.

I shrugged and felt amazingly stupid, now doubting my own eyes and memory. "It's hard to explain because I didn't even think about it until now, but… well, when I'm in the bedroom, sometimes I see light reflected from the windshields of cars that drive by. It goes through the window and onto the wall. The walls are white in there so the whole room flashes brighter as the light sweeps across the room. It's a pretty groovy effect. Well, I was just starting the dishes and I saw something like that flash—but not quite—sort of a flash, um, just a few times on the *kitchen* wall. I suppose I should've thought more of it, then, but I've never seen a flash like that there before, the sun off cars shouldn't reflect off that direction this time of day. Does that have anything to do with anything?"

He was scribbling away. "Possibly. UFOs are often reported in earthquake areas."

"*What?*" I almost screamed. "There wasn't a saucer out there. "Was there?" I held my belly, hoping I hadn't been impregnated. But then I remembered I'd been ripped off and didn't have a womb. They'd left a surgical tool inside of me anyway. I looked at my manicure for comfort. "A flying saucer at my house making an earthquake! Wow! Now I have the creeps!"

"I doubt you had a flying saucer."

"What else could it have been? It must be a flying saucer! What else could it be?"

"We don't know why but the ground may emanate an energy that can be seen in the form of light. Sometimes entire sheets of flashing light have brightened an entire night sky as if it's day. This phenomenon has been reported just before earthquakes."

"No way! That's just too creepy for me to deal with." I shivered and goose pimples raised right out of me. I rubbed my arms. "*Scary!*" I looked up at the sky and expected to see something hovering up there that looked like a pie plate. But there wasn't even a cloud.

"It won't be scary," the earthquake detective stated, his face having that bland comfort of science look, "when we figure it all out enough. Maybe someday we can predict earthquakes using these signs."

I grabbed him and kissed him on the mouth. He pushed me away. I looked at him angrily and opened my pink fuzzy gown to let him see my fabulous body. "Let's go inside now and see the earthquake damage. I want to show you how the bed moves if you rock it real hard."

He just looked at me as if I were about as interesting as a kitchen chair.

"Are you gay?"

"No."

"Just because you're a science guy doesn't mean you can't have some good primed up mink every now and again!"

"I already have a wife who's trying to get pregnant, a girlfriend who's a nymph, and a subscription to Madam Bush's Whorehouse that I just renewed. I'm just plain sapped out right now."

"My luck!"

After he left, I just wanted to sit on the clutter and watch TV. But the power was off so I couldn't. I got a hammer that was still in its drawer (but the drawer was across the room from its chest) and went around the house tapping all the nails the rest of the way back in. It was the perfectly neurotically tedious thing to do, since I'd become furious with Bod for being away during such a crisis. I was under the house whacking away at the rows and rows of escaping nails when Bod walked in. He was so tanked he didn't seem to see that the house was trashed. Though the bed was now against the other wall of the bedroom, he still somehow fell on it.

"Bod!" I tried to talk to him, "Where have you been? There was a terrible earthquake and I was left here all alone and all the dishes crashed right down on my head! I was alone and I needed a man! I needed attention! I needed any old man! There's times a woman shouldn't be left alone! Not after a hormonal douche! Not after an earthquake!" He just mumbled something that turned into snoring. He was useless. So I pushed the couch against the wide-open front door to try and block it up a bit against coyotes, burglars, rapists and rubber mask murderers, before calling it a night.

*****

The next morning when I was almost ready to deal with cleaning up my messy house, Sue the door-to-door hippie came back.

"Come in! Come in!" I called out to her from the other side of the debris. "Just be careful where you walk. The place is full of landmines."

"What happened to your house?" Sue asked. "Did the government come sack it? I never heard about that. Nobody told me!"

"Come in. Come in. You'll just have to climb over the couch to get past the door."

She did, and had an awkward time of it, since she was wearing a long busy intricate butterfly tie-dyed caftan that caused my eyes to involuntarily rake up and down her. She lugged a heavy strawberry red suitcase dotted in hideous cartoon strawberry seeds, which utterly clashed with the robe and her odd woven straw headband that was dripping with her cute Indian braids.

"I had an earthquake," I apologized. "I guess you didn't feel it."

Her eyes widened. "Earthquake? At just this house? *Groooo-vy.*"

"The field next to the atomic power plant did it worse. And this side of the hill or something," I said, pissed. "You didn't feel anything at all? That's not fair."

As she shook her head, I got close enough to see that the aqua button on her lapel read, 'dolphins love everybody.' She asked, "Did you get any pictures of the power plant during or just after the earthquake?"

"Yeah right," I said. "Have you ever tried to do *anything* during an earthquake? It left everything such a mess I had to pound all the nails back into the house."

Sue daintily pushed down on her odd woven straw headband and asked, "You pounded nails? You a lesbian?"

"Are you a spy?" I asked.

Sue jolted as if guilty, which was very odd. "Why? Who told you what? Why would you say that? A spy? Me?" Then she laughed in rather bad acting, pushing hard on her Indian braids as if they might suddenly blast off if she didn't.

"Cool it," I hushed her. "I was joking, thinking you might've been a spy from the Suzy Homemaker Award people, as if they'd really come here to my house and flunk me for having an earthquake. And no, I'm not a lesbian. I wasn't pounding the nails because I wanted to." Since we were speaking of nails, I looked at my hands and saw that my manicure was trashed. They almost looked like I had boy hands. It saddened me.

Sue laughed again, this time for real. "Oh, you were joking. Of course. Groovy."

"So what are you up to these days?" I asked, hiding my boy hands. "Still trying to make the power plant go away?"

She nodded. "Sure."

"It almost did." I said. "It almost just soaked into that field."

"That doesn't sound safe," she said, her eyes screwing together in concern. I thought the effect would've been much better if she'd worn black mascara. Then she held her suitcase out before her. "But I'm not just protesting the power plants. I'm also selling *Apple Cosmetics*, these days. Have you tried them before? They're groovy. I joined the FBI… I mean… the FB*A!*" She laughed nervously. "The new Feminist Business Association."

"What's that?"

"To fight sexism in business," Sue explained. "We become self-employed so we don't have to work for *the man*. He stinks."

"This has certainly become a life full of issues," I grumbled, pushing a few items on the floor around with my foot.

"Women should think about issues," Sue mildly pretended to scold me in a way that made me wonder if she'd practiced her spiel in the mirror. "The biggest problem in the world is men. They cause war and oppress women and create repressive rape culture! Women are so much better than men. Women are the source of all creation." Her eyes looked off and tried to find to some distant glory. "Women are the only creatures on earth who are truly creative, because they give birth. Birth is, you know, the greatest act of creativity!"

"Getting fertilized is not my idea of art," I said. "Movies are. And movies are not eggs getting knocked up. Movies are… just swell!"

"Movies! Movies!" Sue huffed. "The camera lens is nothing more than a rape."

"Huh?"

"It has its long phallic lens zoom in and in and in and in and out like a dirty filthy man humping away. It objectifies women by doing that."

"What? Objectifies? What's that? The lens–humping? What?"

"You know," Sue answered. She had righteous fury building in her, making her voice rather shrill. "It turns women into objects. Instead of just letting them be… you know… *people*."

"Well… I'm not as worried as you are about men today. I was just screwed by Mother Nature and that's all. I get all the luck." I pushed a coffee mug with my foot.

"We must stop all sexism by first agreeing that men are destructive monsters that rape the world. We must stop them. We must stop men and stop sexism. They stink! Especially on a hot day! Step on them! Crush them! Lock them all away into camps!"

The idea of stepping on Bod's head gave me a rush of pleasure. Then I had to wonder why I was always imagining Bod being hurt. "Sure," I agreed. "Let's stop sexism, now. Turn 'em all into slaves! What's a good way to start the revolution?" I asked, looking at her suitcase. "Shop? Mom told me once that if capitalism is good, greed is a virtue."

"What?" Sue looked a bit confounded, then looked down at her wares.

"Oh, never mind. Mom's probably just bitter that she's not rich. Let's just talk about shopping!"

Sue looked back up at me. She smiled sweetly. "Groovy. Have you ever heard of *Apple Cosmetics*?"

I shook my head. "Nope."

"They're, like, made from vegetables!" She set the suitcase on the floor next to the clear plastic coffee table.

I set the table upright for her suitcase. "I thought apples were a fruit."

"Oh!" Sue laughed. "No, it's just called *Apple Cosmetics*, but it's really made from vegetables."

"Oh, how interesting." I wasn't interested. I already had enough cosmetics spilled to the four corners of the house. "This place looks like a really stoned sorority house, huh?"

"They're all natural so they won't give you cancer or germs and only come in natural colors and won't poison you when you eat it off at dinner."

"I do like that one over there," I pointed to a lovely pale honey-colored lipstick.

"It's called *Organic Dawn. Organic Dawn*," Sue repeated as if it was a magic spell. "It won't poison you. It's all organic. *Orgaaaaanic Daaaaawn!*"

"It looks like it has bits of metal in it," I said. "Pretty. But is metal organic? Is it healthy?"

"Oh definitely," she assured me. "It's not metal, it's gangrene."

"Rotting flesh?"

"No… um… I mean guanine, I think the word is, an all natural pearly stuff made from fish scales of a certain fish that aren't rotting. Don't ask me what kind."

"Fish scales?" I made a face. "Yuck!"

Sue smiled. "Fish scales are shiny. It's better than the *other* companies who use aluminum and synthetic pearl in their frosties. That's not natural. Petroleum isn't natural. Gives you cancer!"

"Petroleum gives you cancer?" I asked. "Oh critters! I'm surrounded by it!"

"Yes, it's a very dangerous world!"

I decided, "I'll take your *Organic Dawn*. Then I just might feel a bit better. I need to start buying things to help me feel better after all that's happened here."

"Yeah," Sue agreed. "You'll feel healthy while you wear it! You'll feel so groovy!"

"And that. And that!" By the time I finished trying the *Flawless Feel Foundation*, I felt even better. I bought that too, along with an array of eye makeup, so I wouldn't be putting petroleum derivatives on my precious eyeballs. I was screaming for more. "I'll take this *Alpha Zen Glitter*, *Ying Yang Blue*, *Clean Sea Green*, and *Pure Karmic Soul*, to boot." While I was unearthing the contents of the house, inch by inch, to find my wallet, she invited me to a nuclear action meeting.

"Nope." That was going too far, I thought. It was one thing to *shop* to save the world but it was going too far to expect me to *show up* for anything. I told her I was busy. I was. My house was one big junk drawer. Still, she handed me three business cards… for the feminist group, the nuclear group, and her own makeup business.

I asked, "Why are your cards so brown?"

Sue smiled. "Bleaching paper will ruin all our drinking water."

I held the card close to my eye. "But it's hard to read off such a dark brown color."

"Drinking is more important than reading."

"Oh, of course. That's great." I took the dark brown business cards, trying to smile as sincerely as she was. I looked around, wondering where I would put them. "Haven't the grocery stores become stingy?" I asked, "I really have a time with those free sample people!"

She shook her head. "I think that's just your hobby."

"Maybe," I admitted. "I never thought of free-sample hunting as being hobby-like before. Boy, what a dumb hobby."

She asked, "Is that why you put so much of my stuff all over your face before you bought anything? To see how much your face fit for free?"

I smiled. "I dunno." I had.

"You should join our feminist group!" she continued. "It'll be very good for you and the world. Women are better than men. So we have to stop sexism, pollution, rape and war. All you have to do is start a business," she explained, making it sound as breezy as a movie musical number.

"I'll let you know. First I have to deal with this mess."

Sue beamed at me in the way women beam at each other when they know they're superior, I think, and said, "Bye. Oh, and one more thing," she added. "Keep your all natural makeup in the freezer so it won't spoil. It doesn't have chemical preservatives in it that'll poison you."

I heard a car pull up, and in an instant, a man in an ugly tan leisure suit and rubber lizard mask ran to the door but was stopped by the couch. He pulled out a gun. From a slit in her butterfly caftan, Sue pulled out a gun and pointed it at him like a seasoned police woman. I gasped in alarm. The man's black beady lizard eyes spotted Sue and *he* gasped in alarm. He turned and ran out and his car squealed away, throwing bits of gravel against the house.

"What the hell was that?" I asked, holding my heart.

Sue put her gun away. "It was… I don't… he was…"

"It was like he was going to shoot me but was afraid of you? What? The friggin psycho is afraid of hippies?"

"Oh that man!" Sue dismissed him, a bit too exuberantly. "He's… he's… he's just a fan!"

"A who?"

"Yeah! A fan who goes around trying to get autographs."

"What?" I said louder than I meant to. "How do you know that?"

Sue said, "You know… I read it in the paper. He's famous for being so odd… even by this town's standards. He chases stars and then when he gets to them, *that's it*, he gets shy and runs away."

"With a gun?" I reminded her, not convinced.

"It's a squirt gun," Sue blurted. "In this heat, you always need a squirt gun with you."

"In this heat, he can friggin start by just taking off the rubber masks. The creep must have a pile of them."

"He's shy, as I said." Then Sue quickly excused herself, seeming very nervous. "Gotta go!" She climbed up onto the couch, fell over the other side, and was gone.

I wondered if I was a bit psychic, because I felt that something was horribly wrong in the deepest deep of my guts, and wrong in a way I'd never felt before. Yes, there was a mask-wearing gunman who'd killed whats-his-face. And he was still popping up here and there. Yes, I was in a stilt house! An earthquaked one. Yes, I was living with a rude slob. But also, there was something weird about that hippie. There was just something not right about her Indian braids. I stated aloud, "Everything from the headband down is fake!" I said it again because it sounded so true.

Since the fridge was backwards, I barely squeezed my arm around to slide all my new cosmetics in. I sadly appraised the house. I decided that, without help, I was in no mood to clean anything. Bod lived here, too. After picking the kitchen ceiling tiles out of the bathtub, I filled it to the very top, and soaked, wondering how I was to rub a frozen block of makeup on my face.

I could tell when Bod came to. I heard wild hysterical screaming. "What the hell did you do to my house? You crazy fuckin *bitch!*"

"I had an earthquake," I yelled back, "and since you weren't here to help me through it, you can just clean up this mess all by your friggin self!"

"What?" He popped his head in the bathroom and stared at me, looking very freaked out.

"You were the idiot to buy a shanty on the side of a hill. Well, this is what it gets you!"

"You had an earthquake?"

"Yes!" I splashed some water at him in anger. "And you were such an insensitive jerk, you didn't even feel it! And then a crazed man with a squirt gun in a rubber mask ran in. But then he saw the hippie and ran out. She looked like she was going to squirt him! And why would he want Snako's autograph before he killed him… if he indeed had anything to do with Snako being electrocuted in the pool, since he's shy and was wearing a different mask then. It could have actually been somebody else, since anybody can wear a rubber mask. And I think I'm psychic because I can feel that something is very very screwed up around here!"

Bod was not up to speed with what I'd been thinking, so he nodded vacantly before he excused himself with an, "*Eh*," and crashed heavily back into bed again. Fear jolted through me. What if

I electrocuted in the bathtub? I jumped out so fast, I took half the water with me and fell into the dirt of a spilled plant.

Hours later, Bod got up again. When he saw the house was so messed up that he couldn't even eat something if it required a pan, he just walked out. I really didn't expect him to clean, or even help, not *really*, so I was actually very relieved to have him out of my sight.

When he came back, drunk, I snapped, "If you don't lay off the juice, your liver's gonna fall out on the sidewalk." He ignored me. "Your liver is gonna turn the size and color of a school bus and just drive off without you!" Still, no response. I guess a bad time to talk to a person about his chug-a-lugging is when he's passed out.

Next morning, I cleaned awhile, mostly just pushing big things around and trying to get dried toothpaste out of the carpet. Bod moaned from his bed for eggs. "Scrambled?" I asked, thinking I was doing a funny.

After he ate his eggs and drank a pitcher of water, he became human by noon. Then it grew so hot we mostly just sat around and looked at the mess, sucking *Polarbears*, wondering how we could have forgotten where things were supposed to be. After the *Polarbear* box was gone and my tongue was bright plastic blue and my stomach felt like a concentrated curdled punch bowl, we decided to leave the house for the day. We needed to find an air-conditioned bar. We needed to be able to breathe. On the bus, we weren't the only ones looking like filthy disaster-movie scum. Heat is a great equalizer. At a watering hole, I asked the bartender if he'd heard of the earthquake. When he shook his head, Bod scoffed, "She had a tantrum in my house and now she's blaming an earthquake." I kicked him so hard under the table he knew damn well that I wasn't amused by that horrible accusation.

I said to the bartender, "I had an earthquake."

The bartender nodded and said, "Sure."

Five brews later, Bod regressed as I expected, relieving my mounting suspense. "I could've been *sooooo* rich," he whined, starting in on the ancient tirade. "I was gonna make the best movie! The best! A true story always sells. *Twins Of Evil* would still be playing. *Ah!*

The residuals! I had a damn good cast and script. It was so real, just like the real events; brains in bread-bags in the deep-freeze, movie star mom phoning the kids every day to try to buy or sell pills, the seductions, the victims becoming just like the stars they stood-in for. The enemas. The raw goat. I made up a scene where she chases the goat through the city, just to have an action scene. I made up a scene where the evil twins go to a movie star look-alike whorehouse just to bag their own Mom. Super creepy. I made up a scene where she's found floating above her bed, her eyes popping all the way out, and she's saying her movie script lines backwards!"

"Amazing."

He grumbled. "I could be a millionaire. I could be so rich I'd be living above the dam."

"You think so?"

"It's as clear as beer!"

Returning home, we were too drunk to feel our feet, but we sure felt the heat and the stagnant city air rubbing into our face like a giant armpit. We spent the rest of the afternoon sitting around like dripping wax works. It was too hot to breathe. When the friggin sun finally set, it looked and felt like an ominously glowing furnace with the door left open. The sun hated us.

I asked, "Do you really think Os killed Snako?"

"Hell no," Bod said. "Don't even say that."

"What if the man in the rubber monster masks is Os?"

"Impossible."

"Yes, I suppose," I agreed. "He's too thin and moves too young to be Os. But he has to be somebody."

Bod looked at me and nodded. His eyes screwed up like in a clock spring in an attempt to think intelligently about it. "*Eh.* He has to be somebody."

"The hippie girl said he had a squirt gun."

Bod chuckled. "She's stupid."

"She had a gun, too."

"It wasn't a squirt gun."

I thought about that one. "*Hmm.* What's a hippie doing with a gun? Something's not right."

Chapter Eight

Then, I went on to play the part of a bored shrill housewife. I lived to wallow around the house and re-cook precooked overly marketed freezer conglomerations. I had a toaster. All the while, I often announced, "I'm bored!"

Sue, the door-to-door hippie, came back to sell more cosmetics, wearing another head-to-toe tie-dye wonder. When she knocked, I was on the floor in the middle of my tummy-tightening workout.

"Hi. Are you OK?" she asked. "Should I call a doctor? Did you just over-dose on drugs? Is it too much speed? Where do you buy the drugs? Do you know if they're just from a middleman or what? Who's the kingpin? Do you know his name and where he lives? Who smuggles them into the country? What are their names? Where do they live? Do they come up from Mexico? Do you know? Do you know the contact in Mexico? Do you know names?"

"They're called *sit-ups*, dear. This is how I keep my belly so flat, sheer iron muscle along with most my internal organs having been removed." I waved at her so she'd see how pretty my nail polish was. "What was that about Mexico?"

"Oh," Sue nodded as if impressed. "I thought you were having a seizure. I came by because I have so many new groovy colors that have come out since we last visited. I just know you'd want to be seen in the latest colors."

Sweating like a pig in the awful heat, I felt totally untrendy. I had to break the sad news that I didn't need any replacements. "Sorry."

"Not yet?" she fretted. "Haven't you been wearing makeup? Are you depressed?"

"Honey," I explained, "the sad fact is, your all-natural brand has been in the freezer, so it won't spoil in this freakin heat. So I haven't even started any of them yet."

Sue's face dropped. "No?"

"The petroleum laden department store cosmetics are unhealthy, perhaps. And they kill whales, I'm sure. But they're handy! They're so full of toxic preservatives, they're right there for me."

"Like drugs?" Sue asked. "Have you seen any drugs around? Do you know if anybody has been taking pictures of the nuclear power plant? Have your neighbors been having meetings to sabotage it? Did anybody take pictures of the power plant just after the earthquake?"

"Why do you care?" I said. "Is it illegal?"

Sue's face grew angry. "Blowing it up is!"

I said, with too much hysteria wavering in my voice, "It's probably going to blow up all by itself. If it's just going to sit out there in this awful heat like it does, then it doesn't have a fat chance! Damn the sun's hot!"

Since I was not in a buying mood, Sue left. I wondered if she was a spy, again, but this time seriously. Then I thought about how Indian braids looked very hippie. So I realized I was being stupid. Then I remembered how fake they looked. I was so confused.

I mopped myself with a paper towel then decided to clean house, starting with dresser drawers. This was an unusual thing for me to do since I hardly ever think about dressers being dirty. When I lifted out Bod's jeans, I sniffed cautiously at the crotches to see which ones needed to go in a laundry pile. I came upon a pile of girly magazines. After the surprise wore off, I looked through them and felt jealous of the girls. They were younger. I felt grossed-out to be seeing so many of them naked and sprawled out like that. Then I felt strangely angry. I wasn't sure why. I put my bathrobe on and went to my prince charming. "Bod? Hey! Bod! What are these disgusting things doing in the house?"

"Where'd you get those?" he asked angrily. "Have you been snooping through my things? How dare you?"

"They embarrass me and turn my stomach. And I'm trying to clean."

"How can they turn your stomach? *You* do that! You're a dumb porno star."

"I'm not a pornographic actress," I corrected him. "I'm an actress who does semi-nude scenes in order to advance her pathetic little career. If you weren't such a dick-wad you'd see the difference. I'm really a very serious artist at heart." I made an even sterner face to show how serious I was.

He said, "Whatever? Put them back."

"What do you need with these? What do I have to do to satisfy you? Slap a mink on my forehead?"

"I need the magazines for research. I'm a producer. Remember? I need to see how these things are photographed."

"Fine," I smiled like the Wicked Witch of *Endor Mountain* before she blasts the entire miniature forest to try and kill Tricky the Squirrel. "I accept that." I smiled again. "I *want* you to improve yourself. We all applaud your attempts. Me, myself and I. Now that you've studied the exquisitely lit girls, I think we can toss them!"

"No!" he insisted, suddenly coming to life. "You can't throw those away! Those are mine! Those are none of your business! You're nosey!"

"They *are* my business!" I said, feeling suddenly righteous. "It goes into my eyes and into my mind, and it did something to my stomach. It made me want to have diarrhea. So it is my business!"

"How?" he whined. He grew angry but wisely kept a lid on it. He obviously sensed my cosmic universality of female power. My crisp stunning black liquid eyeliner helped. He pouted, "How can this be any of your retarded concern?"

"I accidentally came across them while cleaning this pig-sty. And they made me upset. They made me sick to my stomach. They ruined my chores! I like to clean pretending I'm Mabell Charms from that TV show, but now I just feel like me and I feel icky. *That's* why it's my business! *I don't like being made fun of!*"

"I'm not making fun of you!" Bod blushed, squirmed and otherwise acted very ashamed. "You just don't understand something about men. Men are very visual."

"So are women. I look at you and I want to scream! From now on you just look at pictures of *me*! God knows there's been plenty of them taken and they look just as good as anything! I'm not fat. I'm not ugly. I'm not old. So wank to me, baby. Your superficial wank is only to me. I'm now the goddess of superficial wank!"

After that glorious oration, he was speechless. I wouldn't allow the conversation to continue, anyway. After I huffed a bit more, I dumped the magazines in a garbage barrel in front of the house and threw in a match. Bod didn't bother to stop me so I guess that proved I was right and he was wrong. After the flaming blaze grew to a bright inferno and things began to stink really bad, I realized I needed to find some water, and fast. The big black garbage pail was very modern and plastic. It was all beginning to pour down the gravel driveway.

When that was over, Bod walked up to me. It was obvious he had worked on something clever to say so he could have the last word. "We're not married, you know. We're just shacking up. So don't even think of acting like a dumb wife." If that was his idea of a last word then he could have it. It was too pathetic to contemplate. I just looked at him as if he'd said, "*gesundheit.*" I nodded a thank-you and then went back to cleaning. There were still dust-bunnies under the dresser and they had to die.

*****

Then I got tired of trying to do anything. Even the TV commercials of food couldn't pep me up. I went to bed and stayed there. After days on end, I couldn't bring myself to get up, even to freshen my mascara. "I'm tired!" I complained. "Leave me alone!"

"You're pathetic," Bod scoffed. "Your pillow is black."

"That's my mascara. Go away."

"Move. I'm not into corpses."

Through all this personal de-evolution, Os was so kind to me. He kept stopping by. He'd sit gingerly on the very edge of the bed so I wouldn't bruise. He tried to encourage me. "Don't be depressed, Jilly. Cheer up. We'll start the dinosaur flick soon. Very soon. We've got a great part for you. Bod wrote it for you, special. You'll play Dixie Dawn Don's sister! And you get eaten by a giant plant!"

"Her!" I moaned. "How does a cave-tramp pad her bra? Oh, I know… stuff her bra with shark teeth, pointed inward. That sounds prehistoric."

Os said, "You don't need to pad anything."

"I wasn't talking about me. And what does *soon* mean? I don't want to get eaten by a giant plant. Can't that icky Dixie Dawn Don get eaten by a giant plant?"

"It'll be a great scene," Os insisted. "The plant bites you in half. Then we cut to a dummy, of course. Candy Cane has made a fake torso that is so bananas it shoots real pig intestines. That one shot, alone, will sell half our tickets."

I started to bawl. "I don't want to be bitten in half!"

"But Bod wrote the scene just for you… special."

"Let *her* get bitten in half. And then just have pork and beans come out of her. She's got no real guts." For some reason, in my mind's eye, I couldn't see me, but only Dixie Dawn Don getting snapped into pieces by a big giant plant. The audience would openly weep for joy. Or maybe the giant plant could just catch her by her fat hair and whip her around until her neck broke. Or maybe the giant plant could try to eat Dixie Dawn Don. But then it dies of toxic shock. My mind raced until I started to laugh and laugh and laugh, louder and louder. I got so loud, I was screaming. Os just looked at Bod like it was all his fault. For that, I would have been happy. But I was too sad.

*****

My birthday came near, making me feel old, old, old. I didn't want another holiday to come and go without cards. So I got out of bed, walked to the end of the road, caught a bus to the drug store, and bought cards.

The one I bought from Bod to me said: "You're getting old, time to iron your Birthday suit." Sounded like something he'd say.

The one from Os to me said: "Happy Birthday to the biggest star in the land. Go on a diet." Sounded like something he'd say.

The one from Mom to me said: "My little girl has grown older and wiser (one of these is a lie)." Sounded like something she'd say.

The one from Andernach to me said: "Happy Birthday." He was not rude so it would have to be generic.

The one from the Sue, the door-to-door hippie said, "It's your birthday. Groovy." There's a picture of a whale going to Heaven.

The one from Dixie Dawn Don, I wrote in, "Jilly, I'm your biggest fan. You're my total idol. Your poster is on my wall and I kiss your toosh every day. I love your hair. I love you. I love you more than anything. I am nothing compared to you. I think I'll go slit my wrists now."

I forged everybody's signature as best as I could and placed them on my headboard. I went back to bed. When Bod finally noticed the cards, he looked at me like he was afraid of me, but he didn't say a word.

*****

The day of my birthday hit me like a head-on train crash. I crawled out of bed again to look closely in the mirror and realized I looked very smooth and dewy for my age, like a teenager. That was probably due to the light bulbs on the bathroom mirror. I'd long ago colored them all over with a dark pink marker. My knockers even seemed to defy gravity. I do have to admit they were all wrapped up in cellophane tape. Still, while slowly exhaling, I took it all as a sign of my impending stardom. I vowed to continue my facial avocado treatments, just in case it was true that the skin could eat.

Bod shamed me. "You finally get out of bed just to rub your lunch all over yourself? You've lost your mind!"

"You don't understand and I'm too busy to explain."

"Take that off!" Bod said as I slipped on my party dress. "We don't wear clothes in this house.

"I *will wear a party dress*! It's *my* day and I'll do as *I* please!" I threw him a lime green tie with orange shamrocks on it. "You can at least wear this." Bod tied it around his waist and it was just wide enough to give him some unprecedented modesty if you looked at him from only the very front.

I scampered out to the mailbox to see if it was crammed full of letters and cards from fans all around the nation. There was just one odd unsigned letter that read, in cold impersonal type, "Jilly, if you marry Os, you will be murdered with him. You will die. I will kill you. I mean it, you will be killed with him! This is the only warning you will get before he is killed. I will kill you, too. Get it? I will shoot you dead. Is this clear? If you marry Os, you are a goner." Not wanting to upset Os when he came over, I threw away the horrid letter from my one inappropriate fan.

Os gave me a bra he spray painted silver. "Happy Birthday! Here! You need steel for those bananas!" Then he stood at attention, he was so proud of it. Bod laughed real hard. Too hard. "What did you get your little lady?" Os asked Bod.

"Oh, I was just going to ball her for her birthday." He laughed, lifting up his tie.

Os frowned and looked at me with pity. So I said, "Let's tell the paper we're getting married. It'll be fun."

Os chuckled. "You hate Bod that much?"

"Sure. And it's press. I need some press." I had suddenly remembered that threatening fan letter I got in the mailbox. The threat was such a good idea. I would have never come up with such a good idea myself. "Don't engagements always make good press?"

Os asked, "Where'd you get such a good idea? Who made you a press agent?"

I smiled. I shrugged. "I guess I'm just brilliant at promoting myself."

The next day, I called the tabloid but the woman who answered the phone said she didn't know who I was. She hung up on me.

*****

Days later, Os announced that I'd appear before the camera in a matter of mere months in the caveman flick AS THE LEAD! My original part had been entirely red-penciled. I was *it!*

"Why isn't that *precious* Dixie Dawn Don in the lead?" I asked. "Did she get fat? Did she get a face lift and it snapped?"

"She's gone," Os said without a hint of emotion. "She's going to marry some filthy rich businessman in Iran. They say that by the end of the sixties that country became very Western, modern and liberal.

So she'll live in a new modern country. She'll live in Iran happily ever after, I'm sure. That's the end of her talent. With her gone, you're now our number one Flicker Farm star."

I smiled greedily at getting the lead part, but was also disturbed that somebody as irritatingly bimbo as Dixie Dawn Don could find a rich man and maybe be happy. So I decided to make myself worthy of Flicker Farm. I decided to put myself in top form. I bought all the new diet pills that promised to melt my love handles like butter, even though I didn't really have any. I taught myself how to climb a rope without ripping up the insides of my legs. I taught myself how to throw a spear while running barefoot across gravel with a lovely calm smile on my face. I lifted gallons of heavy chocolate milk until my body was hard muscle. I was an obsessive mess, but people are obsessive, and I always wanted to fit in. As the final days approached, I ate nothing but celery and pills. For dessert I sucked a few frozen currants and pretended they were movie theater candy.

Finally, the other projects—*Metal Sex Robot*, Dawn Don vs. aluminum foil and *Jungle Fox*, Dawn Don vs. an ape suit—had cleared out of the barn so the prehistoric film—Jilly vs. art—could begin. A paper cave set was crumpled up in a corner. The set really was paper. Wide sheets of dark grey paper were unrolled from huge spools and then crumpled and taped to a scant wood frame. Paint was then speckled all over it in fashionable purple and blue stratums.

"A sneeze could knock this over," I said to Candy Cane, who, of course, was doing all the work.

"Ca-ca. Then don't sneeze. This is serious, man!"

I asked him, "Where'd you get that charming bracelet? It looks rich."

"Dixie Dawn Don's around here somewhere giving everybody good-bye jewelry. They say her husband is soooo rich, how lucky. Where's your jewels?"

I shrugged, trying to pretend utter indifference. He didn't buy it. "Ca-ca!" Candy Cane splashed the paper awhile longer and then clomped off with his paint cans. I stubbornly stayed put. If icky

Dixie Dawn Don was going to give me jewelry, she'd have to find me and come to me. I wasn't going to go crawling to her.

I stood for about a half hour, my feet utterly glued to the floor, casually swinging my purse, dreaming of a diamond ring or earrings. After I got something nice, then I'd forgive her a little bit for being so icky. Finally, Bod told me it was time to go. He now had an expensive watch. In the car on the ride home, I asked Bod why I didn't get anything from the greedy hairy bitch. "Why? Why? Why?"

"Maybe you're too new. She just thanked us old-timers."

At home, I opened my purse and screamed bloody murder. Most of my purse's contents spilled out along with the horrible *thing* that had somehow gotten in there. Bod came running and couldn't figure out what I was pointing at. "Look!"

"What?"

"Look!"

Bod was stupid. "What am I looking at?"

"It's a voodoo curse!" I bawled. "I've been cursed!" I was pointing at a woven-straw voodoo-looking doll. How it got into my purse was a mystery. "*Aaaaaah!*"

"What?"

"Bod! It's an evil voodoo doll!"

Bod grabbed it impatiently and ripped it up, which took a bit of effort since it was woven rather tightly. He flushed the shattered remains down the john. "There! Are you dead?" he asked me. I wasn't dead, so I shook my head. "Well then, *eh!*" he concluded, "It wasn't a voodoo doll of *you*."

*****

The next day the picture started. We spent most of the day just setting up in the barn. Candy Cane had to be pulled away from the paper cave set. It had sagged a bit during the night, so he obsessed trying to fluff it up. I wore a brand new blonde wiglet to the barn. It was a long voluptuous model called, *Chignon Top On.* It wasn't quite my color, but Bod assured me it was good enough.

He said, "Film stock is not as sensitive as the human eye."

I asked, "Are you sure?"

"Yellow is yellow is yellow to Chrome-A-Shift film stock. The cheapest in town."

"Why use the cheapest film stock?"

"Why waste our money on true color. Who knows what colors really looked like at the beginning of time."

"Oh. Of course. I knew that."

Bod looked at me like he knew I was stupid and I knew he was smart. Then he walked away.

The costume Candy finally issued to me was a scandal. It fit in the palm of my hand. It was a tiny rabbit fur g-string thing. "Isn't it cute?" he asked. Today his eyelids were painted a grass green, which went very well with his attempt to dye his hair blonde. It went bright orange and stuck out all over like a fright wig. His t-shirt read, "My face seats six."

"What covers my breasts?" I asked, putting my hands up over them.

"A few long plastic curls of your hair. *You tease!*"

"What keeps it in place?"

"Duct tape, of course."

"Duct tape?"

"Seriously. Duct tape is very serious, man!"

"Oh. Of course." Then I asked, "Why am I wearing pink lipstick, pink nails, and baby blue eye shadow?"

"Because you look *so bad* in it."

"But… I'm a cavewoman!"

"Ca-ca! Don't put yourself down," Candy Cane scolded me, wagging a finger. "You have a mind, also."

I complained. "I'll look ridiculous!"

He curled the corner of his lip. "Who knows what they really looked like, *eh?* I bet if we saw a real one, we'd puke."

"This is bullcrap. Just bullcrap! The sets are paper. And my makeup is modern and the movie doesn't even have a title, yet, except Bod called it *The Missing Stink*, and the script has more spelling errors than I've ever seen before for so few words, and it doesn't even have a plot… just Bod's stoned rantings, and I haven't even seen my co-star! And I'm upset!"

"Here," he offered. "Snort some coke. It'll help you feel *bad*."

I grabbed the little envelope from him and shoved it into my nose. I was already feeling bad enough, but I wanted to melt a few more pounds away. "I wish life was really so simple!"

"It is… believe me."

"When do I see my co-star?" I sniffed.

Candy Cane said, "When you film in the desert. All his scenes are there. Oh no, wait. He does have some cave scenes. You'll see him soon. Boy-oh-boy, is he humongous and he gets to poke your beaver in the waterfall."

"Excuse me?"

Candy smiled. "The prehistoric putt! The genetic beginning of the human race. God poke America!"

"What?" I started to fumble with my script. I had to add, in almost as much alarm, "You're putting water near this set?"

"Have some more coke."

I didn't, I was already forgetting six thoughts at once from what I'd already snorted. My brain started to feel like a lime gelatin mold put in the freezer by accident. I concentrated real hard and asked, "Are the dinosaurs going to be little lizards with fins glued all over them like in that one movie… what's it called…"

"*The Bones of Blood Valley*?"

"Yeah! That one!"

"Oh no," he assured me. "Too expensive. Real lizards won't direct. They don't go when I say 'go' and stop when I say 'stop.' We can't waste film stock waiting for one to decide to crawl somewhere."

"So what are you going to do? I guess if a lizard decided to crawl, it would be *away*. You'd only get their backsides."

"I'm making a monster suit that I'm going to wear myself, of course."

"You play the dinosaur?"

"Seriously. Who else would be dumb enough to do that in this heat, but a dumb underpaid horny fag."

I asked, "How do you make a monster suit?"

"I take long johns and duct tape scales all over it. And then I have this rubber monster mask. A lizard monster. It will work just fine."

I became suspicious. "How many rubber monster masks do you have?"

"None of your business. But I'm the costume department so I have lots of all kinds of things like that. Why? Why are you looking at me like that?"

I shivered. I didn't want to accuse him of being a psycho killer, so I wrinkled my face in utter snobbery. "So… this film only has one gay dinosaur?"

"That's all we can afford," Candy Cane said with a shrug. "Uno. Me. Bad! Seriously!"

"I just keep running away from the same rubber monster mask? I mean… monster?" My mouth went dry. I looked on his jeans for signs of blood stains.

"Oh! I almost forgot these," he added, handing me a shiny rosy-colored monster-tooth necklace and matching dangly earrings.

"Great," I said sarcastically. "A final touch of realism!"

Candy Cane said, "Every picture needs glamour. And this is a Jilly picture! You want to look like a real cave woman… or a star!"

"Gotcha." I winked. "If you want a real cave woman, go to a cave. Of course."

*****

My first scene was to scream at the yet unseen long johns and rubber monster mask. I was supposed to be hiding in a cave, but I couldn't touch any of it or else it would wiggle. I also couldn't move my head to the right or they told me it would be cut off by the monster. They were going to matte that in later over a space designated as the cave opening. They would film that later and it would be called a *double exposure*. This was going to be one fancy picture!

I tried my best to be a good sport—working up a true worry like a good actress—but with great apprehension. I wondered how Dixie

Dawn Don would have done it, and I did the exact opposite. After a few shots of screaming myself completely hoarse at the special effect, Candy Cane finally thought to inform me that it'd all be dubbed later. I didn't need to hurt everybody's ears. In embarrassment, I looked around and noticed the lack of microphones or Molita. "Cut! Great Jilly, you're a natural!" the cameraman praised me.

"Zowie!" Candy Cane exclaimed. "You're gonna get an award!"

"I just creamed my jeans" a moronic young helper called a *grip* remarked, as if it was a cool thing to say. It wasn't, really. He was new.

"I just screamed my jeans," I said to try to help keep his dumb comment from bombing so completely.

*****

That night at home as I lay on the floor, stretching my legs, Bod asked, "How's the cave woman movie?"

"I just don't think I understand it," I confessed. "What's the point of making it?"

"Money," he explained. "Why are *any* movies made? *To-make-money*! Money! Money! Money! Period!"

I asked, "Aren't movies our very mythology and life stories about everything that matters about who we are as a culture? Don't movies tell us how to act and who we are and where we came from and where we're going and what to wear? For you to say that now, is like, just so totally despairing!"

"Money is not despairing," Bod insisted. I think he liked to hear the sound of that word as much as anything. "Money. We do this to make money. Money."

Chapter Nine

On the second day of shooting I met my co-star and cringed all over again.

"Here's the humong of the hour!" Candy Cane said, today wearing a lime-green t-shirt that read, "My mother had a botched abortion, what's your excuse?"

"Hello Miss Jilly," he smiled a big toothy smile. "I'm a big fan of yours."

I looked at him, curiously, trying not to be rude. His forehead wasn't makeup. It really was that pronounced. Candy Cane couldn't wait to help him into his costume, I suppose, since he was already tightly strapped in it. I stared. His g-string was a bit bigger than mine, but only out of architectural necessity, his meat and potatoes barely having a place to hide in the well chewed leather. So I just stared in alarm, imagining Candy Cane making many, *many* fittings to get it just oh-so-*right*.

Os walked on the set, smiling proudly like a father. "Great to see you looking so thin, Jilly, when everybody else has gone bananas. Here, snort some more coke. Stay that way."

"Thank you, Os," I said, and snorted some. "You're such a good dad to me. I should marry you. But not after a big press release!"

He gave me a soft nudge on my shoulder. "It'd be great press. Wouldn't it? I'd tell the world that you're going to inherit all my kingdom. What a headline. *Jilly To Inherit All!*"

I kissed his cheek. "Now don't get me all greedy. I'm supposed to play a character who lives on raw lizards. They have me smashing a lizard on the head with a rock and eating it. I don't know if I can do that. Why did Bod write that scene for me? Why does Bod do things like that? What's his problem?"

Os said, "In fiction, a good gross-out always picks up the pace."

"Gross!"

"Don't worry. It'll be plastic."

"I eat plastic. Oh. OK."

Os yelled to the room, "All right, this film is costing me a fortune! Let's get some footage of this pretty lady's assets."

"Front or back?" I asked. He laughed. I laughed. Then I forgot what I was talking about. Then blood dripped out of the side of my nose that the coke had gone up. I tried to blame Bod, but I couldn't remember his name. I scampered off to fix my makeup. All hyper from too much coke, I put on *a lot* of makeup and maybe looked more like a demonic Cleopatra than I did a cave woman.

In my first scene with my co-star, we pretended to do the big nasty under a garden hose waterfall. For this we had to leave our costumes behind so the water wouldn't ruin them, or so Candy Cane claimed. "We don't have backups!"

"Action! Go at it!" We were sprayed with water. My co-star went at it, trying to make it more and more authentic as the moments passed. Just as I began to fear he might make Darwin happy—and you know what I mean, don't make me describe what he was trying to do to me down there—somebody screamed, "Cut! Print."

"Great! Hurry!" Os ordered. "Cut the water before we kill the well! We need some water left for coffee!"

"Get off of me," I insisted, trying to hurt him with my elbows. "He said cut, not *poke!*" He was so heavy on top of me that I could barely breathe. "Damn! Now! Get up! *Now!*"

"I'm in love."

"I'm *not!*"

"I'm in love."

"Get over it. Get off me! Now!"

The dejected caveman went off to the men's room.

*****

The next morning we took Os's car out toward the revered place that had depicted so many of Flicker Farm's great and famous scenes (I say that with some facetiousness). "Where's Molita?" I asked. "Why isn't she coming with us?"

"We don't need sound," the cameraman driver said.

"Why not?" I asked.

"Do you see any dialogue in the script?" Candy Cane asked. Today his bright orange T-shirt read, "Eat me raw."

I admitted, "It's all grunts."

"Ca-ca is easy to dub."

"Oh," I griped. "I wish Molita was coming with. She's fun."

"I'm glad she's not here to call me 'ofay' all day," the cameraman driver said as if he didn't really like her.

"What's that?" I asked.

Candy Cane laughed at me. "You don't know what an ofay is? Seriously?"

"Don't laugh at me. What is it? I guess I've heard it before, but that doesn't mean I know what it is. Sue me."

"An ofay is a white person."

We drove and drove; I started getting drowsy. "Why not just film in Flicker Farm's backyard?" I asked. "Isn't there enough sand there?"

"Oh, no, Jilly," Candy Cane explained. "We're going to a special place in the desert. Not just any ole desert. Just wait and see."

The car crested a hill and we plunged steeply down into a wonderful canyon. The roller coaster thrill of it caused me to squeal. Everybody else laughed. We didn't drive all the way to the bottom. That would have been a very long ear-popping descent. But the car turned onto a shelf and stopped.

"This is perfect!" I gasped in awe, slowly stepping out. The wide expanse had the strangest sound of wind. It was a hot wind that smelled positively dry, clean, and empty. In the far distance, the valley narrowed, shadowed, and was so purple and deep I couldn't see the bottom. "I can see why you all like to film here. It's a rather eerie place, like another planet."

"We like it," Candy Cane agreed.

I added, "The sky over there is strange looking. What's going on over there? Those clouds look so scary."

Candy Cane said, "Those aren't clouds. It's smoke. It's the fires. Half the state is burning down again."

"It sure will look dramatic-like for our movie, huh," I said. Candy Cane smiled in a way that made me wonder if he or Os would actually set fire to a distant forest just to get a dramatic sky effect for a movie. "I wish Molita could be here to record the sound of that valley," I said. "It's the coolest sound."

"She already has. Os comes out here too, so he can grumble and complain how we're all inept because we're unable to capture this place on film as it really is." Candy Cane started to unwind duct tape with a crack. "Here," he said, "hold up your feet."

"What's that for?" I referred to the big roll of tape looming before me.

"The bottoms of your feet," he explained. "Now give 'em to me."

"I don't need that. I worked weeks to toughen them up. My soles are as thick as shoe leather."

"You'll need it," Candy Cane insisted. "Everything in film needs duct tape. Seriously. Duct tape is so bad, man. Without duct tape, the movies couldn't exist. When duct tape was invented, the movies were invented. Did you know the cave set seams were duct taped? Did you know the camera filter is kept on with duct tape? I use it on the back of costumes. I once wore it to play a robot mummy alien from a spaceship from a lake in Peru, which was a miniature. It didn't splash very realistically. Bite me."

I asked him, "Did the duct tape take longer to get off than it did to put on?"

"Sure! It took off all my hair."

Three car tires were taken from the trunk and tossed behind some piled stones. After Candy Cane doled out our coke and then had successfully ignited all three tires, "Action!" was yelled by our cameraman in a rather surprisingly sarcastic tone. Neanderthal man and I ran about in mock fright with the simulate volcanic activity billowing behind us. "Cut!"

"No," Candy Cane yelled at the cameraman. "Quick, get some more shots at different focal lengths before the tires burn out!"

"I'm not using up all my film stock on the first day of shooting."

Candy Cane insisted, "We've got to milk these special effect for all we can! This is serious, man!"

Regardless of the cameraman calling him a stupid fruit, he was right. So we did a few more shots. Then Candy Cane walked behind me and hiked up my sagging, furry g-string that had worked its way askew.

"Next time, just pantomime me to tidy my costume!" I snapped at him, viciously. "I can very well give myself my own wedgie!"

"Fussy!" Candy Cane left me and went over to my co-star and did the same to him. When Candy Cane reached around and shifted the front of his g-string to make sure it hadn't gone askew, my co-star just looked straight ahead in astonishment.

"Watch it, dude, that tickles."

Candy said, "Don't be temperamental. This is serious, man!" He petted the costume a few times like he needed to smooth it down.

"Hey man, that tickles even worse!"

"I'm in charge of costumes and they have to look just right."

"You do that anymore and the costume won't fit at all!"

The cameraman suddenly acted like he'd die of fatigue, disgust and boredom as he curled up in a fetal position in the sand.

Embarrassed, I turned away toward the awful sky. "Why don't we all road-trip and film at the forest fire? That would look real."

"What? You ca-ca?" Candy stopped fussing with the caveman's costume and glared at me. "Do you really want to die?"

"Die?"

"The fire is racing along the ground faster than anyone can run. That's what they said on TV? Every other day it gobbles up some fireman or slow reporter."

"Oh." I rubbed my arms and realized in complete horror that I had a painful sunburn. Candy Cane thought he could solve the problem by spitting into his cocaine and rubbing it on me. That did not make me feel fresh. So I hid in the hot car to avoid any more unnecessary exposure. There, I realized my heart was beating way too fast. "Slow down," I told myself, "Slow down!" It was all the darn coke, I realized.

"Jilly!" Candy Cane called out for the next set up.

I should've known something was wrong when I was unable to say, "Coming." My lips just barely moved. When I stepped out of the car and into the bright sun, I fainted dead away but came to, moments later. The precious cold-water ration was being blotted onto my face and neck with a little single piece of toilet paper.

"Ca-ca! Don't ruin her makeup!" Candy Cane yelled. "Just blot her forehead!"

"God, she fainted," cameraman moaned. "How temperamental!"

Candy Cane and the cameraman caucused and decided that the next shots would have to be the ones where Neanderthal man carries me over his big broad shoulders. I was thankful such inactivity had been invented for me in the script (I refuse to say *written*), since they hadn't even considered canceling the day's shooting.

"God, you're heavy," my co-star complained, lugging me up on his broad shoulder.

"It's all muscle," I muttered.

"She's heavy!" he griped.

I said, "Well, then, it's your turn to faint." Then we noticed that my earrings had fallen off.

Candy Cane screamed, "It took me hours to make those! Find them! This is serious! Find them now! *Man!*"

The cameraman insisted, "Forget it, we don't have time!"

"Screw you, you ofay!" Candy Cane screamed at him.

"Cool off, man," I mumbled, delirious, "Or you'll be next. And besides, you're not supposed to call him an *ofay*. Molita is. You're supposed to call him a gringo."

"Screw you, you ofay!" Candy Cane sulked, not giving up on his search for the earrings. He kicked the desert around as if it could be punished. Lucky for me, a steady pounding breeze finally picked up enough. It started to throw lethal clouds of dusty grit toward the camera. That could hurt its gears if it got inside. It could scratch the film. So the day was called. The camera was hurried into the safety of a black bag in the trunk and we headed back up the hill.

"Do you think this car will make it?" I asked as its wheels began to spin impotently in the loose sand.

"If not," the cameraman driver said, "I got three pushers." Luckily the car didn't stop altogether and we crested the steep hill and got out of the valley. On the open desert, I felt a claustrophobic panic attack overwhelm me. I tried not to burden my coworkers with this.

Candy Cane, sitting next to me, noticed it. "God, girl, you're really jonesing out on us."

"I'm just… I don't know… I can't breathe…"

"You're not the well woman we once thought you were."

"I think I'm having a heart attack," I whispered to him, knowing I'd be dead before the journey's end and was frightened by the prospect. I knew it wouldn't be an easy death. And it saddened me that I'd be disappointing Os. "Tell Mom I almost loved her. Tell Os I almost married him."

"And what do I tell Bod?"

"Bod who."

"Nonsense," Candy Cane replied without concern. "You just had too much junk. Here, don't be so serious. Pop a downer. You'll feel fine." In spite of my stomach's screaming at me that it didn't want any more chemical garbage, I swallowed the blue pill and soon felt intensely groovy. The car's ceiling bent a mile away as I felt a feather pillow shoved between my eyes and brain. "The pill's working, isn't it?" he laughed. "God girl. You feel love."

"I feel love. I want another pill."

"God, girl. Anymore of these and you'll have a baby."

I laughed, not caring about some monster-movie baby that had ripped out all my guts. My head rolled to the side and I drooled down my chin. I couldn't find my fingers, hand or even my arm to rub it away. Maybe a volunteer would step forward. "Love me?"

"We all love you."

"Tell me you love me," I repeated.

"I just did."

"I missed it. Tell me you love me again." My eyes rolled back into my head and I had a moment of total clarity. It was as if the world's puzzle smashed together before my very face and I wanted to put this vision of the meaning of everything into super-dooper communicatable words. I wanted to share my deep ultra wisdom. "These films are like… omigod… miles of tiny little pictures, aren't they? Just lots of little pictures all in a row. Lots. And I mean lots! *Wooo-ooow!*"

"There, now," Candy Cane soothed me, "please don't get heavy."

"Just little tiny pictures. Lots of them. *Soooooo cool!*"

"Yes, Jilly."

"Lots," I repeated as if I was unbelievably profound. "Little! Lots! If only you could understand it like I do."

"*Si*, Jilly."

"I miss my mother."

"We all miss our mothers," Candy Cane said. "So what?"

"I miss my baby," I started to gush tears of remorse and sadness.

"We all miss our babies."

"Oh my poor baby," I bawled. "I killed him! I gave him to the military scientists in silver raincoats! And they had duct tape! They put it over everything!"

"Seriously?"

"I'm sure they used duct tape! They'd tried everything else. Why not that too!"

Candy Cane humored me. "Yes, duct tape goes over everything, very good Jilly, and no, you're making no sense, Jilly. You have to focus, now, and come back to us or I fear we may lose you for good."

"Lose me where?" I asked as I watched the lifeless desert outside. Then I realized I was not outside. I was inside. I tried to make the ceiling of the car come closer. As it came closer, I realized that it looked padded, like a padded cell, like a padded bra! Dixie Dawn

Don was coming down from the sky to smother me in her giant padded bra! I gasped. I forced a deep breath as I deliberately shook the horrific image from my head, willfully trying to run from my impending coma. All the cactus animals, outside, started waving at me. "Hello, cow!"

When we finally pulled in behind Flicker Farm's barn, I saw that someone had gotten out a shovel and built-up a giant sized anthill. "What's that?"

"A doll-sized volcano," Candy Cane answered.

"Doll-sized?" I pondered that. "Can I fall into it and melt? I have become a doll."

"Yes, I'm afraid you have," Candy Cane admitted. "A Flicker Farm doll."

I passed out. I woke up in bed with the driest mouth and a sharp pain on my head. My wiglet was still pinned in, but twisted sideways. It hurt. I ripped at it until it was off. Then I looked at it in sad disappointment. "It's fried!"

"What?" Bod mumbled, just waking up next to me.

I explained, "They said in the catalogue to keep wigs away from heat. I was in a desert all day and the sun is bigger out there. My wig is fried!"

Bod said, "It always looked like road-pizza to me."

"No!" I protested, trying to curl out of bed and crawl. I had to find water. "It was a lovely wiglet! It cost a lot of money!"

"You can clean the sink with it."

"You're so rude," I said with a growl. "Who can put up with you?"

"*You* do," he said, like a snot.

I stopped trying to quarrel with him. That required a thought process. My brain felt swollen. "I want new hair!" I moaned.

"I can't afford it."

"I'm not going back to the desert until I have new hair!"

From where he lay, he reached out and slapped my head. "Shut up, you dumb Polack!"

I was startled. My heart leapt. "*What* did you call me?"

"I called you a dumb Polack," he said.

I started to tremble. "I've killed for less!"

"Well, don't get so upset. *Hey!*" Then a cruel teasing grin spread across his face. "That really bothered you, didn't it. I knew there was something odd about you, that you were really something different than what you appeared to be. Are you really a Polack? Polack! Polack! Polack!"

I turned red. "Of course not! Polacks screw light bulbs in wrong and I am *not* retarded!"

"Polack! Polack! Polack!"

"Stop it!"

Bod said, "How do you drive a Polack crazy? You put her in a round room and tell her to go pee in the corner."

I clenched my fist, tight, without even thinking twice about it, and hit him in the face as hard as I could. I screamed, "Screw you, you crapping son of a bitch!" My hitting him sent him into his own wide-awake rage. He picked up the pressboard night table and swung it around. I yelled, "You *creep*!" With furniture now in the bed, we rolled off onto the floor and started a brawl to the death. "You son of a bitch!"

"Goddam you!" His elbow clobbered me hard in my face. We stopped dead in our tracks and looked at each other, suddenly realizing that my face was soon to be photographed.

I accused him, "You're trying to kill me!"

"You wanted to kill *me*! I had to protect myself."

I yelled, "I wanted to kill *everybody!* You, I suppose, just wanted to kill *me!*"

"Don't be so pious."

"Look at me!" I screamed. "You pathetic woman beater, my face looks like a balloon! How can I be pious! You should crawl with shame! Freakin woman-beater!"

"What about me?" he yelled. "You hit my face, first!"

"You don't count!" I countered, "So what? You don't have to be photographed!"

"Goddam it!" He yanked the refrigerator door open. "Put some ice on your stupid movie star head! You've got a full day of shooting ahead of you."

"Swell. Wait until I tell Os that you're a woman-beater." I took the big wax paper bag of frozen cheese flavored hash brown and sausage breakfast hearts from him and buried my eyes in it.

"Don't you dare!" he gasped, suddenly panicking. "Don't you dare tell Os!"

"Why not," I said with a laugh, trying not to cry from pain. "I thought you men loved to brag about how you beat your women."

"You liar!" he yelled. "You hit harder than me!" He stomped out and slammed the door so hard the top hinge popped out from the plywood.

I sat, licking the wound inside my swelling mouth, and rehearsed a scene in my head.

Os: What happened?

Jilly: Oh, nothing.

Os: You look like you've been beat up! Did Bod do that to you?

Jilly: Oh, you know how he drinks so much and just loses his head.

Os: I'm gonna whoop his head!

Jilly: Would you like to borrow these brass knuckles?

Os: You have brass knuckles?

Jilly: I just so happen to have some in my purse. Imagine that.

Os: You're bananas!

Chapter Ten

The next day at the studio they were filming some special effects for the cosmic opening, but I wasn't there. I wasn't supposed to have evolved yet. Luckily they weren't filming anything with me until sunset. Anything before then and my joints would have creaked. I needed a whole day of drinking lots of water and icing my face. As we were driving through town to get back to the canyon location, there was an endless gas line at the pump. We waited an hour to add two gallons, since that's all the cash we had on all of us together.

"The damn Arabs won't sell us any more oil!" Candy Cane cursed. "Ca-ca!"

"Then what will they live on in Arabia?" I asked. "Do they really have that many cars of their own?"

"Are you a politician?" the cameraman driver asked.

"No," I said. "I just know camels don't run on oil. Something is very odd about America and oil and I can't put my finger on it."

"Ca-ca." As we zipped off, Candy Cane predicted that oil would soon be more valuable than gold, and Banks would put it in their vaults and we'd be pouring oil into cash registers.

At sunset it was finally my turn to work. I was buried in heavy waterproof makeup that covered the purple spots on my face. Candy Cane tried to soothe my feelings by saying, "My dad hit my mom once, and she said, if you ever do that again, remember you have to sleep sometime. I'll get you back when you're asleep."

I looked in the hand mirror and thought I looked like a tan candle. "Don't let the camera get too close. And don't worry; Bod won't do it again. I told Os what happened. Bod's in the doghouse."

"Cool!" Candy Cane said. "Bod is such a jerk isn't he? Why don't you become a lesbian?"

"I am wearing far too much makeup right now to even consider it." I checked to make sure all my nails were pretty.

He asked, "Does your face hurt?"

"Not in a way that really bothers me. It's feelings that really get hurt when people fight, and I think I'll wake up in the middle of the night and fume about this one for the rest of my life."

I fluffed my hairpiece. Then I was whisked to a dramatic rocky cavy part of the beach. Just as the bloated red sun dropped low enough to skim the water. I swam up from beneath the shimmering red waves as if I'd just evolved from the ocean. Since the moment was so poetically lit, I lingered and dragged the shot out as long as I could, pretending I was in slow motion, pretending I was in a big-money perfume commercial. Since this was the first time I'd be seen in the movie, I wanted everybody to just crap.

*****

The next day's work was started before dawn even cracked, so we could get some photography of the dim pink sunrise crawling up the desert. I wondered if this type of arty stuff would get us an award. Then we filmed some shots of Neanderthal man rock climbing. I wondered why something so dangerous wasn't done last in case he fell, but I didn't say anything. I didn't want to invite bad luck. The way his butt looked while he climbed was shocking enough.

I opened a can of pop and tried to get into character. When stimulants of a higher order were offered my way, I decided to pass. "Why?" Candy Cane asked in surprise, as he put a silly umbrella hat on his head.

I regarded his hat with envy, as I also wanted shade. "I don't need to faint and spaz-out *two* days. In fact, I think that coke is evil."

"Seriously?"

"Seriously!"

Candy Cane said, "Whatever. Be fussy."

The sun was now high enough, so I opened a big yellow beach umbrella for myself. An umbrella hat was groovy but it was not for me. It would've crunched the dead plastic mutt on top of my head. And also, a published photo of a cavewoman in an umbrella hat wouldn't look right.

On, "Action," (barked rather sarcastically again), I did my scene, pretending I was meeting a Neanderthal man. Easy enough. We circled around each other, squatted, stood, squatted, stood, and did wordless charades of fear, confusion, curiosity, and then lust. I grabbed my bosom and heaved and heaved. He wiggled his hips. I heaved some more. He wiggled faster. At our distances, we silently went up and down.

Then he did the twist so fast he whipped out of his g-string. Luckily he noticed it so he kept his back to the camera. I tried not to stare, but it was hard. Then we did deep knee bends, trying not to look too much like rhythmic P.E. warm ups. During one squat, I spotted my lost earring and clawed it out of the dirt. "Cut," the cameraman said as if bored and disgusted. My co-star quickly tucked himself back in and re-arranged his costume before Candy Cane noticed all had gone askew and willingly came to his aid.

I distracted him anyway. "Candy Cane! Look! The lost earring!"

"Seriously? Wow! Bad man, put them on!" When Candy Cane freshened my makeup, he shook his head indignantly, plastering extra foundation on my bruises. "I'm going to beat Bod's ass when I see him for hitting you like that."

"I didn't realize you cared about me so much," I said with a big grin.

He dabbed on more lipstick. "Ca-ca on you. I was thinking more about your close-ups."

It got dark enough for my favorite scene. I was to do the primal fire spirit dance of universal womanhood, the dance of me to myself the Fertility Goddess of Creation, a true source of sexist box-office profits, or something like that. While waiting, I held myself, shivering, amazed at how quickly the desert cooled down after being so cruelly hot.

"Are you sure you don't need any blow for this?" Candy Cane asked, now wearing a jacket.

I shook my head and made a "stinky" face. He looked at me like he didn't take me seriously. So I said, "That stuff is really rude."

"When you fall of a horse, you jump back on."

"I'm acting, right now," I told him. "Acting doesn't need coke. I did without it all day. I don't need it now."

"Whatever." He put the envelope away and then went and lit two big fires to illuminate the scene. A few torches were also lit in the background, to give the shot some depth. Otherwise the background desert at night is rather dark and that doesn't show up well. I stood between the bonfires and waited in my warm place, breathing deeply, trying to meditate my mind to a primordial place of righteous matriarchy. My bones ached from running around in the sun all day but I couldn't allow myself to show that in front of an uncaring camera. I had to seem immortal.

"Action," the cameraman shouted. Though we were now *all* dead tired, he sounded interested for once. I shot off like a cannon ball, jumping and thrusting and gyrating. I screamed like a mad woman. I twirled. I bravely kicked at the fire. I vibrated and shimmied so my butt-cheeks wiggled. I threw sand up into the air. When I ran out of things to think to do I fell to my butt, gasping from exhaustion. "Cut."

For my effort, I receiving a well-deserved applause from the cameraman, caveman co-star, and Candy Cane, as I fell the rest of the way back on my back.

"Zowie you jumped!" Candy Cane gasped. "That was serious! Wow! You all right?"

"I bit my tongue," I admitted to him. "I hate it when I do that."

With our marathon day of shooting ended, I was so glad I hadn't done any drugs. I liked the feeling of having my head clear as we headed home. I wanted to see and smell the night desert for what it really was. The moon was a bright flashlight. The sand had a fantasmagorghic glow. The black cacti looked deceptively like cushy mod furniture.

After awhile of the night drone, of nobody talking, of nobody taking me out of my own thoughts, I started to imagine Indians riding horses alongside the car so intently they became real. The engine started to sound like throbbing drums. I saw dancing ghosts.

All was groovy with the world, but when we approached the barn, we saw eerie red twirling lights surrounding it.

"Cops! Ca-ca!" Candy Cane screamed. "Hide the drugs!"

He dumped his snow out the window as the cameraman driver kept right on as if we didn't even know the studio was there. "What's going on?" I asked, looking out the back window.

"We'll read about it in the papers."

*****

The next day, I read the story in *Movieland Nova*, by reporter Tim Cline:

"Jilly, such a star now, she brings down an entire studio, albeit, the studio is Flicker Farm and would have blown over with a poodle fart. Sleazy Flicker Farm busted; drug trade porno production. Man known throughout town Oscar, Os by colleagues. Ring leader cult gang thugs."

"Cool," I said to Bod, then observed, "Why do the papers always read so funny?"

"Cool? Cool?" he screamed at me. "How can you call this cool?"

"We were all called thugs!"

"That's not cool!"

"Calm down, darling," I assured him. "He won't spend any time in jail for this, believe me. All this will do is give Os great publicity. I'm sure he called the cops on himself."

"This isn't funny," Bod sulked as he crawled into bed.

I didn't know what to make of all of this, so I scrubbed the house down and re-bleached the spice-rack behind the stove.

*****

I was officially summoned to a hearing at a courthouse made of pale simulated wood. If it had been real wood, the tree should have been ashamed of itself. I concluded that this was all the cheap veneer of a movie set, and it might as well have been, since I became a media star. Drawings of me appeared on the local news every night as I testified in the tiny cramped courtroom.

I said I had no knowledge of pornography and had nothing to do with it myself. The lawyer directed me to say my performances were "not pornographic, but interpretive art of authentic human intimacy done in tasteful restraint." I gave it my best, but being so nervous, the challenging tongue twister came out as, "tatnet repliant."

I swore I didn't do drugs, since I'd turned down coke that last shooting day. I truly never wanted to see it again. The hearing was the best performance of my life. Footage of me even showed up on the nightly *Star Gaze*, for a week. The new fans asked, "Who is this Jilly? Who is this criminal star?" But *everybody* was being dragged in to bull crap some sort of a deposition, so I didn't stay in the spotlight long, but I tried to milk it for all I could.

After I was out of the news for a week, I called up Timothy Cline and proclaimed, "Os and I might get married." He squealed at the news, so I chattered on and on, "I'll inherit a super fortune of diamonds and motor oil he has hidden in a secret place, and I'll live on a yacht with a dog and you'll all weep at how rich and well-dressed I am! I'm even going to get one of those new microwave ovens! They say they're fast!"

It made the next day's *Movieland Nova*. My flippant attitude infuriated Bod, who insisted, "This is the end of us all!"

"Os hasn't done anything wrong and it'll all blow over," I scoffed, shaking my wiglet out like a rug, dust flying. "It's great publicity."

"If they want to run Os over, and you over, and *me* over, they will!"

"I can't worry about that now," I said, slapping the wiglet to death against the wall, more dust flying. "We have a big movie in our hands."

*****

As soon as the Flicker Farm lawyer got the footage released from police custody, Bod himself "went to town." He started to cut it together with an upright hand crank movie editor with a tiny little screen, and other equipment Candy Cane smuggled from the studio for us.

Then Candy Cane kissed me good-bye. He said he was skipping town for a while. "This is serious, man!" He explained that he was going to escape the cops and visit his mother in Mexico.

Just when I was ready to get sad at the loss of his company, Bod hyped me up with his own "golly gee, the show must go on" spiel. He said, "We've got to get this out to the theaters in time to capitalize on all the Flicker Farm hype."

"So what're we calling this?" I asked. "B.C. Boobs? Pterodactyl Trash? Neanderthal Nuts?"

"Great ideas," he smiled, grinning like a little boy about to read new comics and rubbing his palms together.

"No, seriously. What's it going to be called?"

"Os hasn't told me yet," Bod confessed. "He says he's still thinking on it."

"He has a lot of time to think in jail. I can't stand the thought of him in there. I wish they'd leave him alone. He's such a nice old man."

Bod agreed. "Poor guy."

I asked, "What are we doing about music?"

"Molita has a tape of African percussion that she says has no copyright, so, it's ours. But we'll play it backwards just to be safe."

"What about the monster?" I asked. "Candy Cane skipped town."

"Os told me to change the script. We're going to fill the prehistoric valley with giant turtles."

"What?" I objected. "Come on. Stop pulling my leg."

"I'm serious," Bod assured me, and stopped cranking the footage through the machine to look me in the eye. "It's all Os's idea, so don't argue. You've got to help me get those shots together."

"How are we going to shoot them?" I asked. "How do you make a turtle look ten feet tall?"

"Clear out the weeds down the hill," he ordered. "It's going to be a miniature prehistoric valley back there, now. We'll add some swirls of colored fishbowl sand here and there. We got to make it all purdy as if Candy Cane was still poofing around. I'll buy a few turtles from the pet store."

"Wow!" My imagination started to spin. "It's like an adult version of playing in the sandbox."

"You've got it. Now if you could start that for me while I cut this first scene together, I'd be so obliged."

I went to work on the back hill, stuffing weeds into garbage bags, determined to transform it into the coolest prehistoric valley the movies had ever seen. I didn't have any gardening gloves so I lost a little blood but didn't mind; I became a naturalist. I asked Bod, "Honey? Why does only one kind of plant grow around here?"

He shrugged. "If it's hearty enough to grow around here, it's hearty enough to grow in Hell."

"Oh, here's the pencil I lost a long long time ago off the balcony! I think our luck is changing!"

*****

The three turtles were not very big and not so easy to direct, in fact, they were doggone belligerent. Bod spent entire days on his belly in the dirt, behind the camera sunk in a hole so the lens was flush to the ground, waiting for them to do something scary. Or just do *something* so he could run a bit of footage through the camera. I tried to prod them along. But they would just hide inside themselves like turtles are so famous for doing. I blasted them with a self-defense whistle to no avail. Mace got a few good shots in the can, but the breeze would always work against us. Turtle food, we found, worked the best.

I asked, "Why didn't we think of turtle food first?"

Bod said, "Because we're not turtles."

*****

The film's few double exposure shots also needed to be finished. They were almost as tedious as the turtles, but exhilarating in that sciency sort of way. There was a scene of Neanderthal man and me running toward the camera, running away from a colossal wall of fire, seen all at the same time in the same frame—us and the fire. We'd already filmed "us," way back when, in the desert. The shot would now have to be finished behind the house with the wall of fire on a much smaller scale than originally planned.

The fire would be raging in a piece of gutter. Bod pulled it off the roof saying it never rained anyway. A fire in something like a strip of gutter was all we dared. We feared a larger scale inferno would take advantage of the drought and engulf the neighbors. Bod covered the bottom half of the lens with a piece of black construction paper. The bottom part of the frame was where Neanderthal man and I would be seen running. If that area weren't covered with black, to prevent it from exposing some more, you'd see the gutter, and we'd look like ghosts against it. The fire would be at the top, over our heads. If we were lucky it would look like it was far behind us. It would seem to be a hundred feet tall.

I poured gasoline into the gutter and lit it

"Action!"

I squirted more lighter fluid its way to keep it at a tiny roar until the footage counter signaled that the exposure had run its course. We shot the gutter fire for just as many frames of film as we had shot us running. As I'd said… sciency.

"When can we see how it looks?" I asked impatiently.

Bod frowned. "It takes a week to get the footage processed and returned. We can't see this for a week, *if* our check doesn't bounce. So if we want to eat this week, we better go out and find some free samples. We only have extra money for beer."

"So we don't even know if what we just did matched up?" I complained. "It might not even turn out?"

"Nope. Life's not fair."

Another such "matte shot" was a tight turtle close-up. I now had a turtle face matted into the cave opening that was supposed to be Candy Cane's rubber monster mask. I wondered how silly that could possibly look. "I'm screaming at giant turtles!"

"I hate Os," Bod said with a grumble. "I'll never forgive him for this. I can't believe he has me directing turtles. They're so dumb!"

"We love Os," I reminded Bod. "You'd direct spiders for him if you had to."

"At least spiders are scary."

The last split screen shot had me waving my arms around wildly at the top half of the frame. I'm doing a little skipping about like one does when one fears falling into a deep crack in the earth that goes all the way to China. The crack is supposed to be just at my toes. I'm acting like I'm afraid I might be swallowed whole, as I'm just looking down, screaming and screaming. The bottom half of the frame wasn't shot yet. It was going to be what I'm screaming at, the crack opening up. The mechanics of our effect were utterly ingenious. As Bod rolled the camera, I pulled the kitchen table leaves apart. It had been piled high with dirt so no one would know it was our kitchen table. You just see the dirt falling through a crack.

We also did this a few more times so we could have the turtles falling through. They went to a pillow below so they wouldn't get hurt. We'd need them again. And we also pulled the table apart just for shots of the crack, alone, assuming it would be very exciting to see the earth opening up again and again, from different angles, as if the whole world were splitting apart.

"This is so exciting everybody in the theater will get a head to toe hernia!" I said.

Bod replied, with a moan, "God, I've got to edit all this."

Then he plotted revenge against the three turtles. I didn't like that. By now I'd named them. "You can't do that to Lump, Chunk and Bump!" I complained. "That's cruel. The audiences will protest. *I* protest. The Animal Society will protest!"

"The audience will love it. They all love cruelty and gore. They just pretend they don't."

"I want to keep them as pets! I've grown attached to them. They're so cute! You can't kill them! They have souls!"

"Buy your own damn turtles, then. These are prehistoric turtles. They must face the consequences!"

"You're so cold!"

"Survival of the fittest. Do you see any giant turtles around the city, now? No. They all died. We can't fuck with nature." So the turtles were set in place. They must have felt their impending doom, because they started crawling away at top turtle speed. Perhaps turtles are very very smart and we just don't know it, since we don't know the language.

"Great!" Bod said with a grin. "They're moving for once! Hurry! Get into place!"

"I'm ready." I was nervous, knowing we had no chance to retake this shot.

"*Action!*"

I lit a bucket of gasoline. The explosion seared my arm. *"Aaaah!"*

"Hurry! *Hurry!*"

I knocked the blazing bucket over with my ball bat. The flaming fluid splashed out and poured down the hill just like an exploding river of watery lava, washing over the sprinting turtles.

"Great!" Bod screamed behind the camera. "It'll be the best shot in the whole film! I wish I could somehow splash some blood out there!" He forgot to say, "Cut." He was busy kicking sand over his blazing shoes. So I took it upon myself to tip the three garbage cans of water positioned above the gas bucket, which washed down the hill and extinguish the whole mess, Bod included. It was far more water than needed, but once again we were in mortal fear of burning down the block.

I joked, "Does the film need a tidal wave?"

"I suppose it does. The camera was still rolling. So it has one, now. It was rolling almost 80 frames a second, so it plays back in slow motion, so it looks real big."

"I was joking."

"Oh. Well, we'll get some surf shots and add a tidal wave to the movie. I did see a hell of a lot of water before I turned the camera off. We might as well use everything. I can't waste a frame or Os will kick my ass. And a tidal wave will look rich on the poster. When you make a movie like this, it's really all about what looks good on the poster."

I grinned big. "Now, it's an epic."

As I dug into the ground, to bury the poor abused turtles, Bod looked at me curiously. "What happened to your hair?" he asked.

"My *what?"* Horror suddenly hit me like a skillfully aimed brick. *Heat*! I ran, crying, to the house, tripping up the hill a few times. In the bathroom mirror, I let out a wounded sigh. I *had* toasted one side of my wiglet. I wanted to put my fist through something. Bod appeared at the door. *He* would do!

"Are you all right? Did you burn yourself? That was quite a flash of fire, wasn't it?"

"Oh... *Oh*... like... *screw yourself!"* I screamed in total hysterics, my fists tightly clenched. "*Just go SCREW yourself!"*

In great wisdom, he quickly turned and left.

*****

Molita was over the next day wearing the grooviest orange disco jumper. She came in lugging all the sound equipment she'd been able to get her hands on. She grumbled that it wasn't much. She'd need to make the picture seem much more than it really was. "Sound either adds or it takes away," she sadly explained.

I said, "It'll be psychedelic!"

"Right, girl." Molita gave me a withering glare, obviously upset that everything was so flim-flam. We recorded a few sound effects. Bod tried to make rumbling volcano noises with his mouth, and I made hissing noises, while we shook the table. It was piled with pieces of broken concrete and rattled.

Then Molita just stood up and started to scream. I'd never seen such a tantrum. Bod fled the house and got beer. A bit drunk and a bit more lackadaisical, Molita went back to work. I almost belted out a laugh when she got so drunk she decided to be the voice of the monster turtles. She roared deep in her throat, sucking in air. I didn't dare actually laugh out loud, though. That would've ruined the take.

*****

For the World Premiere, the unspooling, we went to a small run-down theater in a poor part of town. Being blissfully upbeat, I dressed in a faux-fur coat over a purple dress and twirled my brand new wiglet so it looked like a yummie glop of vanilla ice cream.

After we saw where we were and who was there, Bod and I prudently decided to hide in the projection booth. The theater was full of obnoxious kids. When the time came and the room was full, the lights faded and we started the noisy projector.

The *Turtasaur* opening title flickered a bit. A lyrical creation montage of gloomy footage followed it. The camera wandered through the Flicker Farm barn cosmos, which was layers of backlit cigar smoke. Candy Cane had shot this in an artistic tangent long before the police chased us out. Then shots of the ocean came on through a dark red filter so it looked like rolling, splashing, ebbing waves of the blood of life, or lava or something cool. Molita's voice came on in a voice over, in a heavy drunk urban black accent. "The seeds of life are in the debts, honey-chile, and they ain't comin' out till ya'all breathe and breathe and the pulse in your righteous places begins with ya-all prayin' and prayin' to Jesus, as life begins, in the (small burp) bed of all hot mama gravy. *Ooooh* some *real* hot mama gravy! In the bed of life. In bed! Just rockin' and rockin' the holy Jesus out of ya-all!"

I asked Bod, "Did you write that?"

Bod shook his head. "No. That crazy woman just made that up. Must have been when we left her to go ball. I knew we shouldn't have left her alone with the microphone. Not after all the beer she'd had."

"Oh crap."

The crowd stopped laughing and then got noticeably bored with a too-long series of desert shots. The crowd perked up at the first shot of turtles. There was some explosive sniggering. They appeared as mere turtles. A few shots of them were in blurry focus. When they all started to roar at each other, their mouths didn't move and they all sounded like the same drunk black woman. A few people angrily stormed out. I began to sweat.

I asked, "Is this a bad movie?"

Those who remained started spontaneously screaming when I crawled out of the golden sunset waters like a goddess. They went bananas. I was horrified. I had wanted to look like a slow motion perfume commercial. The slow motion on my behalf looked more like I was fighting off a paralyzing stroke—and losing. I was supposed to look like a big tease with my extra wet wig hair over my knockers. It just looked like a drowned collie was stuck to my front. I said to myself, "That woman should have gone extinct."

"What's wrong with you?" Bod asked. "Is that your idea of acting or something?"

"I was trying to move in slow motion to be real cool."

Bod sadly shook his head. "Didn't work. Did Candy Cane direct this?"

"Nobody did. Hey. What's going on down there? Bod?" I asked, pulling my coat closed. "What are they doing? They're not laughing or booing. They're screaming even louder! They've all gone mad!"

"Hell if I know! You look great dripping water."

I spotted a person in one of the theater seats wearing a rubber monster mask. It was of a green zombie monster. He kept looking at all the wild kids like he was looking for somebody. "Look!" I pointed him out. "They are really into it. They even dressed up! A rubber mask!"

Bod rubbed his chin. "*Hmmm.* People *do* wear rubber masks in this town, don't they? I wonder why."

"Let's get out of here!" I shuddered. "He might be a psycho killer creep. They wear rubber masks, too!"

"We're safe up here. The dumb rubber mask man doesn't know we're even up here."

I backed into the dark shadows of the booth's far corner and watched the screening go impossibly downhill. The soft focus shots got loud "*boooooos!*" from the crowd. This same footage hadn't looked soft in the editor, but the large projector lens and the big screen were unforgiving. When the caveman crouched under his killed killer-plant lean-to, one of his big hairy balls popped out of the side of Candy Cane's impractical fashion. Jeering hysterics shot through the crowd.

"Boner! Boner!" the kids yelled, as if that should fly out of the g-string next.

"Why did you leave that in?" I asked Bod. "You could have cut the shot before his ball showed!"

Bod shrugged, red-faced. "I couldn't see details like that in the editor. You know how small that viewer is! What do you think I am? A fag? Good God! Balls jettisoning everywhere! I'm not a fag!"

The caveman finally noticed that he was flashing and put his hand over himself. Then he then looked directly into the camera like an idiot. Everybody in the crowd screamed even louder.

I said, "Of course you're not a fag. I'd never accuse you of having personality."

By the time my fire dance came on, the crowd was dancing in the isles, screaming like they were insane. I think, by then, the African drum music had already been terribly overused. It was causing a dangerous trance. So, when they saw *me* dancing to it, it just made things worse. My two long locks of hair that had been duck taped to my knockers just stuck absurdly down as all my other hair was bouncing up in the air. "Jugs! Jugs! Jugs!" they screamed until it fell into perfect unison.

"The damn punks are all stoned," Bod tried to assure me. "Don't take it personally."

I nodded. I could see and smell stinky cheap pot wafting up through the projection beam. "Stoned."

When Neanderthal man carried me over his shoulder, one could spot that he'd started to pop out of his g-string again, another pink-a-boo from Bod.

"Boner! Boner! Boner!" they screamed. In the waterfall scene, caveman's wiggling wet butt looked utterly comical as the garden hose dribbled on his back, bringing the riot to an anarchistic frenzy.

"Bod," I moaned. "Some church is going to close us down."

"Is he really doing it to you?"

"Of course not. Look at my elbows. I'm trying to hurt him."

"He looks like he's really doing it to you."

"Bod! Damn you! You're obsessed with my really doing it on film. You're so jealous! Have you ever heard of *acting?*"

"Your co-star sure has a rather authentic and intuitive method of acting." Bod's eyes got wider; he stepped close to the window. "Shit. I couldn't see his balls like that when I was editing. Damn he's got balls! Shit. We're all going to prison."

"I was referring to me doing the acting," I reminded him, now feeling so irritated I wanted to scream. So I did. It ripped out of my throat and felt very good. Bod and the projectionist looked at me like it scared them. Good.

At the end of the movie, when the volcano discharged its gasoline, Neanderthal man and I ran in terror. A few burning tires actually showed up in the frame. A full-scale riot began. "Tires! Tires! Tires!" I think I saw about four boys punching each other.

The man in the green rubber zombie mask stood up and turned to look at the projection booth. "He has a gun!" I pointed, not seeing a gun. I just knew he was going to shoot us.

Bod said, "So."

I said, "He could be psycho!"

"They all are, down there. We made them that way."

"He could kill us!"

Bod answered, "Give it a few more minutes and the movie will kill him."

"He scares me. Let's *go!*"

The projectionist sadly waved us off. "In all my years as a scab projectionist," he said, "I've never seen such a god-awful movie, nor have I ever seen such a crazy bunch of drugged, perverted rapists for kids."

"Screw you," Bod thanked him as we slipped away before we had a chance to see how the surf footage led into the burning turtle soup. Bod had done a lot of cutting and hoped it would be snappy. I hoped that a previously unseen surfer would appear from that stock footage. Then we could pawn the whole mess off as an "art film."

We quickly escaped the theater. Out in the street, the man in the green rubber zombie mask was standing and waiting under the marquee. When he spotted us, he started running towards us.

"Freak!" I screamed out. We ran. I thought we were dead. I became so scared. A guy chasing you in a rubber mask is always terrible. But then a big black van pulled up onto the sidewalk next to him. In a flash, men in black jumped out. They punched him in his rubber zombie face, and then pulled him into the van. They drove off so fast I had to wonder if it all had really happened. "Did that really happen?" I asked Bod.

"It must have been a drug deal," Bod said, shaking. "Don't deal drugs if you want to live long."

"Drug dealing at our premiere?"

"What else was it good for?" Bod shrugged.

Chapter Eleven

The one review our epic movie received, in *Movieland Nova* from Timothy Cline who was obviously now following my career, read:

"Historic worst film, *ever.* Flicker Farm's swan song unintentional comedy with nuts, *Turtasaur*, drove audience into complete raving. Don't miss it! Poor Jilly alternating unmatching shots, looks like ready to slay turtle one instant, next, mauled by entire tribe missing links. Only one close-up, absurdly fem makeup seemed fully intact.

"Earrings come and go as if of magical origin, as coif, which changes from flowing curls, to blitzed macramé straw bale. Biggest gimmick of *Turtasaur*, of course, beyond three napping blurry turtles, volcanic sparkler, idea of filming girl wearing two extra wigs for bra and boy with jack in the box in his box! Guarantees finance. Desert-sand-is-much-too-hot-for-me barefooted dance number a must see. If you find yourself screaming for no apparent reason at end of picture, look around, not alone. Everyone screaming, and *more*! So much more I needed a bath."

I had to read this a few times over. I seemed to be losing my ability to comprehend what I read, but since it'd been awhile since I'd been home schooled, I assumed that was natural. Then I wondered why Mom hadn't let me go to regular school, until high school, and then with a set of pretty dresses. And then I let some boy almost lay me, he hurt me badly, and then they found a surgical clamp inside of me and that was why. I was immune to anesthesia for some reason. So the pain drove me mad. But then after that operation, the pain finally went away for good. I had been in acute pain from one thing or another since I'd been born. I'd been in such pain the hypnotist told me to forget about it. And I really did want to forget about it. I liked the pretty dresses too much. So I looked at my arty electric blue press-on nails and forgot about it.

"Honey," I called out from the living room couch to Bod who wouldn't get out of bed, "They predict great financial success from our movie. We've got a hit!"

"It's a piece of unmitigated shit."

"It didn't turn out right," I agreed, "but we can't help it that the studio was arrested before it could be finished properly."

"It was always a piece of shit. I think Os arranged his own arrest just to get himself out of it. I'm going to kill him."

"It's the police's fault."

"I blame Os," Bod insisted. "In this case, the cops were innocent pawns. It's a plot!"

The phone rang. A voice squealed, "You've got a cult classic on your hands! We've got to capitalize on that!"

I said, "Who is this? Andernach? Is that you? Slow down."

"Sure," Andernach said, "Don't you remember my voice? Remember me?"

I was so happy to hear from him. "How could I forget your girly voice? How you doing?"

"I'm more famous now than I was before," he bragged. "Your photos really helped. You photograph so well. The left side of your face is so even to the right side of your face. Do you know how rare that is? Let's do some more photos! More! More! More!"

I asked, "You heard about *Turtasaur*?"

"Haven't *seen* it, yet," Andernach admitted, "I have to say I'm not sure if I'm brave enough."

"Oh come on!" I scolded him. "The turtles aren't that scary. We didn't give them fangs."

"The word around town is that the entire picture has a quality about it that drives people into screaming madness. Haven't you been listening to the radio? One man even swallowed his tongue!"

I knew that couldn't be true. I hoped. "No."

"Well, believe me, people are talking about it! It's mass hypnosis!"

"Good. Maybe it'll make some money. For some reason, I seem to go through wiglets like other stars go through vodka bottles."

He chuckled. "I can tell this town has worn you down a bit."

"How?" I asked.

"The weariness in your voice. It no longer has any *golly* left in it. Let's get you out of the doldrums and think about your bright and shiny future."

"What's that supposed to mean?" I asked, suspiciously.

Andernach said, "You've gotta keep on truckin. Let's do another photo shoot."

"Snako's nudie magazine has all shut down."

"Let's go for a best selling poster!"

"Let me check with my agent, first, that's what he's paid for. Bod?" I screamed out in my shrillest shrew voice. "Andernach and I are going to take some more pictures!"

"Good," I heard him respond in a tone that told me he couldn't care less.

*****

The next morning, I looked up the number of the cancer society. "Hello? This is Jilly. Do you know who I am? I'm the famous actress of that cult film, *Turtasaur*. Since I'm known as a topless actress, I'd like to be your spokesperson for breast cancer." The phone clicked dead in my ear. "Hello? Hello?"

Bod had heard the attempted conversation and said, "That is the dumbest thing I've ever heard. Why would you want to get involved with those squares and do charity?"

"You'd never understand." I badly needed to address my poor self-esteem. I took out the card with the Feminist's Business Association's number and gave it a ring. "Hello? Is this the Feminist's Business Association?" Bod heard this and walked up to me, glaring angrily as if I'd just called the communists. "Yes, I have just started a fan club and that makes me a business owner, right? My name is Jilly. It's a fan club to me."

The woman on the other end of the line had heard all about me. At their meetings they had been talking about how I degraded myself, which degrades all women, and "whored myself to the rape culture of men (who were sexist pigs) which festered slavery or really bad pay, objectification, and general all around contempt." If I were to be in their mix, I'd have to renounce all my old ways, let my armpit hairs grow, and be born again.

I said, "But then I couldn't have a fan club."

She suggested that I sell food containers, car insurance, makeup, and encyclopedias. If I were attractive enough, I could sell cemetery plots. I hung up on her, gasping indignantly. I decided to ring up Sue. I'd pretend I'd actually taken my organic cosmetics out of the freezer and needed more. Of course I hadn't. I wasn't *that* organized.

"*Groo-oovy* Sue and her Apple Cosmetics!" she said in an insipid singsong. "How can I help you?"

"Hello honey? This is Jilly. Say, what's new in lip color? I'm really in the mood for the latest thing. I need new lips!"

"I'm sorry, but I'm not supposed to talk to you. You've been ex-communicated," she said, very quietly. "You're dead to me."

"What's that mean? My credit is still good!"

"No, ex-communicated!"

"What's that?" I demanded, never having heard such a dumb long word in my life.

"Not sure," Sue admitted sheepishly.

I sighed. "OK, hon. So, I've… been extra-curriculared or something. You'll have to try to tell me. Is it like I'm going to get a big award or something?"

"No, no it's n-nothing like that," Sue said. "I'm not suppose to talk to you anymore because you've betrayed all women."

Feeling stung, I finally figured it out and couldn't believe it. I became so mad I didn't know what to say, so I said any old thing. "And you… *you've been fumigated!*"

Bod laughed. "Why would you want to join a bunch of losers?"

Andernach pulled up to the house and sprinted up to the front door in excitement. After doing a grandly melodramatic two-footed pirouette, he pulled out a newspaper.

"What's that?" I asked, my head whirling.

"P on *Turtasaur!* Parents, police, preachers and psychiatrists want this sick film banned from theaters for sake of public health."

"What's that mean? Can we all be thrown in jail for causing mass rioting? I didn't mean it! Really! I didn't mean to cause social disarray! I just want to be a star." Tears of frustration welled up in my eyes.

"No, no," Andernach assured me. "It's all just really good press. That's all."

"It's a scandal!" I gasped. Below my stupid picture (I was nearly cross-eyed since I was gazing into a lens too close to the tip of my nose), it read, "Jilly is a riot."

"Which is good press!" Bod snatched up the picture and pinned it up on our bright yellow cork note-board by the avocado colored telephone. "Now go take some pictures and I promise they'll sell."

*****

Sans anything but the fake hair on my head, I carefully climbed a big dead tree as Andernach snapped three rolls of film, trying to line me up behind the branches so my nasties wouldn't show and my poster could sell in the drug stores. "Andernach? What do you know about feminists?" I asked while sucking in my tummy as tightly as I possibly could.

"Not much. The only ones I know of are radical lesbian types. But then, you know, that's the circles I'm in."

I asked, "What are lesbians like?"

He shrugged. "Depends on who you're talking about. They're all as different as anybody else, but not like gay men who are all alike, dancing to the same disco hit, chasing the same new meat, wearing the same fashions."

"You sound like you don't like your own people."

Andernach chuckled. "*I* can say it. But if a straight man says it, I will slap his teeth into his tonsils."

"You're so butch."

"OK, I admit it, I'd probably cry my way through a twelve pack of beer."

"No, I mean you're so butch, now. Taking pictures really brings out something strong in you. I wonder what will bring out the *me* in me. Do you think I should start a fan club?"

"I'd let a fan start a fan club," he recommended. "That's what they're for. Let them do all the work. OK, now lean over the branch towards me."

I noticed my position up in the tree. "But doesn't that make my knockers look like cow udders?"

"Oh. I guess so. Sorry. OK, arch your back."

"Andernach?"

He shouted an order. "Smile! If you talk I might catch your lips in a funny angle."

"I just wanted to ask. Do you think I'm degrading myself?"

He shook his head, exasperated. "I don't know. I don't think so. But then I'm going to get filthy rich off your pictures so what am I supposed to say?"

"We're not good people, are we?" I accused.

Andernach nodded as if he agreed. "Good people don't make money." He shrugged as if it couldn't be helped.

"What does it mean to be a boy or a girl?"

"What? Hell if I know. Some say the difference is all learned. But I don't know." He glanced down at his pants. "Boys like to shoot their wad and girls like to make a house. At least that goes for all boys, gay or straight. I don't know about all girls. Don't ask me. Don't ask me why people are the way they are. I don't even know why I am the way I am. I don't know what makes people gay but people look at me like I'm supposed to know everything about being gay just because I know how to scratch my gay itch. Outside of all that, I just want to make some money taking pictures. For a start."

"I don't know who I am. I don't know what it means to be a girl and why that's different from being a boy, in such a big way. Why?"

Andernach smiled naughtily. "Maybe for boys it feels bigger than for girls. I don't know why. Maybe the boner. It really is a distraction. It's always great but it's also always completely in the way. I don't know if girls ever get anything so urgent. I don't know. You tell me. You're the expert on being a girl."

I couldn't think. "I don't feel like I know anything at all."

"Maybe because it isn't talked about when we're growing up. We're supposed to learn all the things we're supposed to learn but there's a lot they won't talk about."

"What is life all about?" I asked with a sad moan. "My life. Your life. Everybody's life."

"The game of life? Oh that. Crap." Andernach made a face at me. "I don't know. Get by. But always tell yourself you're doing a bit more than that. Or else you get discouraged. Eat all you can but don't get fat. That's a good start. And have all the sex you can but don't get the clap. And I ain't full of *Reddi Wip* so sometimes it takes a while to have sex."

I wrinkled up my nose. "Yeah, Bod sometimes wants to take all day before he does his big final heave-ho, like there's nothing else to do in the world, and I just want to get it over with so I can dust and do the dishes and catch my soap."

Andernach said, "Sometimes you just have to set aside a couple of hours for sex. Now that's life! And nap all you can. That's another important thing that life is all about. A few good naps here and there. And another thing… try to have clothes that are pretty clean even though the damn laundry room is all the way down in the basement. And beer. Beer is life. But that goes back to point one. Drink all the beer you can, but don't get fat. And when you get really discouraged about your life, watch an old western. Westerns are so boring, like having to sit through a church service with a bad organ, but westerns somehow give you a good stiff upper lip. I don't know how it works, but that's life. Yep. That's life. Beer. Sex. A stiff upper lip."

I wanted to weep. "There has to be more to life than that. What about when you die?"

"Make sure it isn't at middle age in a cold wet ditch behind the poor house. Avoid that. Make sure that when your time comes it's because you really are all worn out and there's just nothing more that can be done for you, being such an old fart. Make sure that when your time comes, it's in a bed the size of a yacht. And you want lots of people around you who are crying for no good reason. They're just there because you're so big and important or something. And that's why they're crying. Like when the President dies."

I asked, "What about *after* you die?"

"Jilly, shut up! You think I can figure all that out? Me? You really think that for one second I can figure something out like that? I can't even figure out my checkbook!"

"Well, hurry and use up your roll," I ordered him. "I'm getting bark prints."

"Oh wow! You've been crying a little. You're eyes are so beautiful now. They glisten. Look straight at me and let the camera do all the work! That's art. Art is to make everybody forget their own crap. Life is crap. Art is a brief little vacation from crap."

"Yes. I am art." I didn't believe it for a second. I felt like a fraud.

Andernach finally ran out of exposures, so I gingerly began to climb down. "My nails!"

"Hurry up, you old lady," he called up to me. "Get your clothes back on before the cops come!"

I got down and things went uphill.

*****

Without my having to pound the pavement or knock on doors, a publicity opportunity fell in my lap. An A.M. radio station called at 6 o'clock Sunday morning and jarred me awake. While I was still in bed trying to focus on what was happening, the host started asking me questions. "Were there backwards Satanic messages in *Turtasaur?"*

"There wasn't enough money in the budget to put forward wind sounds on it," I honestly answered. "What you thought was wind, was just some bad machine noise that got in there by mistake when we were mixing it."

"Who's on the phone?" Bod interrupted me.

"Shut up and roll over! I'm getting interviewed!"

"Who's interviewing you?"

"Shut up! I'm trying to concentrate!"

"If that's a tabloid," Bod warned me, "Your patootie is fried."

"Shut up, you retard, I'm on the air *right now!"*

"Well then don't call me a retard over the radio!"

"Hello?" the host said. "Who was that? Was that Satan?"

"Yes. I mean, no. That's Bod. But some people think he's dead. So maybe I shouldn't be in bed with him right now."

"You're in bed?"

"Yes, and Bod get your hand off my ass!" I slapped his hand away. He was not being fresh, but was crawling over me like a klutz to get to the radio. By the time Bod angrily found the station, it was all over. I was disappointed. I didn't feel like I'd said anything to let the world know who I really was. I also had a mind and stomach and soul. "What a stupid interview." I rolled over.

"Who listens to the radio at six on a Sunday morning?" Bod grumbled. He clicked it off.

"People getting up for church."

"Screw them!"

"They're the good people who will shut me down," I predicted.

*****

Later, I found more girly magazines in Bod's drawer. My stomach twisted and I felt guilty for doing a nude shoot with Andernach. "I will not feel guilty," I said aloud to myself. "I'm not a prude. I'm as naked and gorgeous as Sally Mea at the end of that hippie movie, *Live a Life*, where she goes all happy at the end and runs through the field of flowers and screams, 'I am the sun!'!" I took a big fat black felt marker and drew moustaches on all the women and wrote "Hi!" all over the place, and, "I am the sun!" That was so fun, I decided to also draw suns all over the pages.

Then I called *Movieland Nova* and asked for Timothy Cline, but he wasn't in, so I just told whoever it was on the other end, grandly lying, "Os and I are married and I'm carrying his child and if he isn't released from jail soon, I'll have a spontaneous miscarriage from the stress alone, all over the courthouse steps, and it will be on your conscience." I tried to make it *really* good. I think I over did it. This time the woman who answered the phone knew who I was, and even had photos of us, already spliced together and handy. I couldn't wait to tell Bod of my publicity stunt.

Bod asked me scornfully, "Who would believe you're married to Os? He's not studly looking like I am."

I looked at Bod head to toe. "But the boss is still somehow so much more appealing."

*****

Bod and I visited Os in jail. As planned, I brought along a small bag of oranges. Os's two oranges had been carefully injected with vodka. "It doesn't smell on the breath," Bod had assured me.

"This one is yours, Os." His had the name brand stickers *Florida Fun* still on them.

I asked Os, "Did you like my publicity stunt, saying we're married? Do you think anybody cares? I hope so. I hope it brings me a lot of attention."

He nodded. "Out there? No. They're all bananas. In here? *Oh yeah!* They treat me better in here, now. Thanks."

"How do you explain me away?" Bod asked Os. "I *live* with her."

Os winked. "I told everybody you're a homosexual."

Bod turned red. "Gee thanks, pal."

When munching happily on our oranges, Os began to quickly loosen up. "Commies everywhere in this greedy town!" he ranted. "And at every level! It's just bananas!"

Bod nodded. *"Eh."*

"Not so loud," I warned him, "or they'll think you're drunk!"

"Damn them commies! They're making everything illegal unless it's government approved! So what if a bunch of horny kids want to watch a crazy topless girl and run around and scream like a banana? I betcha they all flew solo when they got back to their cars. It's healthy! It's good for the plumbing! If a kid isn't jacking off every two hours, he should be checked for polio!"

Bod asked, "How's your lawyer doing with your case?"

Os scrunched up his face and looked like he was ready to spit. Then he did, but it was just an orange seed. "The damn city had such a hard time trying to pin me with the charges! It's the big studios that did this. My only crime is playing in the free market game. It's supposed to be a fair field! The big studios don't like that. They've always been so commie. They want a monopoly. They want capitalist banking fascists that only crank out government approved commie crap… horrid *family* pictures where everybody looks and acts the *same*!"

"Lower your voice," I warned him again. "They'll think you're drunk."

"Oh, screw them, they're bananas! They didn't stick anything to me," Os persisted. "It's just that the judge was a damn commie, too! All he did was try to shame me for being a bad influence on society. What a barrel of socialist commie cripe! Bad for society? Who else but a socialist would used the word society since they're the very same word? Screw society! I'm not a socialist, I'm a business man!"

"Shhh!" I warned, again, looking around the room nervously. The guard that was standing at the door wasn't looking at anything. His red eyes were blinking a lot. Sometimes he laughed a little. He looked very stoned.

Bod asked Os, "So what were you exactly charged with?"

"Income tax!" Os glowered, slurring just a wee bit now. "Another commie institution to break the little guy's balls. Income tax only breaks the small guy! The rich assholes just laugh it off. The commie government won't be happy until *all* the big money flows through a few government approved circles."

"But the religious people," I dared suggest, "They say that…"

"The religious people are the worst commies of them all! They want to make everybody the same… telling us all what we can and can't do! Telling us all how to think. Telling us all what's good and what's bad. Telling us who is the right kind of person and who isn't. Commie controls! Everything their way! As if we're all too stupid to live our own lives!"

"I'm sorry we couldn't get you a real dinosaur," Bod tactfully changed the topic before we attracted the attention of the guard, who probably wouldn't have come to attention until he'd fallen over. People at the table next to us were blatantly eavesdropping, since our conversation was obviously better than anything they could come up with. Bod added, "The pet stores just don't carry dinosaurs."

Os belted out a laugh. "No, but they sure have some scrawny looking turtles! I've been reading about them in all the papers!"

"You have?" he asked.

"The pet stores should give me some of their profits for all the business we're throwing their way. Ever since *Turtasaur* opened, there's been a crazy run on turtles."

"That's amazing," I said. "I didn't know."

Os said, "Yep! And the even more amazing thing is that most of these kids are too young to get into that kind of drive-in. It's just a new craze. That's all. Turtles!" He chuckled.

I smiled to myself, always knowing deep in my heart that someday I'd have a profound effect on culture.

Bod said to Os, "Jilly tried to join a *feminist* group, as if they'd take her."

"Good! This country needs more trouble-makers." Os quickly added, "I hate feminists. I hate anybody who hates me! If you hate me for any reason I'm going to squash you!"

I looked around nervously, hoping no one would notice how drunk Os had gotten. Everyone was looking at us but the guard, who was now giggling with his eyes shut.

On the way out, Bod remarked, "God, girl, you sure know how to spike an orange! How much vodka can you fit in one?"

I shook my head. "Remind me to never go to jail."

That evening, I noticed Bod had taken it upon himself to throw out the girly magazines I'd defaced. I smiled to myself, having won a victory, although my own hypocrisy hurt my head as I tried to connect the psychic dot-to-dots. That nudie girl bad. Me nudie girl good. Yeah right.

*****

My new poster of me in the dead tree was printed in rich brown tones, only, and that made it look both sexy and unworldly. It quickly climbed the poster popularity charts. The papers even wrote articles about it.

One headline read, WHY IS SHE WEEPING IN THE TREE?

And, Turtasaur… what a surprise. Even though it had been deemed by the press as the worst film ever made, it stayed at the theater. It slowly opened in more and more drive-ins across the Midwest as Bod could afford the extra prints. I, of course, got some of these profits. I was now able to shop. First off was a new vacuum cleaner. Then a pan (all Bod's were warped). Then when I decided the residuals were real, I got a lava lamp for the bedroom and a purple disco lamp and two yellow beanbag chairs for the living room.

Success opens doors. Unusual doors. Bod and I received an invitation to the Gilbore Mansion, home of *Gilbore*. It was the biggest girly magazine empire in the world. We were thrilled with the honor of being a part of one of their famously opulent parties. As I was choosing from my sad selection of formal dresses—one—I thought about an idea. But I didn't tell Bod. I feared that if I did, he'd change his mind about going.

"This party is a great opportunity to wheel and deal," Bod proclaimed on the car ride over. "And did you *really* have to wear that ugly dress?"

"This is as good as it gets." I said. At the tall wide iron gates, a guard in uniform let us pass. "Gosh, this place is a castle." Hundreds of beautiful lamps lined the driveway that wound around the vast shadowy grounds like a fantasy set, causing *even me* to feel like a million bucks.

"It's all run by the mob," Bod divulged, his mood improving at the sight of the massively sprawling white pillared mansion, seeming as big and grand as the downtown library, but much classier. "Look at those trees," Bod pointed out. "Chinese Maple. Thousands of dollars."

"Trees cost money?" I puzzled. I'd never before thought about trees costing money.

"Everything costs money!"

"Look! Look!" I pointed out in excitement. "Look at that row of statues over there! They're giants!"

"This guy has money."

I grew worried. "I hope we weren't invited by mistake."

"I bet he wants to centerfold you," Bod warned… or wished. I wondered if Gilbore would still want to put me in a centerfold by the time the evening was over, with what I had planned. A valet took Bod's little-bitty rust-pitted bug of a car without either a smirk or the subtlest pained look in his eyes. He was obviously a professional who figured that artists come in all packages.

We entered the mansion one awed marble step at a time. We stepped into a grand hall filled with gorgeous people and champagne towers. Superstars and TV stars and bit players, who'd certainly have to be as fun at parties as in their roles, mingled about. "This is beg time," I said, meaning to say *big* time. A Freudian slip.

"Jackpot," he said.

"Bod, can we take one of those chandeliers home?"

"I wish! It's a little too big for the house." Understatement. Our home could have rested *inside* the ornament.

"I'm going to leave you," I said, "and socialize." Before he could protest, I was off, trying to walk in perfect star-pose through the most gorgeous hall I'd ever walked through. My eyes started to leak tears at the awesome splendor of it all.

I spotted a woman in the most dazzling silver beaded gown. It poured down her body like a silver fountain. Without even thinking, I walked up to her in awe and lightly touched it, letting my fingertips graze across the exquisite handiwork below the collar. Her expression could have stopped a clock. Immediately becoming self aware, I realized my horrible crime and stepped back. I turned red. "I'm so sorry," I mumbled. "Your dress is so beautiful… *omigod*… I don't know what overcame me."

The gorgeous woman looked up and down at what I was wearing. "I understand." Then she turned completely away from me.

Bitch.

I cooled myself off with a clinking iced white wine. While I sipped, I enjoyed the wildly beautiful dresses from a respectable distance. The woman I had touched walked by me again and smiled coldly. I felt like a peasant. I gathered my courage with a few deep breaths, crunched down ferociously on an ice cube, and then proceeded to do what I had come here to do. I walked up to an older man who looked rich and tasteful. I smiled my loveliest smile. He noticed me, and smiled back.

"Do you like breasts?" I asked.

He looked at me like he knew he was in a trick question, but had to answer, "Sure."

I wasn't expecting something so minimal. He was smart. I continued, "Then would you like to invest in their safety, beauty, fun and health and donate to the Breast Cancer fund? He seemed confused but I stood my ground, knowing I could. I was righteous.

After a moment, his smile became amused. His left eye even flashed. "And who might you be? I didn't know solicitors were allowed in Gilbore."

"I'm Jilly. Star of *Turtasaur*. You've read about it in the papers, I'm sure. I'm a star, now. And stars do charities between pictures. Of course."

"Oh. Of course. *Oh!* Oh, of course! I've seen an article with a photo. I didn't recognize you with…"

"Clothes on."

"Yes." He nodded respectfully.

Just when I thought I'd gravely embarrassed myself and would be asked to leave with a silent finger pointing to the door, he fished into his wallet and gave me a few one hundred dollar bills. I tried not to bug-eye, gasp, or be gauche and count their quantity. As stone-faced as possible, I stated, "Thank you on behalf of millions of women everywhere." I graciously folded the wad, undid a button, and slipped it away into my bra.

His eye followed where they'd gone. He gave a pert satisfied nod and walked off. I was shaking with nervousness now, but exhilarated. I walked up to man after man, getting a great score each time.

As I paused from my assignment to stare at a woman in utter amazement, her beautiful gown trailing layers of fantastic large gossamer butterfly wings, a stern humorless grey-faced man in a tacky shiny gold suit walked up to me and said, "So you're the woman raising charity money."

"The Cancer Society is my pet project," I answered, trying to sound professional. "I'm always concerned about other people." He looked at me as if he were not amused by some trash who hits up other people for money, though that wasn't *exactly* me. I asked him, "How much would you like to donate on behalf of America's most beautiful breasts?"

"I am Mr. Gilbore."

I paled. I swallowed. I tried to act bold. Then I turned bright red. *"Ah!* Him! You! The man who collects beautiful breasts like none other. Then we both agree that breasts are a national concern. A national commercial treasure! We both agree that breasts are art and love and family and life and mother's eternal sustenance! Would you like to donate generously to preserve both breasts for all women for all time?"

His eyes remained cold and beady. "I have my charities already designated. The Cancer Society has already received my donation for the year."

I joked, "Oh, you already gave at the office!"

He didn't smile, but took a slow thoughtful drag on his cigarette. "I don't know if my guests enjoy being hit up for money at a party, especially something as special as a Gilbore party!"

"Well, *um,* if that's so important to your ambience, I'll stop posthaste if you can just spot me six hundred. Then I have my pledge," I lied so bad.

He looked at me a moment as if he'd shoot me dead right where I stood. He finally removed his wallet and slowly counted out four hundred dollars, like he was afraid of making a mistake. He said, "Just make sure you tell your folks where you got your donations. Make sure the Cancer Society knows this money was collected for breasts at a Gilbore party." He finally broke a wicked wily smile, knowing what his name meant to the wholesome folks of the land. Then his face became sad, his eyes lowering to half-mast.

"What's wrong?" I asked.

"My brother died of lung cancer," he finally said. "Maybe you can do that one, next?"

"We all have those," I said, "We all have to breathe. Now why don't you just put out that cancer-stick you're sucking on and smile again!"

He sucked in a big drag and blew the smoke in my face. I wondered if he was just too rich to be a cad. "I'll live forever," he declared.

Through a massive set of french doors I spotted a man in a rubber clown mask. "Who's *that!*" I gasped in alarm. "It's *him!* The crazed shy fan, or the psycho killer! Who is he?"

"Who? Oh him. He says he's somebody big in the world now," Mr. Gilbore said and then chuckled cruelly.

"He's in a clown mask," I pointed out the obvious. "And he's not here to do clown tricks, is he!"

"No," Mr. Gilbore assured me. "The last clown we hired to do tricks for one of my parties wasn't hung enough and we had to send him home. This one is just a wacko. He says he now owns *Spy Your Skin* magazine. He says he'll inherit it now that Snako's been killed."

"So… who owns it?" I asked. "I thought it closed down after Snako was killed. I thought it was closed down for good."

Mr. Gilmore asked, "You knew Snako?"

"Yeah," I reluctantly admitted. "I met him for the first time the very night he was killed. Really creepy, huh."

Mr. Gilbore shook his head, but not sadly. "*Spy Your Skin* was bankrupt before he was killed. My magazine killed it… *heh heh heh.* Their bills are still all being sorted out in court. They owe me money I'll never get. But I'm going to grab their unpublished negatives for it… *heh heh heh.*"

I asked, "You can do that?"

"It's the happiest debt I've ever had." Mr. Gilbore smiled very big.

"Then who *is* the guy in the clown mask?"

"A nobody who thinks he has something, but he doesn't." He laughed cruelly again.

"He's not big in the world? He doesn't own anything?"

"Nope. Just a nobody relative of Snako. A cousin I think. But I don't know, that would make him Os's kid and they say he was killed by the mob. They say he went up in flames in an elevator. All they found were just teeth or something like that, so the FBI could still identify him. So it can't be that guy. This is somebody else. Certainly."

"Os had a kid?" I marveled.

"Poor clown," Mr. Gilbore went on, ignoring me. "A real dummy, huh, in that red nose. He doesn't even know what's going on. He thinks he's rich. He just doesn't know. I didn't invite him but he came anyway, thinking he was king of the jungle. I couldn't send him away. I'm having too much fun looking at that happy clown mask... *heh heh heh*."

I asked again, "Os has a kid? Os?"

Mr. Gilbore shrugged. "Os had said he didn't have any family, but then we found out he did. And the dumb kid got popped off by the mob. His kid. You tell me. They say he has another kid too, a fairy who is still alive, who he sired in Mexico. But Os won't say who it is."

"Mexico!" I looked at my fingernails.

Chapter Twelve

The next morning, I read the paper. Mr. Gilbore had been murdered at his own party, the one we'd just attended. I shook Bod awake in hysterics.

"Lay off the coke," he said.

"No! It's true!"

"Gilbore? Dead?" Bod was doubtful, in too much shock for it to register. "Murdered?"

I shoved the headlines in his face. "Look! I had just been talking to him and then he was murdered! He was talking about Os having kids somewhere. One burned down. Another one, I don't remember, something about Mexico."

"Gilbore can't be dead! We were just there. He was alive last night; he was rude to me."

I read aloud. "Gilbore found dead in fountain with nose removed."

As Bod silently read the rest of the article, I said, "I wonder if it was the guy in the rubber clown mask."

"No, the paper says he didn't do it. It says right here."

"How would they know?"

"The FBI told them," Bod explained.

"How would they know?" I asked. "At least so soon?"

Bod shrugged. "The government is always spying on those porno people. They know who did it. It's all a cover up."

"You think so, or are you just hung over and paranoid. But I'd have bet the clown did it. It was a rubber mask that wiped out Snako, you know. A rubber mask! But then this guy was a relative. Gilbore told me just before we left, and he wasn't afraid of him. How many people wear rubber masks around here these days? Is this really some new fashion around town? Should I start wearing one?"

"Nobody that I know wears rubber masks. But you could wear some rubber hair. It might last longer."

Then there was a knock on the door. It was the police. They came to ask us questions about the murder, since we were in the area near the time. Of course we couldn't tell them anything clever. After they left, I was in such shock I forgot to send the breast cancer money to charity. So I took it shopping. Badly needing to feel better, and in control of my life, I bused downtown to the *Cuit Fabuleux* dress shop.

*****

Bod saw my new dress and frowned.

"It matches my Indian ring!" I said. "I bought the ring coming into town from real Indians! Now I've got turquoise rocks all over me!"

"That's the ugliest thing I've ever seen. I'm suing the sales lady who sold this to you. How dare she sell such a piece of crud to somebody!"

"Don't be so cruel!" I slapped his chest. "Marsha Thoors' *The Boys of our Wives* is opening downtown this weekend at the Imperial and I'm going to be there in full glamour. It's a big gala premiere!"

Bod wrinkled up his nose at me. "You? I don't know anything about dresses, not being a fruit, but I know that you're not going in public in that? You can't! Oh, and you shouldn't go to the opening anyway."

"Why not? I'm a star! Stars go to those things."

"A strange guy called yesterday to ask if you were going to that. And then he asked me if you really were going to marry Os. I told him to go jump in a toxic lake."

"All the lakes are toxic these days, and see? Everybody's going! Even I'm expected. All the stars will be there! People are even asking about me!"

"But in that dress?" Bod frowned bigger. "You'll cause another riot."

"You exaggerate."

"Just be sure to bring your mace," he suggested. "The old mummy, Marsha, should get a special Celluloid Intelligentsia in the

Film Science and Technology category for Special Effects: her face girdles and butt tapes!"

"Jerk."

*****

Since I had the loose cash to afford a limousine, I nervously called a reasonable company. It was the first time I'd ever sat in one and couldn't believe how big they seemed on the inside, even though mine was a smaller, older budget model. As we pulled up to the theater, my heart began to race. I stepped out, concentrating on fluid grace, clearing my head from the door but knocking my hairpiece, nearly ripping it from my head. But I had too many pins in it for that to ever really happen. So it just hurt like hell as it crackled and pulled against my hairspray. Then I was instantly blinded by flash bulbs. "It's Jilly!" I heard someone gasp. "What's *she* doing here?"

"Isn't she a stripper?"

"No, she's that poster girl. She does porno."

"Oh, look! It's Jilly!"

"What is she wearing?"

"What is it?"

"Look! It's the woman with the hairy breasts!"

"Now she's in… rocks?"

"She causes insanity!"

"They say her movie is so low budget, it causes a vacuum."

"Oh. So that's what sucks everybody's brain out."

I smiled graciously and slightly nodded this way and that for the many photographers. I always knew I'd be famous and now my moment of destiny had finally arrived. My heart sang in my famous bosom like a soaring aria. I'm famous! I'm famous! I walked up to the door and a snobbish man in funeral attire asked, "Do you have a ticket, madam?"

I looked at him in a complete fluster, blinking, my long thick black Fantazma Lashes making me alluring. "A *what?* Why would I need that?"

"I'm sorry," he said, not sounding at all very sorry, looking at my spectacular gown in rude disdain. "But a ticket is required and even the balcony seats have sold out."

I was in disbelief. I didn't realize such events didn't just have magic seating for *stars*. In my pride and great embarrassment, I smiled and coolly replied, "I didn't come here to watch Marsha Thoors, anyway!"

"Oh?"

"No."

He asked, "Then why are you here?"

In a blind panic, I blurted, "To greet my fans! Of course!" I turned to try and spot some. Instead, I saw flashes sparkle all around me. At first I thought they were exploding just for me. I smiled brightly. Then I finally noticed who it was all really for. My mouth dropped open. I was flabbergasted. I would soon be in the vicinity of a star. A real star. A big star. An old star.

The divine Marsha Thoors, herself, in all her buffed and polished glory, and neck-hiding scarves, walked directly toward me. I was directly in her way. I noticed her top lip was over painted to give it perk. A hoard of awestruck worshippers followed her. "*Marsha!*" I could only gasp, since my breath had been ripped out of my lungs from my complete humility and astonishment. I quickly stepped to the side in reverence to let her pass. I bowed.

Then, she was gone. It had all happened so fast, yet I knew I was forever changed. In a daze, I walked to the street to go back to my limousine but it wasn't where it had been before. Marsha Thoors' mile-long limo was pulling away from that spot. In complete disorientation, I looked down the street for mine, but couldn't find where it had gone.

"Oh *crap!*" I cursed very loud. This evening was not going as I'd assumed. I felt so stupid, I wanted the ground to open and swallow me like it did for some of the poor turtles. I took a deep breath, lifted my still-youthful chin in wounded pride and began to walk off into the night, like so many stars walk into the ocean at the ends of their films.

"Jilly! Jilly!" I heard a wonderfully familiar voice call out to me. I spotted Andernach rushing toward me. "What are you doing here?" he asked.

"What are *you* doing here?" I asked him right back, wondering why it shouldn't be natural for *me*, a star, to be at a movie opening.

Andernach smiled sheepishly. "I came to try to get some good shots of Marsha, but got here late and couldn't get through the big crowd. Damn was there a crowd!"

"She's the biggest star in town, isn't she?" I asked with some sadness.

"Well," he nodded. "She's lasted. I guess that makes her the biggest. That's all that matters, you know. You don't have to be a good actress. You just have to last and last and last. Then you're the queen of the land!" He did his trademark two-footed pirouette. "*Love it!*"

"If anybody is a queen," I said in relief, so comforted to have a kind familiar face at my side, "it's *you!*"

"My pearly ass blesses you," Andernach said, and then looked around, oddly.

"What's wrong?" I asked.

"Oh, just wondering if that guy in the rubber mask came back. It was a devil mask."

"A guy in a mask? Here?" I gasped. "*Nooo!*"

"Yeah," Andernach said. "A rubber mask of a red devil. He was just standing over there, like a weird fan or something. Oddly he seemed to be following you. And then a van pulled up and he got in and went away, but it was really weird, like he didn't like the van. I hope he's gone."

My heart leapt with fear. I smiled bravely. Perhaps I was too dressed up to feel real fear. "Probably just a fan. Are you sure it wasn't a green zombie mask or a clown mask?"

"No. A red devil; why?"

"Those masks cost money," I said. "Maybe he owns a mask shop."

"What?" Andernach asked.

I shrugged in confusion. "Somebody out there who is a drug dealer or psycho killer fan or something nerdy or scary, likes rubber monster masks. It was a guy in a rubber monster mask that killed Snako. I bet it was the rubber clown that killed Mr. Gilbore. *I just know it!* And a guy in a green mask was at my movie premiere, just being creepy. He came outside to look at me!"

"Is he after you?" Andernach asked.

"If he is," I said, "Then he's pretty dumb."

"How?"

"Well, I'm still here, aren't I?" I declared in stunning logic. "Still, I have the creeps."

Andernach looked around. "Let's get out of here before he comes back."

"First, take a few quick pictures of me. Then the evening won't be a total loss for us. And make it quick!"

He quickly looked around for ideas. "Why don't you jump into the fountain and do one of those Parisian splashing around things?"

"Are you kidding?" I shook my head. "This gown weighs a ton. I'd drown."

He looked curiously at my dress. "How can you sit in that thing without getting dents in your butt?"

I shrugged. The ride over *had* been hell. But I didn't say a word.

"What are all those rocks?"

"Turquoise! Can't you tell turquoise when you see it?"

"Are you sure?" Andernach thumped at one.

"Careful! That's my tit under there!"

"Are you sure it's turquoise?"

"Of course! Don't you know your rocks?"

"Yes," he said with assurance.

"Then why do you ask?"

Andernach looked at them with suspicion. "They don't look right." He made a sour face.

"What do you mean?"

"Are you sure it's not just pebbles that have been *dipped?"*

"What? Dipped? With the price I paid for this thing it better not be dipped!" After a few harried photos of me posing with neon lights behind me, he drove me to his apartment to see if my pebbles had been dipped. With the blow of a hammer on one of the less conspicuous rocks under the left armpit, we cracked it in two to see that, indeed, it was all grand forgery. I was stunned. I couldn't speak. When I finally could, I said, "Dipped!"

"Well," he offered, to break the awkward silence, "What do you expect from this town? Everything in this town is fake. I bet even the tinsel of this town is just coated paper."

"Huh?"

"Never mind. I'm just trying to joke to make you feel better."

"You knew they were fake the second you saw them, didn't you?"

He gave me a wan smile. "This girl knows her rocks. Now just promise me one thing, Jilly."

"What?"

"When the time comes for you to buy *diamonds*, please don't do it alone. Take me with you."

"Why?"

"Knowing you, you'd pay good moolah for rock candy."

I laughed, heartened to have such an advocate. "I wouldn't dream of buying diamonds without you!"

"Let's get out of here," Andernach urged, looking around nervously again. If I ever see somebody in a rubber monster mask again, and it isn't Halloween, I'll crap."

"Where do you want to go?" I asked, also looking around in great caution.

Andernach suggested, "We can have a few cocktails and watch *Eros on the Beach* with Marsha Thoors."

"It's on TV?" I asked. "Tonight?"

He nodded. "For those who couldn't attend the premiere, they stick on an old movie. I'm sure it's far better. There's nothing better than Thoors in the fifties. She was flawless. *Love it!* Just sandblasted flawless."

"Is she a bigger star than Dunkel Morgendammerung?"

"She's just a lot younger. Dunkel must be a hundred years old by now. So you can't compare."

I asked, "Can we have popcorn?"

"Popcorn and martinis?" Andernach scowled. "Together? Both?"

"Sure," I smiled, embarrassed. "Doesn't popcorn go with everything?"

*****

I got home late. With too much popcorn stuck in my teeth, I admitted everything to Bod.

"*What?"* he screamed, enraged.

I sadly nodded.

"Dipped!"

I looked down in shame, suddenly wishing I'd kept my mouth shut.

Bod yelled, "You wasted all that money!"

"I don't know if it was a total waste." I began to cry, "There were a few pictures taken."

"I'll sue! I'll sue! Give me that stinking dress! I'm gonna beat the fuckin thief to death with it! $1300? Good Jezzez! I bet they're still laughing in that goddam dress shop! They'll stop laughing after they wear this rock quarry down their throats! And don't you ever buy a stone without me by your side to make sure you don't get ripped off again!"

"Yes, Bod." It was at this point I think I realized there was something about the quality of Bod's voice that grated on me. I wondered why I hadn't noticed it before. That night in bed, he tossed and turned, while I just quietly sobbed.

The next morning, Bod was up before me. So he woke me up by tossing the paper soundly on top of my head. "Wake up, sunshine! You made great press last night! You'll be in all the scandal rags across the country for this! You're a star!"

I rubbed my eyes and gazed at a nice full shot of me smiling at the camera from *Movieland Nova.* "That's nice." I smiled. "I have nice teeth."

"*Read* it!"

"OK." I rubbed more mucus away and then had to pull an eyelash from my eye. I read aloud what Timothy Cline had to say:

"Jilly top awards… worst dressed of evening. Did not attend actual premiere. Merely showed to model a clunky abomb… tube of crass blue twill glued over aquarium rocks… before wandering away as if oops attended wrong premiere. Wonder where her knockers went more chic?"

It took a moment for the grief to finish pouring into me before I began to cry, "*I'm ruined*!"

"Turtle shit!" Bod said. "Didn't you listen to what you read? Don't you know how to read and listen at the same time? Are you retarded? This is *great* publicity! Not only is it a full giant picture, because the press knows what the people really want to see—YOU! Mark my words, everyone will start spray-painting rocks and gluing them to their clothes! Or turtles! Just because of you! Look at how you're influencing this town, and this town influences the world! Pretty soon they'll be gluing fake rocks all over China just for fun!"

"I don't believe you."

"And they'll forever wonder where you went in movieland that was cooler than a Marsha Thoors opening."

I opened the paper to read more, but saw a photo that caught the scary man in the devil mask. I jolted.

"Bod! Look! It's him! The psycho!"

Bod looked at the paper and his eyes widened. "Pretty scary."

"Call the cops!"

"But, it's not illegal to be a devil, not in *this town!* Almost all this sick town is dressed inappropriately, if wearing anything at all."

"I should call the cops," I whispered, feeling my flesh crawl.

"Hell, no," Bod warned. "Not them. No cops! Os would forbid it. He says commies control them all and that they're out to squash him. And they've already been over when Mr. Gilbore was killed. You were an idiot. We already knew the clown didn't do it!"

"Is Os in the mafia?" I asked.

"No mafia that I ever heard of."

"Then why no cops? This man could be a psycho killer."

"No cops again unless you want to wig out Os. Just be glad you're in the paper at all and shut up!"

"But it's not a clown, now. I need to tell them that the devil did it!" I turned back to the picture of me and stared for a long time, feeling strange. Although I always knew I'd be a star and that I'd someday profoundly affect culture, I couldn't muster up any feeling of happiness. Not at the moment. My heavy heavy head collapsed back onto the pillow. I closed my eyes. I wanted to escape into the blissful land of sleep. I dreamt that the house was tipping over while I was trying to build a blue rock garden in the living room. Everything kept sliding around, frustrating me.

*****

After my morning coffee, a packet of instant Pep-A-Joe with artificial fudge flavor, I got Andernach on the horn. He reaffirmed everything Bod had said—good press disguised as bad press, with some devil watching on to make it even better press. He had to wonder if I'd arranged it myself. He read to me what the other papers had said.

"Jilly sabotages fashion industry…

Jilly lost at Thoors' premiere…

Jilly thinks she's really a cave woman…

Only Jilly can shape a pile of cheap rocks…

Jilly stalked by Satan…"

Andernach said, "You're famous, toots."

"This is a *sick* sick town." I moaned.

"Lighten up," he assured me. "You had a rocky night. *Ooops!* Sorry. Didn't mean that. Yes I did! After you get your money back, you'll feel better. You'll agree."

I agreed. A refund always helps. And to keep myself from really going to *thee* Devil, I decided that I'd send half the money to the breast cancer charity I'd originally promised. Half is better than none and I still needed to buy some things.

*****

Just in the door, the phone rang and a man's weird angry voice asked if I had really married Os. Mad right back, I said maybe I had and maybe I hadn't and he would just have to find somebody else to marry. He said he would shoot me if I had. That made me even more irritated and so I told him to marry a log. Sometimes I don't think that well on my feet when I'm mad.

"Who was that?" Bod asked from the bathroom.

"We're not sleeping together anymore," I announced, not sure why, but once said, it sounded good enough to me.

"Oh," Bod said, obviously jacking off because he was making strange lotion fwapping noises.

I repeated myself just to be as equally obnoxious as his lotion fwapping noises. "We're not sleeping together anymore."

"Oh," he repeated, pretending to be really listening. Not that we had been doing the big nasty that much anymore anyway. It may have been several weeks since we'd even really looked at each other right in the eye.

I got Andernach on the phone. "I'm leaving Bod. I'm moving in with you. I don't care how small your studio place it. I'll sleep on the ceiling if I have to."

Andernach said, "But I moved."

"Cool. I'll live there too."

"It's even smaller."

"I'm still moving in with you. I'm leaving Bod."

Andernach warned me, "And a dying sex change is also moving in. She'll pretty much just take up the couch. That will make three of us. *Love it!*"

That's how I moved out of Bod's stupid place and ended up where I am now.

Andernach had a third floor apartment with a secure looking balcony overlooking a simple alley. Beyond the alley, and over a row of other people's garages, was a panorama of the city. We could make out miles of glitzy strips of bars, massage and tattoo parlors, ice-cream and hot dog stands, shoe shine boy huts and gas stations, a flower shop, and a gigantic three story dry cleaning empire. Not having to be a nudist anymore, I sewed together a flowing floral pink pastel caftan and matching turban. A new chapter opened in my life. Dignity. I was so happy to see Andernach when he came to collect me that I even did one of his two footed pirouettes with him, his far more organized, but then he'd had years of practice. Then he hugged me and squealed, "*Love it!*"

I sadly said, "Bod never hugged me like that."

Andernach looked at me like he didn't know what to say, so he repeated, *"Love it!"*

Besides the couch, most of Andernach's furniture was the latest "barrel" style, not real barrels but the backs of the swivel chairs were all shiny plastic in a strange pale caramel shade of tan that was molded to look like planks of barrel wood, like it was fun to sit in barrels.

It didn't take me long to tuck my things away, I didn't have all my things. I wanted to move everything I had, it wasn't like I got lazy, but I left so much behind with Bod because he started crying when I removed anything of value. He made a fuss even if I'd been the one who forked out all the moolah for it.

"You can't take the toaster!" Bod shrieked. "What am I going to do without a toaster? Are you trying to starve me? Is that your revenge? You vindictive bitch! You're trying to kill me! I'll starve and I'll die! You should go to prison! You're a murderer!"

"It's mine and I'm the only one who ever used it."

"You can't take the hotdog broiler! How will I eat? I'll die!" He grabbed his stomach as if it had already begun. He went to the freezer and pulled out a box of chili and cheese dogs. "What am I going to do?"

It was Andernach, not Bod, who put his foot down concerning my stereo and matching colored strobe light-boxes that sat on top of the speakers, trying to make you want to dance. They had to stay behind. "But I have headphones!" I argued.

"No room." Andernach insisted. "You're moving into a real apartment, not a sitcom set."

I wanted to cry as Bod tried not to grin too much. As I walked out the door the very last time with a grocery bag full of my clothes, Bod didn't say good-bye, but was sprawled out on the couch, admiring his arm muscles. Macho rock music was blasting from my stereo. *"I'm free from the witch who put a spell on me. A spell that came and went like a winter freeze."*

Outside I looked back at the stupid house and lit a match. I wanted to toss it up on the roof. I imagined it all going up in flames as fast as a crumpled wad of binder paper. I laughed as I imagined Bod jumping out the back hole in the wall where the balcony had been. I imagined him rolling down the back hill with the house rolling after him, it all in a bright ball of fire.

Common sense told me that it was Bod's fate for him to stay behind as I moved on. I blew the match out and said a prayer for him. "Let him forever stay tucked away inside that ugly house."

I went away with Andernach.

*****

To celebrate my new space, I bought a giant burnt orange macramé kit for my new living room wall and knotted and knotted and knotted. When Andernach was first hit by it in all its displayed glory, he said, "That's quite a thing you've got there, Jilly."

I nodded proudly. "It's festive."

He winced and sat, as if his fake barrel furniture were somehow cool and my macramé owl were not. "Are you sure you followed the directions? It looks more like a squashed fishing net. With tits."

"Those are eyes."

"Are you sure?"

"Owls have eyes."

Part Two
Mad for Movieland

Chapter Thirteen

Another resident soon arrived in the small apartment, the dying sex change who would occupy the couch. Miss Spectacle. "What is that horrible knot on the wall?" she asked me, within seconds inside the place. Miss Spectacle was jaundiced, so her eyes were very yellow.

"That is an owl; those are its eyes."

"Fuck me. If you say so. Looks like cow tits."

"I made it."

"*That?* Are you a lesbian?"

"Nope." I flashed her my gorgeously bright pink nails. Then I sadly looked at her own strawberry nails. I had the sudden horrible realization that nails are not a red-hued badge of anything real. Not if she had them, also.

"I'm so broken, just call me Dunkel Morgendammerung, or Dunk, for short." Her voice was far gravellier than mine. It wasn't like a woman's or a man's, per se, but more like my grade school coach. Unlike my coach, Miss Spectacle probably owed her sound more to decades of cigs and gin than yelling at little girls. "UFOs are everywhere!" Miss Spectacle said as she tugged at a pair of green boxer shorts she had over her head to shade her light-sensitive eyes. "They're taking all the water and our brain-cells."

I said to her, "Now that I'm sharing Andernach's bed, I hope they don't take that. Water I mean. It's a waterbed. I'm not worried about my brain cells. They never did much for me. Not yet."

She laughed and her horse mouth seemed big enough to shove a whole a can of hairspray down. "I was born in the wrong century," she complained.

"You want to have been in a time of horses and carriages? That's very romantic."

"No, you empty wig. I want to have lived in the future. If I was living in the future then they could just clone me and then rip out my liver and give me a brand spanking new one, a liver that has never seen ten thousand cocktails."

"How come you didn't want to be a boy?"

"Horrors. I was so horrified by that awful thing sticking off of me that squirted this and that. I was so appalled and horrified that I needed a hell of a lot of cocktails! I like it on other people, but it just didn't wear well on me. A penis should visit a girl, not be stuck on her to fucking flip her whole brain out to hell." Then Miss Spectacle yawned, nodded off, and started to snore like a freaked-out bullfrog.

I asked Andernach, "Do you think they'll ever be able to clone things?"

He shrugged. "The sci-fi writers say 'yes' and the real scientists say 'no.' Which one do you think we should believe?"

"Well, the artists, of course," I said.

"I guess there's no harm in feeling poetic on your deathbed." He looked down at Miss Spectacle's near corpse as if he were appraising it. "Nothing wrong with wanting all sorts of fantastic things."

I looked at my pretty fingernails. "Wouldn't it be nice if that neat stuff was all, like, true? I've often looked into the night sky and wished with all my might I'd see a flying saucer."

"First things first," Andernach cautioned me. "Before you become a cloned reincarnation from the Bermuda triangle, we have to work on making you a star. A real star. Not just somebody who thinks she's one."

"You sound so selfless in the way you say that."

Andernach shook his head. "If you become a big star then it's all the easier for me to sell your photos. Stars always have people riding their coattails.

I softly slapped his shoulder, pretending I was clobbering him. "You can get so cold."

"I can also get hungry."

"That's when you go out for free samples."

"Where?"

"Don't you know?" We took a walk to the nearest grocery store having free samples that day.

*****

The next afternoon, Miss Spectacle got mad at me. We had a contest of wills. "We *will* watch *War Torn* on the telly," she said with a powerful growl. She narrowed her baggy painted eyes at me.

"That's a war movie," I said. "Only beer-belly red-necks like war movies."

Miss Spectacle grew indignant. "You ignorant child! *War Torn* is a fantastic sweep of grandiose epic that'll leave you weeping your tits inside out!"

"But it's a war movie," I repeated.

"I've been laying here all day," Miss Spectacle explained. "I've been having too many memories of when I was a birth defective child, having a hideous thing stuck onto me like that. It was wrong. It ruined my behavior. I was just crazy. I was constantly trying to prove to all the other kids what a total spaz I was. My memories are going to kill me. I don't like remembering being a little retarded boy. I like being a big brilliant woman. And so war is a very fitting distraction, especially with who is starring! Now flip the channel. Now! Or I'll have a k'nip fit!"

I lost the argument when Andernach looked at me like, "Don't argue with a dying diva." I lost the contest and didn't know quite how to deal with my pride. I didn't want to spend two hours huddled alone in the tiny kitchen. So I planted my butt in the shag of the carpet and accepted my defeat and my daiquiri.

The old b&w movie began modestly. Miss Spectacle had seen it enough times to play special narrator. "Just look at that lovely actress," she said to just me. "Her cheekbones could leave paper cuts." And then she added in a religious tone, "European!" I felt my own face. I didn't feel enough cheekbones. I didn't feel worthy to be a star.

Miss Spectacle suddenly realized that in her excitement about cinema, she'd sat up and moved around too much. She lay back down as if every bone in her body hurt badly. Maybe it did. "I'm going to die soon, I'm just so Dunkled."

"What?"

"Morgendammerung," Miss Spectacle moaned, and it was a very deep moan, as if maybe she ran out of hormone pills and couldn't afford anymore. "I want an army of drag queens at my funeral singing 'I'll Fly With Angels.' I want a rainbow to appear over my coffin. I do not want any photographs from my childhood on display."

This made me feel strange, like I didn't know what to say, so I said something not entirely bright. "Well, like, you're not dead right yet, right?"

She looked at me like I could have tried to come up with something far better, but she understood. "I want you to write my life's story for posterity," she ordered me. "Ever since I escaped my pea-brained family and had the surgery, I've had such a fabulous life of glamour."

I asked her, "Why can't you write your own biography?"

"Honey," Miss Spectacle said with irritation, then paused, then blinked heavily, false eyelashes fanning the room (the inside corners not quite glued down all the way), "When an old girl like me has her liver eaten away with the big C, she doesn't have much energy left for her own afternoon douche. Why do you think I make Andernach do my makeup every morning? To be waited on?"

"Well, *yeah,*" I answered. "Sure."

"I keep telling him to stop the purple eye shadow, the bitch. You know what the color opposite of yellow is? Purple. He's just trying to bring out the piss color of my eyes to make fun of me. That bitch is trying to make me look like a Dunkel Evil Twins reject!"

"If you don't like the way he does it then…"

"I can't be wasting my low battery-power on doing my own makeup." She reached into her purse and pulled out a tube, twisted it open and rubbed it on her lips. Then her yellow eyes widened with utter surprise. "What?" she muttered, noticing what she actually had in her hand. She started to scream, wiping manically at her mouth.

"Who's been trying to poison me? Who did this? Who put this glue stick in my purse! I'm going to *kill!*"

I couldn't help but fall into fits of giggles. She looked at me as if I was the assassin. "I didn't do it. Swear."

She finally thought about it enough to laugh, bellowing so loud she rattled the wallpaper, which tired her noticeably. So she passed out again.

I watched her breathing for a while and thought about what she'd said. I'd never actually heard anybody say before, "I'm going to die." That was freaky. Suddenly, her eyes popped open. It was a very short nap. It made me nervous that I was still staring down at her. I jumped away. Still groggy, she said, "I'm gonna die," as if that were the first thing on her mind when she came out of sleep. Maybe she dreamed about it, relentlessly. "I'm gonna die."

I wondered why I didn't dream at night of my own death. It wasn't like I didn't dream about everything else. My own any-time-or-place death should bug me, as much as her. Why not? I shivered and twisted one of my plastic nails until the tape crackled and it all popped off.

"Have you ever thought about it," Miss Spectacle continued. "Have you ever thought about how much pain you will be in just before you croak? How you can't breathe? How you will vomit and piss and crap all over? What a splitting headache you will have so you can't even see straight? How your chest will be pounding and pounding in horror while it feels like dozens of burning spears have been stabbed clear through it? And your mouth is so dry you'd think a camel sat on it. And then everybody in your life that you have always hated will come and stare down at you in your bed with irritating faces. They will make stupid faces of great sadness. They will want your death to be the way they've always thought it should be. That's only because they're making *your* deathbed into *their* drama. Because they know someday they're next. And then your mother comes close and tries to convert you to the family religion, so she'll think she will see you in her Heaven when she dies. And you agree with her and you are saved just so the old bitty will get the hell away from you. And then you can't breathe at all. And then your final credits roll, and final credits always have the tackiest music. Have you ever thought of your own death? Have you ever thought about how it will be tacky and small and not like a grand movie in the least?"

I said, "Sometimes it is like a grand movie." I had a vision of a man in a rubber monster mask stabbing me a hundred times. I'm wearing a beautiful white dress that soon looks like it's been dipped in cherry snow cone syrup. I hoped it wasn't a premonition. I got nervous so I decided to change the topic. "Some of Andernach's sisters are coming over to sew. They call them super-sonic fashions. Gotta clean my pile of junk from off the top of the sewing machine."

"Go on, go on, nobody's keeping you. And if Dunk comes over, tell her to kiss my funky silicone for dropping out of pictures. God, has a camel sat on her."

"Oh certainly," I joked with her. "Dunkel Morgendammerung isn't expected to stop by, but if she does, you'll know about it."

*****

A drag queen sewing party is very noisy:

"Hon," Car Crash marveled to P.P., watching her overdrawn red lips. "I didn't realize you were so oral."

"You know," P.P. said, "I love to lollipop a man all night! If he pops his cork too soon I'm just left with nothing to do for the whole rest of the night."

"You're a lying bitch!" Norma Wife charged, blinking at P.P. with her immense blue foil eyelashes. "With those phony clown lips? The only thing you can suck off is your lip pencil."

"Hon, *talk* about it," Miss Precome urged her. "We're here for you."

P.P. insisted, "My lips are gorgeous because I made them that way!"

Car Crash said, "I just sat on a vibrator and now my teeth are chattering." Everybody looked at her vacantly like they wondered where that came from, and then resumed their sewing. Except for P.P. She was putting together her seams with school glue.

"Did you see the new stripper?" Miss Precome asked, all excited, "Is he humongous or what? Or is that a swollen infection and I should be grossed out."

"He looks like a shot camel," Cindy Scream declared.

"Are all redheads humongous?" Norma Wife stated, matter of fact. She held her hands out about a foot apart.

"Are all camels shot?" P.P. asked, pretending confusion. "Huh?"

Miss Precome said, trying not to giggle, "I once knew a man just like Mars. You couldn't see it with the naked eye." Then she giggled.

P.P. said, "That one is *sooooo* old."

"As old as your stage act," Miss Precome said while giggling. "What color are you making that?"

"Just add more makeup," Cindy Scream ordered as if furious, shaking her entire body.

"Shut up, blister hips," P.P. snapped, and then turned to me. "Honey munches, Jilly, you're the star here. Here, you put this thing over your head! It's not that fat; I hope you don't get stuck. And *you!* These are not safety scissors so watch yourself."

"Yeah, Jilly!" Norma Wife said. "You star of dashboard come."

"Good thing dashboards can't give birth," P.P. added, "Not with Jilly at the drive-in!"

I smiled and said, "I can't compare to you, doll. You're far too luminescent."

"Luminescent!" P.P. gasped. "You melt my eye makeup, *man!*"

"I'm not a man," I finally said, bringing down the house. I was, indeed, the only thing with real knockers in the pad, or so I'd been assuming. I looked at my press-on nails to assure myself of my beauty.

P.P. said, "Who's got a sleeper? I think I took too many yellows this morning and my fingernails are ready to pop."

Miss Precome chimed in, "Honey, those cheap nails of yours will pop with one children's chewable. I worry."

"We all gave up on your cherry popping. Once you're a mummy, we just give up."

As they laughed, I thought. Was I *supposed* to really be a man? Some memory told me to forget about it, but it was hard to remember because the Mexican hypnotist didn't twirl a big candy-stripe funhouse swirl at my face. He just said, 'forget it,' and I looked at my pretty nails that I'd always wanted and I gladly did.

"Fingernails!" I gasped. The memory of my fingers suddenly overwhelmed me. I asked, "How do you girls keep your press-ons from always flying off? I always lose mine." The question was ignored. Obviously, no one wanted to confess her own ignorance of her inability to control molded plastic appendages, which proved to me that the impertinence and impermanence of press-ons was a universal bane. I looked long and hard at my nails and felt like I was back in Mexico.

"Doesn't Jilly have boy hands?" Cindy Scream pointed out. "And I have horny hands. Isn't God funny that way." She grabbed her padded bra. "*Aaaaah!*"

I said, "I think sometimes God puts us together when he's hung over," and put my hands behind my back.

"Could you please turn down that cigarette?" P.P. asked Miss Car Crash, ignoring us. "It's cracking my foundation!"

"I'm sorry to say this," Car Crash said, "but there are a few cracks already there."

"What?" she gasped, turned and daintily shuffled off to the bathroom mirror.

"You're flawless, girl, just a few tiny battle scars, but you're flawless!"

"Flawless?" Miss Precome screamed after her, "You have everything in your makeup kit to fight time. You have everything but a pencil eraser! Just erase your face and you'll look so much more something!"

"You guys are too much," I said as I tried on a half-built hat. "Maybe some loud tissue flowers," I thought aloud. "What colors do we have over there?"

"Why don't you come to the Zoo with us sometime," Car Crash asked me. "I don't know why you're only afraid of us at night. Come to the bar!"

"Yea, Jilly, come with us and play. We're so much fun at night."

"Don't be afraid."

I said, "A big gay bar does sound scary."

Miss Precome said, "The Petting Zoo is the mother of all gay bars. And it's not anything to be afraid of. Unless you're cute new meat. And then expect to be licked head to toe."

Car Crash protested, "*Ah!* You should be afraid of us by *day!* Full sun on a drag queen's face is really scary! It could turn you to stone to have to see such a thing!"

I just smiled at them all, blankly. This vein of conversation always irritated me since I was, conceivably, possibly, really afraid of all of them after dark. Maybe I was influenced by that movie, *Rabid Blood Moon* where things changed horribly after sunset. When I thought about being subjected to The Petting Zoo, for some reason all I could picture was myself running alone through a massive shadowy cornfield at dusk. The stiff sharp leaves slap into my face, slashing long red cuts across my eyelids and lips. I wasn't running away from anything. I was lost and wanted to find my friendly suburban street that cut into the field like a last outpost of civilization. Now what that had to do with a bar, don't ask me, but that's what I thought. When movies play in our heads like dreams, you just can't talk about it and make real sense. So, I just shrugged away Car Crash's comment as I went to the fridge and opened a cardboard cup of cherry flavored gelatin yogurt slush.

"Run! It's a turtasaur!" Cindy Scream screamed for no apparent reason, maybe just covering an awkward moment.

*****

The next day, while watching a dull rerun of *The Meddlers*, I asked Miss Spectacle about her childhood as a he. "Do you remember it?" I asked.

"Why? Don't you?"

"Don't I what?" I was puzzled.

"Screw it. Don't you remember when *you* were a little boy?" Miss Spectacle asked very matter of fact.

I shuddered. "But why would you say I was a little boy?" I splayed my fingers out across my skirt to show off the pretty nail color. "That would make me a sex change. Do I look like a sex change to you?"

"Don't you remember getting a sex change?"

"No, I really don't. And I think I would remember such a thing."

"Well, you are a piece of work," Miss Spectacle commented. "It's like you went under the knife before you hit puberty. You don't look like you got hit with very much testosterone poisoning."

"I think getting a sex change is just genital mutilation. Not to be rude, but that's my opinion."

"And we all have them. Fine. Deny what you are. You can be whoever you want to be. I am. And if you want to talk about mutilation, you should see what I can do to my eyebrows."

"Yeah," I chuckled, having just plucked a bit on my own.

Then she pretended to fall asleep. I shook her leg. She opened her eyes and glared at me, growling again as she said, "You never interrupt a dying woman! It's rude to keep somebody as rich as *God* waiting!" So I let her be and worried about having had a sex change and not knowing it. I put my hands on the sides of my head and tried to push my brain into remembering what it was the hypnotist was making me forget. After a while of blanks, I gave up, flipped through the paper and spotted an ad for a new trendy vegetarian restaurant. The place was fabulously called, *Rubber Meat.* All the stars who were anybody were supposed to show up to be seen, and, so, of course I'd have to be there with bells on. "I have some star work to do."

Chapter Fourteen

I went off to visit with my public at Rubber Meat. I was wearing a neat pale dress with a plunging neck-line and leather belt, owl sunglasses and a trendy white-knit, brimmed "beer can" hat to complete the swank effect. Hopping off the bus and crossing a hot gas stattion parking lot, I saw that there were no stars other than myself. There was just a short line in front of a round orange building with a giant stucco carrot sticking up from the top of the roof. I waved and smiled and tried to work the crowd.

"You one a dem stars?" a man in bright pink flip-flops finally asked.

"Yes, I'm Jilly," I said with a big celebrity smile.

"Nevvah heard ah-yah."

"You're a vegetarian?"

He gave a big zany smile and said, "Rubber meat!" I tried to keep my smile wholesome as I left.

I grumbled and made a quick vegetarian meal of gas station corn chips. The chips didn't settle well in my stomach. Maybe it was the heat combined with the speed with which I shoved the things into my face. I felt like a sideways garbage-pail of salted oil when I hopped the bus to get home. A man boarded a few stops later and didn't look at all right. His eyes didn't seem screwed in properly. Of course he sat right next to me. He fidgeted for a spell and clamped his fist. Then he turned to me and said in a cold matter-of-fact tone, "I'm gonna hit you."

I quickly replied, just as matter-of-factly, "I'm gonna throw up on you." I very well felt totally inclined. At that, he saw my green face, stood and hurried away, standing far down the aisle. At the next stop, he hurried off. I followed, causing him to break into a full run to escape me and my potential projectile. I did purge so quickly and neatly in the bushes that I was able to re-board the same bus and not repay.

I got home and sulked. As I drank some baking soda, I complained to Andernach that there were too many people in the world who didn't know I was a star. He suggested he take me with him to the gay bar that night. "You need to get out and blow some stink off," he ordered me.

"I have a stomach ache."

"Beer always helps a stomach ache."

"It's a gay bar, right?" I said as I began my upper body exercises lifting two milk jugs. In spite of purging the corn chips, I still felt like they had fattened me. "Will I be molested?"

Andernach rolled his eyes. "Shut up."

"Are there lesbians there? I hear they beat up pretty women so their faces are just as ugly as theirs."

"Shut up."

"Well?"

"You don't know anything."

Despite his blurry assurances, I couldn't help but shake some primordial suburban stereotype I had in my head of those stocky manly women who can only come out at night. They have to hide from polite society because they are so manly. So they meet in unlit alleys, unfinished basements, and remote log cabins, so nobody has ever really seen one. But everybody knows they're out there, like Bigfoot. I'm not sure where my explicit picture came from. I never had a real person in my life spell out such a horror to me. It was there in my head just the same. I had a deep fear in my gut, like those women do when they walk down the shadowy dark hall, with the gossamer curtains blowing, in those British vampire movies.

*****

I entered The Petting Zoo's doors with Andernach. It was like falling face first into a huge sci-fi movie. I stepped into a kaleidoscope tinsel spaceship. In awe, I realized I'd stepped into a new ultra candy colored cosmic dimension. I'd entered an alternative strobing crystal fantasy reality. I was in a very loud flashing electric laser-beam light world. It was so far from being common and average I'm sure nobody there even knew how to spell it. Six monstrous flashing Christmas-tree light space-ship chandelier gizmos hypnotically twirled over a black mirror dance floor. Pink mist squirted up, blue bubbles blew down, and the music was loud enough to screw up your pulse. Neon trimmed balconies held clusters of glass tables. Behind that was a wet bar that wrapped around the entire empire. Andernach's smile said, "Welcome to pansy paradise."

Andernach went to the center of the dance floor, wiggled his hips, did his special pirouette, and then skipped off to the bartender. I followed in his giddy footsteps.

*****

When I returned to The Petting Zoo, now well known, the lesbian Bloody Mary ordered me, "If you see Auntie Ant back there in the dressing room, tell her she just can't strut around on stage and flap her jaw. She has to learn some of the words of the song. Tell her I'll kick her ass if she doesn't at least mouth three of the words. Or *you* kick her ass. You're a lesbian, too, aren't you?"

"No." I showed her my beautiful nails, but she didn't seem to regard them with the same admiration. I added, "But Miss Spectacle insists I'm a sex change."

"Oh *her.*" Bloody Mary laughed. "Once you're a sex change; *everybody's* a sex change!"

I went to the drag queen dressing room and popped my head through the door. "Hi girls!"

"Oh hi, Jilly, what's up?" Miss Precome smiled, shaking out a sparkling red wig, releasing a cloud of glitter.

I air-kissed her, and then pointed to Aunt Ant. "*You!* Learn your lyrics or Bloody Mary will get you and kick your little butt."

"Oh," he made a face. He wasn't in a dress, yet, so he was a *he* and not a *she.* "I'm so glad we have our very own bitch squad here. Like we need her to hand out her own sanitary napkins like parking citations."

"Yeah," Norma Wife laughed. "If the other cops come, we can just tell them they're too late. Bloody Mary has already taken care of everything. We have been absorbed." We laughed.

With these tricksters of cosmetics in their cocoon of transformation, I always played up my part of the Flicker Farm star. I did it with aplomb. "Now where's my throne?" I glided over to a beat-up 1950's beauty chair in the corner, topped off in red Christmas lights. This endless camp and fun led to my, finally, regardless of my authentic equipment, being hailed as an honorary, full-fledged bonafide *Petting Zoo* drag queen.

"Hail Jilly, queen of the under-arm fairies!"

Then I was promoted to an even higher honor. I was asked to help host the Drag Queen Follies on their modest but enchanting proscenium stage. "Yes, ladies and gentlemen, I am Jilly, the super star of the greatest motion picture ever made, *Turtasaur*."

Not a prodigy, I almost died out on stage the first few weeks. But I kept at it. I kept playing the audience and learned how to keep them in the palm of my hand. I learned that if an audience becomes apathetic they would become disrespectful. It's really the performer who's rude to assume they know the audience, even if they're the very same people night after night. You have to *look* at them—look into their eyes to see if you have them and are connecting. It's no different than trying to get through a crosswalk. You look at the person in the car to see if they see you and if they'll stop for you or you'll stop for them, regardless of who has the right of way. If you don't pay attention and don't take the millisecond to negotiate this you might become road pizza. Or stage pizza.

I would talk on and on about my big movie career. "My co-star is *so* big that when he gets excited, he faints. He's *so* big that when he watches TV he has his own warm throw pillow. He's *so* big that he wears a hammock. He's so big that when he stops peeing, he's still peeing. He's *so* big that he gets pinched in the elevator. He's *so* big, people say hi to him twice. He's *so* big that he buys shoes in sets of three. He's *so* big that he's always accused of shoplifting beanbag chairs. He's *so* big that he needs two sleeping bags. He is *so* big that our movie was going to be in 3-D but they couldn't get the two cameras far enough apart. He's *so* big that he went to the funhouse and started spinning before he got all he way in. He's *so* big that when he was on an airplane and the person in front of him put their seat back he got excited. The seat in front of him was then pushed so far forward the plane got there an hour early."

They laughed.

"Speaking of dizzy, the divine Miss Emeralda Jewel Suck will perform a strip tease where she ends up wearing nothing more than two fake knockers and a cheater that looks like it could pass for one of my hair pieces left in the desert."

Miss Emeralda Jewel Suck flounced out. The lights flashed. The two-note disco swelled. I snuck away, hearing somebody yell from down a back hall to an alley exit, "Hanky panky gets you a spanky!"

In the dressing room, as I was wiping off my eye shadow, irritated that my Black Forest liquid eyeliner had coagulated, Bod barged in. He looked like he needed a shit, shower and shave. It took me a moment to remember that was his usual look. I'd come accustomed to gay camaraderie and they usually looked quite the opposite. "*Eh*."

"Eeek! A *man*!" Cindy Scream screamed, her hands flying up to cover a few unpowdered zits on her upper bosom.

"Where's the party?" Bod asked, all cheap smiles.

"In your mouth!" Cindy Scream answered. Bod shot back a cranky tight-lipped glare.

"Bod!" I admonished him. "Don't you knock? There's ladies present!"

He looked around absently. "Where?"

"*Me!*" I pointed out.

"*Eh*," he had to agree.

"And here!" Miss Precome shrieked and grabbed her fake boobies, jerking them up and down and left and right all at the same time.

"And *here*!" Norma Wife shrieked even louder, to compete, grabbing her black fishnet behind. Then as if in total surprise, she gasped, "I caught a fish!"

"Were'd ya find that one?" Bod asked. "Under something?"

"Under my oven."

Bod looked lost. "Eh."

"Bod," I said. "Why are you here? I hope it's a job for me. A movie?" The room quieted. Jilly, *the star,* had spoken. The queens' ears started their flapping, stirring up a mental breeze. Lipsticks and brushes froze in midair.

"Nope," he shook his head, trying to act sad, but Bod is a very bad actor. "Got a job, but it ain't no damn movie."

"What?" I asked, trying very hard to play cool. "It can't be a record deal."

He smiled. "Bingo."

I was thrilled. "Wow!"

"*Girrrrl!*" the queens praised me.

"You're going to be a star!"

"A real platter splatter!"

"What?" I was in disbelief. "A record deal? Who? What? Omigod… oh my gosh! I've got to get home and start writing songs about great love, truth, femininity and meaning!"

"Hold on," he stopped me. "It's just a disco demo. One song. It's called *Sunny Side Up*."

"Well," I shrugged. "It's a start."

"Damn right. It could make us both so rich we'll sue each other." Bod glanced about. "Gotta go." He stepped out into the hall then I heard him shout, "Good God! Somebody's getting a blow job back here!"

I yelled back, "If it's Andernach, tell him to hurry up so we can catch a bus before the schedule changes."

"I heard Andernach yell back, "Hold your horses. I ain't full of *Reddi Wip!*"

*****

I never did a disco song and I never saw Bod again. But first, before I go off on that grand bizarre tragic saga of suicide, death or murder, Candy Cane and Andernach met each other. They saw the "*bad*" pools of shimmering whatever in each other's eyes and pants and they didn't see anything else. That's how I'd put it if I wanted to be romantic. Actually it went more like this.

Candy Cane: I'll blow you if you give me supper. Serious, man.

Andernach:*Love it!*

Andernach did four celebratory pirouettes in a row, and then fell backwards and spread his legs. Candy Cane bleached his hair back to orange to celebrate new love. I had to move to the living room floor. There was no more sharing the waterbed for me. Candy Cane had all but moved himself in. To show I was a good sport about it all, in tribute to new love, I bought their bed a new fangled gadget. It was a magical poly optics lamp that sparkled out two feet off a wood-like base. It actually looked a lot better in the store where it was plugged-in and the tips of each thin strand of plastic lit up like a sparkle of fairy dust. At home, the lamp cord wasn't long enough so it just sat there dark.

One night as they were jumping around on the bed, Miss Spectacle finally complained. "Nuts! Noisy cads, huh?" She and I were trying to watch *Wild West Ho.*

"Don't mind them, at least the toilet's available." I dismissed the boys as I wondered if Mom was watching the very same show at the very same time, which would've been somehow cosmic.

"I still don't trust the Mexican," Miss Spectacle said, her head nodding to the bedroom door, her glare flashing a yellow evil eye.

"Get off Candy Cane's case," I begged her. "Just because he's a little different doesn't mean he belongs to a coven."

"There's a lot of covens in this town," she warned. "You wouldn't believe the respectable looking doctors, judges, pastors and politicians who are really members of evil covens."

"Well," I deduced, "Candy Cane doesn't look anything like *respectable* so he can't be one of them."

"You just never know," Miss Spectacle warned again, shaking her head suspiciously. "You never know." Then she smacked her lips in a manner that meant she was changing the subject, and added, "I'm going to die soon, I just know it. We should get Magic Dan over here to read my future to tell me how long I have."

"Magic Dan?" I asked.

"He's the best psychic in Tinseltown," Miss Spectacle insisted. "He checks the Five Solarwind Star Zones."

"What's that?"

"You don't know?" She asked me in a shaming tone.

"Why would I?"

"Well, let me tell you!"

"*Tell me*!" I insisted.

Miss Spectacle became stone serious. "He reads your eyes. That is your mind. Then he reads your tongue. That is your appetites. Then he reads your heart. That is your soul. Then he reads your anus. That is your personality. Then he reads the lines on the bottom of your feet. That is your future."

"How does somebody read an anus?"

"He sticks his finger up it and feels your vibrations. Your personality all is concentrated right there."

I winced. "Huh? I can't imagine anybody not being read as uptight, with that going on."

Then a miracle happened and it wasn't Magic Dan. The unthinkable! We'd long given up on such a possibility. Thunder!

"Oh my!" Miss Spectacle screamed. "Oh my! Oh *my!*"

Candy Cane and Andernach ran out of bed in alarm, smelling like spit. "What was that?"

"Listen!" Now nothing else mattered in the universe but the desert town getting water. In childlike excitement we turned off the TV and sat with our ears tuned to the outside in total silence and awe. "Rain!"

"What if it misses us? What if it just thunders and the rain misses us?"

"The UFOs are doing something evil; I just know it!"

"Stop that, Miss Spectacle," I warned. "You always say things that scare me!" More thunder rumbled crisply over the city, jiggling all the windows. "It's not UFOs. It's Thunder!"

"Strangest thunder I've ever heard!" Then there were haunting glimmers of lightning. "Sweet Mary! It's coming!" Miss Spectacle gasped. We could feel the electricity on the backs of our necks, like we were about to be hit. I shivered.

The sound of giant heavy raindrops hitting everything was, indeed, an unusual sound for this town. I remembered how back home it had been such a common sound amongst cornfields, while I drove with windshield wipers futilely trying to erase the blur of too much water pouring down all at once. And I almost forgot it. "Did anybody even predict rain?"

"No, even the radar gave up."

"Maybe they unplugged it to save juice."

"*Shhhh!* Listen!" The sky grew an awful green color. Then raindrops fell until there was enough of them and they all mingled together into a true blue bonifide explosive cloudburst. "*Raaaaaain!*"

It came down in such thick gray sheets that we couldn't even see halfway down the alley anymore. Our city view completely vanished. We jumped around and acted like idiots, all but the ailing Miss Spectacle who was too tired or composed. It was primal fun. "It's raining, it's pouring, and Jilly's films are boring," we sang, even I. It was *so* freakin funny—both the rhyme and having rain. Then hail fell and I got scared.

After such drought, the water just skipped across the sun-fired terra firma like floodwaters. It washed the city's hollow plaster architecture this way and that, like a garden hose on a sand castle. But this downpour wasn't a quaint, splashed movie miniature. The stars didn't just have to scream in front of a rear projection screen and then go home to even drier martinis. This was a real drench! Just as we were watching garbage cans float down the middle of the street, posthaste, the power went out.

"Ca-ca! I can't see!" Candy Cane yelled.

I said, "It's dark."

Candy Cane cried, "This is serious, man!"

"When you're bedridden," Miss Spectacle said. "It doesn't matter. Screw it. Who're you going to trip over?"

"I'm afraid!" Candy Cane screamed. "Serious! I can't see!"

Andernach found a candle and lit it while moaning like a ghost. It put us into a thoroughly gothic mood. And then because we were all looking at him, because he had the candle, he got happy and did his ninny pirouette. It blew out the candle.

Miss Spectacle yelled, "Stop it! You spaz!" It was relit and then handled with care. "Let's call the dead!" she said.

"Hell*oooooo,* Miss Spectacle," Andernach moaned some more.

"Shut up!" Miss Spectacle snapped. "I'm not there yet!"

"A séance?" Candy Cane asked.

"No!" I insisted. "That's rude. Bothering dead people must be rude."

The phone rang, which startled me since I didn't realize it could still work with the electricity out. Andernach grabbed it and then looked at me with a sour face. "Is it for me?" I asked. He nodded and glared at the phone as if a crazy person were on it. Well, I suppose that was true. "Hello?"

"Deet*sa*-ver*um*-Jilly*ous?"* The sounds came out in a sliding singsong, every word ending on a very high note.

"Huh?" I couldn't tell if the elderly woman on the other end was European, badly drunk, crazy or some combination.

"Jillyo*us?"*

"Yes, ma-am, I'm Jilly."

"Aaaaaaaaaah, daahli*ng!* Do you know who I am?"

"I haven't the slightest. Sorry."

"Oo*oh?"* There was a long pause. "Oooh, I seeeee. Velllll, I vas mostly in silents—soooooooo—how would you know my voice? Reeeeally, now. No*ooo?"* Again, her sentence ended on a very high note.

"I also have to confess," I said, "that I haven't seen very many silents. They don't put then on TV."

"Yesss… yesss. Dis tis tawooo."

"I asked, "It's what? Ta-wooo?"

She replied, "No! Not tawoooo. *Tawooo!"*

I got it. "Oh! *True!"*

"Of course stoooopid! Dis tis *tawoooo!* De television is safer. No fire. The old film was always on fire. De heat of projection enough to cause big white flame—everywhere. Burned de poor projectionist. The old film stock vas just very flammable by nature. It would just go up like a zeppelin! How many times I had to run from theater because de film burst forth in flame, I vill never forget. Much smoke. *Ahhh!*"

"What?" I turned to Andernach. "Did film used to blow up in the old days?" He looked at me like I was loony. I turned back to the phone, where she was going on and on.

She said, "I hear about you on television. You 'ave great promise to be a veerrry great big film star."

"What?" I asked.

"I vant to meet vit you, so vee can speak about your future in film."

I looked at Andernach and shrugged like I didn't know what was going on, "Who are you?"

There was a loud peal of thunder so I suddenly had to wonder if the weather could have anything to do with this phone call. The whole world was being drenched because I was on the phone? Well, if they could have heard the haunted-house quality of this voice for themselves they wouldn't have disagreed.

"I am *Dunkel Morgendammerung*! Do you not know who I am? You stupid girl!"

I covered the receiver. "She says she's Dunkel! Can't be," I whispered to the room.

"Serious?" Candy Cane looked concerned, maybe thinking I'd been talking to a ghost.

Miss Spectacle finally caught her breath, gave out a shriek and feigned collapse. "The divine superstar of the silent screen! The divine diva of them all! The biggest divine!"

"Are you sure you're the mother of the Twins Of Evil?" I asked the phone.

"Who?" the voice on the other end asked.

"It can't be her," Andernach said. "She's disappeared for decades now. No one has heard a word from her. She fell off the face of the earth! She's probably just propped up somewhere with an apple in her mouth."

Candy Cane said, "She used to have to put her makeup on with a chisel. That was years ago. What's left of her face? It must have been pulled entirely behind her head by now. She's been lifted so many times her boobs are on top of her head. And they went flat, so she hairsprays them up to look like mouse ears. Seriously, man!"

"Shut up!" I realized that unless she was *dead* dead, why couldn't a person who's been absent from the tabloids not still make stupid phone calls to people like me? "Hello, Miss Morgendammerung?"

"Vist call me Dunkel Morgendammerung! Dis is my name! You come for tea or I be insulted. I see you then. Yaaa*h?* I give you your advice you need, then. Dis town is full of dirty rapists and sodomites; you need good advizzzze." She then went on to talk with me for a long time but most of what she said was not clearly understandable. I did remember the important goody: the time and place of our "tea" and how I was not to somehow insult her.

"*Wow!* You have Dunk's address!" Miss Spectacle said with delight. "You can sell that to the press! They've been trying to nail her since those mass murders! Fuck me! What a windfall! Goody goody gumdrops!"

I said, "I wouldn't dream of betraying a poor old woman. She'd probably throw a curse on me! And she'd probably serve me cold coffee enemas!"

Miss Spectacle said, "The poor old woman! Don't talk about her like that!"

"That is *not* a poor old ca-ca!" Candy Cane added. "She's really creepy, man. She gave her kids cold coffee enemas, turned them evil and then rubbed rare herbs all over herself to try to protect herself from them while she ran after a goat with a fork! I wonder if her recipe included any garlic? God, she must have smelled like a dinner salad all the time!"

"Tell me about her," I asked. "Before tonight, I'd never heard of her, much. I just heard about the Twins of Evil. And I saw lot of glamorous postcards." I was broken off by a deafening peal of thunder, louder than before, which shook the apartment plasterboard and windows with anger. The lights flashed on in the room for just a second as sparks shot out of the power line pole across the street.

We all screamed. Then we were left back in the eerie dark again.

"*Ca-ca!*"

Chapter Fifteen

I asked Miss Spectacle again, because she was an expert, "Tell me about the great star! Tell me about Dunk."

"Well, that old bag wasn't always an old bag and she wasn't the biggest silent star," Miss Spectacle finally explained, after we calmed down from the big lightning strike. "But Dunk outdid them all, hands down, for class. All her enemies from the old days are dead. Outliving your enemies is the best revenge."

Candy Cane said, "It's her witchcraft! That's for sure! Seriously!"

I asked her, "What did she look like back then?"

"She has to be in one of my movie books," Miss Spectacle said. "Andernach, give me my book on *History of Movies*."

A giant picture book, the size and weight of a tombstone, was lifted from a cardboard box and offered. Candy Cane held the candle near the pages. "Not too close!" Miss Spectacle yelled. "I don't want wax all over my prayer book!"

Andernach snipped, "I'm careful. Now you watch that you don't drool."

Miss Spectacle narrowed her yellow eyes on him and shut him up that way, then found Dunkel in the first few pages. "Here she is. Fuck me! She was always in some monumental wig."

I asked, "Whatever happened to her?"

"Well," Miss Spectacle explained, "According to the latest authority in all the magazines, nobody's sure. Her movie career was over before the big trials of her kids, so that didn't wash her up. They say she was doing cabaret at the time and got into pills and kept falling. Her famous long gorgeous legs kept getting all banged-up. Then one day after she got caught shopping with bloody shins, she just disappeared. Then, she calls Jilly and says hello. *Hawooooo!* You'll have to tell us what happened to her."

*****

The next day I called Bod to make sure the jerk was OK from the big storm.

"Come over and help me clean up this mess!" he yelled at me. "A giant mudslide has forced itself right through my front door. The whole house is full of Indian Hill!"

"Mud?" I asked. "You have a house full of mud?"

"About four feet of it!"

"I don't live there anymore."

"So? You've got to come and help me clean!"

"I bet all the cockroaches are finally dead!"

"No. They're mostly on the ceiling now. They're smart. Now get over here and help me!"

"I've cleaned that ugly little house more times than I want to remember!" I reminded him as calmly as possible. "I hope all your dirty magazines didn't get ruined!"

"But I need help!" he screamed louder, as if that were supposed to be persuasive.

"You live there now, *you* clean."

"But I don't know how!" he whined.

"Figure it out," I insisted. "I just remembered… I also left behind my vacuum cleaner. Deal with it!"

He hung up in my ear. I didn't mind. Who wants to talk to someone who has a house full of mud? It can make you feel guilty if you want to dwell on it, but I now lived on the third floor.

I waited a few hours, then hopped the bus. I couldn't imagine him cleaning anything, especially not in the current heat and humidity. I could imagine him giving up and resolving to live out the rest of his life with a dirt floor and very low ceiling.

I knew something was wrong when I turned the bend and saw fire trucks. Then I realized I was supposed to see the house.

I stopped at the edge of the ravine to the culvert, now a much sharper cliff, and my heart leapt at the harrowing sight. I looked down. Trailing down the back of the hill was splintered wood, broken glass, ripped tar paper, twisted kitchen chairs, colorful frozen meal boxes, his grubby clothes, and a few of his bright unbreakable plastic dishes. The only thought I had was, "Why hadn't this happened before?"

"Watch it, little lady," an official voice said behind me. "You better back up. Don't you fall, too."

I turned to look at a very cute fireman, and my tears just poured. He was too cute. His face was smooth and radiant as a child. His shoulders wide enough to carry several distressed damsels. I thought, at once, about that TV series *Fireman Sam* and felt like I was in it, life imitating art, trapped in an unreal world of characters and drama.

"Please back up a bit, ma'am," he ordered, his voice holding such calm authority that I'd have never dreamed of disobeying.

"I… I… I used to live here with him… Bod," I faltered, still feeling dreamlike. "Where is he? Is he all right? Did he get out?"

"We found a fellow in the house," he said, "in two pieces." As morbid images flashed into my mind of what body parts were still connected to what body parts, I threw myself forward and hugged the fireman. I exploded into tears and left a big wet spot on his already damp blue shirt. His chest smelled like lime deodorant soap. I sniffed and sniffed. He gently pushed me away. When I wiped my cheeks and looked up into his face, I saw that it held such perfect tenderness. I could have melted when he finally uttered, "I'm sorry."

"Are you sure he wasn't murdered?" I asked. "Are you sure a car didn't slam into the house on purpose just to push it over the hill? Was a man in a rubber monster mask driving the car? We've had trouble with that kind of thing around here lately."

"Sometimes people aren't murdered," the fireman tried to assure me. "Sometimes they just die."

After I bawled on him some more, and sniffed, he had to go. I walked away with the smell of lime deodorant soap in my nostrils.

*****

It really hit me a few days later when I saw the obituary.

Bod. We thought he was dead, but now he has died. Found in two pieces under mud.

I ran through the apartment in hysterics, screaming drunk, "Bod was the only love in my life! He's gone! I shall never love another! I want to die. I feel so *baaaaaad!*"

Miss Spectacle shook her head, sadly, "You're not the well woman we once thought you were. Were you also a spaz as a child?"

"What? Why?" I asked, wiping my cheeks. "What does that have to do with anything?"

"You said you wanted to die. Usually that's because people can't bear the memories of how much of a spaz they were as a child. Such memories are unbearable and require an immediate suicide. There's nothing worse than memories."

"I'm sad for Bod!"

"He probably had a happy childhood," Miss Spectacle surmised. "Fuck him all over the place! I hate people who had happy childhoods. Who did they think they were?"

The other members of the household were a bit more patient with me as I drank and bawled Bod out of my system.

*****

A week later I came to the day on my calendar where I was not to offend *the star.* I fixed my face extra careful, slightly reinventing the shape of my mouth a little bigger. Then, I nervously answered her summons. I looked her up at the appointed time in a terribly plain modest hotel (not even the usual swimming pool!), and the old scrawny doorman seemed extremely guarded of me when I announced myself. I had to swear many times that I was at her beck and call.

"She rang me out of the blue," I said. "How else would I know where she is? Or who she is?" At that, the doorman gave me a super dirty look. "Well," I added, "she was a bit before my time."

"Where's your tape recorder?"

"I don't have one," I said, "if you'd like to frisk me." He gave me a different dirty look and gestured for me to just show the inside of my white jacket and under my brimmed hat. I had dressed in an old-fashioned, formal way, even having white gloves borrowed from Miss Precome.

The doorman escorted me to her door. "I'm not an assassin," I assured him. He dug deep into his left pocket for a key, then waved it at me, then knocked.

"Veee*ez?"* a soft suspicious voice cooed from inside.

"Madam," he called through the door. "Did you send for a Miss Jilly?"

There was a long pause. "Who? Ooo*oh?* Did I? Todaa*aay?"*

"It's what she claims," he said gruffly. He glanced at me. The way he did it made me want to poke him in the eye.

"Is she hee*ere?*" the woman asked in a confused voice. "Here now?"

"Yes ma'am."

I began to feel very nervous. Something wasn't right. Why would she invite me and then act like she didn't remember?

"I veem not ready to see aaanyone, Carl. Come in… *alone*."

"Excuse me." He slid through the door so I couldn't see in.

I heard some hushed conversations, the toilet flushing and water running. I wondered why I was standing in the hall for so long. I wondered if anybody had any intention of seeing me at all, ever. I almost turned and slinked away when the door opened. "She'll see you now, Miss Jilly," he said with some ceremony.

Though I'd waited at least a half hour, it warmed me to suddenly realize such a friend she had in this doorman. In my smile he must have seen this. He hurried off. I stepped in.

Dunkel Morgendammerung asked, "Who are you?"

"Jilly."

"Who? Are you de nurse?" an old *old* laid-up woman said with confusion. I was taken aback, looking at a bedridden elderly woman, wrinkled and mottled and wearing no makeup. She didn't look like the woman in the postcards. She looked like her grandmother. "Are you?"

"Nurse!"

I looked around a dim room full of layers of memorabilia clutter. "My name is Jilly," I reintroduced myself as my eyes caught a glorious Celluloid Intelligentsia placed before a huge grandly framed mirror. My eyes widened greedily. The highest award in the world! Next to it was a gold ornamental perfume tree with a flacon of french perfume in a shallow cup at the end of each curving branch. It must have been a very old gifty-gift, for it was dripping in hundreds of sweeping dusty tendrils of undisturbed cobwebs.

"Veez, veez. Carl has already cleaned the bedpan. You late, you rotten girl," she crabbed, anger brightly flashing in her grand eyes. The power in them made her suddenly seem as spooky as a rabid dog. Her turkey gobble wobbled. "You too late to help me today! You can go now! You no use to me, now! You keep coming so late and I will have to dismiss your service!" Her strange accent seemed to leave her, in this tantrum, and she started sounding American. I had to take a moment to really appreciate what she must have once been. On the very surface, she looked like one of my failed grade-school papier-mâché projects, but her bones were fine and her demeanor full of dignity, like a queen. Her hair was like white dandelion fluff, unevenly short as if she'd cut it herself while blind drunk.

"Dear Miss Dunkel Morgendammerung, I'm not a nurse," I slowly and carefully explained. "I don't know the first thing about being a nurse. I am a film actress."

The fire of righteous anger suddenly melted. Great confusion washed across her. She quickly looked around the room for there to be people about, but there weren't. Lines suddenly appeared everywhere on her face, then melted away to leave a baby smooth countenance. "Oo*oh*. Film. Oooh!" She eyed me up and down, her gaze turning into suspicion at my attire. "And what is that ugly white uniform?" Her preposterous accent returned.

I looked at my dress in alarm. "I thought it was classy." The drag queens had approved, saying I looked just like Besty Clam in *Doll House for Two*.

"Dee only ding I can zay about dat is you burn it! You rip it off and burn it now! Burn it now!"

I fought from blushing, flustering, or becoming angry. As I spoke, I slowly maneuvered myself to get a closer look at the award, slowly, so as not to cause alarm, trip an alarm, or provoke anything. "Sorry about my dress. I must have made a mistake when choosing it. Remember you offered to help me? Help me with suggestions… with my career… by offering a little kind advice." I sidestepped deeper into the room, in front of the mirror, and the small breeze it stirred brought the dusty cobwebs of the perfume tree to life. "Remember?" I asked again. "You said you could help. You said you could give me tips for my career."

"Ooo*oh?*"

"Yes!" Bingo. She finally warmed to me.

She finally even gave me a girly smile, creating a pile-up of lines around her eyes. "Oooh. Vat did you zay your name?"

"Jilly." I came toward her and sat in a chair waiting a few feet from the bed.

Recognition did not light in her eyes. "Very well, Jilly. Virst, ve find vu sumptink to vear!" She gestured to a closet at her left. "Open dee doors!" I did, and somehow felt like a criminal as I slid the shutters aside. "Take out *dat* vite one. No! No! *Dat* vite one! Yah yah!"

I finally found the dress she wanted me to find. It was a beautiful, ancient, long treasure of white satin and translucent beads. It was a crime black and white couldn't capture its subtle purple and pink refractions. She pointed. "Put dat on!"

I looked at her closely so I wouldn't misunderstand her. I asked, "Me? Put this one on? Now?"

"Ves! Put it on right here and now! I show you beautiful gown!"

"Is your powder room through there?" I asked.

"No! You dress in front of me! I see that you do it correctly!"

"Sure." I shrugged and stripped.

"All of eeet!" she bellowed when I stopped at my underwear. "We must have no lines in de gown. You put it on naked!"

I stripped off my bra and panties, wondering if Dunkel Morgendammerung liked shaming me or if these things really were worn like this. Stripped, and about to don the apparel of a 20s movie star, I wondered if maybe some luck would rub off. Maybe I'd zap back in a time tunnel to days of old. When I held the gown up to myself, my heart sank. I was way too big and tall. The dress was really just one long thin pants leg. I sadly shook my head. When I regarded where her feet ended in the bed, I could see she really was a surprisingly tiny little thing.

She saw it, too. Her gaze dimmed. Then she became furious. "We took care of ourselves in ze old days! We ate only oysters to stay thin. All of today's stars fat cows! You eat fat cows with cheese! You become fat cows with cheese!" As she continued her tirade, her accent was gone again. I returned the gown to its fat stuffed purple satin hanger. As I stuck my nose in her closet, again, I said, "My ass isn't fat. See? See what a pretty little ass I have? It's just that I'm a bit odd everywhere else. Perhaps you have a circus tent in here for me to wear."

"Why pretty dresses do not fit on you? Are you a lesbian?"

"No. I'm just too much of a lunk, I guess."

She fell deeper into her pillow. "I be tired now. You can go. But before you go, I tell you about ze ole days." And she went on to tell me a string of memories, which I couldn't follow completely. I think she switched languages on me a few times. But I couldn't be sure.

On my way out, I asked the doorman, "Why is she bedridden? What happened? I was afraid to ask her, myself. I think that would've been rude."

"That was considerate of you, ma'am," he said, almost like a count. I wondered if he weren't a doorman, but some guardian angel, incognito, protecting vulnerable has-been stars.

I repeated, "So, why is she bedridden?"

"Her legs have gone out from under her and she has had falls. This way, it is safer for her."

"Has she seen a doctor?"

"She has a spiritualist in every Sunday."

*****

The instant I was back home, I related as much of this as I could humanly remember to Miss Spectacle. She openly wept, causing her yellow eyes to look even stranger. "Oh my *god!*"

I recounted, "After I'd redressed in my own clothes, we talked. Or I should say *she* gave a monologue about every other star she'd known, never once saying anything about herself."

Andernach asked, "What did she say about the Twins Of Evil?"

"Not a word."

Miss Spectacle asked, "Are you going back?"

I shrugged. "It depends."

"Depends? Screw you!"

I pointed out the obvious. "I have to be invited."

"Well," Miss Spectacle smirked, obviously scheming, "It sounds to me like the old bat's totally touched. Her mind is going fast. It could be from all the evil. Maybe she has seen spirits. Maybe she really is the monster mother they used to say she was and her body is possessed."

"Don't say that!" I insisted, feeling sorry for her.

"So, just return and make it like she invited you," Andernach suggested. "Maybe she won't remember *not* inviting you."

I thought about it and couldn't muster any enthusiasm. Miss Spectacle noticed my lip curling into a snarl and said, "Honey! How can you pass up the opportunity to visit with such a superstar? Maybe you can write a book about her someday, and make some cash! Those types of deathbed books always sell hot! Sneak some snapshots while she's on her bedpan! You'll make a mint. Remember the fuzzy photo of Gloria Bottles' last seconds of life, sitting up in bed, screaming, shaking her fist at the ceiling. It was in every paper. Even the real papers!"

"You're sick."

"Well then, think of all you can learn about *ze ole days!*" Miss Spectacle tempted me, grinning wickedly. I pictured myself at the feet of a true movieland sage. So I reluctantly decided I'd return in a week. I smiled. She smiled. She winked. "Screw it!"

Chapter Sixteen

It was easy breezing into her apartment for the trick visit, since she pretended she knew all along that she'd invited me, or pretended to pretend. I don't know. She'd slapped on a simple blonde wig and cat-eye sunglasses, so at least she knew she wasn't getting the nurse. Still, I felt crappy pulling the wool over such vulnerable crinkled-up eyes. After some chit-chat, Dunkel Morgendammerung easily slipped into a long-term memory lane.

"In *Cleopatra*, a real snake bites my bosom. We used a bigger snake than was real for the photography. Veeel, it didn't veeelly *bite*, not veeelly. It tried, but veterinarians removed its fangs. De snake tried to bite and I could feel its angry little mouth snap down on my booby. Then… *oooh*. I zuppose you never saw that. No one has in years. Dey zay all the prints catch in great fires. It was de chemical they made them out of. Nitrate. *Cleopatra* burned down the Apex Theater in 1928. It vaz the biggest movie palace in the valley, you know. I vaz told the projectionist died with that fire. He could have run out, but instead, he tried to put de fire out to save the rest of the print. He burned alive. He did it for me."

As she talked, she looked out beyond the confines of the room, seeming to see great armies of fans or extras or angels. As I listened, I paged through thick musty scrapbooks, constantly comparing her impossibly divine face in the photos with the elderly one at my side. As I looked beyond her haunting face, to the rest of the photo, I couldn't believe the variety of glamorous places she'd visited and the important people she'd once been with, even the Queens of Sweden and England! In every photo she wore a different gown, all smart or fantastic, except one party where she was only covered with a few pieces of tiny fern. She stood next to an Adonis whose matching fern only covered the hair above his pee-pee. I was in total astonishment that there were nudists back then too.

"We all prank all the time back then. We were all like children. We always play. Anybody would do anything for a laugh. In *Gilda Was a Woman*, they put a big whoopee cushion in the sofa. In the scenario, my husband is dead at war and I fall weakly into it. I know the camera cannot hear the sound so I ignore it until the director cuts the scene. Then we laugh. We all laughed for hours. Those stories about me get so twisted over time, though. In Gilbert Johns' book he says I had the hiccups and had to mask them. Not true! I would not go so far as do the scene with hiccups! That is silly! All my stories get remembered so wrong! Especially the ones with my poor children and their terrible difficulties. They even say I gave them coffee enemas! Ridiculous!

"My youngest—and no, they were never twins—the youngest had not passed his bowels in three days. I give him cold coffee with honey to drink, thinking to help him pass his bowels. The child grows ill and we take to hospital where ze find his intestine has twisted. All is made better though. We were afraid for many days that he might lose his colon. I cry and pray for long time. I am sorry for all my gaiety and neglecting my boys. Then the story comes out about enemas. Where the hell did that come from? We have no enemas around here! We drink too much champagne to ever need that.

"Oh, such horrid stories that everyone believes. I did no evil to make my boys do what they later came to do! I may not have done enough good for them. I did not do evil, though. I have many big parties that children cannot go to, but I not evil! And they say I make love to the Devil, because I had a goat! It was just a gift after I did that mountain movie, the big hit of 1923! It was a silly gag gift. They didn't care if the goat dropped dead after that party. Everybody was so irresponsible. But I went on to take care of that goat as a pet. And I loved my goat. But not in any disgusting way. Not in any improper way. I loved my goat as a pet.

"Oh, my poor pet goat. One day she jumps over the fence and was hit by a car. I was so sad. The papers only said mean things about it. They said I ate raw goat meat. They always say such terrible things about me, because I have glamour!"

Tears rolled from under her dark glasses and down the uneven contours of her cheeks. I was moved to cry myself. I couldn't believe how one story could turn so weirdly into another. I couldn't believe she was so misunderstood.

"My children still love me. They write me from where they are," she added. "I got a letter just the other day. They say sweet things. They are sorry. They want to come home and be good. I will give them time then. I will not throw big party. I will spend time with my children and not all the men who come to drink and laugh and make love."

I didn't have the nerve to remind her they'd been murdered and dead for ten years, and that she was far too old for gentlemen callers. For the next few hours she told me more about the good old days, but most of it was very hard to follow or she was just repeating.

On the way out of the building, I asked the doorman how an old person's arteries could harden so much to cause a senile condition scientifically. He didn't say a word, but looked at me like I was a rude person. I suppose I was, or he had no idea what she was suffering from. Maybe no one knew such mysteries of the limitless cosmos of the mind. I pondered the question of whether the brain could rot away from a specific disease, or if it were just the inevitable fate of growing old. There was a difference between the two; *one* could surely be cured with a pharmaceutical prescription. The *other* was grounds for suicide.

I got home. My roommates didn't believe my retelling of the Dunkel Morgendammerung myths.

"You're so gullible," Miss Spectacle chided me. "Of course she has to tell herself she isn't the mother of pure evil. If she were truly as innocent, she wouldn't have been driven out of her own mortal mind with her own unrelenting guilt! It is pure evil inside her head and it is melting it!"

Miss Spectacle also told me to return and steal every photo I could get my hands on, especially the nude-with-fern one.

*****

The next time I stopped by the corner gas station for corn chips from the vending machine, the attendant smiled and sneered. "I hear you're pretty rude."

As I pulled the big metal silver rod out to release a bag with a loud *ka-bang,* I said, "*You're* rude. You asshole! You don't carry *Corny Peso!* They're my favorite brand!"

"No. I'm talking about the lip you're giving your elders."

"What?" I had no idea what he could have been talking about.

"The tabloid," he gestured towards the rack. I tore open the *Movieland Nova* until I came to a very unflattering picture of me spliced together with a fabulous one of Dunkel Morgendammerung. Her picture was circa 1920 with a few unconvincing pencil lines drawn in, not only on her face to attempt to age her, but silly bags were drawn under my eyes.

I thought we looked like some kind of morbid vampire sisters. *Morgendammerung Reports Jilly Undisciplined*, the shocking headline read. I felt momentarily dizzy from seeing such a thing. My stomach flipped. I had to sit on the floor. "Oh my god, I'm ruined!" In utter fright I read the article so fast that I didn't read a word. I finally took a deep breath and read it again:

"Star of silent screen mother of Twins Of Evil reports to *Movie Weekly* that Z-movie booby starlet, Jilly, unpolished and unprofessional as washerwoman, wears nothing better than pillowcases full of rocks, but we already knew that, too fat for normal fashion. Her films embarrassment to industry dedicated to beauty improving lives of family."

The article went on say (*lie!*) that Dunkel Morgendammerung had delivered all this candid gossip at an exclusive *Movieland Nova* banquet where she looked radiant with health. Her famous legs were in top form and she danced a cautious tango with mature, but still working, bohunk, Huge Stock.

"Do you want to buy that or are you going to read the whole thing here?" the clerk behind the register asked. "This is not a library!" I jumped up and threw the flimsy little paper at him with the earnest intent to injure. I stormed back to the apartment and ate my chips.

Hours later, when Carl, the doorman, saw me, he paled as if it were he who'd committed the great crimes. He insisted, "You cannot see madam Dunkel Morgendammerung, today. She is resting."

"I just want to ask her one little thing!" I said, shamelessly thrusting my hand deep into his left pocket, I felt more than his key, causing him a jolt. "Don't worry, I won't murder her. There won't even be a scene. I may even bathe her, brush her nubby hair and sterilize her bedpan."

"Stop or I'll call house security!"

"Try." I skipped up the steps, and when I entered her hall, I heard loud screams. I wondered if she'd been called and forewarned? Worried and feeling the need to explain myself, I still charged on. I knocked a few times and then keyed open the door.

Dunkel Morgendammerung turned to me and screeched in mortal terror, "Get that hag out of here! Get her out of my room! Get that old *damned* bitch out! Hurry!" I looked at what she was screaming at. She was pointing to her own reflection in the huge vanity across from the foot of her bed. The great movie star continued screaming,

"She just sits there like a witch and stares and stares at me! Throw her out. Throw her bony old ass out! Out of my house!"

Carl hurried past me, into the room. "I'm so sorry, madam but she stole your key."

"Who are you?" She yelled at him, her face blotching redder with fury. "Are you the preacher? If you've come to haul that old goddam witch away, then you certainly took your time! She's just staring at me and pointing, driving me mad! Drag her away and burn her at the stake!" He looked at the mirror to where she was pointing, in confusion, and then looked to me as if I might have an answer.

I suddenly thought I might have a plan. I walked to the mirror, picked up the Celluloid Intelligentsia that was displayed before it and hammered the mirror with all my might until the glass was completely smashed to pieces. The perfume tree knocked over and bottles rolled out across the floor, trailing dusty cobwebs. Luckily the bottles didn't break. That would have smelled. At that dramatic display, the elderly woman quieted, smiled, and seemed to calm down. Then she heavily collapsed her head into her pillow. "Is that ugly witch gone? Is she gone for good?" she asked, exhausted.

"I don't see her. Do you?" I answered with a question.

She picked her head back up from the pillow and looked around. "I don't see her. Aaaah! You took her away. *Aaaah!*"

I assured her. "Gone. The witch is gone."

"Yes! She's gone! Thank you, nurse," she smiled and fell into the bed again, her skeletal body jerking with her heavy exhausted panting. As Carl stood at the door confused and distraught, I walked out, shaking. I wondered if I could go to jail for what I'd just done. It felt illegal. I had just touched a Celluloid Intelligentsia that wasn't mine!

The next tabloid headline in that trashy little flimsy-papered two-cent tabloid the *Slanderbox* was even more of a loo loo: "The Great Morgendammerung Survives Jilly Exorcism."

"Silent movie great, Morgendammerung, haunted by ghost of Twins Of Evil! Jilly performs heroic ritual to put her back, Morgendammerung's soul saved from coven! Jilly kills the evil of the twins. Dunkel vomited loads of snakes and toads. A goat was seen running through nearby streets. Cold coffee enemas ran down the walls. All true. Top sources reveal."

Miss Spectacle loved the paper and wanted to refuse to believe *my* tale, the true story.

"There are many evil covens," she insisted. "It's all true! And everybody knows the Twins Of Evil are still haunting the studio soundstages. You hear about it all the time. Movie star stand-ins are always running around screaming about having seen their heads floating around in bread bags."

I was aghast. "You don't know anything. I do. I was there. I was with Dunkel Morgendammerung. It went nothing like that and you know it! And a head can't even fit in a bread bag! That's just a stupid story!"

"Screw it!"

"The poor old lady was confused," I explained, "and her reflection scared her."

"How could a great star not recognize her own damn reflection? How could anyone not know a mirror when they see it? It was a curse! It was her own children haunting her for having abused them. That's it! That's the only explanation! It was pure evil!"

"I tell you, there were no Twins Of Evil in the mirror! It was just a normal mirror. She saw her own reflection and didn't recognize it. Maybe she forgot that she'd gotten old."

"You're in denial!" Miss Spectacle screamed at me. "There were the Twins Of Evil in the mirror and you can't accept that! I don't know why not! Everybody else can accept it. Old mirrors show that kind of thing, ghosts and demons, everybody knows that. You're just a rude atheist!"

"Screw the tabloids," I said. "They'll say anything to sell copies. And people are dumb and want to believe fantastic things because people are just dumb! But I was there!"

"You're so full of shit, Jilly, so full of it that your eyes are brown!"

"I promise it," I said, crossing my arms stubbornly. "Remember what the paper said about her attending a party and dancing with Huge Stock? She can't dance. She can't even get out of bed!"

"Bullshit! You made this all up just so you don't have to steal the picture for me of them only wearing ferns. Screw it, Jilly! I'll never forgive you, you selfish bad-actress porno wanna-be!"

I was so upset I turned on my heel and went to the refrigerator, burning with guilt though I hadn't done anything wrong that I could figure. I even began to imagine the Twins Of Evil appearing in that mirror. It was an easy thing to do—far more fantastic—like a movie. Then I heard loud snoring.

An hour later Miss Spectacle woke up. She was slowly running her fingers up her rib cage, singing, "The itsy bitsy spider crawled up my water spout…" She looked completely dazed and out of it. I didn't even try and talk to her. At six-twenty p.m., Miss Spectacle turned extremely yellow, asked for her toothbrush because she didn't feel fresh, and then drifted away into a coma. Andernach called the grim reaper people. They came in white jumpsuits to take her to the cancer hospice. I was so scared, I hid in the bathroom, looked at myself in the mirror and tried to think only of my face and nothing else.

*****

I thought and thought, hating myself the more I did it. Thinking is obviously very dangerous to mental health.

I thought about Miss Spectacle's last passionate request to possess some old photos that I may have been able to nab if I tried. I didn't. So I may have been the one who pushed her right over the edge into her coma. I felt everybody had mountainous power over me.

Andernach? I'm sponging off of him. Shame on me.

Bod? If I'd cleaned his house right away, it wouldn't have collapsed from the weight of all that mud.

Miss Spectacle? I denied her last dying wish. Stealing is nothing compared to letting a dear friend down to the depths of a hospice.

Dunkel Morgendammerung? I betrayed an old woman whose life had gone tragically horrific. I came and went like a little shyster with the morbid curiosity of a cheeky cad.

My mother? I was as rotten a daughter as she was a mother. How does the expression go? We reap what we sow?

Sue, the door-to-door hippie? I didn't buy enough organic cosmetics and now my fingernails will get cancer.

Well, that was about as exhaustive a list as I could come up with at the time. Of course life is messy, so I'll have a far bigger enemies' list as I grow older.

Then I got a call from a grim reaper and was informed that Miss Spectacle had promptly bought her farm only three hours after checking in. This black news took me away from my own self-pity.

All emotion just seemed to float away. I felt nothing. I pinched my cheek and didn't feel it.

Not one to just lie in somebody else's sandbox and desist, I decided to busy myself with a complicated papaya facial peel. One doesn't have to have feelings to lose oneself in cosmetics. I had to look my best. There was a funeral to attend. One has to look her best for a funeral so that people won't think you're the one coming up next. After my facial mask was rinsed off, I found sorrowful classical music on the radio and lit candles and sprayed the air with my best perfume, *Aura of Aria.*

I put all my skin products on my face and neck, then put my elastic chinstrap on and decided to keep it on until the funeral. Then without even washing my hair, I lunged for the conditioner and started rubbing it in. I would keep that in, as well, to have a lion's mane. I rubbed perfumed cream all over my knockers, thinking how the loving care would certainly scare away the evil of cancer.

"You have lost your mind," Andernach accused me, sadly shaking his head.

"Ca-ca! She took my avocado," Candy Cane griped. "Seriously! And she didn't even eat it! What a loco!"

I proclaimed, "I must be flawless for the funeral. Everybody looks at you. That's what funerals are for. Everybody who otherwise wouldn't be together gets together! They're terrible!"

Candy Cane and Andernach left me, so my eyes scanned the counter for a product I may have missed. I didn't see any so I didn't do anything. I didn't think, I didn't move, I just sat—all plastered up with products. I just sat and breathed in and out. I wondered why I was indulging in sad behavior. I didn't even know Miss Spectacle that well. Maybe sometimes a person needs a funeral just to get something out of their own system, and it has little to do with a dead body. Not if you don't know them that well. But I couldn't be sure.

*****

The funeral felt like swallowing broken glass. The mortician did Miss Spectacle's makeup like they did any old lady. Miss Spectacle was not any old lady. Lucky for her dead face, drag queens aren't shy and plan ahead. At the climax of the service, four queens swooped down on her with false eyelashes, liquid eyeliner, lip pencil and glitter in hand. "Now we have a dead queen," they told the mortified mortician who was hovering nearby.

Afterwards, outside the front of the funeral home, people stood around amongst the phony 2-D pillars and chatted. "I'm not sorry the bitch is dead," one queen declared. "I can't be sorry. She was such a fang."

"But she changed before she died," somebody else defended her. "She became a nice person."

"People always become nice when they know they're going to die. So it don't count, then."

I wanted to tell a few stories but then I stopped myself. They weren't really nice enough. This disturbed me so I went over to Andernach. He said, "She was the most wonderful person. We will miss her gift."

"She was a righteous warrior."

"A true inspiration to us all."

"A trail blazer."

"I don't know what we'll do without her."

All I could think about was a chat I'd had with her. I'd asked what she had learned in life. Miss Spectacle looked at me hard with her yellow eyes, and answered, very matter-of-factly. "When I was younger, all I wanted was to be cool. But I was such a dork. I was a stupid spaz. Every year I look back to the one before and think, I was such a dork. When I finally get to where I think I'll know anything, I'll drop dead, and then I'll be back to square one. When you're dead, you're a dummy."

Once I was back in the apartment, seeing the couch without Miss Spectacle lying there, was unbearable for me. I didn't like the feeling. I didn't know what to do with myself. I kept pacing and looking out the window and sitting in the kitchen. But I was doing nothing. So I wanted loud music, lights, and booze to fill my head.

"Let's go out," Candy Cane urged me, as if reading my mind. He and Andernach whisked me off to the glamour of The Petting Zoo where I bumped bosoms with the same crowd from the memorial service. My morose thoughts on death went away completely, as I danced with everybody, even couples who didn't want me intruding on their foreplay. I didn't care. I couldn't stop laughing the entire time, so most people just laughed back.

When I was finally tired of laughing, I went to the back dressing room and collapsed in my beauty chair throne. "Get a paper towel," a queen shrieked as she rushed in. "I just stepped on a pooplette out there in the hall."

Another queen shrieked, "Oh God, somebody out there has a stinkweed tonight."

"And it'll probably end up in your mouth."

"Oh, if that comment wasn't in bad taste."

"Miss Mary, thing, could you go out there and sniff a few butts and tell us where it came from?"

"I suppose *you* can't do it, your nose is too full of coke to smell a rose."

"At least I paid for it with my own money and didn't steal it from my mother."

"If I want any shit from you, I'll squeeze your head!" the offended queen screamed as she dipped her hand in cold cream and slapped it across the offending queen, sending her elaborate makeup straight to hell.

"You bitch! I was supposed to go on in ten minutes!" the offending queen screamed back as she threw powder at the offended queen, which wreaked total havoc on her black strapless mini.

"Kill!" In a flash (these things must happen often) the few other queens who were nearby wrapped feather boas around the two and stopped the fight. The two messy mamas were separated until order could be maintained. This matter would have to proceed according to rules.

"Vogue! Vogue! Vogue! Vogue!" we all chanted as we followed them out to the dance floor. There, the crowd gathered around and watched as the two feuding sisters tried to out-dance each other, not with gymnastics or energy, per se, but an intensely angular dance mostly defined by its stylized pantomime. They tried to point out what was supposedly flawed in the other person, done in drop-dead attitude, their eyes blazing like two iced-over gladiators.

After the song was over, they stomped away in different directions. I wondered who won, if anyone. So I asked Miss Precome who was standing next to me. She shrugged and said, "They both looked like they faced each other pretty good. This one'll probably end up at Miss Supreme Courtney."

"What?" I asked. She went on to explain that that meant a three hundred pound black drag queen from the old school (over forty and no longer counting) named Miss Supreme Courtney would have to be summoned to referee the rematch. She would decide who had out-faced the other. Her word would be final. Urban myth had it that she pioneered the vogue in a spontaneous moment of artistic genius in an alley fight when she refused to parley with broken bottles. She had seen too many faces and careers ruined by getting all sliced up.

I asked, "What does the winner get?"

Miss Precome answered, "You just win, that's all."

"Oh, that's nothing," I scoffed. "I was expecting the loser to get thirty lashes, or something."

"Getting thirty lashes, losing thirty lashes. It's hard to tell when our eyes have so many."

"This was a fight, after all," I reminded her.

"Winning a vogue is the ultimate," Miss Precome insisted, smiling like a cartoon femme fatale. "You win a vogue and you're on top. Knowing that you won a vogue is better than anything. Queens love to win. Winning is *winning!*"

Then we all danced again. I joined a bunch of guys doing the bump until I was re-reduced to insane laughter, laughing at everybody until we were no longer doing the bump but rather the car-crash. Then Candy Cane ran up to me in wild terror as I nearly tackled him from a hip smacking rebound. He grabbed me and stopped me from spinning. "Os has been shot dead!" he screamed loud enough to be easily heard over the monumental disco. "He's dead! Shot! This is really serious, man! Serious! Shot! He's dead!"

My face dropped. "*What?*" We hurried to the back makeup room to talk. I asked, "How? What happened?"

Candy Cane said, "It was just all over the TV! The instant he was out of the slammer, he was popped off. It has to be the mob! Seriously!"

Andernach rushed into the room with a few queens. "There you are! Os! Killed! You heard!"

I ran into his arms and hugged him, feeling lost. "If it's the mob," I said with a moan, "then we'll never find out who did it! There'll never be justice!"

"Daddy!" Candy Cane screamed out. "Daddy!"

"We all thought of him as our sugar daddy," Andernach agreed.

"*No!*" Candy Cane howled. "He screwed my mother! He really is my daddy. I really am his little fairy!"

"But... Why didn't you say that before?"

"He hated me because I wouldn't play baseball with him and I hated him because he wouldn't buy me red pumps!" Then Candy Cane lay face down on the floor and wailed louder, "*Daddy!*"

I said, "He didn't mention being married." I frowned. "Hey!"

Candy Cane said, "They got a divorce the second he looked at me."

Andernach said, "I thought he only had one son who was blown to bits by the mob in an elevator? You're lying."

"And there's no studio to inherit!" Candy Cane continued to wail. "The government has it surrounded and it's in probate and they're sitting on it for being a nasty drug den of sin, but so what. My uncle is dead and my brother is dead and daddy is dead and I have *nothing*! The ca-ca government took my barn!"

"How did your brother die?" I asked. "What was his name?"

"Maximino. And mean, was he, oh—to the max!" Candy Cane sat up and suddenly seemed to calm. "And it's all a very good story. He wasn't shot. But it was a mob hit, they say. They *say* my brother was electrocuted in an elevator that caught on fire and cremated him. Seriously, man. Poof!"

"Then how do they know it was Maximino?" I asked. "And who is *they?"*

Candy Cane said, "The FBI. His teeth didn't burn. They're still in a drawer somewhere in Washington D.C. and nobody can look at them. But who wants to look at them? I don't want to look at his teeth! I seriously don't!"

Then I had to ask, "It could have been an accident, right?"

"I hope not," Candy Cane said. "I take elevators all the time."

When we stepped out toward the dance floor to leave, I jolted in fear and pulled everybody back into the hall. "It's *him!"* I cried.

"Who?"

"*Him*! The psycho killer! He's wearing a rubber mask!"

"A monster mask?"

"No! It's a gay bar! He's in a fairy mask! It's a mask of Titania Queen of the Fairies, from the cartoon, *A Midsummer Night's Fairy.* And he's also wearing an ugly as sin white leisure suit! I'm so scared!"

"*Where*?"

"Out there, he's just looking around! Looking for me! I bet he has a gun!"

"Ca-ca!"

The boys cautiously peeked around the corner of the hall and then grabbed me as we all ran out the back door in terror. We ran a few blocks before we caught the bus at a far away stop.

Chapter Seventeen

The next morning the door buzzed. "It's him!" I cried. "He's gonna shoot us all!"

"How does he know where you live?" Andernach asked. He peeked through the peephole and sighed with relief. "It's not him." He opened the door to receive three official looking letters we had to sign for. We had to go to court.

"Subpoenaed!" I cried. "Candy Cane! Andernach! All of us! I'm going to have a breakdown. We all have to go to court!"

Candy Cane said, "Not me. I have just decided I need to visit mama." He started packing in haste. "Serious! I'm outta here!"

"Calm down," Andernach insisted to the both of us. "Breathe. You have to breathe, or you *will* die."

I took a deep breath, to say, "I'm not going! I'm not leaving the apartment! I'll be gunned down if I do! It's not safe out there!"

"If you don't go," Andernach warned me, "you'll be in contempt and you'll go to jail."

"I'm not going to ca-ca!" Candy Cane said. On his way out the door, he kissed us and said, "Call me when this is over. *Ciao!*"

I said, "What? I can't call Mexico! What would I say?"

"Then bye for a while."

"Oh come on," I ribbed him. "If I can go to jail, you can go to jail, too." But he was gone. Then the phone rang and a man's voice I didn't recognize asked for Candy Cane. I could say in all honesty that he wasn't there, had left town, left the country, was in Mexico, and he shouldn't call again.

First thing the next morning, and still shaking so bad I lost a nail in the rotary of the phone, I called the judge's office. I said I couldn't come because a psycho killer was after me. They said they'd send a cop out to pick me up. I had to show up or be in contempt. I asked if I could go into protective custody and still be a celebrity movie star.

They said no. Still on the phone, I threw up a bunch of corn chips I'd been eating way too fast.

I went to the courthouse. Just before my hearing, it dawned on me that I really hated the Flicker Farm lawyer, but couldn't pin down why. When we walked up the court steps there were way more cameras flashing at me now than the first time. Of course I reflexively smiled, regardless of my fear and nausea.

"Do you know who killed Os?" they asked.

"My lawyer," I loudly declared, pointing, causing him to give me an intensely dirty look. I snarled back. I now knew why I didn't like him. No humor.

Then that horrible psycho killer, now in a lime green leisure suit and goofy rubber president mask, pushed forward and asked, "Are you married to Os?"

"Are you a psycho killer?" I asked, freezing in terror. "It's *him!*" I pointed out to my dull lawyer.

He hadn't thrown himself between him and me. He hadn't tried to protect me. "We can't do anything about him now," my lawyer said, pulling me along.

"Why not!"

"He's not charged with anything. You are."

"You're worthless!"

I was shoved into the courthouse, this time rather violently. If I'd worn a hat or false teeth, they would have gone flying. The last thing I heard from outside, was that horrible guy in the president mask yelling, "Did you marry the son of a bitch? Do you inherit everything of his? Do I have to kill you to get you out of the way of my inheritance?"

The courtroom smelled funny, like car tires. The judge was very round and had big lips. All he needed was a powdered wig and then we'd have been *Song of Salem,* the sequel. "What do you have to say about spreading filth to our country's young people?" the judge asked in such a serious and humorless voice that I instantly thought about how he should get along quite well with my dull lawyer.

"Filth?" I tried not to bawl. I didn't know how to answer. To my way of thinking, filth was what one encountered when cleaning Bod's house. "What do you mean by that?" I finally asked, finally working up real tears, wondering what any of these questions had to do with Os's murder. It was like the judge didn't even care about Os.

"Your prehistoric turtle movie!" he explained. "You exposed your breasts! You fornicated!"

"Oh *that*." I groaned. "So what about my knockers? There's nothing wrong with them. Every part of me is wonderful. It had to be in the movie; they're like camel humps. Cave women needed them when they crossed the desert, and that is really very nice. Now we're not extinct because of them. But I had my hair duct taped over them anyway, and you know what? That really hurt!"

"And you fornicated!"

"Oh that. I didn't really *do it* in the movie. It was just all play-acting. Besides, even if we had, which we didn't, I wasn't dating my co-star, but even if we had, so what? What's wrong with two cave people having sex? We're all here now because cave people had sex. What's wrong with *anybody* having sex? The big studios make war movies and mob movies and psycho killer movies all the time and I think war and the mob and being psychotic is what should be considered offensive. Why aren't they on trial for making offensive movies?"

He grandly shifted his weight in his seat and looked disdainful on me. "Are you a lesbian?"

"*No!* For the final time, I say *no!* Now stop asking me that!" I impatiently flashed him my manicure. "The bottle says it's 'Glazed Terra-cotta.' It's most tasteful, and *fabulous!*"

"I only asked you once. And I asked you because you're being so difficult! Little lady, how can you think war movies are offensive?"

I pondered a moment, thinking of the scene in the unforgettable *War Torn* that Miss Spectacle had turned me on to, and I thought of the horrible vivid scenes that were surely as real as the real thing. Mom and kids were running down the street with the sound of a bomb dropping. There was bright fire. Then we see one of the kids' shoes wedged up in a tree.

"Well, speak up!" the judge ordered.

I thought about Os again and wondered if the judge had any intention of even pretending to care about him. I felt myself percolate. "Lots of gorgeous young men get blown up and shot," I sobbed, as if he shouldn't already know this, being a person who supposedly reads. "Towns get bombed and burned. People run around, scared out of their wits, blood just dripping." I was now thinking of more scenes in *War Torn* and began to really wind up. "Big expensive boats get sunk leaving people to get eaten by sharks. Girlfriends get left behind and all they do is cry and have affairs. Somebody always double-crosses and you just don't know what's going to happen next. Those things are all horrible to any civilized person. War is just a mess and I don't..."

The judge said, "That's enough of your sensational, unfounded views on life."

"Well, why am I here?" I asked, flustered. "A great man was murdered. A psycho killer is running circles around this courthouse as we speak and nobody arrests him. I didn't do it. Where is justice?"

"*You* are here for conspiring with that man to break every local obscenity law in this town."

"What?" I asked. Either I'd read my subpoena wrong or this judge was belligerent. "War is obscene!"

"Don't you have any pride in yourself as a woman? Do you enjoy debasing yourself with this pornography? Pornography belittles, objectifies, and debases women!"

I said, "Some porno movies show women getting slapped around and then balled real good and fast, sure. Maybe *most* porno movies are rude to women. That's probably because uptight middle-class men in business suits wish they had more control over their wives who are smarter than them. The porno movies are made for those loser men to get happy at. I don't know. Most men have to feel in control over things. Porno movies give men what they can't get in real life. Why is that?" I looked at him as if he would know from personal experience.

His face grew stern in response. Then it flashed red. "I ask the questions in this court!"

"Well, anyway. I was never in a film where I was abused. I was a modern woman, well, a cave woman, whatever. So what if it looked like I was getting balled for real. Sex is nice for people. If Mother Nature couldn't be happier about it, then why shouldn't I?"

All during this tirade, I couldn't help but be distracted by my good-for-nothing lawyer's tie. Why would anyone wear something tight around his neck that looked like a hangman's noose to a trial? Maybe he *had* killed Os. I gave him a dirty look then turned back to the judge. "Why aren't I on trial for conspiring to burn down three helpless turtles? That's the only offensive thing that happened in *Turtasaur!* Where are all the animal rights activists? Where's the protests? Why am I here?"

"You do not ask the questions!"

"Why do you think you can judge me?" I stupidly asked, growing weirdly angry, feeling like I was the only person on the planet who really had any common sense, and feeling unfairly picked-on. "Why do you think you have power?" My brain was obviously shutting completely down from stress and despair. My fingernails dug into the varnish of the railing until they popped off. "How does your sitting there in a dumb witch's dress make you better than me?" The judge pounded his nutcracker on his desk. I continued, "You're so stuck on my knockers that you don't even care about mob murder! It was the courts who killed Os! He was a successful businessman and the courts tore him away from his work until he was vulnerable and his enemies squashed him, but you don't care about the free market! The commie courts ruined a good businessman and squashed competition and now want to blame my free speech that I'm having right now this very minute! *My* movies!" I wailed, clawing at the box of tissues a compassionate guard placed on the railing just for me.

The judge pounded his nutcracker so hard it broke, which was perfect poetic justice for what had happened to my press-ons. My nervous philosophical observations got me just what I was trying to avoid. Judicial wrath. Contempt. Commie-insinuating retribution. Jail. Three weeks! At the sound of that horrible word, my lungs went into a seizure. My face went so pale and my eyes popped open so wide the compassionate guard made me sit down before I fell.

I was led down a stark grey hall with a glossy cement floor to the ghastly unnatural inhuman torture of confinement. I almost expected to be mobbed by battalions of hysterically angry cannibal lesbian satanist rapists. "Am I safer in here or out on the street with a psycho killer?" I asked my guard. Of course I got no answer.

As we walked, mostly what I saw in the jail cells was not gang lesbian satanists with dry skin. I just saw a bunch of bemused-looking non-white people—Oriental, Black, Mexican—who were from the wrong side of the studios. "Hey white girl, whatcha in for?"

"My knockers."

Hearing that, the guard looked at me and finally spoke. "Aren't you that Jilly chick?"

"Yep. It seems I'm just no good."

"I heard all about your turtle movie. It was all over the religious radio stations."

"Yeah, that's why I'm here. I was jailed for making a bad movie. Is that a first?"

Then we stopped walking. "Here's your new home. What do you think?"

"Impossibly smaller than my last apartment." I groaned. "Where's my gerbil wheel?"

"What do you think this is?"

"I'd rather just be flogged in front of the shopping center, and be denied free samples, and have it over with than spend one minute in there."

The guard pushed me forward. "Make yourself at home."

"Has it been disinfected?" I wasn't even given false assurances. The guard left me, and I stood in the middle of my claustrophobic cell, inspecting every finite surface. I couldn't decide if the paint was a dirty white or a clean pale grey. The light was strange and the space was so inhumanly small I could smell my own breath. No person otherwise ever spends any time in a space so small without obsessing on how to leave, or at least breathe.

I thought of that scene from the film, *Windflowers*, where the lovers run in slow motion and converge in a vast field of blowing flowering weeds. I realized that jail was designed to deprive us from that very experience, any real experience. I thought about the submarine movie, *Under*, that some people called *Underwear* because of a certain scene, and I wondered if my space was like that. I wondered if the insides of submarines smelled like cold metal.

I grew tired of standing. I finally sat on the narrow metal shelf, their idea of a bed, knowing I just had to give into the germs sooner or later, having no intention of standing for three weeks. I started to cry and it wasn't a quiet cry.

"There now, honey," I heard a soothing voice come from the next cell. I couldn't see her, but she sounded like a black woman. She had to repeat this a couple of times. "There now, honey, don't fret." I finally wound down my crying enough to apologize. She asked me, "Why are you here?" I couldn't speak. Words were so far away, as if they were a lost art. I began to question if I were still on the same planet I'd started my day on. Many moments of silence passed. She said, "I'll tell you why *I'm* here. I killed my husband. I beat him over the head about a hundred times with a hot frying pan."

Suddenly I didn't feel like I was such the monster. I couldn't even remember what I had done. In the safety of my cell, all I could feel was danger as I saw rubber masks coming at me, the Queen of the Fairies being one of the scariest, especially in a white leisure suit. "But you sound so nice," I finally said to the psycho killer woman.

"People thought I was nice, once," she answered. "Obviously, I'm not. What did you do, honey? It can't be as bad as me."

"I didn't kill nothing or nobody." I moaned. "My boss got killed by the mob or something and I'm here rotting in jail because I'm the only one who cares." In the vacuous silence that followed, I was forced to wonder if that made sense.

"Don't be ashamed of your heart, hon," the woman finally said, maybe thinking I was in some sort of grand denial.

"I'm not in here for anything," I insisted and wasn't being smart-alecky. I began to cry.

"But then why did you cry?" she asked. "People only cry when they realize a moment of truth. A lying person never cries. A lying person just thinks of the next thing they're going to say."

"When I was in high school I went to a summer camp for the first time," I began to confess, slowly, in a low solemn voice. "I was such a shy pretty girl and it was the first time Mom ever let me go anywhere like that, all by myself with other normal people. I had new dresses. I had all kinds of new girl things. Mom told me to make friends with all the girls and be a nice girl. There was a very pretty girl in my cabin. She was far prettier than me. She had all the right clothes, and she was very popular with the boys who fussed over her like she was the queen that she was. She was very, very pretty." I stopped.

"Go on, honey. It ain't that bad when you air it out."

"I was jealous of her but also liked her, because I wanted to be like her. I tried to get her to notice me, to like me but she was in a class above me. She only talked to the few other rich girls at the camp who were so pretty and tiny. I was always too tall."

"Oh, I hate it when that happens," the black woman agreed.

"Then one day, I don't know how this happened, but it seemed a rumor flew through the boy's side of camp that this girl who had seemed so perfect, wasn't. She was defective. She was… part Polack! So of course she was shunned and she just couldn't figure it out. But boy did the Polack jokes fly behind her back! And back then almost every joke was a Polack joke and everybody told them all the time, everywhere, to anybody. Finally one of the braver boys asked her right there in the mess hall if she was a Polack. The boys laughed. She screamed strongly that there were no Polacks in her family. She insisted that she was perfectly white. It didn't matter. The damage had been done. The suspicion had been cast against her. She became the face of the Polack. She didn't seem very foxy anymore.

She started to look ugly, actually. She was shunned the remaining days of camp and it totally destroyed her. The other girls avoided her too. It was just as if she had instantly turned into a bad creature or something."

"What's so bad about being Polish? That's white, right?"

I said, "No, it's not… quite. There's a horrible difference. Well, they look white, but they're not the same. They're the *wrong* kind of white. You know what I mean? I don't know why. It just is. Polacks are people who are all wrong in a really horrible way!" I started to cry again, not able to hold back the ancient pain that bubbled up again in my heart. I thought my heart was being stabbed by a knitting needle.

"It's all right, sister," the woman assured me. "You don't have to cry for the sins of the world."

"No, no. You see—how can I say this—I've never admitted this to anybody, but since you're black maybe you can understand."

"What? Is your mother black?"

"No, it's a personal shame. It's something I've never told anybody. My memory of it isn't sure. But it's too horrible! It's too horrible!"

"Out with it."

I admitted, "I think my father was a Polack."

"So?"

"My mother never talked about it; it was that shameful. That would mean we were the stupid people. I remember it being talked about once when Aunt Betsy May was over, but then they hushed each other up, warning that the child might hear. At summer camp, I didn't even think about it until this popular girl was accused of having Polack blood in her. Then I became horribly afraid that they would find out my secret. I was a jumpy nervous wreck those remaining days of camp that somebody might point a finger at me and say that I wasn't who I claimed to be. That I had a horrible secret. That I wasn't right. That I was a Polack. Then everybody would hate me.

"My stomach was sick. My hands were numb. It hurt to smile. It would have been better if they just did it and then got it over with. Sometimes I wanted to stand up in the mess hall and scream that I was a freaking retarded Polack just to get it out of my system. But I couldn't. It was too horrible to be a Polack.

"I couldn't wait for camp to be over, and when I got home, I just cried and cried that I'd barely escaped. What had been a summer camp became a Nazi camp. To barely escape a Nazi camp is hard on the nerves. Mom asked what was wrong but I couldn't tell her. I was so ashamed to be a Polack and I knew that she must be ashamed of it too, to have a child half Polack, and I didn't want to humiliate her. We've never talked about it."

"Kids are mean. Your mama ain't mean, though. You need to talk about this with your mama, because it's only when secrets are buried that they have any power. And I still don't know what this Polack thing is. Hell, I don't even know where Poland is on the damn map."

I wiped my tears and shook my head. "I don't either. But they say that it's a place where everybody is a complete joke. They fall in holes. They fall off chairs. They can't figure out where to go pee. It takes lots of them to change light bulbs. It's just horrible!"

"That's nonsense! It's just prejudice like any other. I bet if you went to Poland you'd find that it's like any other place of white people. They may speak Polish, but whatever. Maybe they make cookies in a different way. That don't make 'em 'tarded, honey!"

I felt a ton of torture chains lift off my shoulders. "I'm sure you're right." I started to laugh at myself and felt ashamed. "Of course all Polacks aren't retarded. I guess it was just all the Polack jokes that I grew up with that made me feel this way."

"I never heard no Polack joke," the woman admitted.

I paused, dumbfounded. "What? Everybody tells Polack jokes!"

"Maybe you white people do to try and find prejudice among yourselves when there ain't nobody else around to look down on. I don't know no Polack jokes."

"How many Polacks does it take to change a light bulb?"

"*No!* Now don't you be telling me any!" the woman scolded me. "You have pride in yourself, now! You give your daddy some respect!

If you have Polish blood running through you then you be proud of that. And you take a hot frying pan and you beat the mother-shit out of any friggin fool that tries to make you feel small!"

I stood up and clutched the bars and started to scream, "I'm a Polack! I'm a Polack! I'm a Polack and I'm as beautiful and as darn smart as anybody else!"

"Shut up down there," somebody yelled at me.

"So you're a Polack," somebody else said. "And I'm the Queen of Mars."

I felt such liberation. I wanted to scream at everybody that I was a Polack. I was now a righteous Polack. "I'm a Polack and there's nothing anybody can do about it!"

Then a guard came. "What's the crisis, Jilly?"

I sat back down. "Oh, nothing, just stretching."

"Good. I hope you're all stretched out. Now shut up."

The guard walked away and I just kept mulling over and over again, "I'm not retarded and yet I'm a Polack."

I heard the woman next to me chuckle to herself.

Chapter Eighteen

The longer I was in the slammer, the more I liked it. I didn't have to think. My mind adjusted to the small size of the cell and it became like a glove. The days were timeless, the meals bland but consistent, and for the first time in my life I didn't puke corn chips and my bowels became regular. I became agoraphobic. I loved my walls and they braced me. They were my buttresses. They were my skeleton. The room was the inside of a skull. I was the mind.

When I was released, I trembled to have to walk down the long hall to go outside. Once outside, the blue cloudless vastness of it threatened to suck me up off my feet. It was blazing hot and the breeze had a weird gas station smell. Andernach was there to pick me up and he couldn't even muster up a halfhearted pirouette for me. He noticed my fear. "Jilly? What's wrong?"

"It's so big out here," I said in the awe of a little girl. "Big."

"What did they do to you in there? Torture you?"

I looked around, trying to peer into the distance. "Have you seen the scary rubber mask man?"

"No," Andernach comforted me. "It's been as quiet as your honey pot."

"That's quiet. Wow." I didn't enjoy my return to freedom until we were on the bus and I saw the city fly past us in all its rubble, seediness, and glory. Birds swooped down to hunt for crumbs on the sidewalk. They looked free. A Mexican Indian child danced on roller-skates, shutting the whole world off, feeling like a star. A mob of black men sat outside a tobacco shop talking. I felt my strength return. I thought about my mother. I thought about my childhood. I thought about shame. I thought about how I missed the waterbed. Andernach kept glancing over at me like he was scared of me. I tried to smile a very nice smile to reassure him, but I knew I wasn't doing it right.

*****

There was a cute as buttons Mexican girl in the apartment wearing my clothes. "Who are you?" I asked.

"Jelly, star of *Girdle-Sore*!" she sang.

Hearing the voice I realized it was Candy Cane. "You're in my clothes!"

"They fit a boy's body so fine. Seriously. And these shoes do too. Do you know how hard it is to find girl's shoes that fit a boy?"

I looked at my fingernails. I looked at his fingernails. Mine were nicer. "You didn't leave town!" I said.

"*Si*, but I had to come back. My mama was dead."

"What?"

Candy Cane nodded. "Seriously dead."

"What happened to her?" I asked. "Did she have a heart attack at all this bad news?"

"No, she was poisoned."

"*What?*" I gasped. "Murdered?"

Candy Cane shrugged, and very sadly. He wiped a tear away. "They say it was food poisoning. How can you ever know for sure? People die of it all the time and aren't murdered. Anyway, that's what the FBI said, that it was just food poisoning." More tears began to roll down his cheeks. "But she smelled like bug spray. What kind food poisoning is that? Is it all the chemicals they spray on their food? We're going organic! Today! Seriously! We're all going to become health food nuts!"

"Why would the FBI be involved… in Mexico?" I asked.

"My mother was special enough for the Pope to investigate!" Candy Cane cried. "At least to me! Maybe it was a pesticide banned in the U.S. and they were inspecting it! I don't know. Maybe she was eating that ca-ca DDT! *Oh my mama!*"

"Was she really an important person?" I asked, "for the FBI?"

"No," Candy Cane admitted with chagrin, wiping his cheeks. "How screwy. She was just a good simple woman who sewed me some great dresses and grew fields of pretty red flowers."

I wondered if it could've been psycho murder. It had to be. But who could have done such a thing? Was there a rubber mask man in

Mexico, too? And why? It seemed someone was trying to inherit a rinky-dink trashy movie studio that went bust. And who was left in that family? "*You* are the only one left in that family!"

Candy Cane asked me, "Why you say it like that?"

"Are you the only one left to inherit anything?"

"I didn't kill my own mother for a movie studio! It's been taken away by the cops and is gone. Even if I was cold-hearted and a complete loco, I'm not that much of a complete loco. But now I'm back, and in disguise to keep myself alive, just in case there's a real loco out there! I figured it'd be easier just to disguise myself as a total taco bitch! Your clothes fit. I love your underwear! It feels so good on my gonzos."

"Hey! Where's the owl?" I interrupted in alarm, pointing to the wall.

Andernach wrinkled his nose and shook his head. "I rolled it up and it fell out the window. Macramé is so seventies and the seventies are so tired."

"So what's next?" I asked. "What's the eighties going to be? What crafts could they hold? Isn't it a bit early to look so far ahead?"

"I don't know what the eighties will be," Andernach said, "it will probably be a new and glorious age of gaydom. Maybe we'll all get to have gay sex in outer space with no gravity to say who's the bottom. I don't know, but I do know it won't have macramé in it, and no mobsters or psycho killers. I would even hope that rubber monster masks go out."

Candy Cane kissed us with, "Bye, cold bitches," and then he sadly shuffled outside, dragging my high heels he was wearing.

Pondering the future, aspiring to mop up the past, I rang up my own mother. "Mom? Are you still alive? It's me."

"Oh, hi stinker."

"Mom, why didn't you ever talk about my being a Polack? Why did you hide that from me?"

There was a brief pause and then, "What in the hell are you talking about?"

"Wasn't Dad Polish?"

"Hell no, he was Swedish French Irish Something or Other."

"What?"

"And I'm German Irish Danish Something or Other."

I gasped. "What?"

"Yes, honey, that just makes you a mutt."

I said, "What a relief! I didn't know that, Mom. Why didn't you tell me?"

"Why would I tell you that you were a mutt?"

"No, I mean about not being Polish." I was very puzzled.

"I also didn't tell you about not being Italian," Mom said, sounding like she thought I was crazy. "Sorry. Besides, who cares? People that are Euro-mutts are called *white* nowadays, anyway, which isn't really anything, being so vague, so who cares?"

"But?" I was suddenly so confused. "Didn't your sister call Dad a Polack?"

Mom laughed. "Maybe. But that's just a word people use, like calling somebody a Jew because of money. Or Welsh for telling a fib. You know how people use words. So what? It's not nice but so what! Since when did anybody care enough to be nice?"

"So what? But. Well then, why did your sisters not like Dad?" I asked, feeling derailed, suddenly feeling like jail had been a waste of time.

"Oh, they were just being uppity. Everybody thinks they're better than everybody else. God knows why. Betsy May sometimes referred to your dad as a *dumb dirt farmer*. That's supposed to be a Swede. I don't think your father has ever seen dirt. It's just more name calling."

Not wanting to talk about Dad or other boring stuff, I cut the conversation short. But before hanging up, I asked, "Mom?"

"What, stinker?"

"Remember when I was in the hospital?"

"They put you away?"

"*No Mom…* when I was in high school?"

"How could I forget." she moaned. "We almost lost you two times. At least."

"I know this is a dumb question because you probably think I should know this, but… why was I in the hospital?"

"In high school?" Mom said. "You had that problem with the surgical clamp that had been left inside you. You're all better now."

"Mom, I know this is going to sound dumb, but my memory of it is like a weird faraway dream that I can't trust whether it's true or not. The memory has gotten weirder and weirder ever since I moved out here. It's like the scene in the hospital is now on the cutting room floor and I can't make out the string of little pictures anymore. At one point, I even wondered if I've had a baby and somehow it was stolen away from me. Did I? Was I once a boy? How come I feel like I was a boy when I was little, but I never had a penis? I would certainly remember having had a penis."

"You are now a very weird girl." Mom sighed "But maybe that's due to all the drugs they gave you. They had so much trouble keeping you under. I wasn't there but they say you kept waking up and you'd just look at everybody right in the eye in perfect horror. That's *not* supposed to happen in an operation! They say you probably felt every little thing and it may have driven you out of your mind."

"I did! They snipped and yanked and it hurt really bad. But all I remember is the pain and the yanking, not the why. Why was I being cut up? Why did I have all my woman parts removed? And why did I feel so much pain if I was put under? And was there really a werewolf there?"

"You hallucinated a few things, that's for sure. I don't remember the technical words for it, and all that they did. You did take it real hard. After they brought your body back, we wondered for a while if we'd ever see your mind again. I'm beginning to wonder, now, if it really ever did come back. You are a little weird." Mom was silent for a spell. "Maybe it was just the pain. They did say they had so much trouble keeping you under." Mom's voice started to trail off. "You were in the middle of surgery and still waking up and staring at everybody in utter horror."

"Well, tell me!" I asked.

"Oh," she said, and then sighed very sadly. "You had those bad female troubles and some women just aren't fit to have babies and your being a woman almost killed you." She drifted off again.

"Mom?"

"You were always an accident waiting to happen." Then Mom came back, full force. "You could fall off a cliff at the drop of a hat, but I never ever thought my own kid would die before me! I'd always imagined you bawling at my funeral but now I had to imagine it the other way around! You didn't fully appreciate the experience of almost not making it through surgery because you were so loony from it, so pumped full of every drug in the book, but I had that experience for you and I've never looked at life—yours, mine, the cat's, *anybody's*—the same since!"

"Mom?" I asked, and then stopped, feeling a sharp shard of ice jab up my spine. I suddenly became spooked and felt very afraid of talking about past things, not wanting to conjure up the raging ghosts so full of sharp teeth, so I blurted out, "I love you. Bye!" and forcibly hung up with a loud plastic crash. But I felt very unsatisfied.

"How did it go with Mom?" Andernach asked.

"She didn't get poisoned, she's still alive, I should be grateful. Poor Candy Cane. What are we going to do?"

"It went that bad?"

I nodded sadly. "Why is it that people are afraid to talk about certain things?"

"Like what?"

"Maybe moms are just afraid to admit that their little girls had grown up. Maybe moms like us better as little girls. Little girls are not dirty like grown-ups are."

Andernach scolded me. "Don't ever talk crapola like that again. That's a bunch of stupid *stupid* crapola! Everybody knows that being a damn kid is hell. For everybody. Especially for weird kids."

"Oh. Yeah." I nodded an agreement and quietly drifted over to the couch and gave in to it.

Andernach left the building so I started reading the backs of my beauty bottles and wondered why they really didn't do what they promised. "Years younger. Erases fine lines. Smooths. Clarifies Tightens. Reduces pores. Fountain of youth."

"Bull!" I grumbled aloud. They'd filled me with so much hope at the time of their pricey purchase. When would I learn?

The door buzzer startled me. I fearfully opened it, praying it wasn't a psycho killer with sharp implements and a monster mask. It wasn't, but I was still surprised.

"Timothy Cline!" I squealed like a ninny, delighted and not quite able to believe I was a *somebody* enough to get a visit from such a well-known journalist from my favorite rag, *Movieland Nova.*

He smiled, glad I was happy to see him. "May I interview you for my paper?"

"Moi? Me? I?" I led him to the couch.

Timothy Cline said, "My ouija board said you are going to become a big star. Some transformation was going to take place. But then it wouldn't tell me any more. So can I interview you?" He put a microphone at my lips.

"Transformation?" I said, mulling it over. Then I began to remember things, and I heard the voice of the hypnotist in Mexico who had said that hypnosis only works on a person when they want it to, and so I started to weep buckets and shook like a leaf.

"You okay?" he asked. "You want me to come back later? Is this a bad time?"

"I'm ready to remember," I said gravely to the microphone.

"Remember what? Tell it to the *Movieland Nova.*"

"Even though I'm looking hard at my nails, I can remember now. The hypnotic spell is broken."

"OK. Go on."

"I was a boy! I've had a sex change. I remember it all now. I was born with a really weird penis, and the doctor wasn't paying attention to how deformed it was and botched it up even further when I got my circumcision. And then my testicles never dropped. So all while I was a kid, I was in trouble. I was in terrible pain, because my urethra was also deformed. What was my penis would become a big fat round red water balloon before any pee would come out. I always had kidney infections. Mom kept me home and taught me how to read and stuff, there.

"I loved dressing up in her clothes, and I loved all the old lady hats she had—lovely fussy things with veils and frills and beads. Mom let me dress up like that because it was the only thing that distracted me from my horrible body. It made me happy. Oh and did I mention all Mom's old lady earrings—the good big fat sparkly clip-on kind! I just loved those things!

"Anyway, when I was eight or nine she took me to Mexico for an illegal operation to change me into a girl before male hormones kicked in from my damn testicles that never dropped. The Mexican doctor had never seen a little boy as royally screwed up as me, and the nurse even screamed a couple of times. I was awake the entire time they operated. The anesthesia didn't work, and Mom blamed it on it being too hot in Mexico.

"Then I came back to Plaksville and finally went to high school. One day I let a horny boy try to ball me and that's how I found out half the operating room had been left inside of me. New surgery had to happen. They had to fish out a clamp. That created complications and I almost died a few times, and the Plaksville anesthesia didn't work, either, and it wasn't hot out. It was Christmas! So I was wide awake the whole time they were trolling through my guts all over again.

"But then after I healed, I never felt pain again in my life, except of course when I pluck my eyebrows or fall down the stairs or eat corn chips too fast, and stuff like that."

There was another buzz at the door. "Oh God!" I griped. "I'm expecting a psycho killer at any moment. Hold on."

It was a tall lawyer-looking man. "Jilly?"

I said, "If you're here to tell me that I have to go to court again, screw yourself."

He smiled. "No. I'm from the studio, *Starcadia*."

I went blank. "What? Starcadia?" That was the biggest and best dream factory in the history of movies. "Oh, do come in and please don't screw yourself." I ordered the reporter, "Hurry! Go to the kitchen and bring us all some Seamans!"

"Why, thank you," the man said, in a cheesy tone of voice.

"Why did you come all the way from the right side of the tracks to visit with moi?"

The lawyer said, "We want you to be in a big zany Starcadia comedy about this grand ole town called, *Opening Credits*. It'll be an all superstar epic with you playing a B-movie actress, a part not unlike yourself, who's trying to break into a major studio picture, and will do *anything*! We'll do a lot of physical bawdy stuff. You'll even have a stunt-double so we can *really* slap you around. It'll be great."

"Omigod!" I grabbed my beer from Timothy Cline and took a giant gulp.

"It'll be the story of your life so the audience not only will buy it, but adore it. The other stars play along a more fictional line, of course. We certainly couldn't have Dick Majors play himself. Getting drunk and beating your wife is certainly not comedy."

I grabbed the lampshade and put it on my head. "But I don't know if I can be funny! How do you know if I can be funny?"

He chuckled. "The producer is as queer as cucumbers and he used to see you busting up at The Petting Zoo. He's a big fan of yours. He thinks you're just a riot."

"Oh really?" I tossed the lamp shape aside. I wondered how drunk he'd been to find all that so memorably funny, *and*, if we could get all of our movie theater audience just as drunk, or if Miss Precome could at least trot out and warm them up first.

"Besides," he added. "Your cave woman bit is now considered a comedy classic in all the cult circles. Do you realize how many respectable theaters are showing it at midnight now? They can't call it porno even though you can sometimes see things you shouldn't, and I don't just mean him balling you in the cave that's wobbling as if it's in on it too, because you were a genius to make your performance so completely German expressionistic, especially when you first come out of the ocean and you're moving like some kind of a palsied robot. It's utter art, like modern dance. Pure, radical, edgy, sexually-liberated art!"

"Is *that* what I did! Oh yes, expressionism! I have a lot of them!"

"Your presence in the movie will be just the quirky bit of casting genius we need to give us some buzz."

I grinned so big my face hurt, saying, "I'm going to be a big star! After this class A picture, I'm in the big league! I'll be offered more big pictures! I've really finally made it! My foot finally got in the door! I can join a union! Say, can I sing in this picture? I almost did a disco song, but it didn't happen."

The man thought a moment and shrugged. "Maybe. Maybe we can tag a really horrible disco song on the closing credits."

"You think so?" I beamed.

"Sure. The cinemas expect us to put really bad music at the end of the movies these days so the house clears out faster."

"How ingenious."

The agent smiled and pulled a pile of forms from his briefcase. "Read these over and sign them."

"You need a lawyer for that stuff," Timothy Cline warned me. "You can't just sign without a lawyer."

"Who gave you such a practical education," I snapped, "and made you so smart?" I smiled at the agent. "I'm sure they're all in order. Why would Starcadia screw me? If they tried and the public found out, the public wouldn't think well of you guys, now would they? You know how the public falls in love with the screwed underdog superstar. If you ripped me off, it'd be great publicity for me, at your expense."

He smiled. "It's all standard stuff."

"I'll sign them now, then. Hey, Cline, hurry, go in the kitchen and find me a pen." He did. "I'm going to be a star!" I nearly sang as I signed everywhere, even a few places I shouldn't have. "A superstar!"

"Now don't count your chickens before they hatch," Timothy Cline warned me in a stupid wet blanket proverb.

"Get off me," I said to him. "Did I expect my tap dancing on a pool table would lead to a western that would lead to the worst movie ever celebrated to *this*?"

Timothy Cline got up to leave. "Thanks."

"You done? You leaving? Did you get enough dirt for an entire article?"

"I think I'll be starting a book."

"Call it *Jilly Is The Best!*"

He nodded. "Sure."

"Are you gonna finish your beer?"

"No."

"Well then, give it to me."

*****

I sent Mom a postcard. I finally had something consequential to scrawl… *I may not be as smart as you, but I'm a star!*

Postlude

Andernach got off the phone and walked over to me. "That was a reporter who says he knows you… Timothy Cline. How do you know him? You can't know him; he's real."

"What'd you tell him?"

"I told him you were too hung-over from champagne to come to the phone. And that you've been shot. He thought that was so cool. He says he's writing a book about you and getting shot always helps a book sell."

"Bless him."

"Aren't you going to ask why he called?"

"Why'd he call?"

"He called to say he saw you on the award show last night and your sexy dress made him swear. And when the backdrop broke and snagged the host, he just knew you had something to do with it. His ouija board spelled *ape,* but he knew it was really you."

"Did he ever go see my movie? Did he like it? Did he laugh? Did he like me best?"

"Yes, he liked the stupid movie. He said you were the only one the audience really liked. He liked the scenes where your bra gets caught in the paper shredder, and the security gate, and the cop car door, and the limousine trunk, and the escalator, and the cuckoo clock, and the Ferris wheel, but he said he finally gave up and started to think that was normal for you."

"He liked it, though? He liked all those parts? He remembered all of them?" I asked, rubbing my knockers as if they should be hurt from all the bra chewing, though the movie had used a stunt man for all those shots.

"He's a guy, Jilly. He remembers bra scenes."

"But did he like the movie? Journalists always lie. It's their number one instinctive survival skill."

"He wants your autograph."

"Timothy Cline wants *my* autograph? Is he a member of my fan club?"

Andernach looked disapproving upon me. "You'd make him buy your autograph?"

I nodded. "That is rotten, isn't it."

"To the core."

I shrugged. "He's a journalist, sure, but he's still gotta pay his own way through life."

Andernach frowned down on me. "Now that you're famous, I bet we haven't seen *anything* yet."

"I'll try," I assured him, "not to turn into anything as fossilized as Dunkel Morgendammerung." My voice strangely started gaining an important sounding accent. "Not yet, anyway. Not for the next few awards."

"Good."

"I *will* expect a little more respect, though," I added, with a seductive smile. "I have to play this star thing to the hilt, you know. At least long enough to know what it feels like."

"Oh?" he said suspiciously.

"Yes, love. There's some new blueberry butterfly shaped waffles in the freezer that I'm just drooling for, right now. Could you be a *dahling* dear and just drop a few in the toaster for me?"

He looked at me as if I were mistaking him for someone else.

"And then there's that new Butter Rich Bunyan Syrup in the fridge," I continued like a dragon, "and if you could just accidentally-on-purpose spill some on, for me, I wouldn't complain."

He crossed his arms over his chest, giving me a sideways glare. I looked back as innocently as I thought I was, blinking my eyes and fluffing my pillow-messed hair. "So, I'm acting like a star; it's my destiny."

Briefly jostling his crotch in a very rude "I loathe you and can't express it with intelligence" gesture, he reluctantly turned toward the kitchen to do my bidding.

Then the door broke open with a violent kick and the chain popped off. I was horrified to realize how flimsy it had always been.

A man in a dark orange leisure suit and white rubber skull mask busted into the apartment swinging a machine gun. I saw Andernach duck behind the counter, so I rolled off the couch.

Rat-a-tat-tat bullets blew out of the barrel and blasted the walls to pieces. Bits of plaster fell everywhere. Our plastic light fixture flew away in several directions at once. My life flashed before my eyes. I was a dumb kid falling off a swing set. I was a dumb kid jumping off the roof into my wagon. I was a dumb kid getting laid. I was a dumb kid screaming at giant blurry turtles. I cringed that my tiny life had been such an endless parade of stupid things. I looked up to see if I could locate my sharp fondue fork that I had stupidly thought would save me in a psycho killer attack. He completely missed us. I guess rubber monster masks badly impair a person's peripheral vision.

Then I saw lightning fly across the ceiling. I heard shouting voices. I quickly peeked up to see several men in black quickly race into the room, holding long odd guns. The crazed gunman lay lifeless. His very flammable rubber mask was on fire. One of the men in black ripped the mask off and I saw it was the same ugly man from the award show. I would've called the cops but it seemed something more official had already arrived and matters were in hand.

"A…" I began to speak.

Without even a hello-goodbye, they dragged the ugly man out. The room stunk like burnt hair. Then, I had to rub my eyes, for I could *not* believe who was walking in my door. "You? Sue?" I asked. "Sue the hippie door-to-door saleslady Sue? You can't be here to sell me lipstick, now!" Her Indian braids were still in place but she was wearing a swank dark blue suit. "What are *you* doing here? I'm not going to buy cosmetics right now. I'm…"

"FBI," she announced. She flashed her badge too fast for me to even see. "Don't worry, that man is still alive. We just zapped his tits off." She laughed maniacally.

"But… you used to come by as a saleslady hippie?"

"I spy," she smiled naughtily. "It gets me into everybody's house."

"You're a door-to-door spy?"

Sue nodded. "The cosmetic thing even gets me into big druglord houses. Everybody wants zit cover."

"But… those men that came. The men in black with those laser gun things. I saw them backstage last night, too."

"They're all FBI."

"But those zapper guns!" I gasped. "They have to be from outer space!"

"Just stun guns," Sue explained. "They go through a lot of batteries, but they're not from outer space."

"But why do they keep zapping that horrible killer? Why zap him like that and not just shoot his damn head off and make him dead? And why is he trying to kill me? Is he a right winger or something who has a thing against sex changes?"

"No, that was J. Edgar Hoover and he was gay. Your stalker is in protective FBI custody. He's not supposed to exist, but we sometimes have to curb him, to protect him from blowing his identity and blowing our program."

"The Witness Protection Program?" I asked.

Sue nodded. "Yep."

I said, "But he's killing people. He shot me last night! He came to kill us all!" I began to sob at the very idea of it.

"We can't control the behavior of everyone we have in FBI protective custody." She gave the tattered shot-up walls a dirty look. "And this one's a real ding-a-ling."

"That's Candy Cane's brother, isn't it? Maximino!"

Sue nodded her head. "And what a good name for him. He's mean to the max."

"And Maximino didn't really die in a blazing elevator. It was all an FBI cover up. Then he tried to kill all the inheritors of a puny movie studio that he wanted for himself, didn't he?" I said, realizing he was stalking me long before I came out to the world as a sex change star. "That *jerk!*"

Sue nodded. "And he was so busy at it, even killing his mother in Mexico; he made her eat model airplane glue. And he was looking like hell for his brother, Candy Cane, to kill him, but he couldn't find him because he was looking for a boy. The dress really worked. If he'd just watch TV for once he'd see how we took Flicker Farm off the table. What a *ding!* We told him six times, 'you don't inherit anything. You don't exist.' But he just went on like a broken record."

"And you let him just murder everybody?" I asked in utter disbelief, "like, cutting off Mr. Gilbore's nose at his own party and tossing him in his fountain?"

"As long as that nitwit was knocking off people like Snako and Mr. Gilbore and Os who were criminals, we didn't care. We couldn't get those men otherwise. We just thought of him as our very own special FBI hit man. Even his own mother was growing enough poppies in Mexico to turn the landscape red. If she'd been growing roses for export we wouldn't have let him touch her."

"And he goes to prison now?"

"Of course not," Sue answered, absently tugging on one of her Indian braids. She tugged it right off. She looked at the braid in her hand for a moment in irritation before she stuck it back up on the side of her head. "He doesn't exist."

"You mean he…" I went ashen white. "He gets away with all this?"

"It's the FBI J. Edgar Hoover way," Sue answered. "And I'd frame *you* with all these murders to keep you buried in prison for the rest of your life, for knowing too much, and nobody can know anything, but you're a dumb movie star. So if you blab about any of this, you'll just be laughed off the screen." Sue turned to leave, but paused to add, "You'd be better off saying a flying saucer came while you were in Atlantis." She chuckled.

"You *bitch!* That psycho gets away with all this because he's in protective custody? You would protect the mob?"

"And you would question the J. Edgar Hoover way?" Sue asked me very gravely. "You know we have the big picture and you don't know squat. You think you're a somebody, but you're a nobody. You're just a citizen and don't you forget it. If you question, then I'll have to ask you if you're a commie. Don't make me have to ask you that."

I began to cry.

Sue suddenly took pity on my suffering and smiled sadly down on me. "I'll tell you what will happen to our client, if it will make you not see me as such a monster. His jig is up. He's going to spend the rest of his life in a more secure location. To keep him so safe everybody else will be safe, too."

"Where?"

"He'll be relocated to a small town in Okrug."

"Where's that?" I asked.

"Siberia."

"But that's Russia, right?" I asked. "I thought we were at a sort of war."

"We exchange spies and submarines and things all the time," Sue coldly explained. "They're hip to the idea of getting such a big gangster. They don't have any mafia there. Their commie system doesn't allow free enterprise, the devils. We made a deal with them to do a switch. We're gonna exchange him for two old ladies who spy in parking lots. Don't ask me what it is the hell they do or how they do it. And don't worry. He'll suffer. The Russians assure us that all he'll get to eat is half-rotted cabbage, since that's all anybody gets that far up north anyway. The retards.

"He'll wish he were a U.S. citizen again and on death row after living their northern life for a while. He'll beg for the electric chair but will get far worse. He'll have rotten cabbage and wool underwear. The radio only picks up marching songs. He won't be singing along. His new town is also a tuberculosis colony. He'll be begging just to breathe."

I had to smile at the thought of all that. "Groovy."

"Anyway," Sue concluded, standing in the door. "Be glad you're just a star and your story won't be believed if you're dumb enough to repeat it. Or else we'd have to waste you or something. It's the Hoover way, you know. We can't allow the White House to be embarrassed."

"*Bye!*" was all I said. So loudly, she left.

Andernach finally stood from where he'd been hiding in the kitchen. He was pale and shaking. "I'd be dead or framed if they knew I was here and listened to all that. And what the hell is a Hoover? Isn't that something that sucks dirt off the floor?"

"Listened to what?" I feigned ignorance. "It makes no sense anyway, but then again, we're not in government and don't have the big picture. And I probably would do better saying it was a flying saucer that just did all this. The FBI will probably back me up just to shut me up! My new book about my flying saucer experience will sell quad-zillions. There will be a big picture of me on the back cover! And on the front cover! Of course you'll take the pictures!"

"You're a whore."

"I'm trying to have a *career!* I need residuals! So I saw a flying saucer! It shot up the apartment with a machine gun. It will sell! People like to believe in space aliens. I'll be rich!"

Andernach nodded. "I suppose so. I taught you well. Remember when I took your pictures up in the dead tree? I told you to just get rich any way you can, or something like that. And that is the meaning of life."

Molita walked in. "Congrats on the award. Hey. What kind of a party did you all have here?"

"Who are you?"

"I'm Molita and you're a crazy woman. Are you going to tell me you don't remember me after all we've done together? You must have been flying on some bad shit more than I realized to have blanked it all out so much you don't know me!"

"No," I said, "It's just that Sue came in and she wasn't Sue. So I had to wonder if you're a spy too."

Molita looked around at all the bullet holes in the walls. "Holy pig ears. You give a gun to a black man and you got something righteous fighting for freedom. You give a gun to a stupid honky and you get crazy shit like this."

Then Candy Cane entered the apartment, wide-eyed at the zillion bullet holes everywhere. "Ca-ca! Who farted?"

"A mad gunman!" Andernach blurted out, rushing into his arms, hugging him tight. "The one who shot our Jilly at the awards!"

"Serious?"

"And he had a bad aim, man," Andernach added. He laughed. "*Love it.* Nothing like a little dent in the mop board to give the place a little character."

"Anybody we knew?" Candy Cane asked, still hugging Andernach tight.

"*No!*" I blurted, running into Molita's hesitant arms, not to be outdone. "It was just a crazed gunman… I mean a flying saucer! Yeah that's it! The flying saucer with a machine gun! I wonder how I can say that so many times that it fills a whole book!"

Molita shook me off. "You're wrinkling me, Jilly. And flying saucers have laser guns. Not machine guns. Everybody knows that."

Candy Cane said, "You make it sound sort of commonplace."

"The FBI took the man with the rubber masks away!" Andernach said. "Just now. I was here. All away. He's gone. It's done! We have nothing to worry about anymore with that."

"Wow," Candy Cane said. "That was fast. I wondered why there were cops outside, but they're just talking to some men in black. I just went down to get the mail and *look* it's from the government… the FBI!" He ripped open the letter and read it. "The case against our poor little movie studio is dropped and I own it. I'm all that's left of the great Z-movie dynasty, now that even my poor mama is dead. *My poor mama!*"

"But it's all bankrupt!" Andernach reminded him, taking the letter to see for himself.

"Not exactly, there's no debt on any of it, so not *bankrupt.* And Daddy had, *has*, bank accounts everywhere and I'm the only living relation, since you didn't really marry him."

I frowned. "I wonder if that's why that psycho killer shot at me. He thought I had married Os."

"Well, *duh*," Andernach agreed. "You only told everybody. Wills bring out the worst in people."

"I'll have to start all over. No, *we'll* have to start all over," Candy Cane decreed. "The barn is still there. The lights and camera and sound equipment and stuff are still all there. There's gotta be money enough in the accounts to buy film stock and pay the lab fees and make a print. Wow!" He paused and looked around. "Did a crazed gunman really come in and do this?"

"Of course," I said. Then I threw up my hands. "No! I mean. A flying saucer."

"Yeah right." Candy Cane said.

Molita questioned again. "With a machine gun?"

I blurted, "*Jilly vs The Flying Saucer! A True Story!* That'll be the name of our next movie and it'll make a mint!"

Molita warmed to the idea. "That'll be groovy to do sound for a flying saucer movie. I wonder what a flying saucer *really* sounds like."

Candy Cane grew excited. "Then let's shoot here first thing so we don't have to build a set of when they shoot the place up! And Jilly, you can show off your real bullet hole! That'll be great press! I'll just nummy it up a bit with lip liner and it'll be a really gross hole! And you'll get star billing as the world's biggest award winning sex change star who's been really shot by a flying saucer! Think of it! It's never been done before!"

"We don't even have a script," I warned him.

"Yeah," Andernach sadly chimed in.

"Flying saucer movies never make sense, anyway," Candy Cane assured us. "It's all ca-ca. That's all. Seriously. Ca-ca!"

Molita agreed. "If it has cool sounds, nobody will think. They'll just have goose bumps."

I asked, "What will we use for the flying saucer? A hubcap?"

Candy Cane said, "No. Everybody knows what a hubcap looks like. There's a smoke alarm in the hall. We'll take that. Nobody knows what a smoke alarm looks like. Seriously."

"*Love it!*" Andernach clapped. "This movie's gonna be so *bad!*"

"No," I warned him, "Don't say *bad movie.*"

Andernach corrected himself. "I mean it as in… *bad, man!*"

I was so excited. "And it all starts with an earthquake! There's a big earthquake after the flying saucer has flashed lights at my house! We'll shake the camera and throw dishes at my head. And then a cute scientist guy comes by and I seduce him and we have hot sex. Nobody can deny me. I'm a star. Do you realize how long it's been since I've had any sex!

Molita gave Jilly a dirty look. "Don't tell."

Andernach said, "And we'll have a scene where the flying saucer chases Jilly in a car. She's racing away. There are explosions behind her. That'll look so great on the poster."

I said, "We can't do that. What about the rest of traffic? Explosions? What about old ladies and baby carriages."

Andernach explained, "We'll just have you driving out in the desert, way out where it's far away from anybody else."

I nodded. "Yes! And that's why nobody else saw it!"

Candy Cane said, "Cool! No cops anywhere nearby to give out speeding tickets!"

I said, "Candy Cane and Andernach! You both have to be in it! You're a part of the true story!"

Andernach clapped. "And we get anal probed! And we get anal probed!" He started to wiggle with glee as he thought about it.

I added, "And Molita, you're a part of the true story, too! You have to be in the movie!"

She smiled big. "I can play a real black woman! I wonder if the movies are ready for that, yet. I'll play a black woman who records sounds! Who would believe it! And I use my sound recordings to solve the mystery!"

"No, I'm the star."

"Watch it, Jilly! Never argue with a black woman!"

And so with that, we all sat in an excited huddle amongst broken plaster and shattered knick-knacks and planned at how we'd all begin again.